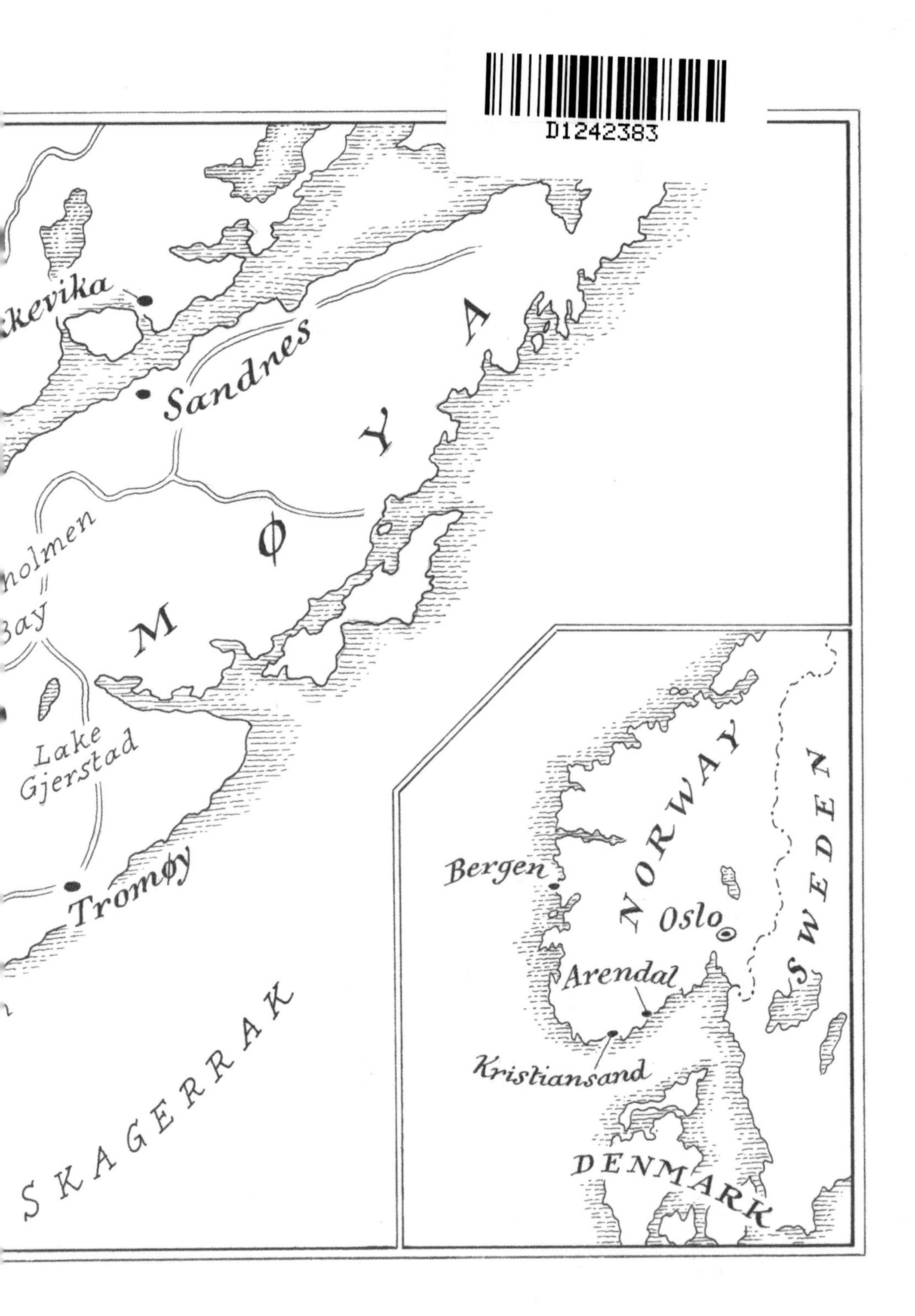
Sandnes
M Ø Y A
Lake Gjerstad
Tromøy
SKAGERRAK
NORWAY
SWEDEN
Bergen
Oslo
Arendal
Kristiansand
DENMARK

MY STRUGGLE: BOOK 3

BOYHOOD ISLAND

Also by Karl Ove Knausgaard

A Time to Every Purpose Under Heaven
A Death in the Family: My Struggle Book 1
A Man in Love: My Struggle Book 2

BOYHOOD ISLAND

MY STRUGGLE: BOOK 3

KARL OVE KNAUSGAARD

Translated from the Norwegian by Don Bartlett

Harvill Secker
LONDON

Published by Harvill Secker 2014

10 9 8 7 6 5 4 3 2 1

First published with the title *Min Kamp Tredje bok* in 2010 by Forlaget Oktober, Oslo

First published in Great Britain in 2014 by
HARVILL SECKER
Random House
20 Vauxhall Bridge Road
London SW1V 2SA

www.vintage-books.co.uk

Addresses for companies within The Random House Group Limited can be found at:
www.randomhouse.co.uk/offices.htm

The Random House Group Limited Reg. No. 954009

A CIP catalogue record for this book is available from the British Library

ISBN 9781846557224 (hardback)
ISBN 9781846557231(trade paperback)
ISBN 9781448155842 (ebook)

The *My Struggle* cycle is published with the support of NORLA

Published with the support of the Culture Programme of the European Union

This project has been funded with support from the European Commission. This publication reflects the views only of the author, and the Commission cannot be held responsible for any use which may be made of the information contained therein.

The Random House Group Limited supports The Forest Stewardship Council® (FSC®), the leading international forest certification organisation. Our books carrying the FSC label are printed on FSC® certified paper. FSC is the only forest certification scheme supported by the leading environmental organisations, including Greenpeace. Our paper procurement policy can be found at www.randomhouse.co.uk/environment

Typeset in Swift by Palimpsest Book Production Limited, Falkirk, Stirlingshire
Printed and bound in Great Britain by Clays Ltd, St Ives plc

Boyhood Island

One mild, overcast day in August 1969 a bus came winding its way along a narrow road at the far end of an island in southern Norway, between gardens and rocks, meadows and woods, up and down dale, round sharp bends, sometimes with trees on both sides as if through a tunnel, sometimes with the sea straight ahead. It belonged to the Arendal Steamship Company and was, like all its buses, painted in two-tone light and dark brown livery. It drove over a bridge, along a bay, indicated right and drew to a halt. The door opened and out stepped a little family. The father, a tall slim man in a white shirt and light terylene trousers, was carrying two suitcases. The mother, wearing a beige coat and with a light blue kerchief covering her long hair, was clutching a pram in one hand and holding the hand of a small boy in the other. The oily grey exhaust fumes from the bus hung in the air for a moment as it receded into the distance.

'It's quite a way to walk,' the father said.

'Can you manage, Yngve?' the mother said, looking down at the boy, who nodded.

'Course I can.'

He was four and a half years old and had fair, almost white hair and tanned skin after a long summer in the sun. His brother, barely eight months old, lay in the pram staring up at the sky, oblivious to where they were or where they were going.

Slowly they began to walk uphill. It was a gravel road, covered with puddles of varying sizes after a downpour. There were fields on both sides. At the end of a flat stretch, perhaps some five hundred metres in length, there was a forest which sloped down to pebbled beaches; the trees weren't tall, as though they had been flattened by the wind blowing off the sea.

On the right there was a newly built house. Otherwise there were no buildings to be seen. The large springs on the pram creaked. Soon the baby closed his eyes, lulled to sleep by the wonderful rocking motion. The father, who had short dark hair and a thick black beard, put down one suitcase to wipe the sweat from his brow.

'My God, it's humid,' he said.

'Yes,' she replied. 'But it might be cooler nearer the sea.'

'Let's hope so,' he said, grabbing the suitcase again.

This altogether ordinary family, with young parents, as indeed almost all parents were in those days, and two children, as indeed almost every family had in those days, had moved from Oslo, where they had lived in Thereses gate close to Bislett Stadium for five years, to the island of Tromøya, where a new house was being built for them on an estate. While they were waiting for the house to be completed, they would rent an old property in Hove Holiday Centre. In Oslo he had studied English and Norwegian during the day and worked as a nightwatchman, while she attended Ullevål Nursing College. Even though he hadn't finished the course, he had applied – and had been accepted – for a middle-school teaching job at Roligheden Skole while she was to work at Kokkeplassen Psychiatric Clinic. They had met in Kristiansand when they were seventeen, she had become pregnant when they were nineteen and they had married when they were twenty, on the Vestland smallholding where she had grown up. No one from his family went to the wedding, and even though he is smiling on all the photos there is an aura of loneliness around him, you can see he doesn't quite belong among all her brothers and sisters, uncles and aunts, male and female cousins.

Now they're twenty-four and their real lives lie before them. Jobs of their own, a house of their own, children of their own. There are the two of them, and the future they are moving into is theirs too.

Or is it?

They were born in the same year, 1944, and were part of the first post-war generation, which in many ways represented something new, not least by dint of their being the first people in this country to live in a society that was, to a major degree, planned. The 1950s were the time for the growth of systems – the school system, the health system, the social system, the transport system – and public departments and services too, in a large-scale centralisation that in the course of a surprisingly short period would transform the way lives were led. Her father, born at the beginning of the twentieth century, came from the farm where she grew up, in Sørbøvåg in the district of Ytre Sogn, and had no education. Her grandfather came from one of the outlying islands off the coast, as his father, and his before him, probably had. Her mother came from a farm in Jølster, a hundred kilometres away, she hadn't had any education either, and her family there could be traced back to the sixteenth century. As regards his family, it was higher up the social scale, inasmuch as both his father and his uncles on his father's side had received higher education. But they, too, lived in the same place as their parents, Kristiansand, that is. His mother, who was uneducated, came from Åsgårdstrand, her father was a ship's pilot, and there were also police officers in her family. When she met her husband she moved with him to his home town. That was the custom.

The change that took place in the 1950s and 1960s was a revolution, only without the usual violence and irrationality of revolutions. Not only did children of fishermen and smallholders, factory workers and shop assistants start at university and train to become teachers and psychologists, historians and social workers, but many of them settled in places far from the areas where their families lived. That they did all this as a matter of course says something about the strength of the zeitgeist. Zeitgeist comes from the outside, but works on the inside. It affects everyone, but not everyone is affected in the same way. For the young 1960s mother it would have been an absurd thought to marry a man from one of the neighbouring farms and spend the rest of her life there. She wanted to get out! She wanted to have her *own* life. The same was true for her brothers and sisters, and that was how it was in families countrywide. But why did they want to do that? Where did this strong desire come from? Indeed, where did *these new ideas* come from? In her family there was no tradition of anything of this kind: the only person who had left the area was her Uncle Magnus, and he had gone to America because of the poverty in Norway, and the life he had there was for many years hardly distinguishable from the life he'd had in Vestland. For the young 1960s father things were different: in his family you were expected to have an education, though perhaps not to marry a Vestland farmer's daughter and settle on an estate near a small Sørland town.

But there they were, walking on this hot overcast day in August 1969, on their way to their new home, him lugging two heavy suitcases stuffed with 1960s clothes, her pushing a 1960s pram with a baby dressed in 1960s baby togs, white with lace trimmings everywhere, and between them, tripping from side to side, happy and curious, excited and expectant, was their elder son, Yngve. Across the flat stretch they went, through the thin strip of forest, to the gate that was open and into the large holiday centre. To the right, there was a garage owned by someone called Vraaldsen; to the left, large red chalets around an open gravel area and, beyond, pine forest.

A kilometre to the east stood Tromøya Church, built in 1150 of stone, but some parts were older and it was probably one of the oldest churches in the country. It stood on a small mound and had been used from time immemorial as a landmark by passing ships and was charted on all nautical maps. On Mærdø, a little island in the archipelago off the coast, there was an old *skippergård*, a residence testifying to the locality's golden age, the eighteenth and nineteenth centuries, when trade with the rest of the world, particularly in timber, flourished. On school trips to the Aust-Agder Museum classes were shown old Dutch and Chinese artefacts going back to that time and even further. On Tromøya there were rare and exotic plants which had come with ships discharging their ballast water, and you learned at school that it was on Tromøya that potatoes were first grown in Norway. In Snorri's Norwegian king sagas the island was mentioned several times; under the ground in the meadows and fields lay arrowheads from the Stone Age and you could find fossils among the round stones on the long pebbled beaches.

However, as the incoming nuclear family slowly walked through the open countryside with all their bags and baggage it wasn't the tenth or the thirteenth, the seventeenth or the nineteenth centuries that had left their mark on the surroundings. It was the Second World War. This region had been used by German forces; they had built the barracks and many of the houses. In the forest there were low-lying brick bunkers, completely intact, and on top of the slopes above the beaches several artillery emplacements. There was even an old German airfield in the vicinity.

The house where they were going to live during the coming year was a solitary construction in the middle of the forest. It was red with white window frames. From the sea, which could not be seen though only a few hundred metres down the slope, came a regular crashing of waves. There was a smell of forest and salt water.

The father put down his suitcases, took out the key and unlocked the door. Inside there was a hall, a kitchen, a living room with a wood burner, a combined bath and washroom, and on the first floor three bedrooms. The walls weren't insulated; the kitchen was equipped with the minimum. No telephone, no dishwasher, no washing machine, no TV.

'Well, here we are then,' the father said, carrying their suitcases into the bedroom while Yngve ran from window to window peering out and the mother stood the pram with the sleeping baby on the doorstep.

Of course I don't remember any of this time. It is absolutely impossible to identify with the infant my parents photographed, indeed so impossible that it seems wrong to use the word 'me' to describe what is lying on the changing table, for example, with unusually red skin, arms and legs spread and a face distorted into a scream, the cause of which no one can remember, or on a sheepskin rug on the floor, wearing white pyjamas, still red-faced, with large dark eyes squinting slightly. Is this creature the same person as the one sitting here in Malmö writing? And will the forty-year-old creature who is sitting in Malmö writing on this overcast September day in a room filled with the drone of the traffic outside and the autumn wind howling through the old-fashioned ventilation system be the same as the grey hunched geriatric who in forty years from now might be sitting dribbling and trembling in an old people's home somewhere in the Swedish woods? Not to mention the corpse that at some point will be laid out on a bench in a morgue? Still known as Karl Ove. And isn't it actually unbelievable that one simple name encompasses all of this? The foetus in the belly, the infant on the changing table, the forty-year-old in front of the computer, the old man in the chair, the corpse on the bench? Wouldn't it be more natural to operate with several names since their identities and self-perceptions are so very different? Such that the foetus might be called Jens Ove, for example, and the infant Nils Ove, and the five- to ten-year-old Per Ove, the ten- to twelve-year-old Geir Ove, the thirteen- to seventeen-year-old Kurt Ove, the seventeen- to twenty-three-year-old John Ove, the twenty-three- to thirty-two-year-old Tor Ove, the thirty-two to forty-six-year-old Karl Ove – and so on and so forth? Then the first name would represent the distinctiveness of the age range, the middle name would represent continuity and the last family affiliation.

No, I don't remember any of this, I don't even know which house we lived in, even though dad pointed it out to me once. All I know about that time I have been told by my parents or have gleaned from photos. That winter the snow was several metres high, the way it can be in Sørland, and the road to the house was like a narrow ravine. There Yngve is, pulling a cart with me in the back, there he is, with his short skis on, smiling at the photographer. Inside the house, he is pointing at me and laughing, or I am standing on my own holding on to the cot. I called him 'Aua'; that was my first word. He was also the only person who understood what I said, according to what I have been told, and he translated it for mum and dad. I also know that Yngve went around ringing doorbells and asked if there were any children living there. Grandma always used to tell that story. 'Are there any children living here?' she said in a child's voice and laughed. And I know I fell down the stairs, and suffered some kind of shock, I stopped breathing, went blue in the face and had convulsions, mum ran to the nearest house with a telephone, clutching me to her breast. She thought it was epilepsy, but it wasn't, it was nothing. And I know that dad thrived in the classroom, he was a good teacher, and that during one of these years he went on a trip into the mountains with his class. There are some photos from then, he looks young and happy in all of them, surrounded by teenagers dressed in the casual way that was characteristic of the early 1970s. Woollen jumpers, flared trousers, rubber boots. Their hair was big, not big and piled up as in the 1960s, but big and soft and it hung over their soft teenage faces. Mum once said perhaps he had never been as happy as he was during those years. And then there are photos of grandma on dad's side, Yngve and me – two taken in front of a frozen lake, both Yngve and I were clad in large woollen jackets, knitted by grandma, mine mustard-yellow and brown – and two taken on the veranda of their house in Kristiansand, in one she has her cheek against mine, it is autumn, the sky is blue, the sun low, we are gazing across the town, I suppose I must have been two or three years old.

One might imagine that these photos represent some kind of memory, that they are reminiscences, except that the 'me' reminiscences usually rely on is not there, and the question is then of course what meaning they actually have. I have seen countless photos from the same period of friends' and girlfriends' families, and they are virtually indistinguishable. The same colours, the same clothes, the same rooms, the same activities. But I don't attach any significance to these photos, in a certain sense they are meaningless, and this aspect becomes even more marked when I see photos of previous generations, it is just a collection of people, dressed in exotic clothes, doing something which to me is unfathomable. It is the era that we take photos of, not the people in it, they can't be captured. Not even the people in my immediate circle can. Who was the woman posing in front of the stove in the flat in Thereses gate, wearing a light blue dress, one knee resting against the other, calves apart, in this typical 1960s posture? The one with the bob? The blue eyes and the gentle smile that was so gentle it barely even registered as a smile? The one holding the handle of the shiny coffee pot with the red lid? Yes, that was my mother, my very own mum, but who was she? What was she thinking? How did she see her life, the one she had lived so far and the one awaiting her? Only she knows, and the photo tells you nothing. An unknown woman in an unknown room, that is all. And the man who, ten years later, is sitting on a mountainside drinking coffee from the same red Thermos top, as he forgot to pack any cups before leaving, who was he? The one with the well-groomed black beard and the thick black hair? The one with the sensitive lips and the amused eyes? Yes, of course, that was my father, my very own dad. But who he was to himself at this moment, or at any other, nobody knows. And so it is with all these photos, even the ones of me. They are voids; the only meaning that can be derived from them is that which time has added. Nonetheless, these photos are a part of me and my most intimate history, as others' photos are part of theirs. Meaningful, meaningless, meaningful, meaningless, this is the wave that washes through our lives and creates its inherent tension. I draw on everything I remember from the first six years of my life, and all that exists in terms of photos and objects from that period, they constitute an important part of my identity, filling the otherwise empty and memory-less periphery of this 'me' with meaning and continuity. From all these bits and pieces I have built myself a Karl Ove, an Yngve, a mum and dad, a house in Hove and a house in Tybakken, a grandmother and grandfather on my dad's side, and a grandmother and grandfather on my mum's side, a neighbourhood and a multitude of kids.

This ghetto-like state of incompleteness is what I call my childhood.

Memory is not a reliable quantity in life. And it isn't for the simple reason that memory doesn't prioritise the truth. It is never the demand for truth that determines whether memory recalls an action accurately or not. It is self-interest which does. Memory is pragmatic, it is sly and artful, but not in any hostile or malicious way; on the contrary, it does everything it can to keep its host satisfied. Something pushes a memory into the great void of oblivion, something distorts it beyond recognition, something misunderstands it totally, something, and this something is as good as nothing, recalls it with sharpness, clarity and accuracy. That which is remembered accurately is never given to you to determine.

In my case, any memory of my first six years is virtually non-existent. I remember hardly anything. I have no idea who took care of me, what I did, who I played with, it has all completely gone, the years 1969–1974 are a great big hole in my life. The little I can muster is of scant value: I am standing on a wooden bridge in a sparse high-altitude forest, beneath me rushes a torrent, the water is green and white, I am jumping up and down, the bridge is swaying and I am laughing. Beside me is Geir Prestbakmo, a boy from the neighbourhood, he is jumping up and down and laughing too. I am sitting on the rear seat of a car, we are waiting at the lights, dad turns and says we are in Mjøndalen. We are going to an IK Start game, I've been told, but I can't remember a thing about the trip there, the football match or the journey home. I am walking up the hill outside the house pushing a big plastic lorry; it is green and yellow and gives me an absolutely fantastic feeling of riches and wealth and happiness.

That is all. That is my first six years.

But these are canonised memories, already established at the age of seven or eight, the magic of childhood: my very first memories! However, there are other kinds of memories. Those which are not fixed and cannot be evoked by will, but which at odd moments let go, as it were, and rise into my consciousness of their own accord and float around there for a while like transparent jellyfish, roused by a certain smell, a certain taste, a certain sound . . . these are always accompanied by an immediate, intense feeling of happiness. Then there are the memories associated with the body, when you do something you used to do: shield your eyes from the sun with your arm, catch a ball, run across a meadow with a kite in your hand and your children hard on your heels. There are memories that accompany emotions: sudden anger, sudden tears, sudden fear, and you are where you were, as if hurled back inside yourself, propelled through the ages at breakneck speed. And then there are the memories associated with a landscape, for landscape in childhood is not like the landscape that follows later; they are charged in very different ways. In that landscape every rock, every tree had a meaning, and because everything was seen for the first time and because it was seen so many times, it was anchored in the depths of your consciousness, not as something vague or approximate, the way the landscape outside a house appears to an adult if they close their eyes and it has to be summoned forth, but as something with immense precision and detail. In my mind I have only to open the door and go outside for the images to come streaming towards me. The shingle in the driveway, almost bluish in colour in the summer. Oh, that alone, the driveways of childhood! And the 1970s cars parked in them!

VW Beetles, Citroën DS 21s, Ford Taunuses, Granadas, Consuls, Opel Asconas, Kadetts, Ladas, Volvo Amazons . . . Well, OK, across the shingle, along the brown fence, over the shallow ditch between our road, Nordåsen Ringvei, and Elgstien, which traversed the whole area passing two estates apart from our own. The slope of rich dark earth from the edge of the road down into the forest! The way small, thin, green stems had almost immediately begun to shoot up from it: fragile and seemingly alone in the new black expanse, and then the rampant multiplication of them the year after until the slope was completely covered with thick, luxuriant shrubbery. Small trees, grass, foxgloves, dandelions, ferns and bushes eradicating what earlier had been such a clear division between road and forest. Up the hill, along the pavement with its narrow brick kerb, and, oh, the water that trickled and flowed and streamed down there when it rained! The path off to the right, a short cut to the new supermarket B-Max. The bog beside it, no bigger than two spaces in a car park, the birches thirstily hanging over it. Olsen's house at the top of the little hill and the road that cut in behind. Grevlingveien it was called. In the first house on the left lived John and his sister Trude, it stood on a plot that was little more than a pile of rocks. I was always frightened when I had to walk past that house. Partly because John might be lying in ambush there, ready to throw stones or snowballs at any passing child, partly because they had an Alsatian . . . That Alsatian . . . Oh, now I remember it. What a dreadful beast that dog was. It was tied up on the veranda or in the drive, barked at all the passers-by, slunk back and forth as far as its tether would allow, whimpering and howling. It was lean with yellow sickly eyes. Once it came tearing down the hill towards me, with Trude hard on its heels and the leash dragging behind it. I had heard that you shouldn't take flight when an animal is after you, for example a bear in the forest; the secret was to stand perfectly still and act cool, so I did, stopping the instant I saw it bounding towards me. It didn't help a scrap. It couldn't care less whether I was motionless or not, just opened its jaws and sank them into my forearm, next to my wrist. Trude caught up with it a second later, grabbed the leash and yanked so hard it was wrenched backwards. I hurried off, crying. Everything about that animal frightened me. The barking, the yellow eyes, the saliva that ran from its jowls, the round pointed teeth, of which I now had an imprint in my arm. At home I didn't breathe a word about what had happened, for fear of being told off, because an incident like this offered so many opportunities for reproach: I shouldn't have been where I was at the time, or I shouldn't have whined or, a dog, was that any reason to be frightened? From that day on terror had me in its grip whenever I saw the brute. And it was fatal because not only had I heard that you should stand still when a dangerous animal attacks, I had also heard that a dog can smell fear. I don't know who told me that, but it was one of the beliefs that people passed on and which everyone knew: dogs can smell if you are frightened. Then they can become frightened or aggressive themselves and go on the attack. If you're not afraid they are nice to you.

How that occupied my mind. How could they *smell* fear? What did fear *smell* of? And was it possible to pretend you weren't frightened, so that the dogs would smell that and wouldn't notice the *real* feelings that lay beneath?

Kanestrøm, who lived two houses up from us, also had a dog. It was a golden retriever called Alex and as meek as a lamb. It ambled after herr Kanestrøm wherever he went, but also after every one of the four children if it could. Kind eyes and, somehow, gentle, friendly movements. But I was even afraid of this one. Because when you came into view on the hill and were about to go in to ring the doorbell it barked. Not tentative, friendly or inquisitive barking, but vigorous, deep-throated and resonant. Then I stopped in my tracks.

'Hi, Alex,' I might say if no one was around. 'I'm not frightened, you know. It's not that.'

If someone was there I would feel forced to carry on, act as if nothing was happening, plough my way through the barking, as it were, and when it was in front of me, its jaws agape, I bent down and patted it a couple of times on its side with my heart pounding and every muscle trembling with fear.

'Quiet, Alex!' Dag Lothar would say, as he came running up the narrow gravel path from the cellar door or rushing from the front door.

'You're frightening Karl Ove with your barking, you stupid dog.'

'I'm not frightened,' I countered. Dag Lothar just looked at me with a kind of stiff smile, which meant 'Don't give me that.'

Then off we went.

Where did we go?

Into the forest.

Down to Ubekilen, to a bay.

Down to the pontoons.

Up to Tromøya Bridge.

Down to Gamle Tybakken.

Over to the plastic boat factory.

Up into the hills.

Along to Lake Tjenna.

Up to B-Max.

Down to the Fina petrol station.

Unless, that is, we just ran about in the road where we lived, or hung around outside one of the houses there, or sat on the kerb, or in the big cherry tree no one owned.

That was everything. That was the world.

But what a world!

An estate has no roots in the past, nor any branches into the skies of the future, as satellite towns once had. Estates arrived as a pragmatic answer to a practical question, where are all the people moving into the district going to live, ah yes, in the forest over there, we'll clear some plots and put them up for sale. The only house there belonged to a family called Beck; the father was Danish and had built the house himself in the middle of the forest. They didn't have a car, nor a washing machine, nor a television. There was no garden, only a drive made from pounded soil in among the trees. Piles of wood under tarpaulins and, in the winter, an upturned boat. The two sisters, Inga Lill and Lisa, went to the local middle school and looked after Yngve and me for the first years we lived there. Their brother was called John, he was two years older than me, wore strange home-made clothes, wasn't in the slightest bit interested in what we were interested in and devoted his attention to other matters, which he never told us about. He built his own boat when he was twelve. Not like us, not like the rafts we tried to cobble together from dreams and a lust for adventure, but a proper, real rowing boat. You would have thought he would be bullied, but he wasn't, in a way the distance was too great. He wasn't one of us and he didn't want to be. His father, the cycling Dane, who perhaps had nurtured an urge to live alone in the middle of the forest ever since his time in Denmark, must have been mortified when the plans for the estate were drawn up and approved and the first construction machinery rolled into the forest just beyond his house. The families who moved in were from all over the country and all of them had children. In the house across the road lived Gustavsen, he was a fireman, she was a housewife, they came from Honningsvåg, their children were called Rolf and Leif Tore. In the house opposite us lived Prestbakmo, he was a school-teacher, she was a nurse, they came from Troms, their children's names were Gro and Geir. On the same side was Kanestrøm, he worked at the Post Office, she was a housewife, they came from Kristiansund, their children were called Steinar, Ingrid Anne, Dag Lothar and Unni. On the other side was Karlsen, he was a sailor, she was a shop assistant, they were from Sørland, their children were Kent Arne and Anne Lene. Above them was Christensen, he was a sailor, I don't know what she did, their children were called Marianne and Eva. On the other side lived Jacobsen, he was a typographer, she was a housewife, both were from Bergen, their children were Geir, Trond and Wenche. Above them, Lindland, from Sørland, their children were Geir Håkon and Morten. Around there I began to lose track, at least as far as the parents' names and jobs were concerned. The children there were: Bente, Tone Elisabeth, Tone, Liv Berit, Steinar, Kåre, Rune, Jan Atle, Oddlaug and Halvor. Most were my age, the oldest seven years above me, the youngest four years below. Five of them would later be in my class.

We moved there in the summer of 1970, when most of the houses on the site were still being built. The shrill warning siren, which sounded before an explosion, was a common feature of my childhood, and that very distinctive feeling of doom you can experience when the shock waves from the explosion ripple through the ground causing the floor of the house to tremble was common too. It was natural to think of connections above the ground – roads, electric cables, forests and seas – but more disturbing to think of them being beneath the ground as well. What we stood on, shouldn't that be absolutely immovable and impenetrable? At the same time all the openings in the ground had a very special fascination for me and the other children I grew up with. It was not uncommon for us to flock around one of the many holes being dug in our area, whether for sewage pipes or electric cables, or for the foundations of a cellar, and to stare down into the depths, yellow where there was sand, black, brown or reddish brown where there was soil, grey where there was clay, and sooner or later the bottom was always covered with an opaque layer of greyish-yellow water, its surface sometimes broken by the top of a huge rock or two. Above the hole towered a shiny yellow or orange excavator, not unlike a bird, with its bucket like a beak at the extreme end of a long neck, and beside it a stationary lorry, with headlights like eyes, the radiator grille like a mouth and the tarpaulin-covered rear, a back. In the case of large construction projects there would also be bulldozers or dumper trucks, usually yellow, with enormous wheels and tread that was a hand's width. If we were lucky we would find piles of detonation cord in or near the hole, which we pinched because the cord had a high swap and utility value. Besides this, there were normally drums nearby, the height of a man, wooden bobbin-like constructions from which cables were unfurled, and piles of smooth reddish-brown plastic pipes measuring the approximate diameter of our forearms. There were further piles of cement pipes and pre-cast cement wells, so rough and wonderful, a bit taller than us, perfect for climbing on; long immovable mats of old cut-up car tyres, which they used during the blasting; mounds of wooden telephone poles, green from the preservative they had been impregnated with; boxes of dynamite; sheds where the workmen changed their clothes and ate. If they were there we kept a respectful distance and watched what they were doing. If they weren't, we clambered down the holes, onto the dumper truck wheels, balanced on the piles of pipes, rattled the shed doors and peered through the windows, jumped down into the cement wells, tried to roll the drums away, filled our pockets with cable clippings, plastic handles and detonation cord. In our world no one had greater status than these workmen; no work seemed more meaningful than theirs. The technical details were of no interest to me, they meant as little as the make of the construction machines. What fascinated me most, apart from the changes in the landscape they wrought, were the manifestations of their private lives that came with them. When they produced a comb from their orange overalls or baggy, almost shapeless, blue trousers and combed their hair, safety helmet under their arm, amid all the droning and pounding of their machines, for example, or the mysterious, indeed almost incomprehensible, moment when they emerged from the shed in the afternoon wearing absolutely normal clothes and got into their cars and drove off like absolutely normal men.

There were other workmen we watched closely, indefatigably. If anyone from Televerket appeared in the vicinity, the news spread like wildfire among the groups of children. There was the car, there was the workman, a telecom engineer, and there were his FANTASTIC climber shoes! With those on his feet and a tool belt around his waist he clicked a harness that went round both him and the pole, and then with a series of slow and deliberate but for us COMPLETELY incomprehensible movements he began to mount the pole. How was this POSSIBLE? Straight-backed, with no visible sign of effort, no visible use of force, he GLIDED up to the top. Wide-eyed, we stared at him while he worked aloft. Not one of us would leave because soon he would be climbing down again, in the same easy, effortless, incomprehensible way. Imagine having shoes like those, with the curved metal hook that wrapped itself around the post, what couldn't you do?

And then there were the men working on the drainage. The ones who parked their cars by one of the many manhole covers in the road, which were either set in the tarmac or placed on top of a brick circle somewhere close by, and who after putting on rubber boots reaching up to their WAISTS!, levered up the round, enormously heavy, metal lid with a crowbar, shifted it to the side and climbed down. We watched as first their calves disappeared from view, into the hole under the road, next their thighs, then their stomachs, then their chests and finally their heads . . . And what was there beneath if not a tunnel? Where water flowed? Where you could walk? Oh, this was just brilliant. Perhaps he was over there now, beside Kent Arne's bike, which lay strewn across the pavement, about twenty metres away, except that he was *under* the ground! Or were these manholes a kind of station, like wells, where you could inspect the pipes and draw water when there was a fire? No one knew; we were always told to keep our distance when they climbed down. No one dared ask them. No one was strong enough to lift off the heavy coin-shaped metal covers on their own. So it remained a mystery, like so much else in those years.

Even before we started school we were free to roam wherever we wanted, with two exceptions. One was the main road, which ran from Tromøya Bridge to the Fina station. The other was the lake. Never go down to the lake on your own! the adults instilled in us. But, actually, why not? Did they think we would fall into the water? No, that wasn't it, someone said when we were sitting on the rocks beyond the little meadow where we sometimes played football and looking down over the edge of the steep face into the water, perhaps thirty metres beneath us. It was the water sprite. It abducted children.

'Who says so?'

'Mum and dad.'

'Is it *here*?'

'Yes.'

We gazed down at the greyish surface of the water in Ubekilen. It didn't seem improbable that there was something lurking beneath.

'Only here?' someone asked. 'If so, we can go somewhere else. Lake Tjenna?'

'Or Little Hawaii?'

'There are other sprites there. They're dangerous. It's true. Mum and dad told me. They kidnap children and drown them.'

'Could it come up here?'

'Dunno. No, I don't reckon so. No. It's too far. It's only dangerous by the water's edge.'

I was scared of the sprite after that, but not as scared as I was of foxes, the thought of them terrified me, and if I saw a bush stir or I heard something rustle past, then I was off, running to safety, to an opening in the forest that is, or up to the estate, where the foxes never ventured. In fact, I was so frightened of foxes that Yngve only had to say I am a fox, and I am coming to get you – he was in the upper bunk and I was in the lower one – and I froze in terror. No, you aren't, I said. Yes, I am, he said, hanging over the edge and hitting out at me. Despite this and even though he did frighten me now and then, I missed having him there when we each had our own room and suddenly I had to sleep alone. It was okay, after all, it was *inside* the house, the new room, but it wasn't as good as having him there, in the bunk above me. Then I could just ask him things, such as, 'Yngve, are you frightened now?' and he might answer 'No-oo, why should I be? There's nothing to be frightened of here.' And I would know he was right and feel reassured.

The fear of foxes must have worn off when I was about seven. The vacuum it left, however, was soon filled by other fears. One morning I was walking past the TV, it was on although no one was watching, there was a matinee film, and there, oh no, oh no, there was a man with no head walking up a staircase! Aaagh! I ran into my room, but that didn't help, I was just as alone and defenceless there, so off I went in search of mum, if she was at home, or Yngve. The image of the headless man pursued me, and not just in the night, which the other fearful visions I had did. No, the headless man could appear in broad daylight, and if I was alone it made no difference that the sun was shining or the birds were singing, my heart pounded and fear spread like fire to every tiniest nerve end in my body. It upset me more that this darkness could also appear in the daylight. In fact, if there was one thing I was really frightened of, it was this darkness in the light. And the worst of it was that there was nothing I could do about it. Shouting for someone didn't help, standing in the middle of an open area didn't help and running away didn't help. Then there was the front cover of a crime magazine that dad once showed me, a comic he'd had when he was a child, showing a skeleton carrying a man over its back, and the skeleton had turned its head and was looking straight at me through its hollow eye sockets. I was afraid of that skeleton as well; it too appeared in all sorts of expected and unexpected contexts. I was also afraid of the hot water in the bathroom. Because whenever you turned on the hot tap a shrill scream travelled through the pipes, and immediately afterwards, if you didn't turn it off at once, they started banging. These noises, which were one unholy racket, scared the wits out of me. There was a way of avoiding them, you had to turn on the cold water first, and then somehow twiddle the hot tap until the temperature was right. That was what mum, dad and Yngve did. I had tried, but the shrill scream which penetrated the walls and was followed by a crescendo of banging, as though something down below was working itself up into a fury, started the second I touched the hot water tap, and I turned it off as fast as I could, and ran out, my body shaking violently with fear. So, in the morning, I either washed in cold water or took Yngve's dirty but lukewarm water.

Dogs, foxes and plumbing were concrete, physical threats, I knew where I was with them, either they were there or they weren't. But the headless man and the grinning skeleton, they belonged to the kingdom of death, and they couldn't be handled in the same way, they could be anywhere and everywhere, in a cupboard if you opened it in the dark, on the stairs as you were going up or down, in the forest, indeed even under the bed or in the bathroom. I associated my own reflection in windows with the creatures from beyond, perhaps because they only appeared when it was dark outside, but it was a terrible thought, seeing your own reflection in the black window pane and thinking that image is not me, but a ghoul staring in at me.

The year we started school none of us believed in sprites, pixies or trolls any more, we laughed at those who did, but the notion of ghosts and apparitions persisted, perhaps because we didn't dare ignore it; dead people did exist, and we knew that, all of us. Other notions we had, coming from the same tangled realm, that of mythology, were of a happier, more innocent nature, such as that of the pot of gold at the end of a rainbow. Even that autumn when we started the first class we still believed the myth enough for us to go in search of the rainbow. It must have been one Saturday in September, the rain had been tipping down all morning, we were playing on the road below the house where Geir Håkon lived, or to be more precise, in the ditch that was flooded with water. At this precise spot the road passed a blasted rock face, and water was dripping and trickling down from its moss, grass and soil-covered top. We were wearing wellies, thick brightly coloured oilskin trousers and jackets, with the hoods tied around our chins, thus displacing all sound; your own breathing and the movements of your head, where your ears met the inside of the hood, were always loud and clear while everything else was muffled and seemed to be happening a long distance away. Between the trees on the other side of the road and at the top of the mountain above us the mist was thick. The orange rooftops on both sides of the road downhill wore a dull sheen in the grey light. Above the forest at the bottom of the slope the sky hung like a swollen belly, penetrated by the pouring rain which continued to dance on our hoods and now over-sensitive ears.

We made a dam, but the sand we shovelled up kept collapsing, and when we caught sight of Jacobsen's car coming up the hill, we didn't hesitate, we dropped our spades and ran down to their house, where the car was parking at that moment. A bluish ribbon of smoke floated in the air behind the exhaust pipe. The father got out on one side, as thin as a stick, with a fag end in the corner of his mouth, he bent down, pulled the lever underneath the seat and pushed it forward, so that his two sons, Big Geir and Trond, could get out, while the mother, small and chubby, red-haired and pale, let out their daughter, Wenche, on her side.

'Hi,' we said.

'Hi,' said Geir and Trond.

'Where have you been?'

'To town.'

'Hello, boys,' their father said.

'Hi,' we said.

'Do you want to hear what seven hundred and seventy-seven is in German?' he said.

'Yes.'

'*Siebenhundertsiebenundsiebzig*!' he said in his hoarse voice. 'Ha ha ha!'

We laughed with him. His laughter morphed into coughing.

'Right then,' he said when the fit was over. He inserted the key in the car door lock and twisted. His lips kept twitching, and one eye too.

'Where are you off to?' Trond asked.

'Dunno,' I said.

'Can I join you?'

'Of course you can.'

Trond was the same age as Geir and me, but much smaller. His eyes were as round as saucers, his lower lip was thick and red, his nose small. Above this doll-like face grew blond curly hair. His brother looked completely different: his eyes were narrow and crafty, his smile was often mocking, his hair straight and sandy brown, the bridge of his nose freckly. But he was small too.

'Put your waterproof on,' his mother said.

'I'll just get my waterproof,' Trond said, and ran indoors. We stood waiting without saying a word, our arms down by our sides like two penguins. It had stopped raining. A light wind shook the tops of the tall slim pine trees scattered round the gardens below. A thin stream ran down the hill, alongside the road, taking with it little heaps of pine needles, the tiny yellow Vs or fishbones strewn everywhere.

In the sky behind us the cloud cover had opened. The scenery around us, with all the rooftops, lawns, clumps of trees, ridges and slopes, was now suffused with a kind of glow. From the hill above our house, which we called the mountain, a rainbow had risen.

'Look,' I said. 'A rainbow!'

'Wow!' Geir said.

Up at the house Trond had closed the door. He started running towards us.

'There's a rainbow over the mountain!' Geir said.

'Shall we go and look for the pot of gold?'

'Yes, let's!' Trond said.

We ran down the slope. On Karlsen's lawn Anne Lene, Kent Arne's little sister, stood watching us. She was wearing a safety harness; it was attached to a rein so that she wouldn't run off. Her mother's red car was parked in the drive. A light shone from a wall lamp. Outside Gustavsen's house Trond slowed down.

'I'm sure Leif Tore would like to join us,' he said.

'I don't think he's at home,' I said.

'We can ask anyway,' Trond said, walking between the two brick gateposts, which were not hung with any gates and therefore subject to my father's ridicule, and into the drive. A hollow metal globe from which protruded an arrow, all carried by a naked man with a bent back, was cemented to the tops of the posts. It was a sundial, and my father made fun of that too, for what was the point of *two* sundials?

'Leif Tore,' Trond shouted. 'Are you coming out?'

He looked at us. Then we all shouted.

'Leif Tore! Are you coming out?'

A few seconds passed. Then the kitchen window was opened, and his mother stuck out her head.

'He's coming now. He's just putting on his rain gear. You don't need to shout any more.'

I had a precise picture of this pot. Large and black, with three legs, full of glittering objects. Gold, silver, diamonds, rubies, sapphires. There was one at each end of the rainbow. We had looked for it before, without any luck. It was important to be quick, rainbows never lasted long.

Leif Tore, who for a while now had been a shadow behind the yellow glass of the door, opened it at last. A wave of warm air streamed out from behind him. It was always so hot in their house. I caught a slight odour of something that was both acrid and sweet. That was how it smelled in their house. All the houses apart from ours had their own smell, this was theirs.

'What are we going to do?' he said, slamming the door behind him and making the glass rattle.

'There's a rainbow on the mountain. We're going to search for the pot of gold,' Trond said.

'Come on then!' Leif Tore said, breaking into a run. We followed, down the last part of the hill and onto the road going up towards the mountain. Yngve's bike still wasn't back in its place, I could see, but both mum's green Beetle and dad's red Kadett were there. Mum had been doing the hoovering when I left, it was awful, I hated it, it was like a wall pressing itself against me. And they opened the windows while they were cleaning, the air indoors was freezing cold, and it was as if the cold was transmitted to mum as well, she had no space left in her for anything else when she leaned over the wash tub wringing the cloth, or when she pushed the broom or the Hoover across the floor, and since it was only in this surplus space that there was room for me, I also got cold on these Saturday mornings, in fact so cold that the chill penetrated my head and even made it difficult to lie on the bed reading comics, which normally I loved, so that in the end I had no choice but to get dressed and run outside and hope there was something happening there.

Both mum and dad did the cleaning in our house, which was not the norm; to my knowledge none of the other fathers did it, with the possible exception of Prestbakmo, but I had never seen him do it and actually doubted whether he would submit to that kind of work.

But on this day dad had been to town to buy crabs at the harbour, after which he had sat in his office smoking cigarettes and perhaps marking essays, perhaps reading documents, perhaps fiddling around with his stamp collection, or perhaps reading *The Phantom*.

On the other side of our creosoted garden fence, where the path to B-Max started, water from a manhole cover had flooded the forest floor. Rolf, Leif Tore's brother, had said a few days ago that it was dad's responsibility. 'Responsibility', that was not a word he would normally use, so I guessed he had got it from his father. Dad was on the local council, they were the people who made the decisions on the island, and that was what Gustavsen, Leif Tore and Rolf's father, had meant. Dad had to report the flooding so they could send someone to do the repairs. As we walked up and my attention was again caught by the unnaturally large amount of water between the small thin trees, with the odd bit of white toilet paper floating in it what was more, I decided to tell him if the opportunity arose. Tell him he would have to report it at the Monday meeting.

There he was! In his blue waterproof jacket, with no hood, his blue denim trousers, which he wore whenever he was going to work in the garden, and his green knee-high boots, he rounded the corner of the house. His upper body was twisted slightly to one side as he was carrying a ladder with both hands across the lawn, and then he dug it into the ground, straightened up and pushed it into position against the house roof.

I turned back and sped up to catch the others.

'The rainbow's still there!' I shouted.

'We can see it too!' Leif Tore cried.

I caught them up at the start of the path, walked behind Trond's yellow jacket between the trees, which shed a shower of rain every time anyone lifted a branch, down to the dark house where Molden lived. He didn't have any young children, only a teenager with long hair, big glasses, brown clothes and flared trousers. We didn't even know what his name was and we just called him Molden as well.

The best way up to the top of what we called a mountain went past their garden, and that was the path we were taking now, slowly, because it was steep and the long yellow grass here was slippery. Now and then I grabbed a sapling to pull myself up. Just below the summit, the mountain was bare and protruded outwards, impossible to walk up, at least when it was as wet as it was now, but at the edge there was a crevice between the rock face and a gently projecting crag where you could get a foothold and easily clamber up the last few metres to the summit.

'Where's it gone?' Trond said, the first man up.

'It was right there!' Geir said, pointing a few metres along the little plateau.

'Oh no,' Leif Tore said. 'It's down there. Look!'

Everyone turned to look. The rainbow was over the forest, a long way down. One end was above the trees below Beck's house, the other near the grassy incline descending to the bay.

'Shall we go down then?' Trond said.

'What if the treasure's still here?' Leif Tore said, in the dialect we spoke. 'We could at least have a peek.'

'It isn't,' I said. 'It's only where the rainbow is.'

'Who took it then? That's what I'd like to know,' Leif Tore said.

'No one did,' I said. 'Are you daft or what? No one brings it either, if that's what you think. It's the rainbow.'

'You're the one who's daft,' Leif Tore said. 'It can't just disappear all on its own.'

'It seems it can,' I said.

'No, it can't,' Leif Tore said.

'Yes, it can,' I said. 'Have a look then. See if you can find it!'

'I want to look too,' Trond said.

'Me too,' Geir said.

'Count me out,' I said.

They turned and walked away, glancing from side to side. I wanted to go with them, I could feel myself drawn, but it wasn't possible now. Instead I looked at the view. It was the best vantage point anywhere. You could see the bridge almost rising from the treetops, you could see the sound, where there were always boats crossing, and you could see the big white gasometers on the other side. You could see the island of Gjerstadholmen, you could see the new road, the low concrete bridge it crossed, you could see Ubekilen Bay from the landward side. And you could see the estate. All the red and orange roofs among the trees. The road. Our garden, Gustavsen's garden; the rest was hidden.

The sky above the estate was almost completely blue now. The clouds towards the town, white. While on the other side, behind Ubekilen, they were still heavy and grey.

I could see dad down there. A tiny, tiny little figure, no bigger than an ant, on top of the ladder against the roof.

Could he see me up here? I wondered.

A gust of wind blew off the sea.

I turned to watch the others. Two yellow dots and one light green one moving to and fro between the trees. The rocky plateau was dark grey, much like the sky beyond, with yellow and, in some places, whitish grass in the cracks. A branch lay there, all its weight resting on the many needle-thin side branches in such a way that the thick main stem didn't touch the ground. It looked strange.

I had hardly ever been in the forest that lay ahead. The furthest I had gone on the path was to a large uprooted tree, perhaps thirty metres inside. From there you could see down a slope where nothing grew but heather. With the tall slim pine trees on both sides and the denser-growing spruces like a wall beneath, it resembled a large room.

Geir said he saw a fox there once. I didn't believe him, but foxes were no laughing matter, so for safety's sake we had taken with us a packed lunch and bottles of juice to the edge of the mountain, where the whole of the world as we knew it lay beneath us.

'Here it is!' Leif Tore shouted. 'Wow! The pot of gold!'

'Wow!' Geir shouted.

'You can't fool me!' I shouted back.

'Yippeeeee!' Leif Tore cried. 'We're rich!'

'I don't believe it!' Trond shouted.

Then it all went quiet.

Had they really found it?

Not at all. They were trying to trick me.

But the end of the rainbow had been on this precise spot.

What if Leif Tore was right and the treasure hadn't disappeared with the rainbow?

I took a few steps forward and tried to see through the juniper bushes they were standing behind.

'Ohhh, cripes! Look at this!' Leif Tore said.

I made up my mind in a flash and hurried over, dashing between the trees and past the bushes, then stopped.

They looked at me.

'Gotcha! Ha ha ha! We gotcha!'

'I knew all the time,' I said. 'I was just coming to get you. The rainbow will be gone if we don't hurry.'

'Oh yes,' said Leif Tore. 'We tricked you good and proper. Admit it.'

'Come on, Geir,' I said. 'Let's go and look for the pot of gold down there.'

Feeling uncomfortable, Geir looked at Leif Tore and Trond.

But he was my best friend and joined me. Trond and Leif Tore ambled along after us.

'I need a piss,' Leif Tore said. 'Shall we see who can piss the furthest? Over the edge? It'll be one great big long jet!'

Piss outdoors when dad was down there and might be able to see?

Leif Tore was already out of his waterproof trousers and fumbling with his fly zip. Geir and Trond had taken up positions either side of him and were wriggling their hips and pulling down their trousers.

'I can't piss,' I said. 'I've just had one.'

'You haven't,' Geir said, turning towards me with both his hands around his willy. 'We've been together all day.'

'I had a piss while you were looking for the treasure,' I said.

The next second they were enveloped in a cloud of steam as they pissed. I stepped forward to see who won. Surprisingly, it was Trond.

'Rolf pulled his foreskin back,' Leif Tore said, closing his flies. 'So he pissed much further from the off.'

'The rainbow's gone,' Geir said, shaking his dick for a last time before tucking it back.

Everyone looked down over the edge.

'What shall we do now?' Trond said.

'No idea,' said Leif Tore.

'Let's go to the boathouse, shall we?' I suggested.

'What can we do there?' said Leif Tore.

'Well, we can climb onto the roof,' I said.

'Good idea!' Leif Tore said.

We zigzagged down the slope, fought our way through the dense spruce forest and arrived five minutes later on the gravel road that ran around the bay. The grassy hill on the other side was where we usually went skiing in the winter. In the summer and autumn we seldom went there, what was there to do? The bay was shallow and muddy, no good for swimming, the jetty was falling to pieces, and the little island off the coast was covered with shit from the colony of gulls nesting there. When we wandered around there it was mostly because we were at a loose end, like this morning. High above us, between the sloping field and the edge of the forest there was an old white house in which an old white-haired lady lived. We knew nothing about her. Not her name, nor what she did there. Sometimes we peered into the house, laid our hands against the window and pressed our faces against the glass. Not for any particular reason, nor out of curiosity, more because we could. We saw a sitting room with old furniture or a kitchen with old utensils. Near the house, past the narrow gravel road, there was a red barn seemingly on the verge of collapse. And at the very bottom, by the stream running down from the forest, there was an old unpainted boathouse with tarred felt on the roof. Along the bed of the stream grew ferns and some plants with, relative to their thin stems, enormous leaves; if you swept them aside with your hands, in that swimming stroke way people do, to see past the unresisting foliage, the ground appeared naked, as though the plants were deceiving us, pretending they were lush and green while in reality, beneath the dense leaves, there was almost nothing but soil. Further down, closer to the water, the earth or clay or whatever it was, was a reddish colour reminiscent of rust. Occasionally a variety of things got caught there, a bit of a plastic bag or a johnnie, but not on days like today, when the water gushed out from the pipe under the road in an enormous torrent and only abated when it reached the little delta-like area where the water fanned out before it met the bay.

The boathouse was grey with age. In some places you could insert a hand between the planks, so we knew what the inside looked like, without any of us having been in there. After peering through these gaps for a while we directed our attention to the roof, which we were going to try to climb. In order to do so we would have to find something to stand on. Nothing in the immediate vicinity was of any use, so we sneaked up to the barn and did a recce there. First of all, we made sure there were no cars up behind the house, there was one there sometimes, the owner was a man, perhaps her son, he would occasionally stop us crossing the drive when we wanted to extend our ski run, which she never did. So we kept an eye open for him.

No car.

Some white cans strewn by the wall. I recognised them from my grandparents' farm; it was formic acid. A rusty oil drum. A door hanging off its hinges.

Over there though! A pallet!

We lifted it. It had almost grown into the ground. Full of woodlice and small spider-like insects crawling all over the place as we lifted. Then we carried it between us all the way across the field and down to the boathouse. Leaned it against the wall. Leif Tore, acknowledged to be the bravest among us, was the first to have a go. Standing on the pallet, he managed to get one elbow on the roof. With his other hand he took a firm grip on the edge of the roof, and then he *launched* one leg into the air. He got it over the edge, for an instant it rested on the roof, but as soon as his body followed, he lost his grip and plummeted like a sack of potatoes, unable to break his fall with his hands. He hit the slanted pallet with his ribs and slid down to the ground.

'Agh!' he screamed. 'Oh shit. Ooohh. Ow! Ow! Ow!'

He slowly got to his feet, studied his hands and rubbed one buttock.

'Oooh, that hurt! Someone else can try now!'

He looked at me.

'My arms aren't strong enough,' I said.

'I'll give it a bash,' Geir said.

If Leif Tore was known for being brave, Geir was known for being wild. Not by nature, because had it been up to him he would have stayed at home drawing and pottering about to his heart's content all day long, but when he was challenged. Perhaps he was a bit gullible. That summer he and I had built a cart, with a great deal of help from his father, and when it was finished I got him to push me around, just by saying it would make him strong. Gullible but also foolhardy, sometimes all boundaries ceased to exist for him, then he was capable of anything.

Geir chose a different method to Leif Tore. Standing on the pallet, he grabbed the protruding roof with both hands and tried to *walk* up the wall, with all of his weight invested in the fingers he was holding on with. That was, of course, stupid. Even if he had managed it, he would have been standing horizontal to the ground *under* the roof, in a much worse position than when he started.

His fingers slipped and he plunged arse first onto the pallet, after which he hit the back of his head.

He gave an involuntary grunt. When he stood up I could see that he had really hurt himself. He took a few determined paces to and fro, grunting. *Nghn!* Then he mounted the pallet again. This time he adopted Leif Tore's method. Once he had his leg over the edge, a series of electric charges seemed to shoot through him, his leg banged against the roofing felt, his body writhed, and hey presto, there he was, kneeling on the roof and looking down on us.

'Easy!' he said. 'Come on! I can pull you up!'

'You cannot. You aren't strong enough!' Trond said.

'We can give it a try at any rate,' Geir said.

'You'd better come down,' Leif Tore said. 'I have to go home soon anyway.'

'Me too,' I said.

He didn't seem disappointed though, up there. Determined would be a more accurate term.

'I'll jump down then,' he said.

'Isn't it a bit high?' Leif Tore said.

'Not at all,' Geir said. 'Just have to put my mind to it.'

He squatted down and stared at the ground while taking deep breaths as though intending to dive into water. For a second all the tension in his body was gone, he must have changed his mind, but then he braced himself and he jumped. Fell, rolled around, bounced up again like a spring and started brushing his thigh to signal composure, almost before he was upright.

Had I been the only one of us to climb the roof, it would have been a great triumph. Leif Tore would never have given in. Even if he had spent all night climbing up and falling off he would have gone on trying to reduce the imbalance that had suddenly become apparent. Geir was different though. In fact, he could pull off the most amazing feats, like jumping five metres through the air into a snowdrift, something no one else would dare, and it meant nothing to him. It was of no real consequence. Geir was just Geir, whatever he got into his head to do.

Without another word, we walked up the hill. In some places the water had carried parts of the road surface along with it, in others there were long sunken dips. We stopped for a while and pressed our heels into an especially soft patch, the wet gravel oozed over the edge of our boots, it was a good feeling. My hands were cold. When I squeezed them my fingers left white marks in the red flesh. But the warts, three on one thumb, two on the other, one on an index finger, three on the back of my hand, didn't change colour, they were a dull reddish-brown colour as always and covered with a layer of small dots you could scratch off. Then we went into the other part of the field, the bit that came to an end by a stone wall and the forest behind it; it was as though it was bordered by a long ridge, quite steep, perhaps ten metres high, clad with a line of spruce trees, broken occasionally by a knoll of bare rock. Walking here or in similar areas, I often happily indulged the notion that the countryside resembled the sea. And that fields were the surface of the sea with mountains and islands rising from them.

Oh, to sail in a boat through the forest! To swim among the trees! Now *that* would be something.

We sometimes used to drive to the far side of the island when the weather was good, park the car on the old shooting range and walk down to the sea-smoothed rocks, our regular spot, not so far from Spornes beach, where of course I would have preferred to be, as there was sand and I could wade out to a depth that suited me. By the rocks the water was immediately very deep. There was, however, a little inlet, a kind of narrow cleft that filled up with water, which you could climb down into, where you could swim, but it was small and the sea bottom was uneven, covered with barnacles, seaweed and shells. The waves beat against the rocks outside, causing the water to rise inside, sometimes up to your neck, and the styrofoam floats on the life jacket I wore were lifted up to my ears. The sheer walls amplified the gurgling and slopping of the water, making them somehow sound hollow. Terrified, I would stand there, suddenly incapable of drawing breath in any other way than with great, shuddering gasps. It was just as creepy when the waves receded and the water level inside sank with a slurp. When the sea was calm, dad would sometimes inflate the yellow and green lilo, which I was allowed to lie on and float close to the shore, where with my bare front stuck to the wet plastic and my back hot and dry from the burning sun I would splash around, paddling with my hands in the water, which was so fresh and salty, watching the seaweed languidly sway to and fro along the rocks it was attached to, looking for fish or crabs or following a boat on the horizon. In the afternoon the Danish ferry came in, we could see it in the distance when we arrived, and it would be in the Galtesund strait when we left, white, enormous, towering above the low islands and reefs. Was it MS *Venus*? Or was it *Christian IV*? Kids all along the southern and western sides of the island, and presumably also the kids living on the other side of Galte Sound, on the, for us, foreign island of Hisøya, would go swimming when it came because its wake was immense and notorious. One afternoon, as I was paddling around on the lilo, the sudden waves made me sit up and I toppled into the water. I sank like a stone. The water would have been about three metres deep there. I thrashed around with my arms and legs, shouted in panic, swallowed water, which only increased my fear, but it didn't last more than twenty seconds because dad had seen everything. He dived in and dragged me to the shore. I regurgitated some water, I was very cold, and we went home. I hadn't been in any real danger and the incident had no lasting effect, except to leave me with the feeling I had as I walked up the hill to tell Geir what had happened: the world was something I walked on top of, it was impenetrable and hard, it was impossible to sink through it, no matter if it rose in steep mountains, or fell in deep valleys. Of course I had known it was like that, but I had never felt it before, the sense that we were walking on a surface.

Despite this incident and the unease I could occasionally feel when I was paddling in the narrow inlet I always looked forward to these trips. Sitting on a towel beside Yngve and scanning the light blue mirror-glass sea that only ended on the horizon, where big ships glided slowly past like hour hands, or looking at the two lighthouses on Torungen, the white a sharp contrast with the bright blue sky: not much was better than that. Drinking pop that had been in the red-checked cooler bag, eating biscuits, perhaps watching dad as he walked to the edge of the rocks, tanned and muscular, and dived into the sea two metres below a second later. The way he shook his head and stroked back the hair from his eyes when he emerged, the rush of bubbles around him, a rare gleam of pleasure in his eyes as he swam to shore with those slow, ponderous lunges of his arms, his body bobbing up and down in the swell. Or walking to the two sinkholes nearby, one a man's depth with distinct spiral marks in the rock on the way down, filled with salty seawater, covered by green sea plants and at the bottom clusters of seaweed, the second less deep but no less beautiful for that. Or up to the shallow, extremely salty, hot pools that filled the hollows in the rock, refreshed only when there were storms, the surface thick with tiny swirling insects and the bottom bedecked with yellow sickly-looking algae.

On one such day dad decided to teach me how to swim. He told me to follow him down to the water's edge. Perhaps half a metre below the surface a small slippery ridge overgrown with seaweed jutted into the sea, and that was where I was to stand. Dad swam out to a reef four or five metres from the shore. And turned to face me.

'Now you swim over here to me,' he said.

'But it's deep!' I said. Because it was, the seabed between the two reefs was barely visible, it was probably three metres down.

'I'm here, Karl Ove. Don't you think I could rescue you if you sank? Come on, swim. It's not in the slightest bit dangerous! I know you can do it. Launch yourself and do the strokes. If you do that you can swim, you know! Then you can swim!'

I crouched down in the water.

The seabed was a greenish glimmer a long way down. Would I be able to float over that?

My heart only beat this hard when I was frightened.

'I can't,' I shouted.

'Course you can!' dad shouted back. 'It's so easy! Just push off, do a couple of strokes and you'll be here.'

'I can't!' I said.

He studied me. Then he sighed and swam over.

'OK,' he said. 'I'll swim beside you. I can hold a hand under your tummy. Then you *can't* sink!'

But I *couldn't* do it. Why didn't he understand?

I started to cry.

'I can't,' I said.

The depth of the water was in my head and in my chest. The depth was in my arms and legs, in my fingers and toes. The depth filled all of me. Was I supposed to be able to *think* that away?

There weren't any more smiles to be seen now. With a stern expression he clambered onto the land, walked over to our things and returned with my life jacket.

'Put this on then,' he said, throwing it to me. 'Now you *can't* sink even if you tried.'

I put it on, even though I knew it didn't change anything.

He swam out again. Turned to face me.

'Try now!' he said. 'Over here to me!'

I crouched down. The water washed over my trunks. I stretched my arms under the water.

'That's the way!' dad said.

All I had to do was push off, do a few strokes and it would be all over.

But I couldn't. I would never ever be able to swim across that deep water. Tears were rolling down my cheeks.

'Come on, boy!' dad shouted. 'We haven't got all day!'

'I CAN'T!' I shouted back. 'CAN'T YOU HEAR?'

He stiffened and glared at me, his eyes furious.

'Are you being stroppy?' he said.

'No,' I answered, unable to suppress a sob. My arms were shaking.

He swam over and took a firm grip of my arm.

'Come here,' he said. He tried to tow me out. I twisted my body towards the shore.

'I don't want to!' I said.

He let go and took a deep breath.

'You don't say,' he said. 'We know that, don't we.'

Then he went to where we had left our clothes, lifted the towel with both hands and rubbed his face. I took off the life jacket and followed him, stopping a few metres away. He raised one arm and dried underneath, then the other. Bent forward and dried his thighs. Threw the towel down, picked up his shirt and buttoned it while surveying the perfectly calm sea. Then he pulled on a pair of socks and stuck his feet in his shoes. They were brown leather shoes without laces, which matched neither the socks nor his bathing trunks.

'What are you waiting for?' he said.

I pulled the light blue Las Palmas T-shirt I had been given by my grandparents over my head and laced up my blue trainers. Dad tossed the two empty pop bottles and the orange peel in the cooler bag, slung it over his shoulder and set off, the wet towel crumpled up in his other hand. He said nothing on the way to the car. Opened the boot, put in the cooler bag, took the life jacket from my hands and placed it next to the bag together with his towel. The fact that I also had a towel didn't seem to enter his head and I certainly didn't intend to bother him with that.

Even though he had parked in the shade, the car was in the sun. The black seats were boiling hot and burned against my thighs. I wondered briefly whether to put my wet towel over the seat. But he would notice. Instead I placed my palms downwards and sat on them, as close to the edge as I could.

Dad started the car and drove off at walking speed; the whole of the open gravel area, known as the firing range, was full of large stones. The road he took afterwards was pitted with potholes too, so he drove equally slowly along there. Green branches and bushes brushed the bonnet and roof, sometimes there was the odd thump, as a branch hit the car. My hands were still stinging, but less so now. It was only then it struck me that dad was also wearing shorts on a red-hot seat. I glanced at his face in the mirror. It was grim and uncommunicative, but there was no indication that his thighs were burning.

When we came out onto the main road below the church he accelerated away and drove the five kilometres home at far above the speed limit.

'He's frightened of water,' he told my mother that afternoon. It wasn't true, but I said nothing. I wasn't stupid.

A week later my grandparents on my mother's side came to visit us. It was the first time they had been to Tybakken. Back on their farm in Sørbøvåg they weren't the slightest bit out of place, they fitted in perfectly, grandad with his blue overalls and black, narrow-brimmed hats, long brown rubber boots and constant spitting of tobacco, grandma with her worn but clean flowery dresses, grey hair and broad body, and hands that always trembled slightly. But when they got out of the car in the drive in front of our house, after dad had picked them up from Kjevik, I could see at once they didn't fit in. Grandad was wearing his grey Sunday suit, light blue shirt and a grey hat, in his hand he held his pipe, not by the stem, the way dad did, but with his fingers round the bowl. He used the stem to point with, I noticed, when later they were being shown around our garden. Grandma wore a light grey coat, light grey shoes and on her arm she carried a bag. No one dressed like that here. You never saw anyone dressed like that in Arendal either. It was as though they came from another era.

They filled our rooms with their strangeness. Mum and dad suddenly behaved differently too, mostly dad, who behaved just as he did at Christmas. His invariable 'No' became 'Why not?'; his ever watchful eyes became affable and a friendly hand could even be placed on my or Yngve's shoulder as a casual greeting. But even though he chatted to grandma with interest, I could see that in fact he wasn't interested, there were always brief moments when he looked away, and then his eyes tended to be utterly lifeless. Grandad, cheerful and enthusiastic, but somehow smaller and more vulnerable here than he was at home, never appeared to notice this trait of dad's. Or perhaps he just ignored it.

One evening when they were with us dad bought some crabs. For him they were the apotheosis of festive food, and even though it was early in the season there was meat in the ones he had managed to find. But my grandparents, they didn't eat crabs. If grandad got crabs in the net, well, he would throw them back. Dad would later tell stories about this, he viewed it as comical, a kind of superstition, that crabs should be less clean than fish, just because they crawled over the seabed and didn't swim as they pleased through the water above. Crabs might eat dead bodies, since they eat everything that falls to the bottom, but what were the odds of *these* crabs having chanced upon a corpse in the depths of the Skagerrak?

One afternoon we had been sitting in the garden drinking coffee and juice, afterwards I had gone to my room, where I lay on my bed reading comics, and I heard grandma and grandad coming up the stairs. They didn't say anything, trod heavily on the steps and went into the living room. The sunlight on the wall of my room was golden. The lawn outside had great patches of yellow and even brown, although dad switched on the sprinkler the instant the local council gave permission. Everything I could see along the road, all the houses, all the gardens, all the cars and all the tools leaning against walls and doorsteps were in a state of slumber, it seemed to me. My sweaty chest stuck uncomfortably to the duvet cover. I got up, opened the door and went into the living room, where grandma and grandad were sitting in their separate chairs.

'Would you like to watch TV?' I asked.

'Yes, the news is on soon, isn't it?' grandma said. 'That's what interests us, you know.'

I went over and switched on the TV. A few seconds passed before the picture appeared. Then the screen slowly lit up, the 'N' of *Dagsrevyen* grew larger and larger as the simple xylophone jingle sounded, *ding-dong-ding-dooong*, faint at first, then louder and louder. I took a step back. Grandad leaned forward in his chair, the pipe stem pointing away from his hand.

'There we are,' I said.

Actually, I wasn't allowed to turn on the TV, nor the large radio on the shelf by the wall, I always had to ask mum or dad if they could do it for me when there was something I wanted to see or listen to. But now I was doing it for grandma and grandad, surely he wouldn't object to that.

All of a sudden the picture started flickering wildly. The colours became distorted. Then there was a flash, a loud *puff!* and then the screen went black.

Oh no.

Oh no, oh no, oh no.

'What happened to the TV?' grandad asked.

'It's broken,' I said, my eyes full of tears.

It was me who had broken it.

'It can happen,' grandad said. 'And actually we like the news on the radio better.'

He got up from his chair and shuffled over to the radio with his small steps. I went into my room. Chill with fear, my stomach churning, I lay down on the bed. The duvet cover was cool against my hot bare skin. I took a comic from the pile on the floor. But I was unable to read. Soon he would come in, go over to the TV and switch it on. If it had broken while I had been alone perhaps I could have acted as if nothing had happened, then he would have thought it had stopped working of its own accord. Although probably he would have worked out that it was me even so, because he had a nose for anything untoward, one glance at me was enough for him to know something was wrong and he put two and two together. Now, however, I couldn't feign ignorance, grandma and grandad had been witnesses, they would tell him what had happened, and if I tried to hide anything it would make matters much, much worse.

I sat up on the bed. I had a knot in my stomach, but there was no hint of the warmth and softness that illness brought with it, it was cold and painful and so tight that no tears in the world could undo it.

For a while I sat crying.

If only Yngve had been at home. Then I could have stayed with him in his room for as long as possible. But he was out swimming with Steinar and Kåre.

A sense that I would be nearer to him if I went into his room, even though it was empty, brought me to my feet. I opened the door, tiptoed along the landing and into his room. His bed had been painted blue, mine orange, in the same way as his cupboard doors were blue and mine were orange. The room smelled of Yngve. I went to the bed and sat down.

The window was ajar!

That was more than I had dared hope for. Now I could hear their voices down on the terrace without their knowing I was here. If the window had been closed I would have revealed my presence when I opened it.

Dad's voice rose and sank in the calm manner it did when he was in a good mood. Now and then I caught mum's brighter, gentler voice. From the living room came the sound of the radio. For some reason I had the impression that my grandparents were asleep, each in their separate chairs, their mouths open and their eyes closed, perhaps they often sat like that in Sørbøvåg when we visited them.

There was a clink of cups outside.

Were they clearing the table?

Yes, because straight afterwards I heard the flip-flop of mum's sandals as she walked around the house.

At once I wanted to have her for myself! Then I would be able to tell her first!

I waited until I heard the door below being opened. Then, as mum came upstairs carrying a tray of cups, dishes, glasses and the shiny coffee pot with the red lid standing on a garland of clothes pegs that Yngve had made at mum's arts and crafts workshop I went out onto the landing.

'Are you inside in this hot weather?' she said.

'Yes,' I answered.

She was about to walk past, but then she stopped.

'Is there something the matter?' she asked.

I looked down.

'Is there?'

'The TV's bust,' I said.

'Oh no,' she said. 'That's a pity. Are grandma and grandad in there?'

I nodded.

'I was just about to go and get them. It's such a fantastic evening. You come out too, come on. You can have some more juice if you want.'

I shook my head and went back into my room. Stopped inside the door. Perhaps it would be wisest to join them outside? He wouldn't do anything if they were there, even if he found out I had broken the TV.

But that in itself could make him even more furious. Last time we had been to Sørbøvåg everyone had been sitting round the dinner table, and Kjartan had been saying that Yngve had had a fight with Bjørn Atle, the boy on the neighbouring farm. Everyone had laughed at that, dad too. But when mum had taken me to the shop and the others were having a midday nap, and Yngve had gone to bed to read a comic, dad had gone in, lifted him up and shaken him about because he had been fighting.

Nope, the best would be to stay here. If grandad or mum said the TV was broken he might lose his temper while he was sitting there with them.

I lay back down on my bed. My chest trembled uncontrollably; another flood of tears was set in motion.

Ohhhh. Ohhhh. Ohhhh.

He would be coming soon.

I knew it.

Soon he would be here.

I put my hands over my ears and closed my eyes and tried to pretend nothing existed. Only this darkness and this breathing.

But a feeling of defencelessness overcame me, and I did the opposite, knelt on the bed and looked out of the window, at the flood of light falling across the landscape, the glowing roof tiles and glinting window panes.

The door downstairs was opened and slammed.

I cast around wildly. Got up, pulled the chair from under the desk and sat down.

Footsteps on the stairs. They were heavy; it was him.

I couldn't sit with my back to the door and got up again. Perched on the edge of the bed.

He thrust open the door. Took a step inside and stopped, looked at me.

His eyes were narrow, his lips clenched.

'What are you doing, boy?' he said.

'Nothing,' I said, eyes downcast.

'Look at me when you talk to me!' he said.

I looked at him. But I couldn't. I looked down again.

'Something wrong with your ears as well?' he said. 'LOOK AT ME!'

I looked at him. But his eyes, I couldn't meet them.

He took three quick strides across the floor, grabbed my ear and twisted it as he dragged me to my feet.

'What did I tell you about switching on the TV?' he said.

I fought for breath and was unable to answer.

'WHAT DID I SAY?' he said, twisting harder.

'That I . . . that I sh . . . sh . . . shouldn't do it,' I said.

He let go of my ear, grabbed both of my arms and shook me.

'NOW LOOK AT ME!' he yelled.

I raised my head. Tears almost blurred him out.

His fingers squeezed harder.

'Didn't I tell you to keep away from the TV? Eh? Didn't I tell you? Now we'll have to buy a new TV and where will we get the money from? Can you answer me that, eh!'

'No-o-o-o,' I sobbed.

He threw me down on the bed.

'Now you stay in your room until I tell you otherwise. Have you understood?'

'Yes,' I said.

'You're grounded tonight, and you're grounded tomorrow.'

'OK.'

Then he was gone. I was crying so much I couldn't hear where he went. My breathing was jerky, as though it was moving up a staircase. My chest was trembling, my hands were trembling. I lay there crying for twenty minutes perhaps. Then it started to ease. I knelt on the bed and gazed out of the window. My legs were still shaking, my hands were shaking, but it was loosening its hold on me, I could feel, it was as though I had entered a quiet room after a storm.

From the window I could see Prestbakmo's house and the entire front of their garden, which bordered ours, Gustavsen's house and the front of their garden, a bit of Karlsen's house and a bit of Christensen's at the top. I had a view of the road as far as the post box stand. The sun, which seemed to become a touch fuller in the afternoon, hung in the sky above the trees on the ridge. The air was perfectly still, not a tree or a bush stirred. People never sat in their front gardens, that would be 'displaying yourself', as dad would say, making yourself visible to all; behind the house was where all the garden furniture and the grills were in this neighbourhood.

Then something happened. Kent came out of the door of Karlsen's house. I saw just his head above the parked car, the coruscating white hair gliding along like a puppet in a puppet show. He was gone for a few seconds, then he reappeared on his bike. He stood up on the pedals, jerking them backwards to brake, shot out onto the road and built up a pretty good speed before braking hard and swerving and coming to a halt in front of Gustavsen's house. He had lost his father, who had been a sailor, two years ago. I could barely remember him, in fact I had only one image of him, once when we were walking down the hill, it was sunny and cold, but there was no snow, I was holding my small orange skates with three blades and straps to attach them to your shoes, so we must have been on our way to Lake Tjenna. I could also remember when I found out that he had died. Leif Tore had been standing by the line of concrete barriers that separated Nordåsen Ringvei from Elgstien, just outside our house, and had said that Kent Arne's father was dead. While he was telling me we looked up at their house. He had been trying to pull someone out of a tank that was being cleaned, it had been full of gas and they had fainted, and then he too had lost consciousness and died. We never talked about Kent Arne's father when he was there, or about death. Another man had just moved in, whose name, strangely enough, was also Karlsen.

If Dag Lothar was number one, then Kent Arne was number two, even though he was a year younger than us and two years younger than Dag Lothar. Leif Tore was number three, Geir Håkon number four, Trond number five, Geir number six and I was number seven.

'Leif Tore, are you coming out?!' Kent Arne shouted in front of the house. Soon after, he emerged, wearing only blue denim shorts and trainers, got on Rolf's bike, and they cycled down the hill and were gone. Prestbakmo's cat lay motionless on the flat rock between Gustavsen's and Hansen's properties.

I lay back on the bed. Read some comics, got up and flattened my ear against the door to hear if anything was happening in the living room, but not a sound, they were still outside. My grandparents were visiting, so it was unthinkable that I wouldn't be given any supper. Or was it?

Half an hour later they came upstairs. One of them went into the bathroom, which was adjacent to my room. It wasn't dad, I could tell that from the footsteps, which were lighter than his. But I couldn't tell whether it was mum, grandma or grandad, until the flushing of the toilet was followed by a loud banging from the hot water pipes, which only grandma or grandad could have caused.

Now I was seriously hungry.

The shadows that descended over the ground outside were so long and distorted that they no longer bore any resemblance to the forms that created them. As though they had sprung forth in their own right, as though there existed a parallel reality of darkness, with dark-fences, dark-trees, dark-houses, populated by dark-people, somehow stranded here in the light, where they seemed so misshapen and helpless, as far from their element as a reef with seaweed and shells and crabs is from the receding water, one might imagine. Oh, isn't that why shadows get longer and longer in the evening? They are reaching out for the night, this tidal water of darkness that washes over the earth to fulfil for a few hours the shadows' innermost yearnings.

I looked at my watch. It was ten minutes past nine. In twenty minutes it would be bedtime.

In the afternoon the worst part of being grounded was that you couldn't go out and you stood at the window watching everyone else outside. In the evening the worst part was that there was no clear dividing line between the various phases which usually constituted an evening. After sitting up for some hours I simply pulled off my clothes and got into bed. The difference between the two states, which was normally so great, was almost completely eradicated when you were grounded, and that led to my becoming aware of myself in a way that I normally wasn't. It was as if the person I was *while* doing whatever I was doing, such as eating supper, cleaning my teeth, washing my face, or putting on my pyjamas, not only revealed itself but also filled my whole being, as all of a sudden there was simply *nothing* else. I was exactly the same person when I was sitting on the bed fully dressed as I was lying in it without my clothes on. In fact, there were no real dividing lines or transitions.

It was an irksome feeling.

I went to the door and placed my ear against it again. At first it was quiet, then I heard some voices, then it was quiet again. I cried a few tears, then I took off my T-shirt and shorts and got into bed with the duvet drawn up to my chin. The sun still shone on the wall opposite. I read some comics, then I put them on the floor and closed my eyes. My last thought before I fell asleep was that it hadn't been my fault.

I woke up, looked at my wristwatch. The two luminous snakes showed it was ten minutes past two. I lay quite still for a while in an attempt to work out what had woken me. Apart from my pulse, which throbbed as if whispering in my ear, everything was silent. No cars on the road, no boats in Tromøya Sound, no planes flying overhead. No footsteps, no voices, nothing. Nor from our house.

I raised my head a little so that my ears weren't touching anything and held my breath. After a few seconds I heard a noise from the garden. A noise so high-pitched that at first I didn't catch it, but the moment I became aware of it I was terrified.

Eeee-eeee-eeeeee-eeeee. Eeeeeee-eeee-eeeeeee. Eeeeee.

I sat up on my knees, drew the curtain to the side and peered through the window. The lawn was bathed in a weak light: the moon above our house was full. A gust of wind made it look as if the grass was racing away. A white plastic bag caught on the end of the hedge was flapping, and it struck me that someone who didn't know that wind existed would have thought that the bag was moving of its own accord. As though I was perched high above the ground, the tips of my toes and fingers tingled. My heart was beating fast. The muscles in my stomach tightened, I swallowed, and swallowed again. Night was the time for ghosts and apparitions, night was the time for the headless man and the grinning skeleton. And all that separated me from it was a thin wall.

There was that sound again!

Eeee-eeeeeeeee-eee-eeeeeeeeeeeeeeeee-eee-eeeeeee.

I scanned the grey lawn outside. Over by the hedge, perhaps five metres away, I caught sight of Prestbakmo's cat. It was lying stretched out in the grass and smacking something with its paw. Whatever it was smacking, a grey lump like stone or clay, was thrown a few metres closer to the window. The cat rose and followed. The lump lay still in the grass. The cat tentatively hit out at it a few more times, moved closer with its head and seemed to nudge it with its nose, then opened its jaws and took it in its mouth. When the squeaking started again I guessed it was a mouse. The sudden noise appeared to confuse the cat. At any rate it tossed its head and flung the mouse in the air. This time it didn't stay where it landed, it made a headlong dash across the lawn. The cat stood watching, motionless. It looked as if it was about to let the mouse go. But then, just as the mouse reached the bed by the gate to Prestbakmo's garden, it set off. Three bounds and the cat had caught it again.

In the room beside mine I heard dad's voice. It was low and mumbling, without beginning or end, the way it often sounded when he was talking in his sleep. A moment later someone got up from their bed. From the lightness of foot I realised it was mum. Outside, the cat had started jumping up and down. It looked like some kind of dance. Another gust of wind swept through the grass. I looked up at the pine tree and saw its tender branches bending and swaying, slim and black against the heavy yellow moon. Mum opened the door to the bathroom. When I heard her lower the toilet seat I put my hands over my ears and started to hum. The sounds issuing from her after that, a kind of hiss, as if she was letting off steam, were awful. Usually I shut out dad's thunderous torrents too, even though it wasn't quite as difficult to endure as mum's hissing. *Aaaaaaaaaagh,* I said, slowly counting to ten and watching the cat. Apparently tired of the game, it grabbed the mouse in its jaws and dashed through the hedge, across the road and into Gustavsen's drive, where it dropped the mouse on the ground by the caravan and stood staring at it. The mouse lay as still as any living creature can. The cat jumped onto the wall and slunk towards one of the globe-shaped sundials on the gatepost at the end. I took my hands away from my ears and stopped humming. In the bathroom the cistern flushed. The cat turned sharply and stared at the mouse, which still hadn't moved. A jet of water from the tap splashed against the porcelain sink. The cat jumped down from the wall, strolled into the road and lay down like a small lion. Just as mum pressed the handle and opened the door a twitch went through the mouse, as though the sound had released an impulse in it, and the next moment it set off on another desperate flight from the cat, which had obviously reckoned on this eventuality as it required no more than a fraction of a second to switch from resting to hunting. But this time it was too late. A sheet of white Eternit cladding left lying on the lawn was the mouse's salvation as it squeezed itself underneath a second before the cat arrived.

The animals' fleet movements seemed to linger on in me; long after I had gone back to bed my heart was still racing. Perhaps because it too was a little animal? After a while I changed position again, put the pillow at the foot of the bed and drew the curtain to one side so that I could look up at the sky bestrewn with stars, so like grains of sand, a beach with a perimeter invisible to us, against which the sea beat.

But what actually lay beyond the universe?

Dag Lothar said there was nothing. Geir said there were burning flames. That was what I believed too; the image of the sea was more because the starry sky looked the way it did.

Mum and dad's bedroom was quiet again.

I pulled the curtain to and closed my eyes. Charged with the silence and darkness of the house, I was soon fast asleep.

When I got up next morning grandma and grandad were sitting with mum in the living room drinking coffee. Dad was walking across the lawn with the sprinkler in his hand. He placed it at the edge of the lawn so that the thin jets of water, which resembled a waving hand, not only fell on the grass but also the vegetable garden below. The sun's rays, on the other side of the house now, above the forest to the east, flooded into the garden. The air seemed to be as still as it had been the previous day. The sky was hazy; it almost always was in the morning. Yngve was sitting at the breakfast table. The white eggs in the brown egg cups reminded me that it was Sunday. I sat down in my regular place.

'What happened yesterday?' Yngve asked in a subdued voice. 'Why were you grounded?'

'I broke the TV,' I said.

He sent me a quizzical look, holding a slice of bread to his mouth.

'Yes, I put it on for grandma and grandad. Then it went *puff*. Haven't they said anything?'

Yngve took a large bite from the slice of bread, which he had spread with clove cheese, and shook his head. I sliced the top off the egg with my knife, opened it like a lid, scooped out the soft white with a spoon, reached for the salt cellar and tapped it with my forefinger so that only a sprinkling came out. Spread margarine onto some bread and poured a glass of milk. Downstairs, dad opened the door. I ate the white of the egg, poked the spoon into the yolk to see whether it was hard- or soft-boiled.

'I've been grounded for today as well,' I said.

'The *whole* day? Or just the evening?'

I shrugged. The egg was hard-boiled, the yellow yolk disintegrated against the edge of the spoon.

'The whole day, I think,' I said.

The road outside was empty and gleamed in the sun. But in the ditch beneath the dense branches of the spruces it was dark and shadowy.

A bicycle came tearing down the hill at full speed. The boy sitting on it, he must have been fifteen, had one hand on the handlebars and the other on the red petrol canister he had tied to the luggage rack. His hair was black and fluttered in the wind.

On the stairs came the sound of dad's footsteps. I sat up straight in my chair, cast a hurried glance across the table to see if everything was in place. A bit of the hard-boiled egg had ended up on the table. I quickly brushed it off the edge into my waiting hand and immediately put it on the plate. Yngve delayed the moment until it was almost too late to push his chair into the table and sit up straight, but only almost, for when dad came in his back was erect and his feet were firmly planted on the floor.

'Pack your swimming togs, lads,' he said. 'We're off to Hove for the day.'

'Me too?' I wanted to ask, but I held back, because he might have forgotten he had grounded me and the question would have jolted his memory. Also, if he remembered but had changed his mind, it would be best not to mention it, as it could be interpreted as his having made a mistake yesterday, his having done something wrong, and I didn't want him to think that. So I went for my trunks and a towel from the line in the boiler room, put them in a plastic bag with the diving goggles, which would come in handy if we were going to one of the two beaches in Hove, and sat down in my room to await departure.

Half an hour later we left for the far side of the island, on what was perhaps the best day of the year, with the sea so calm it barely made a sound and therefore lent the surroundings, the previously so silent bare rocks and the previously so silent forest above, a semblance of something unreal, such that every footstep on the rocks and every clink of a bottle sounded as if it was the very first time, and the sun, which was at its zenith in the sky, appeared as something deeply primitive and alien on this day, when you could see the sea curve and disappear down into the depths beyond the horizon, above which the sky floated so airily with its light, soft, misty blueness; and Yngve and I and mum and dad put on our swimming costumes and each of us in our own way dipped our bodies, hot from the sun, into the lukewarm water, while grandma and grandad sat there in their finery, apparently unmoved by their surroundings and our activities, as though the 1950s and Vestland were not only features that had stamped themselves on them superficially, through their clothes, behaviour and dialect, in other words externally, but also internally, to the depths of their respective souls, to the innermost core of their respective characters. It was so strange to see them there, sitting on the rocks, squinting into the bright light coming at us from all directions, it seemed so alien.

The day after, they went home. Dad drove them to Kjevik, grabbed the opportunity to visit his own parents while he was there.

Mum took Yngve and me to Lake Gjerstad, the idea being that we could swim and eat biscuits and relax, but first of all mum couldn't find a road to the lake, so we had to go on a long detour through a forest full of scrub and thickets, secondly the part of the lake we arrived at turned out to be green with algae and the rocks slippery, and thirdly it started to rain almost as soon as we had put down the cooler bag and the basket with the biscuits and oranges.

I felt so sorry for mum, who had wanted to take us on a nice trip, but it hadn't worked out. There was no way to express this to her. It was one of those things you had to forget as quickly as possible. And that was not at all difficult; there were so many new experiences in store for us during those weeks. I would soon be starting school, and as a result so many new objects would become mine. Above all, a satchel, which, the next Saturday morning, I went to Arendal with mum to buy. It was square, blue and all shiny and glossy, with white straps. Inside there were two compartments, where I immediately put the orange pencil case I had also been given, containing a pencil, a pen, a rubber and a pencil sharpener, and one of the notebooks we had bought, with orange and brown squares on the front, the same as on Yngve's, plus some comics I put in to plump it up. There, nestling against the leg of the desk, it stood every night when I went to bed, not without some mental anguish for me, for there was still quite a time to go to the big day when I, along with almost everyone I knew, would be starting the first class. We had already been to school for a day, in the spring that was, we had had a chance to meet the woman who was to be our teacher and to do a bit of drawing, but this was different, this wasn't anywhere near the same, this was the real thing. There were those who said they hated school, indeed, almost all the older children said they hated school, and strictly speaking we knew we should too, but at the same time it was so alluring, what was about to happen, we knew so little and we expected so much, in addition to the fact that starting school in itself elevated us into the same league as the older children, from one day to the next, in one fell swoop we were like them, and *then* we could certainly afford to hate school, but not now . . . Did we talk about anything else? Hardly. In fact the school we applied for, Roligheden, where both dad and Geir's father worked and where all the older children went, had no room for us, the year's intake was too big, too many families had moved into the area, so we had to go to a school on the east of the island, five or six kilometres away, with all the kids we didn't know from around there, and we were to be transported by bus. It was a great privilege and an adventure. Every day a bus would come to pick us up!

I was also given a pair of light blue trousers, a light blue jacket and a pair of dark blue trainers with white stripes over the instep. Several times, when dad was out, I put on my new clothes and paced in front of the hall mirror, sometimes with the satchel on my back, so when the day finally arrived and I posed on the shingle outside the door for mum to take a photograph of me, it wasn't just the excitement and the uncertainty giving me butterflies but also the strange, almost triumphant, feeling I would have when I wore particularly attractive clothes.

The evening before, I'd had a bath, mum had washed my hair, and when I woke in the morning it was to a quiet sleeping house, with a sun that was still climbing behind the spruce trees down beyond the road. Oh, what a pleasure it was to take my new clothes out of the wardrobe and put them on at last! Outside, the birds were singing, it was still summer, behind the veil of mist the sky was blue and immense, and the houses that now stood quiet on both sides of the road would soon be teeming with impatience and anticipation, like on Independence Day. I took the comics out of my satchel, hung it on my back, adjusted the straps and took it off again. Pulled the zip on the jacket up and down and speculated: it looked best with the zip up, but then you couldn't see the T-shirt underneath . . . Went into the living room, looked out of the window at the sun, a reddish-yellow fiery orange behind the green trees, went into the kitchen without touching anything, peered across at Gustavsen's house, where there was no sign of life. Stood in front of the hall mirror, pulling the zip up and down . . . the T-shirt looked so good . . . it would be a shame if it couldn't be seen . . .

Clean my teeth! I could do that.

Into the bathroom, out with the brush from the tooth glass, a drop of water and on with the white toothpaste. I brushed energetically for several minutes while studying myself in the mirror. The sound of the brush against my teeth seemed to fill the whole of my head from the inside, so I didn't notice that dad was up until he opened the door. He was wearing only underpants.

'Are you brushing your teeth before you've had breakfast? How stupid can you be? Put that brush down at once and go to your room!'

As I set foot on the red wall-to-wall carpet on the landing he slammed the door behind him and started pissing loudly into the toilet bowl. I knelt on my bed and looked up at Prestbakmo's house. Was that two heads I could see in the darkness of the kitchen window? Yes, it had to be. They were up. Would have been good to have a walkie-talkie so that I could talk to Geir! That would have been perfect!

Dad left the bathroom and went into the bedroom. I could hear his voice, and then mum's. So she was awake!

I stayed in my room until she was up and on her way to the kitchen, where dad had already been clattering around for a while. In the shelter of her back I sat down at my place. They had bought cornflakes, we almost never had them, and after she had put out a bowl and a spoon for me, and I had poured milk over the golden, somewhat perforated, irregularly formed flakes, I came to the conclusion that cornflakes were best when they were crispy, before the milk had soaked into them. But after I had been eating for a while and they were beginning to go soft, filled as it were with both their own taste and that of the milk, plus the sugar, of which I had sprinkled a liberal quantity, I changed my mind; *that* was when they were at their best.

Or was it?

Dad went into the living room with a cup in his hand, he didn't usually have breakfast, but sat in there smoking and drinking coffee instead. Yngve came in, sat down on his chair without saying a word, poured out some cornflakes and milk, sprinkled sugar over the top and started wolfing them down.

'Looking forward to it, are you?' he said at length.

'Bit,' I said.

'It's nothing to look forward to,' he said.

'Yes, it is,' mum said. 'You certainly looked forward to starting school anyway. I can remember it well. Can you?'

'Ye-es,' Yngve said. 'I suppose I can.'

He cycled to school, usually a little while before dad left, unless dad had some work to do before the first lesson that is, which was sometimes the case. Yngve was not allowed to have a lift, except on very special occasions, such as when it had snowed a lot overnight, because he wasn't to have any advantages just because his father was a teacher at the school.

When breakfast was finished and they had left, I sat with mum in the kitchen. She read the newspaper, I chatted.

'Do you think we'll have to write in the first lesson, Mum?' I asked. 'Or is it usually arithmetic? Leif Tore says we'll have drawing so that we can relax a bit at the beginning, and not everyone can write, can they. Or do sums. Only me actually. As far as I know at least. I learned when I was five and a half. Do you remember?'

'Remember when you learned to read? What do you mean?' mum said.

'That time outside the bus station when I read the sign? "Kaffefetteria?" You laughed. Yngve laughed too. Now I know it's called "kafeteria". Shall I read some headlines?'

Mum nodded. I read aloud. Bit staccato, but everything was correct.

'You managed that nicely,' she said. 'You'll do really well at school.'

She scratched an ear as she read, the way only she could, she held her ear between her fingers and moved them back and forth incredibly fast, just like a cat.

She put down the newspaper and looked at me.

'Are you looking forward to it?' she asked.

'And how,' I said.

She smiled, patted me on the head, got up and started to clear the table. I went to my room. School didn't begin until ten o'clock as it was the first day. Nevertheless, we ended up being short of time, which was often the case with mum, she was pretty absent-minded when it came to matters like this. From the window I saw the excitement mounting outside the houses where there were children starting school, that is in the families with Geir, Leif Tore, Trond, Geir Håkon and Marianne, hair was combed, dresses and shirts were straightened, photographs taken. When it was my turn to stand outside, smiling at mum, with one hand shielding my eyes from the sun, which had moved above the tops of the spruce trees by this time, everyone had gone. We were the last, and all of a sudden we were late, so mum, who had taken the day off work for the occasion, hurried me along, I opened the door of the green VW, pushed the seat forward and got in the back while she rummaged for the key in her shoulder bag and inserted it in the ignition. She lit a cigarette, reversed after casting a quick glance over her shoulder, put the car in first gear a few metres up the hill and drove down. The roar of the engine resounded off the brick walls. I moved to the middle of the car so that I could see between the seats at the front. The two white gas holders across Tromøya Sound, the wild cherry tree, Kristen's red house, then the road down to the marina where we almost never went, along the route where in the course of the next six years I would become familiar with every tiniest clearing and stone wall, and out to the small places on the east of the island, where mum didn't know her way, which made her a bit agitated.

'Was it this way, Karl Ove, do you remember?' she said, stubbing out the cigarette in the ashtray as she peered into the mirror.

'I don't remember,' I said. 'But I think so. It was on the left, anyway.'

Below there was a shop by a quay and a clump of houses encircling it, no school. The sea was a deep blue, bordering on black beneath the shadow of the buildings; untouched by the high temperatures, this fullness distinguished it from most of the other colours in the landscape, which were as though bleached after the weeks-long heatwave. The sea's cool blue contrasted with the yellow and brown and the faded green.

Now mum was driving along a gravel road. Dust whirled up behind us. As the road narrowed and nothing of any significance seemed to lie ahead, she turned and drove back. On the other side, down by the water, there was another road she tried. That didn't lead to any school either.

'Are we going to be late?' I asked.

'Maybe,' she replied. 'Fancy not bringing a map with me!'

'Haven't you been here before then?' I said.

'Yes, I have,' she said. 'But my memory's not as good as yours, you know.'

We drove up the hill we had come down ten minutes earlier and turned onto the main road by a chapel. At every sign and crossroads she slowed down and leaned forward.

'There it is, Mum!' I shouted, pointing. We still couldn't see it, but I remembered the green to the right; the school was at the top of the gentle gradient that followed. A narrow gravel road led down to it, there were lots of parked cars, and as mum turned into it, I spotted the school playground swarming with people and a man everyone was staring at was gesticulating on top of a rock, beneath the flagpole.

'We've got to hurry!' I said. 'They've started! Mum, they've started!'

'Yes, I know,' mum said. 'But we have to find somewhere to park first. There, maybe. Yes.'

We had ended up right down by the woodwork-room-cum-gym hall. A large white building from the olden days, and outside it, on tarmac, mum parked the car. We weren't exactly familiar with the school layout, so instead of going to the end and taking the short cut across the football pitch, we followed the road on the other side up to the playground. Mum scooted along with me in tow. The satchel bumped up and down so wonderfully as I ran, every bump reminding me of what I had behind me, shiny and glossy, and hot on the heels of that thought, the light blue trousers, the light blue jacket, the dark blue shoes.

When we finally reached the playground, the crowd was slowly moving into the low school building.

'We seem to have missed the welcome ceremony,' mum said.

'That doesn't matter, Mum,' I said. 'Come on!'

I caught sight of Geir and his mother, ran over to them with mum holding my hand, they smiled in greeting, and we went up the steps in the middle of the crowd of parents and children. Geir's satchel was identical to mine, as most of the boys' satchels were, whereas, from what I could glean in passing, the girls sported quite a wide variety.

'Where are we going? Do you know?' mum asked Martha, Geir's mother.

'I'm afraid I don't.' Martha laughed. 'We're following their teacher.'

I looked in the direction she nodded. And there, sure enough, was our Frøken. She stopped in front of the staircase and said that all those who were in her class should go ahead, and Geir and I ran down the stairs, through all the people, and along the corridor to the end. But Frøken stopped in front of a room close to the staircase, making us not the first, as we had imagined, but almost the last.

The room was full of children dressed in smart clothes and their mothers. Through the windows you looked down onto a narrow field; the forest was close behind. Frøken stood at her desk, which was on a little dais; on the blackboard was written HELLO, CLASS 1B in pink chalk with a flowery border around it. On the wall above the desk there were maps and charts.

'Hello, everyone,' Frøken said. 'And welcome to Sandnes School! My name is Helga Torgersen, and I'm going to be your class teacher. I'm really looking forward to this, I can tell you! We're going to have a lot of fun. And do you know what? You are not the only ones who are new to this school. I am new too. You are my very first class!'

I looked around me. All the adults were smiling. Almost all

the children were craning their necks and glancing at one another. I knew Geir Håkon, Trond, Geir, Leif Tore and Marianne. And the boy who used to throw stones at us and had that frightening dog. I had never seen the others before.

'Now we are going to do a roll call,' Frøken said from the dais. 'Do you know what a roll call is?'

No one answered.

'You call out a name and the person with that name answers,' I said.

Everyone looked at me. I put on a broad smile over my protruding teeth.

'That's correct,' Frøken said. 'And we start with the letter A. That's the first letter in the alphabet, you see. You'll learn all about that later. So, A. Anne Lisbet!'

'Yes,' said a girl's voice, and everyone turned towards the sound, I did too.

The voice belonged to a thin girl with shiny black hair. She looked like an Indian.

'Asgeir?' Frøken said.

'Yes!' said a boy with big teeth and long hair.

After the roll call we sat down at our desks while our parents stood by the wall. Frøken gave everyone a recorder, an exercise book and a jotter, a timetable with our lessons printed on, as well as a money box and a leaflet with a picture of a yellow ant on from a local savings bank. Then she told us about some of the events that would be taking place during the autumn, one of which was a swimming course to be held in a pool at a school on the next island, as there wasn't a swimming pool on Tromøya. She handed out a piece of paper with a slip you could fill in and return if you were interested. Then we did some drawing, with our parents still there watching, and then it was over. The following day school would start in earnest, we would catch the bus on our own and be there for three hours without our parents breathing down our necks.

As we left the classroom I was still wide-eyed with all the newness and strangeness, and the feeling continued when everyone in the new class got into their respective cars with their parents, normally it was only on the seventeenth of May that there was this level of vehicle activity, that a location was left simultaneously by so many children, but as we were driving home disappointment began to set in, and I became more and more dejected the closer we came to home.

Nothing had happened.

I could read and write, and I had counted on having a chance to show that on the first day. A bit at least! And I had been looking forward to having break-time, to the bell ringing at the end of one lesson and the start of the next. To using my new pencil case and the compartments in the satchel.

No, the day hadn't lived up to my expectations, and I had to take off the clothes I looked so good in and hang them up in their place in my wardrobe, to await future formal occasions. I sat on the kitchen stool chatting to mum while she made dinner, it was rare I had her to myself in the middle of the day, and on top of this she had been with me when it counted most, so I exploited the opportunity for all it was worth, and babbled away.

'I wish we had a cat I could play with,' I said. 'Can't we have a cat?'

'That would be nice,' mum said. 'I like cats. They're good company.'

'So is it dad who doesn't like them then?'

'I don't know,' mum said. 'He's just not that interested, I think. And he probably thinks they're a bit too much work.'

'But I can take care of it,' I said. 'That's no problem.'

'I know,' mum said. 'We'll have to wait and see.'

'Wait and see, wait and see,' I said. 'But if Yngve wants a cat, that'll make three of us.'

Mum laughed.

'It's not that simple,' she said. 'You'll have to be patient. Who knows what will happen.'

She put the peeled carrot on the board and chopped it up, lifted the board and slid the pieces into the large pot where there were already bones and bits of meat. I looked out of the window. Through the many small holes in the orange curtain mum had crocheted I could see the road outside was empty, which it invariably was in the middle of the day.

There was a sudden pungent smell of onions, and I turned to mum, who was peeling one with her arms outstretched and her eyes full of tears.

When I turned back I saw Geir come bounding down the hill. He had also changed into his normal clothes. A second later I heard a crunch of gravel through the half-open window as he walked up the drive.

'Karl Ove, are you coming?' he shouted.

'I'm going out for a bit,' I said to mum, slipping off the stool.

'Fine,' she said. 'Where are you going?'

'I don't know.'

'Don't go far then.'

'No, I won't,' I said, and hurried down, opened the door so that Geir wouldn't think the house was empty and go away, said hi and put on my trainers.

'I've got a box of matches,' he whispered, patting his shorts pocket.

'You haven't!' I also whispered. 'Where did you get hold of them?'

'Home. They were in the sitting room.'

'You pinched them?'

He nodded.

I straightened up and went out, closing the door after me.

'Let's set fire to something,' I said.

'Yes, let's,' he said.

'What then?'

'Doesn't matter, does it. We'll just find something. The box is half full. We can set fire to a lot of things.'

'But we'll have to go somewhere no one can see the smoke,' I said. 'Up on the mountain maybe?'

'OK.'

'And we'll need something to put the fire out with,' I said. 'Just a mo. I'll get a bottle of water.'

I opened the door again, kicked off my shoes and went upstairs to mum, who turned to me as I walked in.

'We're going for a walk,' I said. 'I need a bottle of water.'

'Wouldn't you prefer juice? You can take some, you know. It's still your first school day!'

I hesitated. It had to be water. But that might make her suspicious because I always preferred juice to water. I looked at her and said, 'No, Geir's got water, so that's what I want too.'

My heart beat faster as I spoke.

'As you like,' she said. She found an empty juice bottle in the cupboard under the sink, dark green glass, almost opaque, she filled it with water, screwed on the top and passed it to me.

'Would you like some *smørbrød* as well?'

I considered her offer.

'No,' I said. 'I mean yes. Two with liver paste.'

As she took the bread and started to cut it, I pushed the window further open and poked my head out.

'Be down in a minute!' I shouted. Geir looked up at me with grave eyes and nodded.

After she had made and wrapped the *smørbrød*, I put them in a plastic bag with the bottle and hurried back down. Soon we were on our way up the hill. The heat had made the edge of the road soft and crumbly. It was harder where the cars went. Sometimes we lay down on the tarmac like cats and let the heat give us a good baking. But now we had other things on our minds.

'Can I see them?' I asked.

Geir stopped and dug the box up from his pocket. I shook it a little. Full. Then I opened it. All the matchheads were red.

Start a fire, start a fire.

'It's a new box,' I said, giving it back. 'Won't they notice you've taken it?'

'I don't think so,' he said. 'And if they do I'll just say it wasn't me. They can't *prove* anything.'

We had reached Molden's house and set off up the path. The grass was dry and yellow, brown in places. In Geir's house it was his mother who was strict and his father who was nice. In Dag Lothar's they were both nice, perhaps the father was a tiny bit stricter. With all the others, it was the father who was strict and the mother who was nice. But no one was as strict as dad, that was for certain.

Geir stopped and bent forward with the box of matches in his hand. He took out a match and was about to strike it against the side.

'What are you doing?' I said. 'Not here! Everyone can see!'

'Hee hee hee,' he giggled. But straightened up anyway, put the match back in the box and walked on.

At the top of the hill we turned and cast our gaze across the sea as usual. I counted four small white triangles in Tromøya Sound. A larger boat with what looked like an excavator on board. There were two small boats moored on Gjerstadholmen.

Start a fire, start a fire.

As we continued into the forest my stomach was churning with excitement. Sunbeams lay on the forest floor like small quivering creatures of light between the shadows of branches. We stopped by the huge roots of an upturned tree, I took the bottle of water from my bag and held it at the ready while Geir leaned forward, struck a match and held the small, almost invisible flame to one of the wispy blades of grass growing there. It caught fire at once. Spread to the grass beside it. When the flame was as broad as an adult's hand I sprayed water over it. A thin ribbon of smoke floated through the air, alone as it were, independent of what had just happened.

'Do you think anyone could see?' Geir asked.

'You can see smoke from an incredible distance,' I answered. 'Indians saw smoke signals from kilometres off.'

'It caught fire straight away,' Geir said. 'Did you see?'

He smiled and quickly ran a hand through his hair.

'Yes,' I said.

'Shall we try somewhere else?'

'Yes, but this time I want to light the match.'

'OK,' he said, handing me the box and scouring the area for another suitable spot.

Geir was always impatient before any activity and totally absorbed when in the thick of it. Of all the boys I knew he was the one most in thrall to his imagination. Whenever we played – explorers, sailors, Indians, racing drivers, astronauts, robbers, smugglers, princes, monkeys or secret agents, for example – he could keep at it for hours, unlike Leif Tore or Geir Håkon, who were soon bored and wanted to do something else, completely untouched by the gleam that imagination could bring to bear on everything, but Geir was more than happy with the object itself, such as the old car wreck in the clump of narrow willow trees on the flat stretch between the playground and the football pitch, in which the seats, the steering wheel, gearstick, pedals, dashboard, glove compartment and doors were still intact, where we used to play so often, and they just pretended it was a car, which of course it was, pressed the clutch, pulled the gearstick, turned the wheel, adjusted the broken wing mirrors, jumped up and down on the seats to give the illusion of speed while Geir would be entertained by any embellishments you could add, such as being on the run after a bank robbery, and the windows, which were still a shower of glass fragments strewn across the black rubber floor mats, had been shot to pieces; then one of us would drive and the other wriggle out through the window onto the roof to open fire on our pursuers, a game which could be extended to include parking the car in a garage and getting out to share the swag, or even further, for weren't the pursuers close on our heels as we slunk between the trees on our way home in the glow of the evening sun? Or else we might be in a moon-mobile and the landscape around us was actually lunar landscape where, after getting out of the car, we were unable to walk in a normal fashion, we had to hop – or it was one of the many streams we were surrounded by, and of all the boys I knew only Geir would be interested in following it to find the source. What we did most often was to go out in search of new places or to one of the places we had already found. It might be a big old oak with a hollow trunk; a deep pool in a river; a cellar in an unfinished house that was full of water; the concrete foundations of the enormous bridge pylon or the first few metres of the thick cable stays that ran from the bottom of an anchoring in the forest up to the top and which you could climb; a ramshackle shed with planks that were slippery and dark with decay between Lake Tjenna and the road on the other side, which so far was the furthest outpost of our explorations, we had never ventured any further; the two dumped cars; the little pool with the three islands no bigger than tufts of grass, one almost completely covered by a tree, and where the water was so deep and black, even though it was right next to a road embankment; the white crystalline rock from which you could hammer small chunks, beside the path to the Fina station; the boat factory on the other side of Tromøya Bridge beyond Gamle Tybakken, all the factory buildings there, the shells of the boats, the rusty block and tackle and the machines, the smell of oil and tar and salty water which was so good. We criss-crossed this area, which extended over one or two kilometres in all directions, nearly every day, and the whole point of what we found or visited was that it was secret and it was ours. With the other children we played flip the stick or kick the can, kicked a football about or went skiing; when we were alone we searched out places with features that attracted us. That was how it was with Geir and me.

But on this day the magic lay in what we were doing, not where we were.

Start a fire, start a fire.

We walked over to a spruce tree a few metres away. The branches hanging just above the ground were grey and bare and looked extremely old. I broke off a bit between my thumb and first finger. It was brittle and crumbled easily. Grass grew sparsely on the small mound where the tree stood, between a patch of dry soil and a mass of desiccated orangey spruce needles. I knelt down, drew the red match head across the black abrasive surface, and put the flame into the grass, which immediately caught fire. At first the flame was invisible, no more than a quiver of air above the blades of grass, which soon curled and crumpled. But then the tuft caught fire, and from there the flame spread, both quickly and slowly, like a swarm of frightened ants fleeing quickly if you see them as individuals, slowly if you view them as a group. All of a sudden the flames were up to my waist.

'Put it out! Put it out!' I shouted to Geir.

He shook the bottle over the fire, which hissed and shrank, while I beat the low flames in the grass at the edge with my hand.

'Phew!' I said a minute later, when the fire was out.

'That was close!' Geir laughed. 'It really got a hold there!'

I stood up.

'Do you think anyone could see it? Shall we go to the cliff edge and see if anyone's looking up here?'

Without waiting for an answer I rushed across the soft moss and heather-covered forest floor between the trees. The sudden fear seemed to contract my insides, and whenever my thoughts turned to what had happened it was as if a ravine opened in me. It was bottomless. Oh, what would happen now? What would happen now?

At the cliff edge I stopped and put a hand to my brow to shield my eyes. Dad's car was in the drive. He was nowhere to be seen. But he could have been outside and gone in. Gustavsen was walking across the grass. He could have seen and told dad. Or would tell him later.

The very thought of dad, the fact that he existed, caused fear to pump through my body.

I turned to Geir, who sauntered over with my plastic bag dangling from one hand. Down below, a child resembling Geir Håkon's little brother was playing in the sand by the concrete barriers between our road and Elgstien. A car came up the hill, encased in itself, like an insect, the black windscreen its expressionless eye, turned left and disappeared from view.

'We can't go straight down anyway,' I said. 'If someone's seen the smoke they'll put two and two together.'

Why had we done it? Why, oh why?

'They can see us here too,' I said. 'Come on!'

We descended the tree-clad slope beneath us. When we were at the bottom we stumbled homewards through the forest, which was perhaps ten metres from the road. We stopped by the big spruce beside the wide, shallow, turbid stream where all the colours were green and murky, its bark stained with sticky resin, not unlike burned sugar in colour, with the pungent smell of juniper. Between the slender trunks of the nearby rowan trees you could see our house. I glanced at my hands to see if there was any soot on them. Nothing. But there was a faint burned smell, so I plunged them in the water and rubbed them dry on my trousers.

'What shall we do with the box of matches?' I said.

Geir shrugged.

'Hide it, I s'pose.'

'If they find it, don't say anything about me,' I said. 'About what we did.'

'Course not,' Geir said. 'Here's the bag, by the way.'

We started to walk up to the road.

'Are you going to set fire to anything else today?' I said.

'Don't think so,' he said.

'Not even with Leif Tore?'

'Maybe tomorrow,' he said. And his face brightened. 'Shall I take the matches to school with me, do you think?'

'Are you out of your mind?!'

He laughed. We reached the road, and crossed it.

'See you!' he said, running up the hill.

I passed mum's VW, parked on a patch of scorched yellow grass just outside the fence beside the grey dustbin, and stepped onto the shingle. I felt the fear rising in me again. Dad's red car gleamed in the fierce sunshine. I looked down, unwilling to meet the gaze which might await me in the kitchen window. The mere thought of it sent waves of despair shooting through me. When I reached the front doorstep and couldn't be seen from the windows on the first floor I clasped my hands together and closed my eyes.

Almighty God, I uttered silently. Let me get through this and I promise I'll never do anything wrong again. Never ever. I promise by all that is holy. Amen.

I opened the door and went in.

It was cooler in the hall than outside, and after the bright sunshine almost completely dark. The smell of stew lay heavy in the air. I bent down and untied my shoelaces, carefully placed my shoes by the wall, slunk upstairs trying to make my face appear normal and stopped on the landing in a quandary. What would I normally do, go into my room straight away or go into the kitchen to see if dinner was ready?

Voices, the clinking of cutlery on plates.

Was I late?

Had they already started eating?

Oh no, oh no.

What should I do?

The notion of turning on my heel, calmly walking outside, up the hill and into the forest, never to return, came as a joyful clarion call amid all the tension.

Then they would be sorry.

'Is that you, Karl Ove?' dad shouted from the other side of the door.

I swallowed, shook my head, blinked a few times and took a deep breath.

'Yes,' I said.

'We're eating!' he shouted. 'Come on in!'

God had heard my prayer and done as I asked. Dad was in a good mood, I could see that as soon as I entered, he was leaning back in the chair with his legs stretched out, his arms wide apart and his eyes glinting with mischief.

'What was so good that you lost track of time?' he said.

I sat down next to Yngve. Dad was sitting at the end to the right, mum at the end to the left. The Formica table with a grey and white marble pattern and grey edging, shiny legs and grey rubber feet was set: brown dinner plates, green glasses with Duralex written on the bottom, a basket of crispbread, a big pot from which protruded a wooden ladle.

'Been out with Geir,' I said, leaning forward to check if there was a piece of meat in the ladle I lifted out a moment later.

'Where did you go then?' dad asked, lifting his fork to his mouth. Something pale yellow, perhaps onion, was lodged in his beard, on his chin.

'Down to the forest.'

'Oh yes?' he said, chewing several times and swallowing, his eyes trained on me the whole time.

'I thought I saw you on your way up the hill?'

I sat transfixed.

'It wasn't us,' I said at length.

'Rubbish,' he said. 'What devilry were you up to there since you won't admit that's where you were?'

'But we weren't on the hill,' I said.

Mum and dad exchanged glances. Dad said no more. I could move my hands again. I filled my plate and started eating. Dad helped himself to another portion, still with the same apparent gliding movement. Yngve had finished eating, and sat next to me looking down in front of him, one hand resting on his thigh, the other on the edge of the table.

'How was the schoolboy's first day then?' dad asked. 'Did you get any homework?'

I shook my head.

'Was the teacher nice?'

I nodded.

'What was her name again?'

'Helga Torgersen,' I said.

'That's right,' dad said. 'She lives . . . did she say?'

'In Sandum,' I said.

'She seemed so lovely,' mum said. 'Young and pleased to be there.'

'But we got there late,' I said, relief spreading through my body at the turn the conversation had taken.

'Oh?' dad said, looking at mum. 'You didn't say?'

'We got lost,' she said. 'So we arrived a few minutes late. But I don't think we missed anything important. Did we, Karl Ove?'

'No,' I mumbled.

'Don't talk with your mouth full,' dad said.

I swallowed.

'All right,' I said.

'And what about you, Yngve?' dad said. 'Any surprises on the first day?'

'No,' Yngve said, sitting up straight in his chair.

'You've got football practice today, haven't you?' mum said.

'Yep,' Yngve said.

He had changed team, had left Trauma, which was the island team where all his friends played, with its fantastic kit, blue shirts with a white diagonal stripe, white shorts and blue and white socks, for Saltrød, a club in a little town just across Tromøya Sound. Today was his first session there. He would have to cycle over the bridge alone, which he had never done before, and all the way to the training ground. Five kilometres, he had said it was.

'Didn't anything else happen at school today then, Karl Ove?' dad said.

I nodded and swallowed.

'We're going on a swimming course,' I said. 'Six lessons. At another school.'

'There you go,' dad said, running the back of his hand across his mouth, but without removing the ribbon of onion from his beard. 'That's not a bad idea. You can't live on an island and not be able to swim.'

'And it's free too,' mum said.

'But I need a swimming cap,' I said. 'Everyone does. And maybe some new swimming trunks? Not shorts, but the kind . . . well.'

'We can sort out the cap all right. But your shorts will have to do you for now,' dad said.

'And goggles,' I said.

'Goggles as well?' dad said, looking at me with a teasing expression. 'We'll have to see about that.'

He shoved his plate away and leaned back.

'Great food, Mum!' he said.

'Thanks, Mum,' Yngve said, and sneaked off. Five seconds later we heard the sound of his bedroom door being closed.

I stayed at the table for a little longer, in case dad wanted to chat with me. He gazed out of the window for a while, at the four boys hanging over the handlebars of their bikes by the second crossroads, then he got up, put his plate in the sink, took an orange from the cupboard and went down to his study, the newspaper folded under his arm, without saying another word to anyone. Mum started clearing the table and I went to Yngve's room. He was packing his bag. I sat down on his bed and watched. He had proper football boots, a pair of black Adidas with screw-on studs, decent Umbro shorts and some yellow and black IK Start socks. Mum had bought black and white Grane socks for him at first; he didn't want them, so I was given them. But the best equipment he had was the Adidas tracksuit, it was blue with white stripes, in some smooth shiny material, not that matt, crepe, elastic, gym kit-style material that all tracksuits used to be made of. Sometimes I sniffed it, buried my nose in the smooth material, because it smelled fantastic. Perhaps I thought that because I wanted one myself so much the smell was imbued with my own desire, perhaps I thought it because the smell, so thoroughly synthetic, didn't remind me of anything else and therefore didn't seem to belong to this world. And so in some way it bore a promise of the future. In addition to this tracksuit, he also had some blue and white Adidas wet-weather gear.

He said nothing as he packed. Pulled the big red zip to and sat down at his desk. Looked at the timetable lying on it.

'Did you get any homework?' I said.

He shook his head.

'We didn't either,' I said. 'Have you bound your books yet?'

'No, we've got the whole week to do it.'

'I'm going to do it tonight,' I said. 'Mum's going to help me.'

'Good for you!' he said, getting up. 'I'm off. If I'm not back before midnight the headless man's devoured me. I'd like to see how he manages that!'

He laughed and went downstairs. I watched him from the bathroom window, saw him put first one foot on the pedal, then shove off with the other and swing it over the crossbar and pedal as fast as he could in the highest gear until he reached the hill at such a speed that he could freewheel down to the crossroads.

When he had disappeared from view I went onto the landing, stood motionless for a moment to locate mum and dad. But all was silent.

'Mum?' I called softly.

No answer.

I went into the kitchen, she wasn't there, then into the back room, she wasn't there, either. Could she have gone to their bedroom?

I went there and stood outside the door for a moment.

No.

In the garden perhaps?

From various windows I scoured all four sides of the garden without catching a glimpse of her.

And the car was parked outside, wasn't it?

Yes, it was.

Not knowing where she was somehow loosened my hold on the house, it was slackened in a confusing, quite disturbing way, and to counter it I went into my room and sat down on the bed to read some comics; that was when it struck me that of course she was downstairs in dad's office.

I almost never set foot in there. The few times I had, it had been to ask about something, if I could stay up and watch a particular TV programme for example, after knocking first and waiting for him to say 'Come in.' Knocking on the door came at a great cost, often so high that I preferred to go to bed without seeing the programme. On a couple of occasions he had actually asked us to go in, when he wanted to show us something or give us something, such as envelopes with stamps on. We put them in the sink in the spare kitchen which, as far as I knew, was used exclusively for that purpose, to dissolve the gum, and, after drying them for a few hours, we were able to put them in our albums.

Otherwise I never went there. Even when I was on my own at home it never occurred to me. The risk that he would find out was much too great, he would discover anything untoward that was going on, he would sniff it out by some means or other, however well I tried to cover my tracks.

As he had with the hill when we were having dinner. Even though he hadn't seen anything, only us on our way up, he knew we had been doing something wrong. Had he not been in such a good mood he would have brought everything into the open.

I lay on my stomach and started reading a *Tempo*. It was Yngve's, he had borrowed it from Jan Atle, I had already read it many times. It was for older children and for me it had a strong aura of belonging to a distant but utterly radiant world. I didn't have any particular preferences regarding the settings of the comics – it made no difference whether it was the Second World War, as in *På Vingene* or the *Kamp* series, nineteenth-century America, as in *Tex Willer*, *Jonathan Hex* or *Blueberry,* England between the two world wars, as in *Paul Temple,* or the fantasy realities, which the Phantom, Superman, Batman, the Fantastic Four and all the Disney characters appeared in – but my feelings for them were different, they aroused different emotions in me, such that some of the series in *Tempo*, for example the one that took place on a racing circuit, or some in *Buster*, for example *Johnny Puma* and *Benny Goldenfoot*, were particularly absorbing, perhaps because they were closer to the reality that I knew existed. In the summer you could see motorcyclists wearing the leathers and helmets with Formula 1 visors, you could see the low-slung cars with all those spoilers on TV, where they occasionally crashed into the barriers or one of the other cars, rolling over and catching fire, the driver being either burned to death or emerging from the flaming wreckage and calmly walking away.

Usually I was totally engrossed by these stories, without giving them a thought, the whole point of course was that you didn't think, at least not with your own thoughts, you just followed the action. That afternoon, however, I quickly put the comic to one side, for some reason I couldn't sit still, and it wasn't much later than five o'clock, so I decided to go out again. I stopped at the top of the stairs, not a sound, she was still down below. What was she doing? She was hardly ever there. At least not at this time, I thought, bending down for my shoes in the hallway and tying the laces. I knocked on the door to dad's study. That is, the door leading to the corridor into which three rooms opened: the bathroom, the study and the kitchen with the little box room at the end. In fact, it was a self-contained flat, but we had never rented it out to anyone.

'I'm going out!' I shouted. 'Up to Geir's!'

That is what I had been told to do, to tell them if I was going anywhere and say where.

Nevertheless, after a few seconds of silence, dad's irritated voice sounded from inside the study.

'All right, all right!' he shouted.

A few more seconds of silence passed.

Then mum's voice, friendlier, as if to compensate for dad's.

'That's fine, Karl Ove!'

I shot out, closed the door carefully behind me and ran up to Geir's. I stood outside, called a few times until his mother came round the house. She had gardening gloves on, and was otherwise wearing khaki shorts, a blue blouse and a pair of black clogs. In her hand she was holding a red trowel.

'Hi, Karl Ove,' she said. 'Geir went out with Leif Tore a while ago.'

'Where did they go?'

'I don't know. He didn't say.'

'OK. Bye.'

I turned and walked slowly down the drive with my eyes glazed with tears. Why hadn't they called at my house?

I stopped by the barrier between the two roads. Stood for a moment stock-still, listening. Not a sound. I sat down on one of the barriers. The rough concrete chafed against my thighs. Dandelions grew in the ditch below, all grey with dust. There was a grid next to it, rusty and with a sun-faded cigarette packet stuck between the bars.

Where could they have gone?

Down to Ubekilen?

Down to the pontoons?

To the football pitch and the play area?

Had Geir taken Leif Tore to one of our places?

Up the mountain?

I scanned the mountain. No sign of them there anyway. I got to my feet and started to make my way down. At the crossroads by the cherry tree there were three ways to choose between if you were going to the landing stages. I chose the one to the right, through the gate, along the path covered with soil and twigs beneath the deep shadows from the tops of the enormous oaks, down to the field where we usually played football even though it sloped on both sides and the grass was knee-high, trampled from very early spring, there were also sapling trees growing on it, past the cliff with its greyish crags, generally bare but with some low scattered cover, and on through the forest to the road. Beyond it there was the new marina, blasted out of the rock, with three identical quays, all with wooden gangways and orange pontoons.

They weren't there either. I walked along one pontoon anyway; a double-ender had just moored at the tip, it belonged to Kanestrøm, and I went over to see what was happening. Kanestrøm was alone on board and peered up as I stood by the bow.

'So it's you who's out and about, is it?' he said. 'I've been doing a bit of fishing, as you can see.'

The sun glinted on his glasses. He had a moustache, short hair, a little bald patch on top and wore denim shorts, a checked shirt and sandals.

'Would you like to see?'

He held up a red bucket in my direction. It was full of thin slippery mackerel with bluish glistening skin. Some were twitching, and the movement seemed to spread to the other bodies lying so close to one another it was as though they were one and the same creature.

'Wow!' I said. 'Did you catch all of them?'

He nodded.

'All in the space of a few minutes. There was a huge shoal just offshore. Now we've got enough food for several days!'

He put the bucket down on the narrow gangway. Lifted an old petrol canister and put it down beside it. Then some fishing lines and a can of hooks and lures. Humming an old song all the while.

'Do you know where Dag Lothar is?' I said.

'No, I'm afraid I don't,' he said. 'Are you looking for him?'

'Yes, sort of,' I said.

'Would you like to sit at the front here?'

I shook my head.

'Not really. In fact I'm a bit busy.'

'All right,' he said, and stepped onto the pontoon, bent down and grabbed his gear. I hurried off so as not to have to walk alongside him. Ran across the stony car park and balanced on the high kerbstone all the way up to the main road, where a rather steep path plunged down into the forest. It led to the Rock, the place where everyone on the estate went swimming, where you could dive off a two-metre-high rock and swim across to Gjerstadholmen, on the other side of a maybe ten-metre-wide channel. Even though the water was deep and I couldn't swim, I sometimes went along because so much happened there.

Now I could hear voices from the forest. A high-pitched child's voice and a slightly deeper youth's. A second later Dag Lothar and Steinar came into view between the sun-flecked tree trunks. Their hair was wet and they were carrying towels.

'Hey, Karl Ove!' Dag Lothar shouted, catching sight of me. 'I saw an adder on my way down here!'

'Did you?' I said. 'Where did you see it? Here?'

He nodded and stopped in front of me. Steinar also stopped and adopted a posture which made it obvious he had no intention of chatting, he wanted to be on his way as soon as possible. Steinar was in the eighth class at dad's school. He had long dark hair and a shadow on his upper lip. He played the bass and had his room in the cellar with its own entrance.

'I was running down, wasn't I,' Dag Lothar said, pointing along the path. 'As fast as I could, pretty well, and as I was charging round the bend there was an adder in front of me, on the path. I almost didn't manage to stop!'

'What happened?' I said.

If there was one thing I was frightened of in this world it was snakes and worms.

'It shot off like lightning into the bushes.'

'Are you sure it was an adder?'

'Absolutely. It had the zigzag markings on its head.'

He smiled at me. His face was triangular, his hair blond and soft, his eyes were blue and the expression in them frequently intense and passionate.

'You don't dare go there now, do you?'

'I don't know,' I said. 'Are Geir and the others down there?'

He shook his head.

'Just Jørn and his little brother, and Eva and Marianne's mum and dad.'

'Can I go up with you?' I said.

'Of course,' Dag Lothar said. 'But I can't play. We're going to have dinner now.'

'I have to go home too,' I said. 'Have to cover my books.'

*

When we reached the road outside our house and Dag Lothar and Steinar went on to their homes, I didn't go in; I stood around looking for Geir and Leif Tore instead. They were nowhere to be seen. Irresolute, I started walking. The sun, which was just above the ridge, was burning down on my shoulders. I cast a final glance along the road, in case they might have appeared, and then I ran to the path behind the house. The first part went alongside our garden fence, the second skirted Prestbakmo's stone wall, half-hidden behind the many slim aspen saplings growing there, which in afternoons throughout the summer stood trembling whenever the sea breeze blew. Then the path parted company with the estate, ran through an area of dense young deciduous trees, came to some boggy land, at the far end of which was a small meadow beneath an enormous beech tree growing at an angle to a steep incline and immersing everything around it in shadow.

It was strange how all large trees had their own personalities, expressed through their unique forms and the aura created by the combined effect of the trunk and roots, the bark and branches, the light and shadow. It was as if they could speak. Not with voices, of course, but with what they were, they seemed to *stretch* out to whoever looked at them. And that was all they spoke about, what they were, nothing else. Wherever I went on the estate or in the surrounding forest, I heard these voices, or felt the impact these extremely slow-growing organisms had. There was the spruce by the stream, below the house, so incredibly wide at the bottom of the trunk, yet with damp bark and roots that became visible, like coils of thick rope, so *far away* from it. The way the branches cascaded, pyramid-like, to the ground, at a distance apparently stocky and smooth, but, close up, covered with small, dark green, perfectly formed needles. All those dry branches, light grey and porous, that could grow within the canopy of branches which were not grey but almost totally black. The pine tree on Prestbakmo's land, long and slim like a ship's mast, with red-flecked bark and small green lightly swaying whorls at the end of each branch, which didn't start growing until very near the tip. The oak tree behind the football pitch, whose trunk at the bottom was more like stone than wood, but which had nothing of the spruce's compactness because the oak's branches spread outwards forming a sparse vault of foliage above the forest floor, so light that you would *never* believe there was not only a connection between the lowest part of the trunk and the slender extremities of the branches, but it was also their origin and source. In the middle of the trunk there was something that resembled a grotto, as if the tree had bulged out to form a softly contoured yet hard and gnarled oval, the inner cavity the size of a small head. And the leaves, like all leaves, wherever they sprouted, repeated the same beautiful, partly curved, partly jagged pattern, both when they hung from a branch, green, thick and smooth, and when they lay on the ground a few months later, reddish-brown and brittle. Around this tree the ground was always covered with a thick carpet of leaves in the autumn, flaming yellow and green at the beginning, darker and softer as time passed.

And then there was the tree on the slope by the boggy land. I didn't know what species it was. It wasn't compact like the other large trees but grew out from four equally proportioned trunks, they wound outwards, serpent-like, with greyish-green bark full of extended hollows, and in this way it covered just as large an area as an oak or a spruce, but the effect was not as magnificent, it was more subtle. From one of the branches hung a rope and a wooden bar, probably put there by the boys living on the road opposite, they lived as close to this place as we did. No one was there now, and I went up the slope under the branches, grabbed the bar with both hands and launched myself. I did it twice more. Then I stood for a while under the tree wondering what to do next. From the house facing the slope, occupied by a couple with a small child, came the sound of voices and the clinking of cutlery. I couldn't see anything, but guessed they had to be in the garden. Somewhere in the distance there was the drone of a plane. I took a few steps into the dried-up bog, peering at the sky. A small seaplane was approaching from the coast, flying very low, the sun gleaming on the white fuselage. Once it had gone behind the ridge I broke into a run again, into the shadow of the hill on the other side, where the air was a touch cooler. I looked up at Kanestrøm's house, thinking they were probably sitting at the table eating mackerel at this very minute, there was no one outside at any rate, and then I looked down to the path, where I knew every stone, every dip, every tuft and every mound. If a run had been arranged here, from our house along the path to B-Max, I would have been invincible. I could have run along that path with my eyes shut. Without ever needing to stop, always knowing what was waiting around the next bend, always knowing where it was best to tread. When we raced on the road Leif Tore won every time, but I would win here, of that I was in no doubt. It was a good thought, a good feeling and I tried to hold on to it for as long as possible.

Well before I reached the football pitch I heard the voices coming from it, screams and shouts and laughter, as if from a distance, as if heard through the forest, there was something almost apelike about it. I stopped in the clearing. The pitch before me was swarming with children of all ages, many of whom I had barely seen before, most crowded around the ball, with everyone trying to kick it away, the hubbub drifting from place to place, backwards and forwards, in fits and starts. The field was dark trampled ground in the middle of the forest and it sloped slightly up on one side, where quite a number of roots broke through the surface. At each end there was a big goal made with wooden beams, without a net. One side was considerably truncated by protruding rock while the other extended across an uneven patch of large tufts of stiff grass. Almost all my dreams originated here. Running around in this place was bliss.

'Can I join in?' I shouted.

Every kick of the ball returned in a dull echo off the hillside.

Rolf, who was in goal, turned to me.

'You can be in goal if you like,' he said.

'OK,' I said, running towards the goal, which Rolf left with a slow rolling gait.

'Karl Ove's in goal for us!' he shouted.

I positioned myself carefully between the posts and started to follow the game, gradually distinguishing who was in my team, leaned forward and was ready when the ball approached, and when the first shot came, a loose ball along the ground, I crouched down and took it, bounced it three times on the ground and booted it up the field. The ball gave against my foot, it was big and soft and worn, the same colour as the sun-baked ground. The orange tongue flashed beneath the stitching. The ball's trajectory wasn't high, but it went a long way nevertheless, bounced on the right-hand side of the pitch and it was a joy to see the pack of boys running after it. I wanted to be a goalkeeper. I went into goal as often as I could, nothing could compare with the feeling of hurling yourself at a shot and stopping it. The problem was that I could only hurl myself to one side, the left. Hurling myself to the right appeared to be contrary to the laws of nature, I couldn't do it, so if the ball came on that side I had to stick out my leg instead.

The trees cast long shadows across the pitch, and flickering patches of murk pursued the running boys, who merged into a mass and dispersed again and again. But some boys had started walking instead of running, some were bent over supporting themselves on their knees, and to my disappointment I realised the game was coming to an end.

'Well, I'd better be getting home,' one said.

'Me, too,' a second said.

'Let's carry on for a bit,' a third said.

'I've got to be off too.'

'Shall we make new teams then?'

'I'm off.'

'Me too.'

Within a couple of minutes the whole scene had evaporated, and the pitch was empty.

The wrapping paper mum had bought was blue and semi-transparent. We sat in the kitchen, I unrolled a piece and cut it to size; if the edge was uneven and jagged mum straightened it. Then I placed the book on top, spread out the two wing-like flaps, folded the paper over them and Sellotaped the corners. Mum adjusted what needed to be adjusted along the way. Otherwise she sat knitting a sweater that was meant for me. I had chosen it from one of her pattern magazines, a white sweater with dark brown edges, it was different, because the collar was high and straight and there was a split on each side at the bottom so that it hung a bit like a loin cloth. I really liked the Indian style and kept a weather eye on how far she had got with it.

Mum did a lot of needlework. She had crocheted the curtains in the living room and the kitchen, and she had sewn the white curtains in our bedrooms, Yngve's with a brown hem and brown floral print, mine with a red hem and a red floral print. In addition, she knitted jumpers and woolly hats, darned socks, patched trousers and jackets. When she wasn't doing that, or cooking and washing up, or baking bread, she read. We had whole shelves full of books, something none of the other parents had. She also had friends, unlike dad, mostly women of the same age at her workplace, whom she visited now and then, if they didn't come here, that is. I liked all of them. There was Dagny, whose son and daughter, Tor and Liv, went to kindergarten with me. There was Anne Mai, who was fat and happy and always brought us some chocolate, she drove a Citroën and lived in Grimstad, where I had visited her once with the kindergarten. And there was Marit, who had a son, Lars, the same age as Yngve, and a daughter, Marianne, who was two years younger. They didn't come here often, dad didn't like it, but perhaps once a month one or more of them came; then I was allowed to sit with them for a while and bask in the radiance. And occasionally in the evening we went to the arts and crafts workshop in Kokkeplassen, it was the kind of place where you could do all sorts of things, children of other members of staff went there too, and that was where we used to make our Christmas presents.

Mum's face was gentle but serious. She had tucked her long hair behind her ears.

'Dag Lothar saw an adder today!' I said.

'Oh?' she said. 'Where was that then?'

'On the path to the Rock. He almost stepped right on it! Fortunately though it was just as frightened as he was and slithered off into the bushes.'

'Lucky for him,' she said.

'Were there adders when you were growing up?'

She shook her head.

'There aren't any adders in Vestland.'

'Why not?'

She chuckled.

'I don't know. Perhaps it's too cold for them?'

I dangled my legs and drummed my fingers on the table while humming *kisses for me, save all your kisses for me, bye bye, baby, bye bye*.

'Kanestrøm caught loads of mackerel today,' I said. 'I saw them. He showed me the bucket. It was full to the brim. Are we going to get a boat soon, do you think?'

'Take it easy now,' she said. 'A boat and a cat! Well, it's not impossible, but not this year, that's for certain. Next year maybe? It all costs money, you know. But you can ask dad.'

She passed me back the scissors.

You ask dad, I thought, but didn't say anything, trying to slide the blade of the scissors along without making a cut, but it stopped, I squeezed the handles together and made a jagged cut.

'Goodness, Yngve's late,' she said, looking out of the window.

'He's in safe hands,' I said.

She smiled at me.

'I suppose so,' she said.

'The note,' I said. 'The swimming course. Can you sign it now?'

She nodded. I got up and ran along the landing into my room, took the form from my satchel and was about to run back when the door downstairs opened and I realised what I had done as my heart skipped an extra beat.

Dad's heavy footsteps sounded on the stairs. I stood motionless outside the bathroom as his gaze met mine.

'No running indoors!' he said. 'How many times do I have to tell you? It makes the whole house bang and shake. Is that understood?'

'Yes.'

He came up and walked past me, his broad back in the white

shirt. When I saw he was heading for the kitchen all my happiness evaporated. But I had to go back in there, where he was.

Mum was sitting as before. Dad was standing at the window, looking out. I put the form carefully down on the table.

'Here,' I said.

There was one book left. I sat down and made a start on it. Only my hands moved, everything else was still. Dad was mulling over something.

'Yngve's not home yet, is he?' he said.

'No,' mum said. 'I'm getting a bit uneasy.'

Dad looked down at the table.

'What's that you've brought?' he asked.

'The swimming course,' I answered. 'Mum was going to sign it.'

'Let me have a look,' he said, taking the form and reading it. Then he took the pen from the table, wrote his name and passed the form to me.

'There we are,' he said, nodding in the direction of the table. 'Now you take all this stuff to your room. You can finish it there. We're going to have supper now.'

'Yes, Dad,' I said. Put the books in a pile, rolled up the paper and stuffed it under my arm, grabbed the scissors and the Sellotape with one hand, the books with the other and left the kitchen.

While I was at the desk cutting the paper for the last book, a bike rolled up on the shingle outside. Straight afterwards the front door opened.

Dad stood waiting for him in the hall when he came up the stairs.

'What time's this supposed to be?' he said.

Yngve's answer was too subdued for me to hear, but the explanation must have been good because the next moment he went into his room. I laid the book on the paper I had cut out, folded it, and placed another book on top as a weight while I tried to pick the tape free from the roll. When I finally loosened a corner and pulled some off, it tore and I had to start again.

Behind me the door opened. It was Yngve.

'What are you up to?' he said.

'Wrapping my books, as you can see,' I said.

'We had buns and pop after the training,' Yngve said. 'In the clubhouse. And there were girls in the team. One of them was really good.'

'Girls?' I said. 'Is that allowed?'

'Apparently. And Karl Frederik was great.'

Through the open window came the sound of voices and footsteps going up the hill. I stuck the bit of tape I had on my finger on the paper and went over to see who it was.

Geir and Leif Tore. They had stopped outside the drive to Leif Tore's and were laughing about something. Then they said bye, and Geir ran the short distance to his drive. When he turned in there and I saw his face for the first time there was a little smile on his lips. His hand was clenched around something in his shorts pocket.

I turned to Yngve.

'What position are you going to play?'

'I don't know,' he said. 'Probably in defence.'

'What colour's your strip?'

'Blue and white.'

'Just like Trauma's?'

'Close,' he said.

'Come and eat!' dad called from the kitchen. When we went in there was a plate with three slices of bread on and a glass of milk in our places. Clove cheese, brown cheese and jam. Mum and dad were in the living room watching TV. The road outside was grey, and so, almost, were the branches on the trees at the edge of the road, whereas the sky above the trees, across Tromøya Sound, was blue and open, as though it arched above a different world than the one we were in.

The next morning I was woken by dad opening the bedroom door.

'Up you get, sleepyhead!' he said. 'The sun is shining and the birds are singing.'

I pulled the duvet to the side and swung my feet onto the floor. Apart from the sound of dad's footsteps, fading as they went down the landing, the house was perfectly quiet. It was Tuesday. Mum started work early, Yngve had to be at school early while dad didn't have to start until the second lesson.

I went to the wardrobe and searched through the piles of clothes, chose a white shirt, which was the best I had, and blue cords. But the shirt was probably too smart, I thought, he would notice, perhaps ask why I was all tarted up, perhaps tell me to take it off. Better to wear the white Adidas T-shirt.

With my clothes under my arm I went into the bathroom. Fortunately Yngve had remembered to leave the water in the sink. I closed the door behind me. Lifted the toilet seat and peed. The pee was a greenish-yellow, not dark yellow as it often was in the morning. Even though I tried carefully to make sure all the drops fell inside the bowl when I shook myself dry, some landed on the floor, small transparent globules of moisture on the bluish-grey lino. I dried the floor with some toilet paper, which I threw in the bowl before pulling the chain. With the flushing noise in my ears I stood in front of the sink. The water was a pale green colour. Small transparent flakes of God knows what were floating in it. I cupped my hands, filled them with water, leaned forward and dipped my head in. The water was a tiny bit colder than me. A shiver ran down my spine as it settled on my skin. I soaped my hands, rubbed them quickly over my face, closing my eyes as I did so, and rinsed and dried them and my face on the light brown towel hanging on my hook.

Finished!

I pulled the bedroom curtain aside and peered out. The trees in the forest, above which the sun had just risen, cast long dark shadows over the shimmering tarmac. Then I put on my clothes and went into the kitchen.

There was a bowl of cornflakes in my place, with a carton of milk beside it. Dad wasn't there.

Had he gone to his study to get his things together?

No. I heard him moving in the living room.

I sat down and poured milk over the cornflakes. Dipped the spoon in and put it to my mouth.

Oh my God.

The milk was off, and the taste of it, which filled all my mouth, caused me to retch. I gulped it down because at that moment my father came across the floor. In through the doorway, across the kitchen, over to the worktop and leaned against it. He looked at me and smiled. I took another spoonful from the bowl and put it to my mouth. The mere thought of the taste made my stomach turn. But I breathed through my mouth and swallowed it after only a couple of chews.

Oh yuk.

Dad showed no signs of wanting to leave and I continued eating. If he had gone to his study I could have emptied the dish into the bin and covered it with other rubbish, but as long as he was in the kitchen, or on the first floor, I had no choice.

After a while he turned to open a cupboard door, took out a bowl of the same kind as mine and a spoon from the drawer and sat opposite me.

He never did that.

'I'll have some too,' he said. Sprinkled some golden crispy flakes from the box with the red and green cockerel on and reached over for the milk.

I stopped eating. Knowing that a calamity was looming.

Dad placed his spoon in the bowl, filled it to the brim with milk and cornflakes and put it to his mouth. The moment it was inside, his face contorted. He spat it out into the bowl without chewing.

'Ugh!' he said. 'The milk's off! Oh good grief!'

Then he looked at me. I would remember that look for the rest of my life. His eyes were not angry, as I had expected, but amazed, as though he was looking at something he just could not comprehend. Indeed, as though he were looking at me for the very first time.

'Have you been eating cornflakes with *sour* milk on?' he said.

I nodded.

'But you can't do that!' he said. 'I'll get you some fresh milk!'

He got up, poured the carton of sour milk into the sink, shaking his arms wildly as he did so, rinsed it, scrunched it up, put it in the rubbish bin beneath the sink and fetched a fresh carton from the fridge.

'Let me have that,' he said, taking my bowl, emptying the contents into the sink, scouring it with the washing-up brush, rinsing it again and putting it back on the table in front of me.

'There we are,' he said. 'Now help yourself to more cornflakes and milk. OK?'

'OK,' I said.

He did the same with his dish and we ate in silence.

Everything about school was new during this period, but all the days had the same format, and we became so familiar with it that it was only a few weeks before nothing surprised us any more. What was said from the dais was true, and the fact that it was said there made even the most improbable probable. Jesus walking on water, that was true. God appearing as a burning bush at Moses' feet, that was true. Illnesses originating from creatures that were so small no one could see them, that was true. All beings, including ourselves, consisting of tiny, tiny particles that were smaller than bacteria, that was true. Trees needing sunlight to live, that was true. But we not only accepted what the teachers said in this way, we also accepted what they did without a word. Many of our teachers were old, born before or during the First World War, professionally active since the 1930s or 1940s. Grey-haired and dressed in suits, they never learned our names, and what they had to offer as regards knowledge and wisdom never reached us. One of them was called Thommesen. He read a book to us once a week in the break, stooped over the table, his voice a touch snuffled, his complexion pale, almost yellow, and his lips a bluish-red. The book he read was about an old woman in the wilderness, impossible to understand, not a word, so the time he may have regarded as cosy, a friendly gesture towards the small schoolchildren, was for us a torment because we had to sit still while he coughed and mumbled his way through the incomprehensible story.

Another teacher was in his fifties, his name was Myklebust, from somewhere in Vestland, but he lived on the island of Hisøya and was a stern disciplinarian. In lessons with him we not only had to stand in a line and march into the classroom, once we were in we also had to remain standing beside our desks, whereupon he, from beside his desk, would slowly scan the class until there was total silence. Then he would raise himself onto the balls of his feet, bow and say, 'Good morning, class,' or, 'Good day, class,' to which we would answer, 'Good morning, teacher,' or, 'Good day, teacher.' He had no compunction about slapping pupils in heated exchanges or throwing them against the wall. He often ridiculed those he didn't like. His gym lessons were nothing short of drills. There were some women teachers of a similar age who were also strict and formal, surrounded by an aura we didn't recognise but automatically respected and, not infrequently, also feared. One of them lifted me off the ground by my hair once after I said something inappropriate, I remember. Normally they were happy to send notes home, as detentions or early starts were impractical because of the buses. Alongside this band of old teachers, some of whom had been on the staff all their lives, there was also a new generation, the same age as our parents or even younger. Our teacher, Helga Torgersen, was one of them. She was what we called 'nice', that is she never came down heavily on breaches of rules, never lost her temper, never shouted, never hit or pulled hair, but always solved all conflicts through discussion, in a calm controlled voice, and through involving herself as a person rather than playing the teacher role, such that there was little difference between who she was in private, when she was out with friends or at home with her husband, whom she had recently married, and who she was in the classroom. She wasn't the only one, all the young teachers were like that, and they were the ones we liked to have. The headmaster of the school was young too, his name was Osmundsen and he was around thirty years old, had a beard and was strong, not so different from dad, but we were afraid of him, perhaps more than the others. Not because of anything he did, but because of what he was. If you had done something seriously wrong you were sent to his office. The fact that he didn't do any teaching on a daily basis, that he was a kind of shadowy figure in the school, did nothing to diminish our fear. He was also legendary for another reason. The year before, a slave ship had been found only a few metres off the rocks on the eastern coast of the island. It had gone aground there in 1768 and the find had been described in all the newspapers and even shown on TV. Our headmaster, Osmundsen, was one of the three divers who had found it. To me, someone who held diving in greater esteem than anything else, apart from perhaps sailing ships, he was the greatest man I could imagine. It was like having an astronaut as headmaster. Whenever I did drawings, it was always divers and wrecks, fishermen and sharks I drew, apart from sailing ships, page after page after page. Whenever I watched one of the nature programmes on TV, about diving down to coral reefs or diving in a shark cage, I talked about it for weeks afterwards. And here he was, the bearded man who, the year before, had broken the surface with an elephant tusk in his hands, from one of the few intact wrecks of a slave ship that has ever been found.

He came into the classroom on the second day to tell us a little about the school and which rules were important, and after he had gone Frøken said that one day in the not-too-distant future, he would come back and tell us about the wreck he had helped to find. She had been standing by the window with her hands behind her back and a smile on her face all the time he had been there, and she did the same when he returned two weeks later, as promised. My mind was ablaze with the stories he regaled us with, but I was also a tiny bit disappointed when it turned out the wreck lay in waters which were only a few metres deep. That detracted from the achievement to no small degree, I had expected a depth of say a hundred metres, with divers who had to hold the rope for a breather on their way up, taking maybe as much as an hour in all, because of the extreme pressure down below. An overwhelming darkness, flashing beams from their torches, perhaps even a little submarine or diving bell. But on the seabed near the coast, right beneath the feet of bathers, within the range of any boy with flippers and a diving mask? On the other hand, he did show pictures of the find, they had a diving boat moored some way out into the bay, they wore wetsuits and had diving cylinders, and it had all been planned down to the last detail with old charts and documents, etcetera.

Once dad had almost been on TV, they had interviewed him and so on, about something political, but when we watched the news there was nothing, and the item didn't come the next day either, although we all gathered again to see it. However, he had been on the radio once, interviewed in connection with a stamp exhibition, I forgot all about it, so when I arrived home that day it had already been broadcast and he had a go at me.

Many of the teachers wittered on about my name at first, they were colleagues of my father, I suppose, and assumed I was named after him, and I really liked that, their knowing about me, that I was the son of my father. From the very first day I did my utmost at school, above all in order to be the best in the class, but also because I hoped it would reach dad's ears how clever I was.

I loved school. I loved everything that went on there and the rooms where it went on.

Our chairs, low and old, made with iron piping, a slab of wood to sit on and one to lean back against, our desks covered with cuts and ink from all those who had sat at them before. The board, the chalk and the sponge; the letters that grew from the chalk in Frøken's hand, an O, a U, an I, an E, an Å, an Æ, always white, which her hands soon became as well. The bone-dry sponge that darkened and swelled when she rinsed it in the sink, the great feeling it gave you when it rubbed out everything, leaving a trail of water which remained there for a few minutes, until the board was as green and pristine as before. Frøken, who spoke in Karmøy dialect, had big glasses and short hair, wore blouses and skirts, so much she asked us about and told us. She taught us not to speak all at the same time, and not just to shout out an answer but to put our hands up and speak only after she had pointed or nodded to us. Because at the beginning a forest of hands shot up in the classroom, waving impatiently to and fro, with pupils shouting *me, me, me*, because she didn't ask us difficult questions, only ones everyone could answer. Then there were the breaks and all that happened in them, all the children who were there, large groups assembling and dispersing, activities blazing into life and dying back. The pegs in the corridor outside the classroom where we hung our jackets, the smell of ten years of green soap, the smell of piss in the toilets, the smell of milk in the milk lockers, the smell of twenty lunch boxes with a variety of *smørbrød* being opened at the same time in a classroom. The system of monitors, whereby every week a pupil was responsible for handing out whatever had to be handed out, cleaning the board after the lesson and collecting the cartons of milk in the long break. The feeling this gave you of being the chosen one. And the very special feeling of walking down the corridors when everyone else was sitting in class, how deserted they were, jackets hanging from the pegs on both sides, the low mumble from the rooms as you walked past, the shafts of daylight which lent the linoleum floor a dull gleam and on sunny days caused thousands of specks of dust in the air to shimmer, like a miniature Milky Way. A door being thrown open, a boy charging out, could change the atmosphere down the entire length of the corridor, suck up all the attention and significance: suddenly he was all that counted. As though he drew in all the smells, all the dust, all the light, all the jackets and all the mumbling, like a comet in the sky, one might imagine, where all the passing flotsam and jetsam was sucked into its long pallid – by comparison with the shining centre – tail.

I loved the moment when Geir rang the bell and we wandered up to the supermarket, the competition that had already evolved there, where you had to arrive early and put your satchel as far to the front of the queue as possible so that you could get the best seat on the bus. I loved waiting by the shop and watching the other kids drifting in from all sides. Some of them lived right at the top of the estates behind the shop, others came from down in Gamle Tybakken and others still from the estates on the flat land beyond the hill. I especially loved watching Anne Lisbet. Not only did she have shiny black hair, she also had dark eyes and a big, red mouth. She was always so happy, she laughed so much, and her eyes, they were not only dark, they sparkled, as though she had so much happiness inside her they were always filled to the brim with it. Her red-headed friend was called Solveig, they were neighbours and were always together, just like Geir and me. Solveig was pale and had freckles, she didn't say much, but she had kind eyes. They lived on the highest estate in Tybakken, in an area I had only visited a couple of times and where I knew no one. Anne Lisbet had a sister who was one year younger, she informed us when it was her turn to talk about herself in class, and a brother who was four years younger. Another boy in the class lived up there, his name was Vemund, he was a little plump and slow, perhaps even slow-witted, he was the last to run, the weakest, threw a ball like a girl, was useless at football, couldn't read, but he liked drawing and most of the other things you could do sitting indoors. His mother was a big, strong, energetic woman with angry eyes and a piercing voice. His father was thin and pale and walked on crutches, he had some kind of muscle disease, and he was a haemophiliac, Vemund proudly told us. A haemophiliac, what's that? someone asked. That's when the blood doesn't stop coming out, Vemund explained. When dad has a cut and it starts bleeding, it never stops, it just bleeds and bleeds, so he has to take some medicine or go to hospital, and if he doesn't he dies.

Anne Lisbet, Solveig and Vemund's neighbourhood, where lots of other children lived, one or two years older or younger than us, was drawn into our world when we started school. The same applied to all the other neighbourhoods where my classmates lived. It was as if a curtain went up, and what we had assumed was the whole stage turned out to be only the proscenium. The house on the hillside, whose completely level garden we could see from the top, balancing as it were on the edge of a white wall that plunged straight down, maybe five metres, with a green wire fence on top, was no longer just a house but the house where Siv Johannesen lived. Fifty metres further away, behind the dense forest, a road came to an end, and it was along there that Sverre, Geir B and Eivind lived. A bit further down, but in a very different area, a very different world, lived Kristin Tamara, Marian and Asgeir.

They all had their places, they all had their friends, and in the course of a few weeks at the end of the summer everything was opened to us. It was both new and familiar, we looked similar, we did the same things and were thus open to one another. Yet at the same time each one of us had something of his or her own. Sølvi was so shy she could barely talk. Unni worked at the market with her parents and brothers every Saturday, selling vegetables they had grown themselves. Vemund's father walked with the aid of crutches. Kristin Tamara wore glasses with a patch over one eye. Geir Håkon, who had always been so tough, stood writhing with embarrassment in front of the blackboard. Dag Magne had a permanent grin on his face. Geir had received the last rites when he was born because they thought he was going to die. Asgeir always smelled vaguely of piss. Marianne was as strong as a boy. Eivind could read and write and was so good at football. Trond was small and ran like lightning. Solveig was so good at drawing. Anne Lisbet's father was a diver. And John, well, he had more uncles than anyone else.

One day, when we had been at school for the first three lessons, and the bus had dropped us off by the supermarket at twelve, Geir and I walked home with John. The sun was shining, the sky was blue, the road dry and dusty. When we came to John's house, he asked if we wanted to go up and have some juice. We did. We followed him up to the veranda, took off our satchels and sat down on the plastic chairs they had. He opened the door to the house and shouted.

'Mum, we want some juice! I've got some boys from the class here!'

His mother came to the door. She was wearing a white bikini, her skin was tanned, her long hair dark blonde. The whole upper part of her face was covered by a pair of large sunglasses.

'How nice,' she said. 'I'll see if we've got some juice for you.'

She went into the sitting room and disappeared through a door. There was an empty feeling about the room. It looked like ours, but there was less furniture, and there were no pictures on the walls. Two of the girls from our class walked past on the road below. John leaned over the balcony and shouted after them that they looked like monkeys.

Geir and I laughed.

The girls didn't take any notice and went on their way. Marianne, who was taller than all the boys, had a high forehead, high cheekbones and long blonde hair hanging down either side of her face, like curtains. Now and then, when she was angry or desperate, she frowned and had a very special look in her eyes, which I liked. She could also lose her temper and give as good as she got, unlike the other girls.

John's mother came out with a tray holding three glasses and a jug of juice, put a glass in front of each of us and filled it. The ice cubes floated around close together at the top of the red juice. I watched her as she went back in. She wasn't good-looking, yet there was something about her that made you notice her and watch.

'Were you looking at my mum's arse?' John said with a loud laugh.

I didn't know what he meant. Why would I look at his mother's arse? It was embarrassing as well, because he had said it so loudly that she too must have heard it.

'No, I wasn't!' I said.

He laughed even more.

'Mum!' he shouted. 'Come out here a minute!'

She came, still in her bikini.

'Karl Ove was looking at your arse!' he said.

She slapped his face.

John continued to laugh. I looked at Geir: he was staring into space and whistling. John's mother went inside. I emptied the glass of juice in one go.

'Would you like to see my room?' John said.

We nodded and followed him through the dark sitting room to his room. There was a poster of a motorbike on one wall and a semi-naked woman, her skin orange from all the sun, on the other.

'It's a Kawasaki 750,' he said. 'Would you like some more juice?'

'Not for me,' I said. 'I've got to be getting home for dinner.'

'Me too,' Geir said.

The dog snarled at us as we left. We walked down the hill without speaking. John waved to us from the veranda. Geir waved back.

Why would I have looked at John's mother's bum? Was there something about bums I hadn't understood? Why did he shout that out at me? Why did he tell her that? Why did she slap him? And why on earth did he continue laughing afterwards? How could you laugh when your mother has hit you? In fact, when anyone has hit you?

I had looked at his mother, and had a vague sense of guilt when I did so, because she was almost naked, but not at her *bum*, why would I do that?

It was the first time I had been to John's house, and it would be the last. We played football and went swimming with John, but he was not someone whose house we went to. Everyone was a bit frightened of him because even though we said he acted tough but actually wasn't, we all knew that in fact he *was*. He sought the company of boys in the classes above us, was the only one of us who got into fights and was the only boy who would talk back to teachers and refuse to do what they said. He was tired in the mornings because he was allowed to go to bed whenever he liked, and when he talked about his home life in the lessons, which we all did, it was always about some uncle staying with them. Neither he nor any of us questioned the status of these men, and why would we? John had more uncles than anyone we knew, that was all there was to say about that.

A few days later, a Saturday at the beginning of September, one of those early autumn days the summer has stretched into and filled to saturation, when the fields are hot and dusty, the sky dark blue and the first withered leaves whirl through the air almost in a way which is contrary to nature, as the wind is still so mild and all the faces you see are glistening with sweat, Geir and I were walking up through the estate. With us we had a packed lunch and a bottle of juice. We had planned to follow a route we had heard about, it forked left at the end of a long flat stretch, more or less where the path to the Fina station began. To get there we had to cross land belonging to a house we knew very little about, except that the owner could get angry because one Sunday that spring a crowd of us had been playing football on the grass at the far end of his property, bordered on one side by rocks and a stream on the other, when, after half an hour, he had stormed out and started yelling and shaking his fists at us almost before he was within hearing distance, whereupon we all ran away at once. But now we weren't going to play football, now we were only going to cross his fields, along the stream towards the path, which was actually a little track, strewn with small flat mostly white stones. We came to a gate, which we pushed aside, and then we were in a part of the island where we had never been before. The track, lined by tall trees, was in shadow, and it was like walking through a tunnel. Further down there was a curve in the path and white rock glistened in the sunshine. That was the cliff where the stones we were walking on must have come from. We stopped in front of it. It wasn't craggy or semi-rotten, so to speak, the way some more porous rocks might be after being blasted, nor was it flaky or slightly rough, the way bare rock and several of the uncovered crags you could come across in the forest were, no, this cliff was completely smooth, almost like glass, and consisted of many slanting surfaces. Was this a vein of gemstones we had stumbled upon? It seemed like it. On the other hand, it was too close to the estate for that, there was absolutely no chance that we had discovered something no one else had, we knew that, but we still filled our rucksacks with fragments of rock. Then we continued down. The stream followed the track, higher up it ran through a deep gully, then fell, where the slope began, trickling downwards through a series of small terraces. At one point where the stream ran almost level with the track we tried to build a dam. We carried rock after rock to it, covered the crevices between them with moss, and after perhaps half an hour we had managed to make the water flow across the track. Suddenly we heard shots. We exchanged glances. Grabbing our rucksacks, we set off at a run. Shots? Could it be hunters? After a few hundred metres the track levelled out. It lay in deep greenish-black shadow, produced by dense rows of tall overhanging spruce trees. A hundred metres or so away we caught sight of a tarmac road, and we stopped, for the shots were clearer now, and they were coming from our left. We walked between the trees, across the soft cover of blueberry bushes and heather and moss, up a gentle slope, and in front of us, perhaps twenty metres below, bathed in sunshine, there was an enormous clearing full of rubbish.

A refuse tip.

A refuse tip in the forest!

Some seagulls were flying over the far end. Screaming, they circled above the rubbish as if it were the sea. The stench, sweet though still pungent, stung our nostrils. Then the shots rang out again. Not loud, the reports were crisp, like a kind of crackle. Slowly we made our way down to the edge of the dump, and there, a stone's throw away, we saw two men, one standing by a wrecked car, the other lying on his stomach next to him. Both had guns pointing across the dump. They fired at intervals of a couple of seconds. The man on the ground stood up, and then they went into the dump, carrying their guns. We walked over to where they had been. Between the piles of waste, which rose and fell like hills and dales, ran a path which they followed. They were dressed like proper hunters with boots and gloves.

They were grown-ups but not old. Around them I saw cars, fridges, freezers, TVs, wardrobes and dressers. I saw sofas, chairs, tables and lamps. I saw skis and bikes, fishing rods, chandeliers, car tyres, cardboard boxes, wooden chests, polystyrene containers and heap upon heap of fat, bulging plastic bags. What lay before us was a whole landscape of abandoned goods. Most of it consisted of bags of food leftovers and packaging, things that all households carried to the dustbin every day, but in the part where they were standing, and which the two men were crossing, perhaps a fifth of the total area, larger items had been deposited.

'They're shooting rats,' Geir said. 'Look!'

They had stopped walking. One held up a rat by the tail. The whole of one side was shot to pieces, or so it seemed. He swung it round a few times and let go, launching it through the air. It landed on some bags and slid down between them. They laughed. The second man kicked away another rat, putting the tip of his boot underneath the corpse and flicking it.

They returned. Their eyes squinting in the bright sun, they said hello to us. They could have been brothers.

'Are you out for a walk, lads?' one asked. He had curly red hair beneath a blue peaked cap, a broad face, thick lips with a vigorous moustache above, also red.

We nodded.

'A walk to the refuse tip! Takes all kinds, eh,' the second man said. Apart from his hair colour, which was blond, almost white, and his top lip, which was hairless, he was the spitting image of the first man. 'Are you going to eat your packed lunches out there? On top of the piles of rubbish?'

They laughed. We laughed a little too.

'Do you want to watch us shooting some rats?' the first man said.

'Yes, love to,' Geir said.

'Then you'll have to stand behind us. It's important. OK? And stand very still so that you don't distract us.'

We nodded.

This time both of them lay down. For a long time they didn't move. I tried to see what they could see. But only when the shots rang out did I see the rat, which seemed to be hurled back along the ground, as if caught by a sudden violent gust of wind.

They got up.

'Do you want to come and see?' one said.

'There's not a lot to see!' the second man said. 'A dead rat!'

'I want to see it,' Geir said.

'Me too,' I said.

But the rat wasn't dead. It was writhing on the ground. The rear part was almost completely blown away. One of the men jabbed the stock of his gun into its head, there was a soft crunch and it lay still. He studied the gunstock with a concerned expression.

'Oh, why did I do that?' he said.

'You probably wanted to look like a tough guy,' the second man said. 'Come on. Let's go. You can wipe it when we get to the car.'

They went 'ashore' again, with us tagging behind.

'Do your parents know you're here?' one said.

'Yes,' I said.

'Good,' he said. 'I suppose they said you mustn't touch anything here? It's full of bacteria and other shit, you know.'

'Yes,' I said.

'Great! Bye, lads.'

Some minutes later a car started down on the road, and we were alone. For a while we ran around looking at things, emptying bags, pushing over cupboards to see if there was anything behind them while shouting out what we had found to each other. A bag of recent magazines, in good condition, was my biggest find. There was a stack of *Tempo* and *Buster*, a *Tex Willer* paperback, and then some of those small rectangular cowboy magazines from the 1960s. Geir found a slim torch, a small deer embroidered on linen and two pram wheels. When we were fed up with looking, we sat down in the heather with our finds and ate our packed lunches.

Geir scrunched up the greaseproof paper and threw it as far as he could, thinking, probably, that it would end up in the middle of the rubbish, more or less, but it was met by a gust of wind just as he released it and was so light that it didn't even reach the edge and landed in the heather.

'Let's go for a shit, eh?' he said.

'OK,' I said. 'Where?'

'Dunno,' he said with a shrug.

We walked around in the forest for a while looking for an appropriate spot. Shitting in the refuse tip was, for some reason, inappropriate, there was something dirty about it, it seemed to me, and that was strange, because it was all waste, the whole lot of it. But refuse, that was shiny plastic bags and cardboard boxes, discarded electrical appliances and piles of newspapers. Anything soft and sticky was wrapped. So we had to go into the forest to do it.

'Look at that tree!' Geir said.

There was a tall pine tree on its side perhaps ten metres away. We clambered up on the trunk, pulled down our trousers and stuck out our arses, each holding onto a branch. Geir swung his arse just as the shit came out so that it was flung to the side.

'Did you see that?' He laughed.

'Ha ha ha!' I laughed, trying a different ploy, dropping it like a bomb from a plane over a town. It was a wonderful feeling as it came further and further out, the moment when it was suspended in mid-air until it finally let go and plunged to the ground.

Sometimes I would hold it in for days so that I could have a really big one and also because it felt good in itself. When I really did have to shit, so much that I could barely stand upright but had to bend forward, I had such a fantastic feeling in my body if I didn't let nature take its course, if I squeezed the muscles in my arse together as hard as I could and, as it were, *forced* the shit back to where it came from. But this was a dangerous game, because if you did it too many times the turd ultimately grew so big it was impossible to shit it out. Oh Christ, how it hurt when such an enormous turd had to come out! It was truly unbearable, I was convulsed with pain, it was as if my body were exploding with pain, AAAAAAGGGHHH!! I screamed, OOOOOHHH, and then, just as it was at its very worst, suddenly it was out.

Oh, how good that was!

What a wonderful feeling it was!

The pain was over.

The shit was in the pan.

Everything was peace and light throughout my body. Indeed, almost so peaceful that I didn't feel like getting up and wiping my bum. I just wanted to sit there.

But was it worth it?

I could spend the whole day dreading one of those big shits. I didn't want to go to the toilet because it hurt so much, but if I didn't it would only hurt more and more.

So in the end there was no option but to go. Knowing full well that this would hurt like hell!

Once I was so terrified I tried to find another way to get the shit out. I half stood, and then I stuck my finger up my arse as far as it would go. There! There was the shit. As hard as a rock!

When I had located it I wriggled my finger to and fro in an attempt to widen the passage. At the same time I pressed a little, and in that way, bit by bit, I managed to manoeuvre the shit to the side. Oh, it still hurt to work the last bit free, but not *so* much.

What a method that was!

I didn't mind so much that my finger was all brown; it was easy enough to wash it off. The smell was another matter however, because although I scrubbed and scoured, a faint odour of shit hung around my finger all day and all night, even the next morning I could still smell it when I woke.

All these pros and cons had to be weighed up against one another.

When Geir and I had finished, we each wiped ourselves with a fern leaf, and then we went to see the result. Mine had a greenish glimmer to it and was so soft it had already spread across the ground. Geir's was light brown with a black patch at one end, harder and more lump-shaped.

'Isn't it strange that mine smells good whereas yours stinks?' I said.

'It's yours that stinks!' Geir said.

'It does not,' I said.

'Pooh, bloody hell,' he said, pinching his nose with his fingers as he poked around in my shit with a long stick.

Some flies buzzed above it. They too had a greenish glimmer.

'Right,' I said. 'Shall we go? We can see what has happened to them next Saturday, maybe?'

'I'll be away then,' he said.

'Where are you going?'

'To Risør,' he said. 'We're going to look at a boat, I think.'

We ran up to fetch our things, and then we walked home, Geir with a pram wheel in each hand, me with a plastic bag full of comics. I made him promise he wouldn't say anything at home about where we had been because I had a suspicion they would ban us from going if they knew. I had prepared an explanation for the comics, I had borrowed them from someone called Jørn, who lived on the other estate, in case dad found them and kicked up a fuss.

Once inside the porch, I stood still for a moment. I heard nothing unusual and bent down to untie my shoelaces.

Somewhere inside the house a door opened. I took off one shoe and put it next to the wall. The second door opened, and dad was standing in front of me.

I put my other shoe in its place and stood up.

'Where have you been?' dad asked.

'In the forest.'

I suddenly remembered my explanation, and added, looking at the floor, 'And then on top of the hill.'

'What have you got in the bag?'

'Some comics.'

'Where did you get them?'

'I borrowed them from someone called Jørn. He lives up there.'

'Let me see,' dad said.

I passed him the bag, he eyed the contents and took out a *Tex Willer* paperback.

'I'll have that,' he said, and went back to his study.

I went into the hall and was halfway up the stairs when he called me.

Had he sussed me? Perhaps it smelled of rubbish?

I turned and went back down, so weak at the knees that they could hardly carry me.

He stood in the doorway.

'You haven't had this week's pocket money,' he said. 'Yngve had his a while ago. Here you are.'

He put a five-krone coin in my hand.

'Oh, thank you!' I said.

'But B-Max is closed,' he said. 'You'll have to go to the Fina station if you want to buy sweets.'

It was a long way to the Fina station. First of all, there was the long hill, then there was a long flat stretch, then there was the long path through the forest, down to the gravel lane which came out by the main road, where the petrol station was, which was both fantastic and bad. The hill and the flat stretch were no problem, there were lots of houses and cars and people on both sides. The path was more problematic because after only a few metres you disappeared into the trees where there were neither humans nor anything made by human hand to be seen. Just leaves, bushes, trunks, flowers, the odd bog, the odd pile of felled trees, the odd meadow. I used to sing when I walked there. *Gikk jeg en tur på stien*, I sang. Children's songs: *Fløy en liten blåfugl, Bjørnen sover* and *Jeg gikk meg over over sjø og land*. When I sang it was as if I wasn't alone, even though I was. It was as if the singing was another boy. If I didn't sing, I talked to myself. Wonder whether anyone lives on the other side, I said. Or wonder whether the forest continues into eternity. No, it can't do, we live on an island. So the sea is around us. Perhaps the ferry to Denmark is there now? I'd like a bag of Nox liquorice, please, and a bag of Fox lemon sweets. Fox and Nox, Nox and Fox. Fox and Nox, Nox and Fox.

On the right-hand side a vast concourse opened beneath the crowns of the trees. They were deciduous, they were tall and the tops formed such a dense canopy that the vegetation on the ground was sparse.

Straight afterwards I came to the gravel lane, followed it past the old white house and the old red barn, heard the whoosh of the cars on the main road below, and when I reached that, fifty metres away stood the petrol station in all its glory.

The four petrol pumps holding their hands to their temples in their usual salute. The big white plastic sign with FINA in blue letters shone wanly at the top of the high pillar. A juggernaut was parked there, with the driver hanging an arm out of the open window and talking to someone on the ground beneath him. Outside the kiosk there were three mopeds. A car stopped at one of the pumps, a man with a thick wallet in his back pocket got out, grabbed the nozzle and stuck it in the tank. I stopped next to him. The pump began to burr; the numbers on what I thought of as the face sped around. It seemed to be blinking at an incredible speed. The man was looking another way while this was going on, and to me it seemed to be a gesture of nonchalance, not following what was happening. This was someone who knew what he was about.

I went to the kiosk and opened the door. My heart was beating fast, you never knew what was awaiting you in here. Would someone talk to you? Crack a joke and make all the others laugh?

'Ah, here's Knausgaard junior,' they might say. 'What's your father up to today? Is he at home marking essays?'

The customers who hung out went to the school where dad taught. They wore denim, or even leather, jackets, often with brand labels sewn on. Pontiac, for example, or Ferrari or Mustang. Some of them wore scarves. All of them had their hair down over their eyes. And then they tossed their heads back when they wanted to see something. Outside they spat all the time and drank Coke. Some of them put peanuts into the bottle so they could drink and eat at the same time. Almost all of them smoked, even though it was forbidden. The youngest had bicycles, the oldest mopeds, now and then they were joined by even older boys who had cars.

This was where the bad side came in. Mopeds, long hair,

smoking, malingering, playing the machines, everything that happened at the petrol station was bad.

The laughter which always met me when they realised that I was Knausgaard junior gave me nightmares. I had no answer, I had to lower my head and make a beeline for the counter and buy whatever I was there to buy.

'Knausgaard junior is afraid!' they might shout if they were in that mood, for they left me alone as often as they shouted at me. You could never know.

This time they left me in peace. Three of them stood around a one-arm bandit, four sat around a table drinking Coke, and then there were three heavily made-up girls giggling at the table at the back.

I spent all my money on Fox and Nox, it wasn't a small amount, the assistant put them in a transparent plastic bag for me, and I hurried out.

Up the gravel lane, where the air was chilly as the sun had stopped shining there, onto the path. It wasn't so bad, I told myself, looking between all the tree trunks in the vast concourse beneath the branches to see if anything was moving. What should I do? I wondered. Eat the Fox and Nox alternately, or eat all the Fox sweets first and then all the Nox?

To the right of me the bushes rustled.

I stopped and stared at them. Slowly retreated a couple of paces, for safety's sake.

More rustling.

What could it be?

'Hello,' I said. 'Is anyone there?'

Silence.

I bent down and picked up a stone. Hurled it into the bushes and then ran off as fast as my legs would carry me. When I stopped and saw no one was following me, I laughed.

'That taught you!' I said and walked on.

As for spirits of the dead, it was best not to think about them. Keep your mind on other things at all times. Because as soon as you started thinking about the dead, about them being around you, behind that spruce tree over there for instance, all of a sudden it was impossible to think about anything else, and you just got more and more frightened. In the end, all you could do was run, with your heart hammering away and a sort of scream echoing throughout your body.

So even though everything had been fine this time, it was still with a sense of relief that I saw the path and the estate on the flat land open in front of me.

The air, which had been clear and bright when I set out, had turned a little grey as it hovered above the land between the houses along the road.

I ran a few steps.

Two girls were standing outside one of the houses. They watched me as I came across the grass. Then they started running towards me.

What did they want?

I watched them approaching but continued to walk.

They stopped in front of me.

One was the sister of Tom, one of the biggest boys on the estate, who had his own car, red and shiny. I had never seen the other girl before. They were at least ten years old.

'Where have you been?' one said.

'To Fina,' I said.

'What did you do there?' the other said.

'Nothing,' I said, moving off.

They stepped to the side so that I couldn't get past.

'Get out of the way,' I said. 'I'm going home.'

'What have you got in the bag?'

'Nothing.'

'Oh yes, you have. Fox and Nox. We can see.'

'And? I've bought them for my brother. He's eleven.'

'Give them to us.'

'No-oo,' I said.

One of them, Tom's sister, made a grab for the bag. I swung it to the side. The other girl pushed with both arms and sent me flying.

'Give us the bag,' she said.

'No,' I said, wrapping my arms round it while struggling to get to my feet.

She pushed me again. I fell headlong and started crying.

'They're mine!' I shouted. 'You can't have them!'

'Thought they were supposed to be your brother's,' one of them said, grabbing the bag and yanking it out of my hands. Then they ran across the grass as fast as they could to the road, laughing all the while.

'They're mine!' I yelled after them. 'They're mine!'

I cried all the way home.

They had stolen my sweets. How was that possible? How could they just come up to me and *take* them? They were mine! I had been given the money by dad and walked all the way to the Fina station and back! And they just came and took them! Pushed me over! How could they do that?

Approaching my house, I wiped my face on my jumper sleeves, blinked a few times and shook my head a bit so that no one would see I had been crying.

Once when I was five, Trond's little sister, Wenche, threw a rock at me, right into my stomach. I burst into tears and ran over to our garden fence, where dad was working. I was sure he would help me, but he wouldn't, on the contrary, he said not only was Wenche a girl, she was also a year younger than me, it was nothing to snivel about. He said I embarrassed him and I should fight back, surely I understood that. But I didn't. Everyone knew it was wrong to throw stones, didn't they? And that fighting back was bad, a last resort?

Not dad, though, no. He stood there with his stern gaze, and his folded arms, looking across the road to where all the children were playing, nodded his head and said I should carry on playing and stop bothering him.

And since it was girls who had stolen my sweets, there was no hope of any help from dad.

I stood still in the hallway, listened, removed my shoes, put them by the wall, walked carefully upstairs and into Yngve's room while the thought of all the lost Foxes and Noxes hit me with renewed force, and again the tears began to roll down my cheeks.

Yngve was lying on his stomach on the bed reading a copy of *Buster* with his legs in the air. Between him and the comic he had emptied a bag of sweets.

'What are you crying about?' he said.

I told him what had happened.

'Couldn't you just have run off?' he said.

'No, they were in my way.'

'They pushed you. Couldn't you have pushed them?'

'No, they were much bigger and stronger than me,' I sobbed.

'Surely you don't have to blub like that because of it,' Yngve said. 'Would it help if I gave you some of mine?'

'Ye-e-s,' I hiccuped.

'Not a lot, though. But some. This one and this one and this one and this one, for example. And maybe this one. There we are. Is that better now?'

'Yes,' I said. 'Can I sit here as well?'

'You can sit here until you've eaten the sweets. Then you've got to go.'

'OK.'

After I had eaten the sweets and washed my face in cold water it felt as if I was starting afresh. Mum was in the kitchen, I could hear, she was cooking, the fan was blowing. All the time I had been upstairs I hadn't heard anything from dad, so he was almost certain to be in his study.

I went into the kitchen and sat down on a chair.

'Did you buy some sweets today?' mum asked. She was standing by the stove and turning what was probably minced meat in the frying pan. It was sizzling and spitting. There was a pan on the other plate hissing away inaudibly, drowned by the noise of the fan.

'Yup,' I said.

'Did you go all the way down to the Fina station?'

She always said 'the Fina station', never just 'Fina', as we did.

'Yes,' I said. 'What are we having?'

'Casserole with rice, I thought.'

'With pineapples in?'

She smiled.

'No, not pineapples. That's a Mexican dish.'

'Oh, yes.'

There was a pause. Mum tore open a bag and poured the contents over the meat, then she measured some water in a jug and poured that on top. As soon as that was done, the water was bubbling in the pan and she poured in the rice. She sat down at the other side of the table, pressed her hands against her back and stretched.

'What do you actually do in Kokkeplassen?' I said.

'Surely you know, don't you? You've been there many times.'

'You take care of the people living there.'

'Yes, you could put it like that.'

'But why are they there, actually? Why don't they live at home?'

She considered that question at length. Indeed, she thought for so long that my mind was on other things by the time she answered.

'Many of the people who live there suffer from anxiety. Do you know what that is?'

I shook my head.

'It's when you're afraid of something and you don't know what it is.'

'Are they afraid all the time?'

She nodded.

'Yes, they are. And then I talk to them. Do a variety of activities with them to make them less afraid.'

'But . . .' I said. 'Aren't they afraid of one thing in particular? Or are they just afraid?'

'Yes, that's exactly how it is. They're just afraid. But then it passes and then they move back home.'

There was another pause.

'Why did you ask about that? Is it something that's been on your mind?'

'Nope. It was Frøken. We had to tell her what our parents did. I said you worked at Kokkeplassen, and she asked what you did there. I wasn't a hundred per cent sure. But do you know what Geir said? He said his mother taught the people who were where she worked to tie their shoelaces!'

'That's a good way of putting it. The ones she works with aren't afraid. But they have difficulty doing the little chores we take for granted. Like cooking and washing. And getting dressed. So Martha goes there and helps them.'

She got up and stirred the pot.

'They're loonies, aren't they?' I said.

'Mentally handicapped is the expression,' she said, looking at me. 'Loony is a very ugly word.'

'Is it?'

'Yes.'

A door opened on the floor below.

'I'm going to see Yngve,' I said, getting up.

'You do that,' mum said.

I walked as fast as I could without running. If I set off as soon as I heard the first door I would reach Yngve's room before dad had come up the stairs and could see me. If I set off when I heard the second door he would see me.

Now I could hear the first footstep on the stairs as I closed the door behind me.

Yngve was still on his bed reading. He had a football magazine now.

'Food ready soon?' he said.

'Think so,' I said. 'Can I borrow a comic?'

'Help yourself,' he said. 'But be gentle with it.'

Dad walked past outside. I bent down over the pile of comics on the shelf. He kept his comics in collections, so *The Phantom* was in a file, for example, while mine lay strewn all about. He was also a member of the *Phantom* Club.

'Can I take the whole file?' I said.

'Out of the question,' he said.

'The annual then?'

'You can have that,' he said. 'But bring it back when you've finished!'

On Saturdays we had cold rice pudding in the morning and a hot meal in the evening, usually a casserole, always in the dining room, and not in the kitchen where we normally ate. There was a serviette by each place. Mum and dad drank beer or wine with the food; we were given a soft drink. After eating we watched TV. More often than not there was some Broadway-style show from a studio in Oslo, with women dressed in net stockings, jackets and hats and carrying canes, while men in dinner jackets, white scarves and hats and carrying canes came down a white staircase singing some song or other. Frequently it was 'New York, New York'. Sølvi Wang, whom mum liked, usually featured. Leif Juster, Arve Opsahl and Dag Frøland were other regular contributors to Saturday night TV. Wenche Myhre used to perform a sketch playing a young girl in a nursery, or there was the *Eurovision Song Contest*, which, aside from the FA Cup Final, the European Cup Final and Wimbledon, was the pinnacle of the year's TV.

On this evening a man dressed in rags sat on a roof singing and he had an incredibly deep voice. *Oul Man Rivå*, he sang. I was humming the song all evening. *Oul Man Rivå*, I sang as I was cleaning my teeth, *Oul Man Rivå* I sang as I was getting undressed, *Oul Man Rivå* I sang lying in bed and going to sleep.

Mum and dad had closed the sliding door and were in the living room sitting and chatting, smoking, listening to music and finishing off the bottle of wine after dinner. Between the songs I could just hear dad's rumbling voice and was aware that mum said something in the pauses, although I couldn't hear her.

I fell asleep. When I awoke they were still there. Were they going to talk all night, or what? I thought and fell asleep again.

The warm, bright September days were summer's last burst of energy before abruptly crumbling, and in its place came rain. T-shirts and shirts were exchanged for sweaters and long trousers, jackets were put on in the morning and, when the torrential autumn rain set in, rubber boots and waterproofs. Streams swelled, gravel roads were covered in puddles, water poured down the gutters in the streets, bringing with it sand, small stones and pine and spruce needles. Beach life stopped, people no longer went on trips in their boats at the weekend and the traffic to and from the pontoons was all about fishing now. Dad also got out his fishing equipment, the rod, the reel, the lures and the gaff, put on his dark green oilskins and chugged to the far side of the island, where some weekends he stood alone for hours, fishing for the big cod that were there during the winter season. It was very appropriate that the swimming course started at this time because there was something unnatural about the thought of swimming in an indoor pool when the sun was baking hot outside. It was every Tuesday evening all autumn, and everyone in the class had signed up. Since mum left for work before I got up in the morning I reminded her about the course the night before, so that she would remember to buy me a bathing cap on her way home. We should have done it a long time ago, but for some reason or other it hadn't happened. When I heard her car coming up the hill I ran down into the hall and waited. She came in wearing her coat, carrying a bag over her shoulder and, on seeing me, smiled a weary smile. No plastic bag from a sports shop in evidence anywhere. Perhaps it was in her handbag? After all, a bathing cap occupied no space.

'Have you got the cap?' I said.

'Oh no, do you know what?' she said.

'You forgot it? You didn't forget it, did you? The course is today!'

'I did. I was lost in my own world on the way back from work. But you know . . . when does it start?'

'At six,' I said.

She looked at her watch.

'It's half past three now. The shops close at four. I can make it if I go now. I can do that. Tell dad I'll be back again in an hour, will you?'

I nodded.

'Hurry up then!' I said.

Dad was in the kitchen frying chops. A cloud of cooking fumes hovered in the air above the stove. The lid on the potatoes clanked against the side of the pan with the pressure from the steam. He had the radio on and stood with his back to it, one hand holding the spatula and the other resting against the edge of the worktop.

'Dad?' I said.

He swivelled round.

'What?' he said. And when he saw me, 'What do you want?'

'Mum'll be back in an hour,' I said. 'She told me to tell you.'

'Has she been here and gone off again?'

I nodded.

'Why? What for?'

'To buy a bathing cap. I've got my swimming course today.'

The irritation in his eyes was unmistakable. But I wasn't out of the woods yet. I couldn't just about-turn and go.

Then he nodded in the direction of my room, and I went, glad to have got off so lightly.

Ten minutes later he called us. We slunk onto the landing from our rooms, warily pulled our chairs back from the table, sat down, waited until dad had put the potatoes, a chop, a little pile of browned onions and some boiled carrots on our plates before, sitting up straight and utterly still, apart from our forearms, mouth and head, we started to eat. No one said a word during the meal. When our plates were empty, except for the potato skins and the bones, which had been gnawed clean, we thanked dad and went back to our rooms. From the whistling I could hear I concluded that dad was making coffee in the kitchen. After it had stopped, he went down to his study, probably with a cup of coffee in his hand. I lay on my bed reading with my ears tuned to the noises outside the house, the drone of cars passing, and I recognised the sound of mum's VW the moment it turned into the road further down, Beetles were unmistakable and, had I made a mistake nonetheless, I was absolutely certain I was right a few seconds later when it entered Nordåsen Ringvei. I got up and went onto the landing above the staircase. As dad was in his study, it was the best place to wait.

The door opened, I heard her taking off first her boots, then her jacket, which she hung on the hat stand in the corner, and her footsteps across the carpet in the hallway below, which as they began to climb the stairs seemed to merge into the sight of her.

'Have you got it?' I said.

'Yes, no problem,' she said.

'Can I see it?'

She passed me the white Intersport bag she was holding. I opened it and pulled out the bathing cap.

'But Mum, it's got flowers on!' I said. 'I can't wear a cap with flowers on! That's no good! It's a woman's! You bought a woman's bathing cap!'

'Isn't it lovely?' she said.

I looked down at the cap with tears in my eyes. It was white, and the flowers decorating it were not just printed on but small, raised plastic imitations of flowers.

'You'll have to go and change it,' I said.

'Karl Ove, my love, the shops are closed. I can't.'

She laid her hand on my head and looked at me.

'Is it really that bad?' she said.

'I can't go to the course with this. I won't go. I'll stay at home.'

'But Karl Ove,' she said.

The tears were streaming down my cheeks now.

'You've been looking forward to the course so much,' she said. 'Surely a few flowers don't matter that much, do they? You can still go. Then we'll buy you a new cap for next time. I can use this one. I need one. And I think the flowers look lovely, I really do.'

'You don't understand anything, do you,' I said. 'I *can't* go. That's a *woman's bathing cap*!' I shouted.

'Now I think you're being unreasonable,' mum said.

At that moment dad's study door slammed. He could scent a scene like this from a range of several kilometres. Quick as a flash, I dried my eyes and put the cap back in the bag. But it was too late. He was already at the bottom of the stairs.

'Well?' he said.

'Karl Ove didn't like the bathing cap I bought him,' mum said. 'So now he's refusing to go to the swimming course.'

'What rubbish is this!' dad said. He came up the last steps and lifted my chin with his hand.

'You're going to the course with the cap your mother has bought you. Is that understood?'

'Yes,' I said.

'And don't burst into tears over such trivialities. It's pathetic.'

'Yes,' I said, wiping my eyes with my hand again.

'Go into your room and stay there until it's time to leave. Now.'

I did as he said.

'Fancy going all the way back to town to buy it in the first place,' I heard him say as they went into the kitchen.

'But he's been looking forward to this course for so long,' mum said. 'It was the least I could do. I had promised him. And then I went and forgot.'

*

An hour later mum came in to fetch me. We went downstairs to the hall, I had decided not to talk to her, and said nothing, just put on my boots and anorak. In my hand I had a bag with my trunks, towel and the bathing cap in. Opening the door, I saw Geir and Leif Tore waiting outside, each holding a plastic bag. It was getting dark outside, and the air was heavy with drizzle. Their hair was wet; their jackets glistened in the light from the lamp above the door.

They said hello to mum, mum returned the greeting, and then she dashed across the shingle with us close behind. She opened the car door, pushed the seat forward and we clambered onto the back seat.

She inserted the key into the ignition and started the engine.

'Is there something wrong with the exhaust?' Leif Tore said.

'Yes, it's an old car,' mum said, putting the car into reverse and backing up the hill. The wipers dawdled to and fro across the windscreen. The headlamps lit up the black spruce trees across the road, which seemed to take a step towards us.

'Geir can swim,' I said. Then I remembered I wasn't going to say anything.

'Very impressive!' mum said. Flicked the indicator down and glanced through the right-hand window before turning onto the road and driving off, to the next crossroads, where everything was repeated, just the other way around: now the indicator was flicked up and she glanced through the left-hand window.

'And you, Leif Tore, can you already swim?' she said.

The roar of the engine rebounded off the blasted rock face on the other side of the road as we struggled up the hill to Tromøya Bridge. The lights at the top of the mast glowed red in the night. If you didn't know any better you would probably think they were floating in the air, I thought.

Leif Tore shook his head.

'Just a bit,' he said.

The rain-filled gloom had begun to merge the sea and the uplands, I could see as we crossed the bridge. The difference could still be distinguished because the darkness of the land was a shade deeper and denser than that of the calm water, which had a kind of sheen to it. The lights, visible on both sides, seemed to hang in mid-air in the far distance, almost like stars in the firmament, while those closest, whose illuminated surroundings could still be made out, were set in the landscape in quite a different way. Green and red lights shone from lanterns or small lighthouses here and there. We drove down to the intersection beyond the bridge, houses and gardens appeared on one side, industrial buildings on the other, yellow and empty in the light of the headlamps, with the dripping tarpaulin of night hanging above. The wipers were racing across the windscreen; the rain was heavier now. Leif Tore said Rolf had been on the same swimming course. The teacher was an older woman, in her forties, who, according to Rolf, was very strict. But Rolf said so many things. If he got a chance to pull a fast one on Leif Tore, or anyone else, he took it. I said I didn't have any goggles with me, but I could see underwater, so it wasn't a problem. Geir showed us his. They were Speedo goggles with blue glass and white elastic.

'What about your cap?' Leif Tore said.

'My dad's. It's a bit big!' Geir laughed.

'Has your dad got a bathing cap? Mine definitely hasn't. Has yours?' Leif Tore asked, looking at me.

'I don't think so. What's the time, Mum? Will we make it?'

Mum raised her left arm and consulted her watch.

'Twenty-five to six. So we're in good time.'

'Why do only women and children wear caps?' Leif Tore continued.

'They don't,' I said. 'Swimmers who take part in competitions wear them too.'

'I'm going to get one of those white ones with a Norwegian flag on the next time we have any money,' Geir said. 'Dad promised me today. And then he said I could join a swimming club as soon as I could swim properly. In town.'

'But weren't we going to join a football club?' I said.

'Ye-es. I can do both, can't I?' Geir said.

Mum indicated to leave the main road, drove up a gravel avenue leading to an unilluminated school and parked in front.

'I think it's over there,' she said, pointing to a low building behind.

'It is,' Leif Tore said. 'Because that's Trond and Geir Håkon over there.'

'I'll be back to pick you up in about an hour then,' mum said. 'Good luck!'

We piled out of the car with our bags and ran to the entrance as mum's green Beetle turned and drove back the way we had come.

The changing room was cold, the floor a greenish colour, the walls white, the light in the ceiling shrill. A number of cream-coloured wooden benches ran along three of the walls, with a line of hooks above. Five of the boys had come; they chatted and laughed as they undressed. They said hi to us.

'The water in the pool's cold!' Sverre said.

'Freezing cold,' Geir B added.

'Have you been in?' Leif Tore said.

'Of course,' Sverre said.

I sat down on the bench and pulled my sweater over my head. Stood up and took off my trousers. The faint smell of chlorine filled me with happiness. I loved chlorine, I loved swimming pools, I loved swimming. Geir B, Sverre and Dag Magne went into the shower naked. Trond and Geir Håkon followed. We had been told in the strictest of terms that we had to have a shower before we entered the pool. I watched them all as they stood at a distance from the shower, stretched out a hand to turn it on with as much caution as if they were dealing with an unpredictable animal, and checked the temperature of the water as soon as it came out with the other. Once it was warm enough they stood underneath, all with their backs to the wall. Their hair stuck to their foreheads. I took off my underpants, left my clothes in a pile on the bench and waited for Geir and Leif Tore to finish. The door opened, four new boys came in, among them John. There was something I didn't like about being naked when the new arrivals were well wrapped up, so I took the soap container and towel from my bag and went into the showers, to the one furthest away, which was one of three that were unoccupied. Geir and Leif Tore came straight after me, fortunately.

Oh how wonderful it was to stand under the hot water as the room slowly filled with steam! I could have stood there for ever. But my skin went so red whenever I showered, especially my bum, which after ten minutes of really hot water looked like the rear end of one of those monkeys with red rumps. It was impossible not to notice or make a comment on, so after a couple of minutes and a quick check of the colour of my backside, I turned the shower off, dried and went into the changing room to put on my trunks. It wasn't only after a shower that it went red, it also stuck out quite a bit. Dad used to say I had a sticky-out bum. It was true, and it was important for me that no one noticed and made a comment. That kind of thing spread like wildfire.

I sat for a while on the bench, bent forward with my hands on my knees, watching the others coming out of the shower one by one, all with big heads, fair hair, darkened now by the water, pale skin where, after only a few weeks, the clear marks left by a T-shirt and swimming trunks were now disappearing, and skinny bodies; no one was fat in our class, not even Vemund, he was just a bit flabby and had round cheeks, but still he was called fat, the class fatty. Someone had to be. The skin on my arms was developing goose pimples in the cold air and I ran my hands over them quickly a few times. I tried to recapture the happiness the chlorine had filled me with, but now it was as if I couldn't regain it, as if it had been used up or taken over by everything else that was happening.

Through the chink in the open door I saw that the lights in the swimming pool had been switched on.

'It's starting!' someone shouted.

The few boys left in the showers hurried out. The rest put on their bathing trunks, goggles and caps.

A whistle sounded from inside. I took the cap from my bag, crumpled it up in my hand and went to the pool, after Geir, before John. The girls came out of their changing room opposite at exactly the same moment. The teacher stood by the edge of the pool beckoning to us. A whistle hung from a cord around her neck. She was holding a sheet of paper in a transparent plastic polysleeve.

She blew the whistle again. The last boys came running out of the changing room, laughing.

'Don't run!' she yelled. 'We never run in here. It's slippery and the floor's hard.'

She adjusted her glasses.

'Hello and welcome to the course!' she said. 'We'll be meeting here six times this autumn, and our goal is to teach everyone to swim. As this is our first lesson today, we'll take things slowly. First of all, we can play in the water for a bit, and then we'll practise some strokes on the lilos you can see over there.'

'On land?' Sverre said. 'Are we going to learn to swim on land?'

'Yes, that's exactly what we're going to do. Now, there are some simple rules we have to follow. You always shower before getting into the pool. Is there anyone here who hasn't had a shower?'

No one said anything.

'Good! And you must all wear caps. There is to be no running, not even when we have finished. There is to be no ducking! Not under any circumstances! There is to be no jumping into the pool. Always use one of the two ladders you can see.'

'Are we allowed to dive then?' John asked.

'Can you dive?' she asked.

'Yes, a bit,' John said.

'No, you are not allowed to dive,' she said. 'Not even "a bit". So, no jumping, no diving and no running. And whenever I blow this whistle you pay attention to me. Have you got that?'

'Yes.'

'Right, let's start with the roll call. Answer me when I say your name.'

Anne Lisbet was the first to have her name called out, as usual. She was standing right at the back in a red swimming costume, smiling, laughing almost, as she answered. I felt a tingle go through me. At the same time I dreaded my name being read out, hated the way every name was sliced off like a piece of bread and put to one side, until it was my turn. Usually I looked forward to this, sitting in class with everyone's attention drawn to me for a second, how loud and clear my voice was . . . but this was different.

'John!' she said.

'Yes, here,' John said, waving his raised hand.

She sent him a sharp glance before going on to the next.

'Karl Ove!' she said.

'Yes,' I said.

She looked at me.

'Where's your bathing cap? Haven't you got it with you?'

'Here,' I said, raising my hand with the cap so that she could see.

'Put it on then, boy!' she said.

'I'd prefer to wait until I'm in the water,' I said.

'There's no "preferring" here. On with it!'

I unfurled it, drew apart the sides and wriggled it into position on my head. It did not go unnoticed.

'Look at Karl Ove!' someone said.

'He's wearing a woman's cap!'

'A cap with flowers on! That's for old dears!'

'Now, now,' said the swimming teacher. 'All caps are acceptable here. Marianne!'

'Yes,' Marianne said.

But I didn't escape so lightly. All around me there were grins, nudges and amused grimaces. The cap seemed to be burning on my head.

When the roll call was over everyone went as quickly as they could to the two ladders at the corners of the pool. The water was cold, it was best to submerge your body as fast as possible, and I crouched down, launched myself and took as many strokes as I could manage along the bottom. I could swim underwater; the problem was on top. But what a feeling it was, with the bottom only a few centimetres beneath my body and all the water above me! As I broke the surface and stood up, I searched for Geir.

'Did you borrow your mum's cap, or what?' Sverre said.

'No, I did not,' I said.

Geir and Leif Tore had both taken a float, they lunged forward with it in their hands and kicked as hard as they could. I went over to them.

'Shall we go a bit further up and dive?' I said.

They nodded, and we waded off with the slow heavy steps you take when you walk in water, until it was up under our arms.

'Is it true your eyes can be open underwater?' Leif Tore said.

'Yes,' I said. 'All you have to do is keep them open.'

'But it'll sting!' he said.

'It doesn't sting mine,' I said, happy for the opportunity he had given me to shine. For a while we tried to dive the way divers did, swimming on the surface of the water and then bobbing down with their legs in the air. None of us could do it, but Geir was quite close. He was good at everything in water.

When the whistle sounded and we assembled by the thin blue lilos to practise strokes, I had almost completely forgotten about the cap. But then Marianne came over to me.

'Why have you got a woman's cap?' she said. 'Did you think the flowers were so pretty, or what?'

'That's enough about the cap,' the teacher said. She had been standing right behind us. 'OK?'

'OK,' Marianne said.

We lay on our stomachs on the lilos waving our arms and kicking our legs like pale overgrown frogs. The teacher walked around correcting our movements. Then we had to go into the pool again, take a float and practise leg kicks. When we had been doing that for some time, the lesson was suddenly over. After a short get-together at the end of the pool, when she praised us, told us what we would be doing in the next lesson and reminded us to have a shower, we went into the changing room. I sat down on the bench and was about to put the cap in my bag when Sverre bounded over and grabbed it out of my hand.

'Let me have a look!' he said.

'No,' I said. 'Give it to me.'

I lunged at him, but he jumped back. Put on the cap and walked around wiggling his hips.

'Oh, what lovely flowers I have on my cap,' he said in a girl's voice.

'Hand it over,' I said, getting up.

He took a couple more mincing steps.

'Karl Ove's got a woman's cap, Karl Ove's got a woman's cap,' he said. As I ran at him he removed the cap, dangled it in front of me and took a couple of steps backwards.

'Let me have it,' I said. 'It's mine!'

I made another lunge at it. Sverre threw it to John.

'Karl Ove's got a woman's cap,' he chanted. I turned to him and tried to grab it. He gripped my arm and squeezed while holding the cap in front of my face.

I started to cry.

'I want it!' I shouted. 'Give it to me!'

My eyes were almost blind with tears.

John threw it back to Sverre.

He held it up in the air and gazed at it.

'Look! What nice flowers!' he said. 'Oh, how pretty they are!'

'Give it to him,' someone said. 'He's crying.'

'Oh, the poor little diddums. Do you want this lovely cap back?' he said and threw it to where I had been sitting. I walked back, put it in my bag, took my towel and went in for a shower, stood under the hot jet for a brief moment, dried, dressed and was the first to leave the changing room, found my boots among all the others in the front hall, put them on, opened the glass door and stepped out into the playground, where the large shallow puddles, visible only because they were a little shinier than the surrounding tarmac, were lashed by rain. There wasn't a soul around. I walked towards the school building, which was almost identical to ours, and saw the green Beetle parked exactly where mum had dropped us just over an hour ago.

I opened the door and got into the back.

'Hi,' mum said, turning to me. Her face was illuminated by the gleam of a lamp hanging over the edge of the school like a vulture.

'Hi,' I said.

'Did it all go well?'

'Fine.'

'Where are Geir and Leif Tore then?'

'They're coming.'

'Can you swim now?'

'Nearly,' I said. 'But we swam mostly on land.'

'On land?'

'Yes, on some lilos. To learn the strokes.'

'Oh, I see,' mum said, turning back. The smoke from the cigarette she held in her hand hung under the sloping windscreen, thick and grey. She took another drag, then pulled the little metal ashtray and stubbed out the cigarette. From the swimming pool door swarmed a mass of children. A car headlamp swept across the tarmac, then another. The two cars drove almost right up to the entrance.

'Perhaps I'd better tell them you're here,' I said, opening the door.

'Geir! Leif Tore!' I shouted. 'Car's over here!'

They both looked at me, but they didn't come, they stayed with the kids collecting around the entrance.

'Geir! Leif Tore!' I shouted. 'Come on!'

And then they came. Said something to the others first, then they set off, side by side, at a jog across the playground. White plastic bags hanging from their hands, the only things about them that reflected any light and they resembled heads.

'Hello, fru Knausgaard,' they said, getting onto the back seat.

'Hello,' mum said. 'Was it good?'

'Not bad,' they said. They looked at me.

'Yes, it was good fun,' I said. 'But the teacher was strict.'

'Was he?' mum said, starting the car.

'It was a she,' I said.

'Oh,' mum said.

When, four days later, I was walking up through the forest with Geir, Leif Tore and Trond, after the brief and unsuccessful hunt for treasure at the end of the rainbow, the fantasy of being able to swim among the trees there made me pause to wonder whether I would ever be able to swim at all. Grandad couldn't swim, and at one time he had even been a fisherman. I didn't know if grandma could, but I found it difficult to imagine her swimming.

Behind the swaying pine trees clouds scudded across the sky.

What was the time? I wondered.

'Have you got your watch on, Geir?' I said.

He shook his head.

'I have,' Trond said, thrusting his hand forward and up, making his sleeve glide back so that his watch was visible.

'Twenty-five past one, no, past two,' he said.

'Twenty-five past two?' I said.

He nodded and my stomach churned. On Saturdays we had rice pudding at *one.*

Oh no, oh no.

I broke into a run, as if that would help.

'Got a rocket up your arse, or what?' said Leif Tore behind me. I craned my head.

'Lunch was supposed to be at one,' I said. 'I'd better go.'

Up the soft fir-needle-strewn incline, over the little algae-green stream, past the tall spruce and up the slope to the road. Both mum's and dad's cars were there. But not Yngve's bike. Had he been home, eaten and cycled off again? Or he was he late as well?

The thought, unlikely though it was, kept a little hope burning within me.

Across the road, into the drive. Dad might be behind the house, might come round the corner at any second. Might be waiting for me in the hall, might be in his study and tear the door open when he heard me. Might be standing at the kitchen window waiting for me to appear.

I closed the door gently behind me and stood still for a couple of seconds. Footsteps on the kitchen floor above me. Dad's. I took off my boots, placed them by the wall, unbuttoned my waterproof jacket, pulled down my waterproof trousers, took them into the boiler room and hung them on the line there. Stopped and glanced at myself in the mirror above the chest of drawers. My cheeks were red, my hair was a mess, there was some shiny snot under my nose. My teeth stuck out as always. Buck teeth, as people called them. I went upstairs and into the kitchen. Mum was washing up; dad was sitting at the table eating crab claws. Both looked at me. The pot of rice was on the stove, the orange plastic ladle protruding.

'I lost track of time,' I said. 'Sorry. We were having such fun.'

'Sit down,' dad said. 'You must be hungry, I imagine.'

Mum took a dish from the cupboard, filled it with rice pudding and put a bowl of sugar, a packet of margarine and a cinnamon shaker, which hadn't been tidied away with the other spices, beside it.

'Where have you been then?' she said. 'Oh, you need a spoon as well.'

'Round and about,' I said.

'You and . . . ?' dad said without looking at me. He folded the small white bits that stuck out from the end of the hairy orange claw to the side and put the claw to his mouth. Sucked at it with a short slurp. I could hear the meat being released and sliding into his mouth.

'Geir, Leif Tore and Trond,' I said. He broke the empty claw at the joint and began to suck on the next. I put a knob of margarine on the rice, even though it wasn't warm enough to melt, and sprinkled some cinnamon and sugar on it.

'I've cleaned the roof gutters,' he said. 'You should have been here.'

'Oh, yes,' I said.

'But now I'm going to chop a bit of wood. As soon as you've eaten up, you can join me.'

I nodded and tried to look happy, but he could read my thoughts.

'We'll be finished in time for the football,' he said. 'Who's playing today?'

'Stoke and Norwich,' I said.

'Noritsch,' he said, correcting my pronunciation.

'Nowitsch,' I said.

I liked Norwich, I liked their yellow and green kit. I liked Stoke too, with their red-and-white striped shirts. But best of all I liked Wolverhampton Wanderers, who played in gold and black and whose badge was a wolf's head. Wolves, that was my team.

I would have preferred to lie down and read until the match started, but I couldn't say no to dad, and bearing in mind what could have happened I had to count myself lucky.

The rice was so cold that I ate it in a couple of minutes.

'Are you full?' dad said.

I nodded.

'Let's go then,' he said.

He scooped the empty crab shells into the rubbish bin, put the plates on the worktop and went out, with me hard on his heels. From Yngve's room came the sound of music. I looked at the door, nonplussed. How could *that* be? His bike wasn't there.

'Come on,' dad said, already on the landing. I followed him. On with my jacket and boots, out onto the shingle, wait for him. He came a few minutes later with an axe in his hand and a playful glint in his eye. Follow him over the flagstones, then across the waterlogged lawn. We weren't allowed to walk on the grass, but when I was with him, such edicts could be lifted.

Quite a long time ago he had chopped down a birch tree by the fence in the kitchen garden. All that remained of it was a pile of logs that he wanted to split now. I wasn't supposed to do anything, just stand there and watch, to 'keep him company', as he called it.

He removed the tarpaulin, took a log and placed it on the chopping block.

'Well?' he said, raising the axe above his shoulder, concentrating for a second and letting fly. The blade bit into the white wood. 'Everything going well at school, is it?'

'Yes,' I said.

He lifted the log with the axe wedged in and hit it against the block a few times until it split into two. Held the parts and split them, placed them on the ground by the rock face, wiped his brow with his hand and straightened up. I could see from his body that he was happy.

'And Frøken?' he said. 'Torgersen was her name, wasn't it?'

'Yes,' I said. 'She's nice.'

'Nice?' he said, taking a new log and repeating the procedure.

'Yes,' I said.

'Is there anyone who isn't nice?' he said.

I hesitated. He suspended his chopping activities for a moment.

'Yes, since you say that she's nice, there must be someone who isn't nice. Otherwise the word loses all its meaning. Do you understand?'

He resumed his work.

'I think so,' I said.

There was a silence. I turned away and saw the water rising above the grass beyond the path.

'Myklebust, he's not so nice,' I said, turning back.

'Myklebust!' dad said. 'I know him.'

'Do you?' I said.

'Oh yes. He comes to the meetings at the Teachers' Association. Next time I see him, I'll tell him you said he wasn't nice to your class.'

'No, please don't do that!' I said.

He smiled.

'Of course I won't,' he said. 'Don't worry.'

Then there was another silence. Dad worked, I stood there with my arms hanging down by my sides, motionless, watching. My feet were beginning to get cold. I wasn't wearing thick socks. And my fingers were beginning to get cold.

There was no one out. Apart from the occasional car that went past, there wasn't a soul around. The lights in the houses were beginning to get brighter, apparently regulated and intensified by the nascent twilight, which, in contrast with the open sky, seemed to rise from the ground. As though beneath us there was a reservoir of darkness that seeped through thousands, no, millions of tiny holes in the ground every afternoon.

I watched dad. Sweat was running down his forehead. I rubbed my palms against each other several times. He leaned forward. Just as he was grabbing the log and about to straighten up, he farted. Caught in the act.

'You said we should only fart in the toilet,' I said.

At first he didn't answer.

'It's different when you're outside in the open air,' he said, without meeting my gaze. 'Then you can, well, let your farts go free.'

He brought down the axe onto the log and split it in half at the first attempt. The sound of the blow rebounded off the house wall and the cliff above, the latter with a strange delay, as though there were a man up there swinging an axe exactly one second after dad.

Dad swung again and threw the four pieces of wood on the pile. Took another log.

'Could you start piling them up, Karl Ove?' he said.

I nodded and went over to the small pile.

How should I do it? What did he have in mind? Alongside the rock or coming off it? A narrow pile or a wide one?

I looked at him again. He didn't notice. I squatted and picked up a piece of wood. Placed it up against the rock, end on. Placed another piece next to it. When I had laid five in a row, I laid one crosswise on top of them. It was exactly the same length as the width of the five logs. So I laid four more on top, making two equally large squares. Now I could either make two squares next to it, identical, or start a new layer on top.

'What *are* you doing?' dad said. 'Are you completely stupid? You don't stack wood like that!'

He bent down and scattered the logs with his big hands. I watched him with tears in my eyes.

'You lay them lengthwise!' he said. 'Have you never seen a woodpile before?'

He looked at me.

'Don't stand there weeping like a girl, Karl Ove. Can't you do anything right?'

Then he went on chopping. I started stacking the logs in the way he had said. Sobs shook me every so often. My hands and toes were freezing. At least it wasn't difficult stacking them lengthwise. The only question was when to stop. When I had laid them all in a row I stood up with my hands down by my side and watched him as I had done before. The glint in his expression was gone; I saw that as soon as he glanced at me from the corner of his eye. But that didn't necessarily mean something would happen, as long as I didn't say or do anything that might irritate him. At the same time the thought of the match on TV was gnawing at me. It must have started ages ago. He had forgotten about it, but I couldn't remind him, not the way the situation was. My toes and fingers were hurting me more and more. Dad just kept chopping. He paused and occasionally flicked back his hair in a typical gesture of his, a kind of slow toss of his head along with his hand.

We had just been given a PO box in Pusnes, which meant we no longer received mail in our post box on the hill, only a newspaper, and dad had to drive there to collect our post. Last Saturday I had sat in the car with him, and he had combed his hair in the mirror, perhaps for a whole minute, patting his thick shiny locks afterwards, and then got out. I had never seen that before. And when he went in, a woman had turned to look at him. She was unaware that someone who knew him was sitting in the car watching what went on. But why had she turned? Did she know him? I had never seen her before. Perhaps it was the mother of someone in his class?

I put the new logs he threw over on top of the first row. Wriggled my toes backwards and forwards in my boots, not that it helped, they hurt, hurt, hurt.

I was about to say that I was freezing cold, took a deep breath, but then I paused. Turned again and looked at the shiny pool that shouldn't have been there. Watched a large transparent bubble breaking the surface right above the rusty manhole cover. When I turned back, Steinar was walking along the road. He was carrying a guitar case over his back, with his head bent, his long black hair falling over his shoulders and swaying gently to and fro.

'Hello there, Knausgaard!' he said as he passed.

Dad stood up and sent him a nod.

'Hi there,' he said.

'Doing a bit of wood chopping, I see!' Steinar said, without slowing down.

'I am that,' dad said.

He resumed work. I paced backwards and forwards, backwards and forwards.

'Stop doing that,' dad said.

'OK, but I'm freezing cold!' I said.

He sent me an icy stare.

'Oh, you're fweezing, are you?' he said.

My eyes filled with tears again.

'Stop parroting me,' I said.

'Oh, so I can't pawwot you now?'

'NO!' I yelled.

He stiffened. Dropped the axe and came towards me. Grabbed my ear and twisted it round.

'Are you answering me back?' he said.

'No,' I said, looking down at the ground.

He twisted harder.

'Look at me when I'm talking to you!'

I raised my head.

'Do not answer me back! Have you got that?'

'Yes,' I said.

He let go, turned and put another log on the block. I was crying so much I couldn't breathe properly. Dad ignored me and kept on chopping. There were only a couple of logs left now, then he was finished.

I walked back to the low stack of wood and added the new logs. Wriggled my toes in my boots. The tears receded, there was just the odd surreptitious aftershock in the form of an untimely and wholly uncontrollable sob. I dried my eyes on my sleeve, dad tossed four logs over, I put them on the stack, when a thought fluttered in to lift me out of my misery. I wouldn't watch the football. I would go straight to my room and let Yngve and him watch it without me.

Yes.

Yes.

'There we are,' he said, throwing over the last four. 'That's us finished.'

I followed him without a word, took off my boots and my waterproof and hung it up, went upstairs, gathered from the noise in the living room that Yngve was watching the match and went into my room.

I sat down at my desk and pretended to read.

Just so that he got the message.

He did. A few minutes later he opened the door.

'The match has started,' he said. 'Come on.'

'I don't want to see it,' I said without meeting his eyes.

'Are you being headstrong now?' he said.

He came into the room, grabbed my arm and dragged me to my feet.

'Come on,' he said. He let go of my arm.

I stood still.

'I DON'T WANT TO SEE THE MATCH!' I said.

Without another word, he grabbed my arm again and dragged me crying out of my room, through the hall and into the living room, where he hurled me onto the sofa next to Yngve.

'Now you sit there and watch the game with us,' he said. 'Have you got that?'

I had thought of closing my eyes if he forced me into the living room, but now I didn't dare.

He had bought a bag of glacier mints and a bag of English chocolate toffees. The toffees were my favourite sweets, but the glacier mints were good as well. As usual, he had the bags next to him on the table. Now and then he threw one to me and Yngve. Today he did the same. But I wouldn't eat them; I left them untouched in front of me. In the end he reacted.

'Eat your sweets,' he said.

'I don't feel like them,' I said.

He stood up.

'Now you eat your sweets,' he said.

'No,' I said, and started crying again. 'I don't want to. I don't want to.'

'Now you EAT them!' he said. He grabbed my arm and squeezed.

'I-don't-want-any . . . sweets,' I gasped.

He seized the back of my head and pressed it forward, almost down to the table.

'There they are,' he said. 'Can you see them? Eat them. Now.'

'OK,' I said, and he let go. Stood over me until I had unwrapped a chocolate-coated toffee and put it in my mouth.

The next day we were going to Kristiansand to visit my father's parents. We often did that on the Sundays when IK Start was playing at home. First of all we had dinner there, then Yngve, dad and grandad went to the match, sometimes mum did as well, while I stayed with grandma because I was too small.

Both mum and dad had put on better clothes than usual. Dad wore a white shirt, a brown tweed jacket with brown patches on the elbows and light brown cotton slacks, mum wore a blue dress. Yngve and I wore shirts and cord trousers, Yngve's were brown, mine were blue.

Outside, the sky was overcast, but the clouds were of the fluffy whitish-grey variety which, while they may have shut out the sky, did not carry rain. The tarmac was dry and grey, the shingle dry and blue-grey and the trunks of the pines standing tall at the top of the estate, dry and reddish.

Yngve and I got into the back, mum and dad the front. Dad lit a cigarette before starting the car. I was behind him, so he couldn't see me unless I leaned to the side. As we reached the crossroads below the slope up to Tromøya Bridge I folded my hands and said to myself, 'Dear God, please don't let us crash today. Amen.'

I prayed like this whenever we went on longer trips because dad drove so fast, he was always above the speed limit, always overtaking other cars. Mum said he was a good driver, and he was, but every time the car accelerated and we crossed the white line, a feeling of terror took me in its grip.

Speed and anger went hand in hand. Mum drove carefully, was considerate, never minded if the car in front was slow, she was patient and followed. That was how she was at home as well. She never got angry, always had time to help, didn't mind if things got broken, accidents happened, she liked to chat with us, she was interested in what we said, she often served food that was not absolutely necessary, such as waffles, buns, cocoa and bread fresh out of the oven, while dad on the other hand tried to purge our lives of anything that had no direct relevance to the situation in which we found ourselves: we ate food because it was a necessity, and the time we spent eating had no value in itself; when we watched TV we watched TV and were not allowed to talk or do anything else; when we were in the garden we had to stay on the flagstones, they had been laid for precisely that purpose, while the lawn, big and inviting though it was, was not for walking, running or lying on. Yngve and I had never celebrated a birthday at home, and that was rooted in the same logic, it was unnecessary, a cake with the family after dinner was sufficient. We weren't allowed to have friends at home and that was also another aspect of the same logic, because why would we want to be indoors, where we only made a mess and created havoc, when the world outside existed? Our friends would have been able to tell their parents how we lived, and that may well have been a factor; actually the same logic applied here too. Actually it explained everything. We weren't allowed to touch any of dad's tools, not a hammer, not a screwdriver, not a saw or a pair of pliers, a snow shovel or broom, nor were we allowed to cook in the kitchen, nor even cut a slice of bread, nor switch on the TV or radio. If we had been allowed to do that, the house would have been turned upside down, whereas the way it was organised now everything was orderly, as it should be, and if anything was used, by him or mum, it was done in a methodical, appropriate fashion. It was the same with driving: he wanted to progress as speedily as possible, with the fewest possible hold-ups, from one point to the next. In this case, from Tromøya to Kristiansand, the hometown of this thirty-year-old schoolteacher.

Time never goes as fast as in your childhood; an hour is never as short as it was then. Everything is open, you run here, you run there, do one thing, then another, and suddenly the sun has gone down and you find yourself standing in the twilight with time like a barrier that has suddenly gone down in front of you. Oh, no, is it already *nine* o'clock? But time never goes as slowly as in your childhood either: an hour is never as long as it was then. If the openness is gone, if the opportunities to run here, there and everywhere are gone, whether in your mind or in physical reality, every minute is like a barrier, time is a room in which you are trapped. Is there anything worse for a child than to sit in a car for a whole hour, on a journey you know inside out, on the way to something you are looking forward to? In a car full of cigarette smoke from two parents and with a father who hisses with irritation every time you shift position and happen to nudge his seat with your knee?

Oh how slowly time went. Oh how tardy the landmarks were in appearing outside the window. Up the steep hill from the centre of Arendal, through the residential district to Hisøy Bridge, along the whole length of the island coastline, past Kokkeplassen Sanatorium, where mum worked, down the hill and past the shops there, over the bridge crossing the Nidelva river, and then the endless plains with houses and woods and fields to Nedenes. We weren't even in Fevik yet! And from there it was still a long way to Grimstad, not to mention how far it was from Grimstad to Lillesand, and from Lillesand to Timenes, and from Timenes to Varodd Bridge, and from Varodd Bridge to Lund . . .

We sat at the back, silent, gazing out at the varied rolling countryside the road wound its way through. Past straits with islets and skerries, into the dense forests, past rivers and waterfalls, residential and industrial quarters, farms and fields, all so familiar that at any moment I knew what was coming next. Only when we drove past the zoo did we emerge from our torpor because who knew whether an animal or two might appear from behind the tall, long wire fences, free of charge! Then we were past it, and we sank back into our torpor. For an hour we sat on the back seat without moving, for an entire endless hour, before the town began to take shape around us, and the centre of gravity shifted from the car journey to our imminent visit to our grandparents. Entering the town was like entering time, the clock started ticking again, there was the Oasen shop, further down our cousins, Jon Olav and Ann Kristin, the children of mum's sister Kjellaug and her husband Magne; there were the chestnut trees along the road, the tall dirty brick buildings behind them, there was the chemist, there was the kiosk they called Rundingen, there were the traffic lights, there was the music shop, there were the white timber houses, there was the narrow road, and then, all at once on the left-hand side, grandma and grandad's yellow house.

Dad drove some way past the house, down the hill, and then reversed into the lane opposite. Only then could he drive up the short steep drive.

Grandma's face appeared in the kitchen window. When we had got out of the car, which was parked close to the wooden garage door with its black wrought-iron fittings, and were heading for the red brick steps, she opened the door.

'There you are!' she said. 'Come on in!' And when we were in the small hallway: 'Oh, how I've been looking forward to seeing you two boys!'

She gave Yngve a long hug and rocked him back and forth. He looked away, but he liked it. Then she gave me a long hug and rocked me back and forth. I also looked away, but I liked it too. Her cheek was warm, and she smelled nice.

'We might have seen a wolf in the zoo!' I said as she let go of me.

'Did you now?' she said, ruffling my hair.

'No, we didn't,' Yngve said. 'It was just in Karl Ove's imagination.'

'Oh, didn't you now?' she said, ruffling his hair. 'It's good to see you boys anyway!'

We hung up our jackets inside, where there was an open built-in wardrobe, walked across the wall-to-wall carpet and up the staircase. On the first floor the posh living room was on the right and the kitchen on the left. This living room was used only on Christmas Eve and other formal occasions. By the short wall there was a piano on which there stood three photos of the sons of the house wearing student caps, and above them hung two paintings. Against the long wall there were dark display cabinets, with some souvenirs from their travels arranged on top, among them a shining gondola and a golden-brown glass teapot with a very long spout, adorned with what I assumed were diamonds and rubies. At the back of the room there were two leather sofas, between them a corner cupboard decorated with painted roses and in front a low table. Through the large windows you had a view of the river and the town beyond. However, on a normal visit, which this was, we didn't go in there, we took the door to the left, to the kitchen and the two living rooms below, the lowest of which was connected to the best room via a sliding door above a little staircase. Half of the long wall was taken up by a window, through which you saw first the garden, then the river stretching out to meet the sea and, furthest away, the white Grønningen Lighthouse, towering over the horizon.

It smelled good there, not only in the kitchen, where grandma was making meatballs and gravy, which she did better than most, but everywhere there was a fragrance that underlay all the others and was constant, a vaguely fruity sweetness I associated with this house whenever I met it outside, for example when grandma and grandad were visiting us, because they brought the fragrance with them, it was in their clothes, I noticed it as soon as they stepped into our hall.

'Well,' grandad said as we went into the kitchen. 'Was there much traffic on the way here?'

He was sitting on his chair, legs slightly apart, wearing a grey cardigan over a blue shirt. His stomach hung over the waistband of the dark grey trousers. His hair was black and combed back, apart from one lock which had fallen over his forehead. A half-smoked unlit cigarette hung from his mouth.

'No, went like clockwork,' dad said.

'How did you do with the football pools yesterday?' grandad said.

'Not too well,' dad said. 'Seven right was all I managed.'

'I got two tens,' grandad said.

'That's pretty good,' dad said.

'I slipped up on numbers seven and eleven,' grandad said. 'The second one was annoying. The goal was scored after full time!'

'Yes,' dad said. 'I didn't get that one either.'

'Did you hear what one pupil said to Erling the other day?' grandma said from the stove.

'No. What?' dad said.

'He came into class in the morning, and this pupil asked, "Have you won the pools or what?" "No," Erling said. "Why do you ask?" "You look so happy," the pupil said.'

She laughed. 'You look so happy!' she repeated.

Dad smiled.

'Anyone for a cup of coffee?' grandma asked.

'Yes, please. I'd love one,' mum said.

'Let's sit in the living room then,' grandma said.

'Could we go upstairs and get some comics?' Yngve said.

'You can,' grandad said. 'But don't make a mess!'

'Nope,' Yngve said.

Treading carefully, for this was not a house you could run in either, we went into the corridor and up the stairs to the second floor. Apart from grandma and grandad's bedroom there was a big attic room there, and along the wall cardboard boxes containing old comics, going right back to when dad was a child in the 1950s. There was a variety of other objects as well, among them an ancient mangle for wringing tablecloths and bedlinen, an old sewing machine, a number of old games and toys, including a tin spinning top, and something that was meant to be a robot made of the same material.

But it was the comics that appealed to us. We weren't allowed to take them home with us, we had to read them there, and we read plenty from the time we arrived to the time we left. Taking a pile each, we went downstairs and found a chair, and didn't look up until food was on the table and grandma called us to eat.

After the meal grandma washed up while mum stood next to her, drying. Grandad sat at the table reading a newspaper, dad stood by the window in the living room looking out. Then grandma came in and asked if he would like to join her in the garden, there was something she wanted to show him. Mum and grandad sat at the table, they chatted a bit, but mostly they were silent. I got up to go to the toilet. It was on the ground floor, I didn't like it and I had held on for as long as I could, but now I was bursting. Out into the corridor, down the creaking wooden stairs, a quick dash across the carpeted hall surrounded, as it were, by three empty rooms behind closed doors and into the bathroom. It was dark; in the seconds before the light came on I was shaking inside. But even with the light on, I was afraid. I peed down the side so that the splash of the pee hitting the water would not prevent me from hearing anything. I also washed my hands before flushing the toilet because the moment I pressed the lever at the side of the cistern I would have to rush out as fast as I could, as the noise was so loud and eerie that I couldn't be in the same room. I stood at the ready, with my hand around the little black ball for a couple of seconds. Then I flushed, darted into the hall, also scary, because every slightest thing there silently 'transmitted itself', and set off up the stairs, not able to run of course, with a sensation that something down below was following me, until I entered the kitchen and the presence of the others broke the spell.

Outside, in the lane, the stream of people on their way from town to the stadium had increased, and soon also dad, mum and Yngve would be getting ready to go. Grandad always cycled there and left a little later than the others. He was wearing a grey coat, a rust-coloured scarf, a greyish cloth cap and black gloves, I could see him from the window, as he freewheeled down the hill. Grandma took out some rolls from the freezer, we were going to have them when the others returned home, and put them on the worktop.

She sent me a mischievous look.

'I've got something for you,' she said.

'What's that?' I said.

'Wait and see,' she said. 'Cover your eyes!'

I covered my eyes, and heard her rummaging about in the drawers. She stopped in front of me.

'Now you can look!' she said.

It was a bar of chocolate. One of those triangular ones you don't see often that are so good.

'Is it for me?' I said. 'All of it?'

'Yes,' she said.

'What about Yngve?'

'No, not this time. He's been allowed to see the match. You have to have a treat as well!'

'Thank you very much,' I said, tearing off the cardboard packaging to reveal the bar wrapped in silver paper.

'But don't say anything to Yngve, OK?' she said with a wink. 'It's our secret.'

I munched the chocolate as she sat doing a crossword.

'We're getting a telephone soon,' I said.

'Are you?' she said. 'Then we can talk to each other.'

'Yes,' I said. 'We're actually at the end of the queue, but we're getting it anyway because dad's in politics.'

She laughed.

'In politics, Karl Ove,' she said.

'Yes?' I said. 'He is, isn't he?'

'Yes, he is. He is indeed.'

'Are you enjoying school?' she said.

I nodded.

'Yes, very much.'

'What do you like best?'

'The breaks,' I said, knowing that would make her laugh, or at least smile.

When I had finished the chocolate and she was immersed in the crossword again, I went up to the loft and brought down some of the games.

After a while she looked at me and asked me if we shouldn't go to the match as well. I wanted to go. We got dressed, she took her bike from the garage, I sat on the luggage rack, she sat on the saddle but kept one foot on the ground and turned to me.

'Ready?' she said.

'Yes,' I said.

'Hold on tight, here we go!'

I wrapped my arms around her. She pushed off with her foot, put it on the pedal and freewheeled down the little hill, turned right and started pedalling.

'Are you OK?' she asked, and I nodded until I realised she couldn't see me, and said:

'Yes, I'm fine.'

And I was. It felt good holding her, and cycling with her was fun. Grandma was the only person who touched Yngve and me, the only person who gave us hugs and stroked our arms. She was also the only person who played with us. Dad might do it at Christmas, but we always did the things he wanted to do, like playing mastermind or chess or Chinese chequers or yatzy or crazy eights or poker with matchsticks. Mum joined in when we played, but we did most things with her, either on the kitchen table at home or at the arts and crafts workshop in Kokkeplassen, and it was fun, but not like with grandma, who didn't mind doing what we were doing and followed with interest when Yngve showed her something from his chemistry set, for example, or helped me when I was doing a jigsaw puzzle.

The wheels went more and more slowly until they almost stopped completely and grandma got off and pushed the bike to the crest of the hill.

'You just stay where you are, if you want,' she said.

I sat gazing over the town while grandma pushed the bike, a trifle out of breath. Reaching the top, she got back on the saddle and it was a gentle downhill ride all the way to the stadium. A sudden huge groan erupted, as if from an enormous animal, and then there was clapping. Few sounds were so irresistible. Grandma cycled down to one end of the stadium, rested the bike against the wooden fence and let me stand on the luggage rack for a few minutes while she held me so that I could see what was happening on the pitch. The players were a long way away, all the details eluded me, apart from the yellow and white shirts against the green of the turf, and all the spectators standing around the pitch, a black surging mass, but I caught the mood, I inhaled it and in the days to come I would savour it in my mind.

Back home, she began to prepare the meal we would have before leaving, and not long afterwards the door in the hall opened, it was grandad, his expression was grim, and when grandma saw it she said, 'They lost, did they?'

He nodded, sat down on his chair and she poured him some coffee. I never quite understood what the power relationship was between grandma and grandad. On the one hand, she always served him food, cooked all the meals, did all the washing-up and the housework as though she were his servant; on the other hand, she was often angry or irritated with him, and then she gave him a mouthful or made a fool of him, she was sharp and not infrequently sarcastic, while he said very little, preferring not to respond. Was it because he didn't need to? Because nothing of what she said altered anything important? Or because he couldn't? If Yngve and I were present during such sparring, grandma would wink at us as if to say this wasn't serious, or use us in her sally against him by saying such things as 'Grandad can't even change a light bulb properly,' while grandad, for his part, would look at us, smile and shake his head at grandma's antics. I never saw any form of intimacy between them, other than in their verbal exchanges or the closeness that was evident when she served him.

'They lost, I heard?' she said again when mum, dad and Yngve came up the stairs ten minutes later.

'Yes, they did. Eternally owned is but what's lost,' dad quoted. 'Or what do you reckon, Dad?'

Grandad growled something or other.

When we left in the evening we were given a bag of plums, a bag of pears and a bag of bread rolls. Grandad, reluctant to leave his chair, said goodbye to us upstairs while grandma came down with us, gave us each a long hug, stood on the front doorstep and waved until she could no longer see us.

Strangely enough, the journey back always seemed much faster than the journey there. I loved travelling in a car at night, with the dashboard lit, the muted voices from the front seats, the gleam of street lamps as we passed beneath washing over us like breakers or waves of light, the long, completely dark stretches that cropped up intermittently, where all you saw, all that existed, was the tarmac lit up by the headlights and the countryside they illuminated on the bends. Sudden treetops, sudden crags, sudden sea inlets. It was always a particular pleasure to arrive at the house in the night as well, to hear footsteps on the shingle and the sharp slam of car doors and the rattle of keys, to see the light in the hall come on, revealing the presence of all the familiar objects. The shoes with the grommets as eyes and the tongue as a forehead, the chilly gaze from the white two-holed electric sockets above the skirting board, the hat stand in the corner, with its back turned. And in my room: the pens and pencils assembled like a gang of schoolchildren in the pen stand, some insolently leaning against the edge, ready at any moment to discharge a gobbet of spit to prove they were not interested in anyone or anything. The duvet and the pillow that were either tidy and puffed up, looking like something that shouldn't be touched, a coffin or a capsule in a spaceship, or else were moulded in the shape of my last movements, happy to be rearranged, but with no real inclination in that direction. The fixed stare of the lamps. The mouth of the keyhole, the two screw-eyes of the metal fitting, the long, oddly positioned, nose of the handle.

I cleaned my teeth, shouted goodnight to mum and dad and got into bed to read for half an hour. I had two favourite books, which I tried to quarantine long enough to be able to read them again in the same way I had the first time, but it never worked, I picked them up again much too soon. One was *Doctor Dolittle*, which was about a doctor who could talk to animals and one day went on a long voyage with them to Africa, where, after being hunted and captured by some Hottentots, he finally found what he was looking for, the rare sausage animal which had two heads, one at each end. The second book was *Gangles*, which was about a girl who would stand on fountains of water and allow herself to be hurled into the air, and who, after several misadventures, ended up balancing above the sea on a spout of water blown out by an enormous whale. Tonight, however, I chose another book from the pile, *The Little Witch*, which was about a witch who was too small to join the coven in Bloksberg but who sneaked in anyway. She did lots of things she wasn't supposed to do, like witchcraft on Sundays, which was almost unbearable to read about, she shouldn't have done it, she would be caught . . . and indeed she was, but everything turned out fine in the end. I read a few pages, but as I knew the story so well I looked at the pictures instead. After flicking through it, I turned off the light, rested my head on the pillow and closed my eyes.

I had almost let go, perhaps I had even fallen asleep, because it was as though I had suddenly been brought back to my bed and my room, summoned by a ring at the front door.

Diing-dong.

Who on earth could that be? No one rang our doorbell, except guests we were expecting, which in nine out of ten cases were grandma and grandad, plus the occasional salesman, or one of Yngve's friends. But none of them would ring so late at night.

I sat up in bed. Heard mum padding along the landing and down the stairs. Muffled voices from below. Then she came back up, exchanged a few words with dad, which I didn't catch, went downstairs and must have put on her coat there because straight afterwards the front door was slammed shut, and straight after that her car started up.

What in the world? Where was she going *now*? It was nearly *ten o'clock*!

A few minutes later dad went downstairs as well. But he didn't go out, he went into his study. When I heard that I got up, carefully opened the door and sneaked along the landing into Yngve's room.

He was lying on his bed reading. Still dressed. He smiled when he saw me and sat up.

'You're only wearing your underpants,' Yngve said.

'Who was that at the door?'

'Fru Gustavsen, I think,' he said. 'And all the kids.'

'Oh? Why? And why did mum go? Where did she go?'

Yngve shrugged.

'I think she drove them to some relatives.'

'Why?'

'Gustavsen's drunk. Didn't you hear him shouting at them a while ago?'

I shook my head.

'I was asleep. But was Leif Tore with them? And Rolf?'

Yngve nodded.

'Crikey,' I said.

'Dad'll be coming back up,' he said. 'You'd better go to bed. I'll turn in as well now.'

'OK. Goodnight.'

'Goodnight.'

In my room, I drew the curtains aside and looked across to Gustavsen's house. I couldn't see anything unusual. Outside, at least, everything was still.

Herr Gustavsen had been drunk before, he was well known for it. One night that spring a rumour had spread that he was drunk, and three or four of us crept into their garden and stood by the living-room window looking in. But there was nothing to see. He was sitting on the sofa gazing into the distance without moving. At other times we had heard him shouting and yelling through the open windows and on the lawn. Leif Tore just laughed. But perhaps this was something different? Escaping from him, they'd never done that before.

When I next woke it was morning. Someone was in the bathroom, I could hear, probably Yngve, and from the road outside, along the three-metre-high wall surrounding Gustavsen's property and supporting the level lawn, came the drone of mum's car. She had to go to work early today. Yngve closed the bathroom door, returned to his room and then went downstairs.

The bike!

Where was his bike?

I had completely forgotten to ask him.

But that had to be the reason he was leaving so early; he couldn't cycle, he had to walk to school.

I got up, took my clothes into the bathroom, washed in the water he had remembered to leave today too, dressed and went to the kitchen, where dad had made three *smørbrød* and put them on a plate in my place, as well as a glass of milk. The milk carton, the bread, the cheese, sliced meat and jams had been tidied away. He was sitting in the living room, listening to the radio and smoking.

Outside it was raining. A steady drizzle, broken by intermittent gusts of wind, pitter-pattering against the windows and sounding like tiny drumming fingers.

Monday was the only day no one was at home when I came back from school. So I had my own key, which I carried on a piece of string around my neck. But there was a problem with the key: I couldn't get it to open the door. The first Monday it had been raining and I bounded across the shingle in rubber boots and rain gear, the key nestling in my hand, overjoyed at the imminent prospect and filled with pride. I managed to get the key into the lock, but not to turn it. It would not budge however much force I used. The key was unmovable. After ten minutes I started crying. My hands were red and cold, the rain was bucketing down and all the other children had been at home for ages. At that moment one of the neighbours I didn't know so well passed – she was old and lived with her husband in the house at the very top by the forest above the football pitch – on her way down the road, and when I saw her, I didn't hesitate, because she had no connection with my parents, I dashed over and asked, with tears running down my cheeks, if she could help me with the lock. She could. And for her it was no problem at all! She fiddled with the key and it turned. And, hey presto, the door was open. I thanked her and went inside. Knowing there was nothing wrong with the key, there was something wrong with me. The next time this happened it wasn't raining, so I left my satchel by the step and ran up to Geir's. Dad made a comment about the satchel when he came home, I wasn't to leave it lying around, so the following Monday, when the weather was also dry, I simply took it with me, under the pretext of having to do some homework with Geir and thus needing my satchel close at hand.

In the meantime I had worked out a method I could use when the weather got worse during autumn and winter, like today. In the boiler room there was a little window, more like a hatch, but not so small that I couldn't crawl through. It was positioned about half a metre above my head. I had calculated that if I opened the window in the morning, and there was no great risk involved because the window stayed close to the frame even when the two catches were undone, I could pull over the dustbin when I got home, stand on it, wriggle through into the boiler room, open the door from the inside, put the dustbin back, close the window and be indoors without anyone realising I couldn't get the key to turn. The sole doubt in my mind was when to undo the catches. However, if it was raining, it would be the most natural thing in the world to go into the boiler room, because that was where my rain gear usually hung, and all I had to do was lift the catches, impossible to see unless you stood close to the door. And I wasn't so stupid that I would touch anything with dad around in the hall!

I ate the three *smørbrød* and drank the glass of milk. Cleaned my teeth in the bathroom, collected my satchel from my room, went downstairs and into the hot narrow room with the two water cylinders. I stood absolutely still for two seconds. As there was no sound of footsteps on the stairs, I stretched up and unhooked the catches. Then I donned my waterproofs, slipped on my satchel, went into the hall where my boots were, a pair of blue and white Viking rubber boots which I had been given despite my wanting white ones, shouted goodbye to dad and ran out, up to Geir's. He poked his head out of the window and called that he was still having breakfast but would be down soon.

I walked over to one of the grey puddles in their drive and started throwing stones in it. Their drive wasn't covered in shingle as most of the others were, nor brick paving like at Gustavsen's, but compacted reddish earth full of small round stones. This wasn't all that was different about them. At the back of the house they didn't have a lawn but a little patch where they had planted potatoes, carrots, swedes, radishes and various other vegetables. On the forest side they didn't have a wooden fence, as we did, nor wire netting, as many others did, but a stone wall which Prestbakmo had built himself. Nor did they throw all their rubbish in the dustbin, as we did; they kept all their milk cartons and egg boxes to use in a variety of ways and they put all their leftovers on a compost heap by the stone wall.

I straightened up and glanced at the cement mixer. The round green drum was partially covered by a white tarpaulin and it looked like a headscarf. Her mouth was open, it was big and toothless; what was it she could see that surprised her so much?

Down the hill came Geir Håkon's father in his green Ford Taunus. I waved; he lifted his hand from the steering wheel in a fleeting response.

I was suddenly reminded of Anne Lisbet. The thought soared from my stomach and spread like an explosion of joy in my chest.

She hadn't been at school on Friday. Solveig had said she was ill. But today was Monday. She was bound to be better now.

Oh, please let her be better!

I was dying to go up to B-Max and see her.

Her glittering black eyes. Her happy voice.

'Geir! Come on!' I shouted.

I heard his muffled voice from behind the door. The next instant he tore it open.

'Shall we take the path?' he said.

'Let's,' I said.

So we ran behind the house, scrambled over the stone wall and joined the path. From being no more than a mass of tufts with small dried-up channels in between, the bog was now full of water, impossible to cross dry-shod, even in boots, because your foot would sink in a puddle to way above the boot top, but we tried anyway, balancing on the quivering tufts, jumping to the next, slipping, putting out a hand to save yourself and feeling the ground give, the water seeming to *creep* up your jumper under the sleeve of your jacket. We laughed and shouted, telling each other what had happened, crossed the now muddy and slippery football pitch and went between the deciduous trees to the right, up the broad avenue which might once have been a cart track, it was broader than a path at any rate and covered with a carpet of leaves. Red, yellow and brown, they lay there, with the occasional splash of green. At the top there was a tiny field, the grass was long here, a yellowish-white, and lay flat, plastered to the ground. Above it a bare tor towered, on which there stood an old telegraph pole. The former cart track continued for a while, then disappeared, devoured by the new main road running past, maybe twenty metres from the field. Below lay the forest, mostly oak trees, between two of them there was an abandoned car, in much worse condition than the one where we normally played, perhaps a hundred metres lower down, but no less appealing for that, in fact the contrary: hardly anyone ever played here.

Oh, the smell of an abandoned car in a wet forest! The smell of the synthetic material on the torn seats, mouldy and mildewed, but still sharp and fresh compared with the heavy, musty smell of rotting leaves emanating from the ground all around them. The black window seals that had come loose and hung from the roof like tentacles. All the glass that had been smashed to pieces and largely lost in the soil, although there were scattered fragments on the floor mats or in the door openings, like small matt diamonds. And, oh, the black floor mats! Shake them and a whole horde of creepy crawlies ran for cover. Spiders, daddy-long-legs and woodlice. The resistance of the three floor pedals, which you could hardly move. The raindrops that fell through a window onto your face whenever the wind forced them off track or shook them from the leaves on the swaying branches above.

Sometimes we found objects lying around and about near the car: a lot of bottles, some bags of car or porn magazines, empty cigarette packets, empty plastic bottles of screen wash, the odd condom, and once we found a pair of underpants still full of shit. We laughed about that for a good long time, about someone shitting themselves and then coming here to throw away their underpants.

But we used to have a shit in the forest when we were on our walks. We would climb up trees and shit from there, squat on top of a cliff and shit over the edge, or on the bank of a stream and shit in it. All to see what happened and how it felt. What colour the turds were, whether they were black, green, brown or light brown, how long and fat they were, and what happened when they lay there glistening on the forest floor, between heather and moss, whether there would be flies swarming around them or beetles climbing over them. Also the smell of shit was sharper, stronger and more distinct in the forest. Now and then we revisited places where we'd had a shit, to see what had happened to it. Sometimes it had vanished, sometimes there were only dry remains and at others it lay flat as though it had melted in a pool.

But now we had to go to school and there was no time for such activities. Down the hill, across the playground, which consisted of little more than a rusty climbing frame, a rusty swing and a rotting sandpit with next to no sand in it. Up the steep slope, over the high concrete barriers, across the road and B-Max stood in front of us. The line of satchels in the queue was already long. Some girls were skipping despite the pouring rain; others stood under the overhanging roof in front of the shop. But where was Anne Lisbet? Wasn't she here?

At that moment the bus came up the hill. Geir and I crossed the road and reached the bus stop as it turned into the tarmac pull-in outside the supermarket. We got on last and sat right at the front. The big windows misted up with the moisture we brought in with us. Many of the kids started drawing in the condensation. The driver closed the doors and set off towards the main road. I knelt on my seat and scanned the back of the bus. She wasn't there, and it was as if all meaning had leaked from the world. Now I would have to go all day without seeing her and perhaps the following day as well. Solveig wasn't there either, so it wouldn't be possible to find out how ill she was or for how long.

Ten minutes later the bus stopped outside the school, we ran across the playground and into the wet-weather shelter, where we huddled with almost all the other pupils until the bell went and we lined up. I knew most of them by appearance now, some also by name and reputation. We had gymnastics with the parallel class, who had an advantage over us, as they came from this area and were on home ground. This was their school, the teachers were their teachers, to them we were just some kind of immigrant, without any rights. But they were also tougher than we were, that is, they had more fights, they caused more trouble and mouthed off more, at least some of them did, which only the toughest of us, viz Asgeir and John, stood up to. The rest of us were pushed around as they pleased. Any second you could feel an arm around your throat, and then a jerk and you were on the floor. Any second a fist could hit you in the shoulder, where it hurt most, as you queued up or were on the way to the classroom. Any second someone could stamp on your toes in a football game. But they quickly learned they couldn't bully John or Asgeir because they retaliated and gave as good as they got. These boys, who lived on the east of the island, also dressed differently from us, at least some of them did. Their clothes were older and seemed more used, as though they only wore hand-me-downs, and not just from one brother but two or maybe even three . . . Geir's and my greatest fear was that some of these boys would find us when we were in our secret place. But they didn't represent much of a problem, you only had to be on your guard when you were out and everything was usually fine. Perhaps the most significant consequence was that we stuck together more and saw ourselves as a unit and the classroom as a bastion of security.

The bell rang, we lined up, and Frøken, tall and thin as always, appeared at the top of the stairs with her slightly lopsided gait and nervy hand movements, and we marched down to the classroom, where after hanging up our outdoor clothes on the pegs outside we at once sat down in our places.

'Anne Lisbet's ill today as well!' someone said.

'And Solveig.'

'And Vemund.'

'And Leif Tore,' Geir said.

Then I remembered what had happened the night before.

'Vemund's ill in the head!' Eivind said.

'Ha ha ha!'

'No, no, no,' Frøken said. 'We are not nasty to anyone in this class. And certainly not behind their backs!'

'Leif Tore's father was drunk yesterday!' I said. 'My mum had to drive them to a relative's house. That's why he isn't here today!'

'Shhh,' Frøken said, looking at me, holding a finger to her lips and shaking her head. Then she wrote something in her book before scanning the class.

'Anyone else away? No? So, let's make a start, shall we?'

She stepped forward and perched on the edge of her desk. 'This week we're going to learn about farms. Has anyone ever been to a farm?'

Oh, I shot up my arm as high as I could, almost standing up, shouting *Me, me, me! I have!*

I wasn't the only person to have something to say about the topic. And it wasn't my hand Frøken pointed to but Geir B's.

'I've ridden a horse in Legoland,' he said.

'But that's not a *farm*,' I screeched. 'I've been to a farm lots of times. Grandma and grandad–'

'Was it your turn, Karl Ove?' Frøken said.

'No,' I said, eyes downcast.

'It's true that Legoland is not a farm,' she continued. 'But horses are on farms, that's true, Geir. Unni?'

Unni, who was that?

I turned. Ah, that's the girl who was always giggling. Chubby with blonde hair.

'I live on a farm,' she said with flushed cheeks. 'But we haven't got any animals. We grow vegetables. And dad sells them at the market in town.'

'But I've been to a farm *with animals*!' I said.

'Me too,' Sverre said.

'And me!' said Dag Magne.

'You'll have to wait your turn,' Frøken said. 'Everyone has to have a chance.'

She pointed to five other people before I was finally able to take my hand down and say what I had to say. Well, grandma and grandad had a farm, it was big, they had two cows and a calf, and they had hens. I had collected the eggs many times, and I had seen grandma milking the cows in the morning. First she shovelled away the muck, and then she fed them, and then she milked them. Sometimes they lifted their tails and had a piss or a shit.

A wave of laughter rolled towards me. Emboldened by it, I continued. And once, I said, sitting there in class, my face crimson, one of the cows pissed on me!

I looked round and lapped up the ensuing laughter. Frøken said nothing; she pointed to someone else, but I could see from her face that she didn't believe me.

When everyone who wanted to say something had had a turn, she read a passage from a book about Ola Ola Heia. She asked us questions about what she had read out, completely ignoring me until the bell rang, when she asked me to stay behind.

'Karl Ove,' she said. 'Wait here. I need to have a word with you.'

I stood beside her desk while the others hurried out. When we were alone she perched on the edge of her desk and looked at me.

'We can't tell everyone all the things we know about one another,' she said. 'What you said about Leif Tore's father, for example. Don't you think Leif Tore would be upset about that?'

'Yes, he would,' I said.

'He wouldn't want anyone else to know. Do you understand?'

'Yes,' I said, starting to cry.

'We all have a private life,' she said. 'Do you know what that is?'

'No,' I said, sniffling.

'It's everything that happens at home, in your home, my home, their homes, everyone's home. If you see what happens in other people's homes, it's not always nice to tell others. Do you understand?'

I nodded.

'Good, Karl Ove. Don't be upset. You didn't know. But now you do! So off you go.'

I scampered up the stairs, through the hall and into the playground. Cast an eye over the various groups standing there. Some girls were doing French skipping with elastic, some with a rope, some were playing tag. Down on the football pitch I saw a mass of players in front of the nearest goal. The centre of the pitch was covered in a pool of yellowish mud. Geir, Geir Håkon and Eivind were standing by the bench below the little rock with the flagpole on, and I ran over to join them. They were playing with Geir Håkon's boat cards.

'Have you been blubbing?' Eivind said.

I shook my head. 'It's the wind,' I said.

'What did Frøken say then?'

'Nothing much,' I said. 'Can I have a card?'

'You've been blubbing,' Eivind said.

Along with Sverre and me, Eivind was the best in the class. He was the best at arithmetic, Sverre was next best and I was third best. I was best at reading and writing, Eivind was next best and Sverre third best. But Eivind was much faster than me, and of the boys in the class only Trond was faster than him. I was the sixth fastest. And he was stronger than me. I was the next weakest, only Vemund was weaker, and since he was the fattest and the daftest boy in the class, it wasn't a very good situation, no one took any notice of him. Even Trond, the smallest boy in the class, was stronger than me. I was the third tallest in the class, a bit taller than him. I was the fourth best at football; ahead of me were Asgeir, Trond and John, while Eivind was fifth best. I was better at drawing than him, but not as good as Geir, who could draw everything as it really was, and Vemund. As for throwing a ball, I was next to last, again only Vemund was worse than me.

'The wind was in my eyes as I came down the steps,' I said. 'I wasn't blubbing. Can I have a card as well?'

The first card I took was SS *France*, the world's biggest passenger liner, which walloped everybody else in all categories.

In the next lesson we wrote letters of the alphabet in our jotters: *u* as in *ku*, *a* as in *lam*, *å* as in *gås*. For homework we had to write the same letters in our copybooks. Frøken asked whether anyone lived near the pupils who were absent today and, if so, could they pass on the homework.

But I didn't become aware of the opportunity that had presented itself until the next and final lesson, which was gymnastics, as I was running round and round the tiny gymnasium. I could walk up to Anne Lisbet's and tell her what we had to do for homework! I flushed with pleasure at the thought. As soon as we had dressed and left the changing room, on the way up to the place where we queued to wait for the bus, I told Geir about my plan. He wrinkled his nose, go to Anne Lisbet's, why? We had never been there, that was one thing. And Vemund lived there, that was another. Couldn't Vemund take the homework? You don't understand, I said. The whole point is that *we* do it!

He still hummed and hawed, but after I had put a bit more pressure on him, he agreed to go with me.

Instead of making everyone get off at B-Max, this morning the bus went up through the estate and dropped us off on the way. It did that now and then, and it was a strange sight every time, because the enormous bus didn't belong there, on the narrow roads, it towered over everything like a liner in a canal. We stood on the pavement watching it go up the hill, as it groaned with the effort and released clouds of greasy fumes in its wake.

'Shall I go up or will you come down?' I said.

'You come up,' Geir said.

'OK,' I said, walking in the drive, which as fortune would have it was clearly empty. It was no longer raining, but everything I saw was wet. On the dark brown wall there were extensive patches of black damp; on the brick doorstep all the little hollows were full of water; on the spade leaning against the wall raindrops hung trembling from the handle. I unzipped my jacket and took out the key to see if I could perhaps get it to open the door today. But the same happened, the key went in, but the little drum that was supposed to rotate didn't budge. I looked up the road. No one there. So I went to the dustbin by the fence, took out the black half-empty bin bag and put it on the ground, grabbed the dustbin by the handles and lifted it. It was heavier than I had anticipated, and I had to put it down several times on the way to the house. Still there was no one to be seen on the hill. A car came past, but it wasn't anyone I knew, so I carried the bin across the lawn and placed it under the window. Clambered on top, lifted the window and pushed my head and shoulders through. The feeling of losing control, because I couldn't see if anyone was watching me, all I saw was the empty room in front of me, dark and hot, filled me with panic. I twisted and turned, and when I had half my body in, I grabbed the metal pipe on the tank and pulled myself through.

Down to the floor, off with my boots – which I carried through the hall and put on again in the porch – open the door and out again. Hollow with fear and tension, I looked down the hill. No cars, nothing. As long as he stayed away for the next two minutes, and didn't come home because he had forgotten something, or because he was ill, which never happened, dad was never ill, everything would be fine.

A little gasp of joy escaped my lips. I hurried over to the dustbin, carried it to its place, put the bin bag back in, folded it over the edge and dashed back to the window. To my horror, I saw that the bin had left marks in the grass. Quite deep marks too. I ran my hand over the grass and tried to ruffle it to cover the patches where the edge had sunk in and formed a ridge in the muddy soil. Straightened up and regarded my handiwork.

You could still see it.

But if you had no idea it was there, perhaps it was more difficult to see?

Dad saw everything. He would see it.

I crouched down and ruffled the grass some more.

There we are.

That would have to do.

If he saw it I could always deny all knowledge. I doubted he would be able to imagine I had carried the dustbin onto the lawn and put it under the window to climb in. No, if he saw the mark it would be a mystery to him, utterly unfathomable, and as long as I denied all knowledge in a normal voice and with a normal expression he would have nothing else to go on.

I wiped my moist dirty hands on my thighs and went up to my room with my satchel. Opened the wardrobe door and was about to put on my white shirt, warmed by the happy thought that Anne Lisbet would think it looked good, when I came to my senses and dropped the idea in case dad asked why I had changed clothes and I got myself into a tangle which he would be able to unravel.

Then I locked the front door, climbed up onto the hot water tank, turned round, stuck my feet through the window, gently lowered myself until I let go and landed on the ground with a bump.

Picked myself up, down to the drive as fast as possible, acting as if nothing had happened.

There were no cars to be seen now. John Beck, Geir Håkon, Kent Arne and Øyvind Sundt were standing at the crossroads. When they saw me they cycled over. I stood still, waiting for them.

'Have you heard?' Geir Håkon said, braking just in front of me.

'Heard what?'

'A workman on Vindholmen was cut in two by a steel cable early today.'

'Cut in two?'

'Yes,' John Beck said. 'The wire snapped while towing. One end hit a man and cut him in two. Dad told me. Everyone was given the day off.'

I imagined a man on a tug being cut in two, the top half, the bit with the head and arms, standing beside the bottom half, the bit with the legs.

'Have you still got a puncture?' Kent Arne said.

I nodded.

'You can sit on the back of mine.'

'I'm off to see Geir,' I said. 'Where are you going?'

Geir Håkon shrugged.

'Down to the boats maybe?'

'Where are you two going?' Kent Arne said.

'To see someone in the class about homework,' I said.

'Who, if I might ask?' Geir Håkon said.

'Vemund,' I said.

'Do you two hang out with *him*?'

'Nope,' I said. 'Just today. I've got to get going.'

I ran up the hill and shouted for Geir, who came out straight away with a slice of bread in his hand.

Twenty minutes later we walked past B-Max again, along a flat stretch which, after a bend, ascended to the highest point on the estate where the road began that led to where Anne Lisbet, Solveig and Vemund lived. It was also possible to get to it by walking in the opposite direction from our house because the road that linked all the side roads and housing areas on the estate went in a circle, inside which was our own circular Ringvei. As if that wasn't enough, the main road outside also went in a circle, around the whole island. So we lived inside a circle inside a circle inside a circle. A hundred metres past the supermarket the two outermost roads ran parallel, but you couldn't see that because they were separated by a rock face, perhaps ten metres high, moulded into a brick wall. Above this wall was a green wire fence, beyond that there was a rocky slope, and then came the road we were following. But even though we couldn't see the cars whizzing past beneath us we could hear them. The sound of the cars was exciting, and we climbed down to the fence. At first we heard them as a faint drone as they came up the hill from the Fina station, then the volume rose and rose until they were racing past beneath us, the roar of their engines amplified by the rock face. We decided we would throw stones at them. As we couldn't see the cars, the trick was to time the sounds exactly. We each took a stone in our hands and waited for the next car. The stones were big, bigger than our hands, but not so heavy that we couldn't heave them over the fence, from where they fell vertically, ten metres down to the carriageway. Geir started. He threw as the car was beneath us, and missed of course, we heard the faint, hollow clunk as it landed on the tarmac and rolled downwards. When it was my turn, however, I threw much too soon; when the stone hit the road the car was probably fifty metres away.

A woman walked along the pavement carrying a bag in each hand. She stopped and spoke to us, even though we had never seen her before.

'What are you doing down there?' she said.

'Nothing much,' Geir said.

'Come on up,' she said. 'It's steep and dangerous there.'

She set off walking again, but kept an eye on us, so we did as she said and went up.

We balanced on the kerb all the way up to Vemund's house. Outside, his sister was on her knees playing in a sandpit. Her waterproof jacket and trousers were yellow, the bucket blue and the spade green.

'Shall we go and see Vemund first?' Geir said.

'No, let's not,' I said. 'Let's start with Anne Lisbet.'

The sound of her name was electric, thousands of crackling nerve channels opened inside me as I articulated the words in my mouth.

'What is it?' Geir said.

'What's what?' I said.

'You went a bit funny.'

'Funny? No. I'm quite normal.'

After a few steps up the road, which was covered on one side by a film of water running downwards, so thin that it quivered rather than ran, we could see the gable end of the house where Anne Lisbet lived. It was situated at the top of a hill, with a lawn at the front, trees below. A window on the top floor, there was a light on, was that her room perhaps? On the other side of the road was Myrvang's house and the house where Solveig lived, below them the forest, green and dark and wet. We passed them, and the road ended in a gravel turnaround on the edge of the forest. From there a drive led to Anne Lisbet's house. A lamp shone above the front door.

'Will you ring?' I said when we were there.

Geir stretched up on his toes and pressed the doorbell. My heart was fluttering. A few seconds passed. Then her mother opened the door.

'Is Anne Lisbet in?' I said.

'Yes,' she said.

'We're from her class,' Geir said. 'We've brought her homework.'

'How nice of you,' she said. 'Would you like to come in?'

She had blonde hair and blue eyes, so completely different from Anne Lisbet, but she was good to look at as well.

'Anne Lisbet!' she called. 'You've got visitors from your class!'

'Coming!' Anne Lisbet called from above.

'Isn't she ill?' I said.

Her mother shook her head.

'Not any more. We were just keeping her here for another day to be on the safe side.'

'Oh yes,' I said. Footsteps sounded on the stairs, and Anne Lisbet appeared. She was holding a slice of bread in one hand and smiling at us with her mouth full.

'Hi!' she said.

'We thought you were ill,' I said.

'We've brought you the homework,' Geir said.

She was wearing a white jumper with a high neck and a red pattern, and blue trousers. The skin above her lips was as white as milk.

'Wouldn't you like to go outside and play?' she said. 'I've been indoors all day. And I was all day yesterday as well!'

'Yes, OK,' I said. 'Is that all right, Geir?'

'Yes,' Geir said.

She put on her white boots and the red raincoat. Her mother went upstairs.

'Bye, Mum!' she called and ran out. We ran after her.

'What shall we do?' she said, stopping where the shingle finished and suddenly turning to us. 'Shall we go down to Solveig's?'

We did. Solveig came out, Anne Lisbet suggested doing some skipping, so we stood there, Geir and I, with elastic around our legs while Solveig and Anne Lisbet hopped and skipped to and fro in accordance with the intricate patterns they mastered to such perfection. When it was my turn Anne Lisbet showed me what to do. She placed her hand on my shoulder and a quiver ran through me. Her dark eyes sparkled. She burst into laughter when I messed it up, and, oh, I smelled the fragrance of her hair as it flew past my face.

It was absolutely fantastic. Everything was absolutely fantastic. Above us the cloud thickened, the grey had taken on a tinge of bluish-black, the sky was like a wall above the forest, soon afterwards it began to rain. We put up the hoods on our rain jackets and continued to skip. The rain fell on our hoods and ran down our faces, the gravel crunched beneath our feet, the lamp on top of the pole at the end of the turnaround suddenly came on. A little while later a car approached slowly.

'That's dad!' Anne Lisbet said.

The car, a Volvo estate, stopped at the end of the drive, and a large powerful man with a black beard stepped out. He waved to her, she ran over to him, he bent down and gave her a hug, then went in.

'We're having dinner now,' she said. 'What was for homework?'

I told her. She nodded, said bye and was gone.

'I have to go too,' Solveig said, standing there with her sad eyes and rolling up the elastic.

'Us too,' I said.

When we reached the crossroads I suggested running all the way to the shop, which we did. There, Geir suggested we didn't go home via Grevlingveien, nor through the forest, but took the main road down to Holtet. Which we did. A path led from there up through the heath to Ringveien, which we then followed home. But after we had gone a few metres along the road, something strange happened. The bus came down, instinctively I turned and in the window, only a little way from me, at the same height, sat Yngve!

What on earth was he doing there? Was he going to Arendal? Now? What was he going to do there?

'That was Yngve,' I said. 'He was on the bus.'

'Oh yes,' Geir said, not very interested. We crossed the lawn outside the house and walked onto the road.

'That was great fun up there,' Geir said.

'Yes,' I said. 'Shall we go up again later?'

'Yes,' Geir said. 'But perhaps it's best not to tell anyone? After all, they're girls.'

'Well, there's no reason why we should.'

From the top of the hill I could see that dad's car was parked outside our house. Geir's father was home too. They were teachers and finished work earlier than other fathers.

I recalled the dustbin I had used to get indoors.

'Shall we do something else?' I said. 'Go somewhere else? Down to the tree swing?'

Geir shook his head.

'It's raining. And I'm hungry. I'm going home.'

'OK,' I said. 'Bye.'

'Bye,' Geir said, and ran to his house. He slammed the door so hard the glass rattled. I gazed across at Gustavsen's house. There was a light on in the kitchen. Had they come back home or was it the father? They had a garage, so it was impossible to know whether the car was there or not.

I turned and looked up the hill. Marianne's father took off the lid of the dustbin and threw in a scrunched-up plastic bag. He was wearing a woollen cardigan and was unshaven. He always looked angry, but I wasn't sure if he was, I had never spoken to him or heard anything about him. He was a seaman and away for large parts of the year. When he was at home he was there all the time.

He closed the door without noticing me.

From the crossroads came an enormous yellow lorry with rocks on the back. The ground vibrated as it passed. Thick smoke rose from an exhaust pipe at the front.

Yngve had once shown me a picture of the biggest vehicle in the world. It was in a book about the Apollo programme he had borrowed from the library. Everything about it was the biggest in the world. It had been especially built to transport the rocket the few kilometres to the launch pad. But it was as slow as it was big and moved at a snail's pace, Yngve said.

The most appealing part was the launch itself. I could look at photos of it any number of times. Once I had seen it on TV too. You might expect the rocket to shoot off from the platform at an incredible speed, but that was not the case; on the contrary, for the first few metres it rose very slowly, the fire and the smoke it emitted formed a kind of cushion underneath which it seemed to rest on for a brief instant before gently moving upwards, almost waveringly, with a colossal roar that could be heard from a distance of several kilometres. And then it soared faster and faster until its speed was as mind-blowing as you had imagined, and it flew like an arrow or lightning into the crystal-blue sky.

Sometimes I imagined a rocket being launched from this forest. Hidden behind a mountain, it would be erected in secret and one day we would see it rise slowly, very slowly, above the trees just down there, pure and white against the green and grey, with a cloud of fire and smoke beneath it, and then it would be clear of them, almost hanging in the sky for a moment, before gaining speed and soaring faster and faster upwards with the roar from the gigantic engines reverberating between our houses.

It was a good thought.

I jogged down to the house, crossed the shingle to the door, opened it and was taking off my boots on the doormat when dad came into the hall from his study.

I glanced up at him.

He didn't look particularly angry.

'Where have you been?' he said.

'Playing with Geir,' I said.

'That wasn't what I asked you,' he said. '*Where* have you been?'

'We were up at B-Max,' I said. 'Behind it.'

'Oh,' he said. 'What were you boys doing there?'

'Nothing much,' I said. 'Playing.'

'You'll have to go back,' he said. 'We need some potatoes. Can you buy some, do you think?'

'Yes,' I said.

He took his wallet from his rear pocket and produced a banknote.

'Let me see your pockets,' he said.

I stood up and thrust forward my hips.

He passed me the note.

'Put this in your pocket,' he said. 'And don't hang about.'

'OK,' I said. He went back to the kitchen. I put my boots back on, closed the door gently behind me and set off at a run.

Yngve came home shortly before we were to have dinner and just made it to his bedroom before dad shouted that the food was ready. He had fried some chops and onions and boiled some cauliflower and potatoes. Mum informed us that we were going to have a cleaner, an old lady called fru Hjellen, who would come once a week, and she would be popping by this afternoon. Mum had rung her from work, she said, she had seemed very nice. I knew dad didn't want a cleaner, he had mentioned it once, but now he was quiet, so I supposed he must have changed his mind.

I was looking forward to her coming. The few times we had visitors it was always fun, perhaps because when they came they filled the house with something new and different. And it was good because they always showed Yngve and me some attention.

'So those are your boys, are they?' they would say, if they had never seen us before, or, 'How tall they've grown,' if they had, and sometimes they even asked us questions, such as how school was going or about football.

After eating I slipped into Yngve's room. He took a cassette from the rack, it was Status Quo, *Piledriver*, and put it in the recorder.

'I saw you on the bus,' I said. 'Where were you going?'

'To town,' he said.

He lay on the bed and started reading a comic.

'What did you do there?'

'That's enough questions,' he said. 'I had to buy a part for my bike.'

'Is it *broken*?'

He nodded. Then he looked me in the eye.

'Don't tell anyone. Not even mum,' he said.

'Cross my heart and hope to die,' I said.

'It's up at Frank's. You know the bit the handlebars are fixed to, well, it broke. But his father promised he would sort it for me. I get it back tomorrow.'

'Imagine if dad had seen you,' I said. 'In Arendal. Or someone he knows had seen you.'

Yngve shrugged and continued reading. I went into my own room. After a while the doorbell rang. I waited until mum was downstairs in the hall before leaving my room. Shortly afterwards an elderly, somewhat plump or perhaps I should say broad, lady with grey hair and glasses came up the stairs.

'This is Karl Ove,' mum said. 'Our younger son.'

I nodded to her. She smiled.

'My name's fru Hjellen,' she said. 'I'm sure we'll become good friends.'

She patted my shoulder. I felt a warmth suffuse my whole body.

'Our elder son, Yngve, is in his room,' mum said.

'Shall I get him?' I said.

Mum shook her head. 'No need.'

She started showing her around, and I went back to my room. Outside, dusk was falling. The rain was drumming softly on the roof and wall. The gutters were swirling and gurgling. Large raindrops hit the window and rolled down in patterns it was impossible to predict. The headlights from a car lit up the spruce tree above the post-box stand. Jacobsen returning from work. The green boxes and the stand to which they were attached glinted silently in the glare. *No, no*, they said. *Not the light, not the light*. I lay down on my bed and thought about Anne Lisbet. Tomorrow we would go there again. But first of all I wanted to see her at school! And it was enough to see her. I needed no more than that for the pleasure to spread through every part of my body. One day I would ask her to go out with me. One day I would be in her room and she would be in mine. Even though I wasn't allowed to have anyone in my room, she would be allowed to come here, I would fix that. Even if we had to climb in through the little window in the boiler room!

I sat down at my desk, took the books from my satchel and did my homework. Fru Hjellen left, and then I heard Yngve going to the kitchen. It was Monday today, and every Monday he had started making scones or waffles in the evening. I would sit in the kitchen with mum while he worked, it was warm there, the aroma of scones or waffles was good, and we talked about everything under the sun. After Yngve had finished we ate the scones with butter, which melted on them, and brown cheese, or waffles with butter and sugar, which also melted, and drank tea with milk. Now and then, but not often, dad joined us. By and large though, he went back down to his study pretty quickly.

I did my homework at breakneck speed. I could do the

letters of course, it was just a question of scribbling down enough of them, and then I went into the kitchen too. A light shone from the empty oven. Yngve stood stirring a bowl on the worktop with his shirtsleeves rolled up and an apron on. Mum sat knitting.

'Haven't you finished yet?' I said, sitting down at my place.

'Another day or two,' she said, pulling at the wool, as though she was in a boat and jig fishing. 'It depends on how much I get done.'

'Geir and I were up at Anne Lisbet and Solveig's today,' I said.

'Oh?' mum said. 'Who are they? Some girls in your class?'

I nodded.

'Have you started playing with girls now?' Yngve said.

'Yes. And?' I said.

'Are you in love or what?'

I glanced at mum hesitantly, then at Yngve.

'I think so,' I said.

Yngve laughed.

'You're only seven! You can't be in love!'

'Don't laugh at him, Yngve,' mum said.

Yngve blushed and studied the bowl in front of him.

'Feelings are feelings whether you're seven or seventy. It means the same, you know.'

There was a silence.

'But it can't go anywhere!' Yngve said.

'You might be right about that,' mum said. 'But you can feel something for others despite that, can't you?'

'You were in love with Anne,' I said.

'I was not,' he said.

'You said you were.'

'Well, never mind,' mum said. 'How's the mix going? Will it be ready soon?'

'Think so,' Yngve said.

'May I have a look?' mum said, putting her knitting in the basket at her feet and getting up.

'Will you grease the tray, Karl Ove?'

She took the little pan with the melting butter off the heat, passed me a brush and took the baking tray from the drawer at the bottom of the stove. The butter was ready; you could see that by the colour: there were several inlets and some large lagoons of light brown in the thin yellow liquid. If you heated it slowly the colour became fuller and purer. I dipped the brush in the pan and swept it over the baking tray. Butter heated slowly could make the bristles stiffen, so you had to dab rather than stroke it on, whereas with a thin brown liquid it was easier to cover a surface. It took ten seconds and the tray was ready. I sat down again and Yngve started shaping the scones. Downstairs a door opened. Straight afterwards came the sound of dad's heavy footsteps on the stairs. I straightened up in my chair. Mum sat down again, put her knitting on her lap and looked up as dad appeared in the doorway.

'Everything's in full swing here, I can see,' he said, tucking his thumbs through the loops of his belt and pulling up his trousers. 'Soon be something to eat, I presume.'

'In a quarter of an hour or so,' mum said.

'Is that scones you're making, Yngve?' he said.

Yngve just nodded without looking up.

'Right,' dad said. He turned and went into the living room. The floor creaked lightly under his weight. He stopped by the television, switched it on and ensconced himself in the brown leather chair.

I knew that voice. It was the man on the doctor programme. A bit hoarse, it sounded rusty, it issued from a face that always leaned backwards as though addressing itself to the ceiling while his eyes always looked down, as though to direct his voice to the right place.

I got up and went into the living room.

The screen showed an open wound with blood and skin and flesh surrounded by blue linen.

'Is that an operation?' I said.

'It is indeed,' dad said.

'May I watch?'

'Yes, I don't think there would be any harm in that.'

I perched on the edge of the sofa. You could see deep into the body. There was a kind of shaft into it, held open by several metal clips, revealing a layer of flesh which the blood appeared to have just left, and a glistening, membrane-like organ at the very bottom, also stained with blood, all illuminated by a sharp, almost white, light. A pair of rubber-gloved hands rummaged around, apparently at home in these surroundings. Occasionally you saw a fuller picture. Then it became clear the shaft had been opened in a patient lying on a table otherwise completely covered by a blue plastic-like material and that the hands belonged to a surgeon who constituted the focal point of a circle of five people, all dressed in green, the two in the centre leaning over the body under a lizard-like lamp, the other three next to them with trays of instruments and all sorts of equipment I had never seen before.

Dad got up.

'No, I can't watch this,' he said. 'How can they show this on TV on a Monday night!'

'Can I watch it anyway?' I said.

'Yes, of course,' he said, heading for the staircase.

The membrane at the bottom was pulsating. Blood streamed over it, and it sent the blood back, then seemed to rise, until the blood washed across again and once more it had to send it back and once more it had to rise.

Suddenly I realised this was a heart I was watching.

How terribly sad.

Not because the heart was beating and couldn't escape, it wasn't that. The point was that the heart should not be seen, it should be allowed to beat in secret, hidden from our sight; it was obvious, you understood that when you saw it, a little animal without eyes, it should pound and throb inside your chest unseen.

But I kept watching. Medical programmes were my favourite on TV, and especially the few that showed operations. A long time ago I had decided I would be a surgeon when I grew up. Mum and dad sometimes mentioned this to others, it was intended to be amusing because I had said it when I was so small, but I really meant it, that was what I wanted to do when I grew up, cut up other people and perform operations on them. I often did drawings or paintings of operations with blood and knives and nurses and lamps, and mum had asked me many times why I drew and painted so much blood, why couldn't I choose something else, houses and grass and sun, for example, and that was fine by me, but it wasn't what I *wanted* to do. Divers, sailing ships, rockets and operations, they were what I wanted to draw and paint, not houses and grass and sun.

When Yngve was very small and they lived in Oslo he had said he wanted to be a dustman when he grew up. Grandma laughed a lot about that and often mentioned it. In the same breath she said dad had wanted to be an odd job man when he was small. She laughed just as much about that, sometimes so much tears rolled down her cheeks, even though she must have said it a hundred times. My wanting to become a surgeon wasn't funny in the same way, it carried a different message, but then I was also a lot older than Yngve had been when he said he wanted to be a dustman.

Step by step all the clips and tubes were removed from the shaft in the body. Then the host of the show came on camera and talked about what we had just seen. I got up and went back into the kitchen, where the scones were cooling down on the tray on top of the stove, a pan of hot water for tea was steaming beside them and mum was setting the table with plates, cups, knives and a variety of spreads.

The next day the temperature had fallen and the rain had stopped. My winter boots from last year were too small, and mum found some woollen socks I could wear inside my rubber boots instead. The blue Puffa jacket still fitted, so I wore that for the first time since last year. And then, as soon as I was out of the house, there was a blue bobble cap that I pulled down so far over my face that it formed a black ceiling to my vision. Anne Lisbet was wearing a light blue Puffa jacket in smooth shiny material, unlike mine which was coarse and matt, a white cap from which her black hair protruded, a white scarf, blue trousers and a brand-new pair of red boots. She was standing with some girls and didn't return my gaze when I looked at them.

The colour of her jacket was just incredibly attractive.

I wanted one like it.

When we got to school and everyone had left their satchels in a line, I suggested to Geir that we pinch their caps. He would pinch Solveig's and I would pinch Anne Lisbet's. She was standing with her back to us, and when I grabbed it she whirled around with a scream. I waited until her eyes met mine, and then I ran off. I didn't run so fast that she couldn't catch me or so slowly that everyone would see I was waiting.

I could hear her footsteps on the tarmac behind me.

And then she wrapped her arms around me.

Oh! Oh! Oh!

Her wonderfully thick down jacket pressed against mine, she smiled and shouted *Let me have it, let me have it,* and I simply couldn't drag the moment out any longer by holding the cap high above her head, the joy inside me was too strong, I just gave it to her and stood still and watched her put it on her head and walk away.

Then she turned and smiled at me!

And her eyes, oh her eyes, so black and beautiful, they were gleaming! It was like entering a zone of shining light against which everything outside paled and lost meaning. The bell rang, we marched up the stairs, along the corridor, sat down at our desks and took out our books. And I did what we were told, listened when we had to listen, chatted away as usual, drew my sunken wrecks and swimming frogmen, ate my packed lunch and drank my milk, played football in the breaks, sat beside Geir and sang in the bus on the way home, ran through the flock of children with my satchel hanging off my back down the last hill, present in both body and soul, yet absent, because inside me there suddenly existed a new sky under whose vaults even the most familiar of thoughts and actions appeared new.

When we went to see Anne Lisbet that day she was standing in the middle of a crowd of kids on the turnaround outside her house. Two of them were swinging a rope between them like a machine, it lashed the ground like a whip, and one after the other they slipped in, stood and jumped up and down a few times, then slipped out, so that the next person could step in. She was wearing the same cap and the same scarf, and she smiled at us as we stopped in front of them.

'Join in, come on!' she said.

We queued up. I wanted to impress her so much, just slip into the spinning corridor the rope drew in the air, but I didn't manage more than two jumps before it hit my calf and I was out. Strangely, Geir, whose coordination was not that great and whose arms and legs flapped about wildly, managed very well. Jump, jump, jump, jump, jump – and then he hurled himself out with such force and determination that he had to take a few extra steps to prevent himself from stumbling, not dissimilar to a runner throwing himself at the tape.

Now she would think that Geir was better than me.

The sombreness of that thought was gone the very next moment because it was her turn. She ran in and danced inside the rope, an absolute virtuoso, her weight was first on one leg, then on the other while she stared straight ahead, as though her head had nothing to do with what her body was doing. But as she jumped out, no longer needing to concentrate, it was me she looked at and sent a smile to. *Did you see that?* her smile said. *Did you see me just now?*

The water covering the largest sunken areas of the turnaround where we were standing was almost yellow. In the smaller puddles it was a greenish-grey, like the surrounding gravel, only a shade lighter. And shinier, of course. From the forest below came the babbling of a stream. The drone of a machine was also audible. I had never been there before, and walked over to the edge to look down. From the house above me on the edge of the forest a broad rocky slope fell away sharply. Beneath it there was a yellow bog. Behind that pines huddled together. Between the trunks I could see a green workmen's shed and a yellow generator. That was what was making the noise.

Then some drilling started. I couldn't see who was doing it, but the sound, such a monotonous rat-a-tat-tat, with that brittle, almost singing tone of metal on rock lying like a veil over it, was unmistakable. I knew it so well.

I turned back and saw Geir nodding his head in time with

the rope to adapt to the rhythm for his turn. But this time he didn't do so well, his foot got tangled at once, and as the two rope-swingers resumed their mechanical motions, he shuffled over towards me. Behind him Anne Lisbet slipped in. But as soon as she was in position the rope hit her on the arm. She seemed almost to have done it on purpose.

'Are you coming, Solveig?' she said.

Solveig nodded and left the queue. Both of them came over to us.

'What shall we do?' Anne Lisbet said.

'Shall we go and look for some bottles?' I said.

'Yes, let's!' Geir said.

'Where though? Where are there any bottles?' Anne Lisbet said.

'Along the main road,' Geir said. 'And in the forest behind the play area. Round the sheds. Sometimes by the Rock. Never in the autumn, though.'

'At the bus stop,' I said. 'And under the bridge.'

'Once we found a whole *bag* full,' Geir said. 'In the ditch near the shop. We made four kroner on the deposits!'

Solveig and Anne Lisbet looked at him, impressed. Even though the bottle idea had been my suggestion! I had come up with it, not Geir!

Without thinking, we had started to walk. The sky was as grey as dry cement. Not a breath stirred the trees; everything was still, brooding, as if turned in on itself. Except for the pines, that is: they were as open and free and sky-embracing as ever. Standing more as though they were in repose. It was the spruces which were turned inwards, swallowed up by their own darkness. The deciduous trees with their thin trunks and splayed branches were nervous and wary. The old oaks, of which there were quite a few on the slope beyond the road, where we were heading now, were not afraid but lonely. They could endure the loneliness though; they had stood there for so many years and would stand there for so many more.

'There's a pipe there that goes under the road,' Anne Lisbet said, pointing to the slope running down alongside the road. It was covered with black soil, laid recently, no flowers had come up yet.

We walked down. And, sure enough, a pipe did go under the road, made of concrete, perhaps a little more than half a metre in diameter.

'Have you ever crawled through it?' I said.

They shook their heads.

'Shall we?' Geir said. He leaned over with one hand on the edge of the pipe and peered into the darkness.

'What if we get stuck inside?' Solveig said.

'*We* can do it,' I said. 'So you can cross the road and wait for us.'

'Do you dare?' Anne Lisbet said.

'Of course,' Geir said. He glanced at me. 'Who'll go first?'

'You can,' I said.

'OK,' he said, bending down and squeezing into the pipe. It was too narrow to scramble through on all fours, I could see, but not so narrow that you couldn't wriggle through. After a few seconds of twisting and turning his whole body had disappeared. I looked at Anne Lisbet, leaned forward and stuck my head in the pipe. A smell of something fusty, like mildew, filled my nostrils. I placed my elbows on the bottom and edged the rest of my body forward, moving like a grub. When all of my body was inside, I raised myself as far as was possible, and with my forearms, knees and feet pushing against the cement wriggled into the gloom. For the first few metres I could see the shadowy figure of Geir in front of me, but then the darkness deepened and he was gone.

'Are you there?' I shouted.

'Yes,' he answered.

'Are you scared?'

'Bit. And you?'

'Yes, a bit.'

Suddenly everything vibrated. A car or a lorry must have driven over us a long way up. What if the pipe broke? What if it caved in and we were stuck in it?

The tips of my fingers and toes began to tremble with a faint sense of panic. I knew this feeling, it could arise when I was climbing a mountain and then I would be paralysed. Frightened out of my wits, I would stand perfectly still, incapable of ascending or descending, in full knowledge of the fact there was only one way to go, only my own movements could get me out of this. I couldn't move, I had to move, but I couldn't, had to, couldn't, had to, couldn't.

'Are you still scared?' I said.

'Bit. Did you hear the car? Here comes another!'

Again the pipe vibrated around me.

I kept quite still. There was water lying in several places at the bottom of the pipe and it was advancing up my trousers.

'I can see light!' Geir said.

I thought of the enormous weight on the pipe. It was only a few centimetres thick. My heart was pounding. Suddenly I wanted to stand upright. The urge grew wildly inside me, but collided with the recognition that it was impossible, the concrete was wrapped around my body like a cocoon. I couldn't move.

Sometimes Yngve would sit astride me while I was lying under the duvet. He would hold me so firmly that I couldn't move at all. The duvet was tight across my chest, my hands were locked in his and my legs were rendered useless under his weight and the taut duvet. He did it because he knew I absolutely hated it.

He did it because he knew that after a few seconds of being held captive I would panic. That I would summon all my strength in an attempt to break free, and when I couldn't, when he held me in his grip, I would begin to scream as loudly as I could. I screamed and screamed like a being possessed, and I was, I was possessed by terror, I couldn't break free, I was stuck, completely and utterly stuck, and I screamed from the bottom of my lungs.

Now I could feel the same grip around my heart.

I couldn't move.

Panic was growing.

I knew I mustn't think about not being able to stand up, I should crawl forward patiently and everything would be fine. But I couldn't. All I could think of was that I couldn't move.

'Geir!' I shouted.

'I'm nearly out!' he shouted back. 'Where are you?'

'I'm stuck!'

Silence for some seconds.

Then Geir shouted, 'I can come and help you! I just have to get out and turn first!'

The panic attack was like an exhalation of breath, because it was out of me now. I moved my arms forward and dragged my knees after. The material of my jacket scraped against the pipe above. Only a few centimetres above that there were tons of rocks and earth. I stopped. My legs and arms had gone weak. I lay down flat.

What would Anne Lisbet and Solveig think about me now?

Oh no, oh no.

Then the panic returned. I couldn't move. I was trapped. I couldn't move! I was trapped! I couldn't move!

Somewhere in the darkness in front of me something moved. Cloth scraped against cement. I heard Geir breathing, it was unmistakable: he would often breathe through his mouth.

Then I saw him, a white face in the blackness.

'Are you stuck?' he said.

'No,' I said.

He grabbed the sleeve of my jacket and pulled. I raised my back and moved first one arm forward, then the other, one leg, then the other. Geir wriggled backwards without letting go of my sleeve, and even though he wasn't pulling me, because of course I was scrabbling my way through, it felt like he was, and the sight of his white face, pointed like a fox's and unusually concentrated, meant that my mind was no longer on the pipe and the darkness and not being able to move, and so I could move, little by little over the damp concrete, which became lighter and lighter until Geir's feet were out of the hole, followed by his torso and I could poke my head out into daylight.

Anne Lisbet and Solveig were standing close together by the opening and looking at me.

'Did you get stuck?' Anne Lisbet said.

'Yes,' I said. 'For a while there, but Geir helped me.'

Geir brushed down his hands. Then he brushed the knees of his trousers. I straightened up. The space beneath the grey sky was vast. All the shapes were razor-sharp.

'Shall we go down to Little Hawaii?' Geir said.

'Good idea,' I said.

It was wonderful to run on the forest floor. The surface of the water in the little lake was completely black. The trees rising from the two small islands were still. We jumped over to our respective islands. Anne Lisbet and I on one, Solveig and Geir on the other.

Anne Lisbet's lips seemed so vital; they opened and smiled with such ease, now and then of their own accord when her eyes remained unmoved. They seemed to obey the slightest impulse of her mind. She thought of something, they spread across her hard white teeth, soft and red, occasionally followed by an exclamation or a glow of happiness in her eyes, occasionally unconnected with anything else.

'You're sailors,' she said out of the blue. 'And you come home to us. We haven't seen each other for yonks. Shall we play that?'

I nodded. Geir nodded too.

The two girls jumped onto land and went a little way into the forest.

'You can come now!' Anne Lisbet shouted.

We moored, leaped ashore and walked towards them. But we weren't quick enough for them: Anne Lisbet was impatiently dancing from one foot to the other, she set off running towards me, and when she reached me she threw her arms around me and hugged me and pressed her cheek against mine.

'I have missed you so much!' she said. 'Oh, my darling husband!'

She took a step back.

'Again!'

I ran back to the lake, jumped onto the little island, waited until Geir was on the other one, then we repeated our actions with one difference, this time we ran as fast as we could to the girls.

Again she wrapped her arms around me.

My heart was racing, for I was not only standing on the ground in a forest with the sky far above me, I was also standing on the ground inside myself and looking up into something light and open and happy.

Her hair smelled of apples.

Through the material of her thick padded jacket I could feel her body. Her cold smooth face against mine, almost glowing.

We did this three times. Then we delved further into the forest. After only a few metres it sloped down, and as the trees growing there were mostly deciduous, the ground was covered with red, yellow and brown leaves, a floor to the bare walls of trunks. There was the sound of a rushing stream somewhere nearby. The forest tapered to a path running steeply down to the main road, which we couldn't see until we came out a couple of metres above it.

On the other side a field sloped down, beyond lay Tromøya Sound, as grey as clay, while the sky which opened above was a shade lighter.

The traffic was fast-moving, and we kept to the ditch as we walked along. The bottles we usually found here were always new and shiny while those we found in the woods were often covered in grass and had leaves stuck to them, sometimes they were also full of little insects and lifting them up was like lifting up a bit of the field.

Today, however, there were no bottles to be seen. When we reached Larsen's house – a dilapidated, shed-like construction which had once been part of a farm but was now squeezed into a corner between the forest and the road, whose owner was a teacher at the same school as dad and according to rumours had turned up for work drunk several times – we crossed the road and followed the steep gravel road down to Gamle Tybakken. We looked for bottles on the way, but our efforts became more and more half-hearted. Soon we came to a built-up area. Old white houses set far back in well-established gardens full of fruit trees and fruit bushes. Where we were walking, the colours were so sharp, all the leaves were brilliant yellow and piercing red, and so matt in the sky's pale, slightly frigid grey, it gave me a sense I was walking at the bottom of a tin can, with the sky the lid and the hills that rose all around me the sides. After a few hundred metres we walked past a large property with a lawn stretching up towards the forest above. The house at the top was surprisingly small considering the size of the land. A narrow gravel track led up to it, and we stopped by the post box at the end because, outside the house, beside a large stream that plunged down from the forest, an old lady was pulling at a tree that had got wedged in it.

The tree was perhaps three times bigger than her, with a broad network of thin branches around it.

Somehow or other she noticed us standing there because the very next moment she straightened up and looked across at us. She waved. But not in greeting, she was pointing to herself, she was beckoning us to go there.

We ran as fast as we could up the gravel track, across the soft wet lawn and stopped in front of her.

'You look strong,' she said. 'Can you help an old lady, do you think? I need to get this tree out of the stream. It's got stuck.'

Flattered, we got down to work. Geir waded into the water as far as he could and grabbed a branch, I did the same on the other side while Anne Lisbet and Solveig pulled the trunk. At first it wouldn't budge, but then Geir began to shout Heave-ho! Heave-ho! to make us pull in unison and bit by bit we managed to drag it out. When it was free the current caught the end and pushed it onto our side, but we held on and hauled it onto dry land.

'Oh, how wonderful!' the old lady said. 'Many, many thanks! I would never have managed that on my own, you know. You are so strong! Well done. Wait here and I'll give you a little something as a sign of gratitude.'

She scurried off to the house with her head bowed and disappeared through the front door.

'What do you think we'll get?' I said.

'Few biscuits maybe,' Geir said.

'Or a bag of bread rolls,' Anne Lisbet said. 'Mum always keeps some handy.'

'I think, apples,' Solveig said. And when she said that, I agreed wholeheartedly because beyond the gravel track there were lots of apple trees.

But when she reappeared, with her head still bowed, she came towards us empty-handed. Hadn't she found anything?

'Now look here,' she said. 'This is for you with my thanks. Who's going to take care of it? It's for all of you.'

She held out a coin. It was five kroner.

Five kroner!

'I can look after it,' I said. 'Thank you very much!'

'It's me who should thank you,' the old lady said. 'All the best now!'

Elated, we sprinted down the hill. Then without a second thought we walked back the way we had come, discussing what we would do with the money. Geir and I wanted to go to the shop straight away and buy sweets with it. Anne Lisbet and Solveig also wanted to buy sweets, but they didn't want to go to the shop now, it would soon be dinner and they had to go home. We decided to save the money for the day after and then buy sweets.

Anne Lisbet and Solveig took the path home. Geir and I continued along the main road to the shop. Standing outside, we couldn't wait as we had agreed, the five-krone coin was burning a hole in our pockets, it was all we could think about. Waiting to spend it was simply not on, so we decided to buy sweets now and save them until the following day and surprise Anne Lisbet and Solveig with them.

And so we bought them.

However, after we had done so and started walking to the road, Geir's father came along in their Beetle. He pulled over beside us, leaned over the seat and opened the door.

'Hop in,' he said.

'Can Karl Ove come as well?'

'No, not this time, we're not going home. We're going to town. Another time, Karl Ove!'

'OK,' Geir said. Turned to me and said in his dramatic whisper, 'Don't eat any of the sweets!'

I shook my head and stood watching until Geir was in and the car had driven off. Then I ran to the concrete barriers, jumped over them, scampered down the slope and into the play area, past the wreck of the car, across the football pitch, through the forest and along the edge past the bog. Just before I could be seen from our house I stopped and divvied up all the sweets, which until then had been in one bag, and put them into the four pockets of my jacket. I threw the bag away and ran onto the road, down the side of the house – there was a light on in the living-room window – and into the drive. Dad's car was there and, leaning against the wall in its usual place, Yngve's bike!

The little metal part holding the handlebars in position had a very different, and much brighter, gleam than the metal around it. Surely dad couldn't help but notice?

I opened the door and went in. If dad met me I would just hang up my jacket as normal. If he stayed in his study or in the living room, I would go upstairs wearing my jacket, hide the sweets in my room and then go back down with the empty jacket. If he met me then and asked why I was still wearing my jacket I would say I'd had to go to the toilet urgently.

The house was quiet.

There he was. Upstairs in the living room.

I carefully removed my shoes and walked through the hall, up the stairs and into the bathroom. Opened my fly, wriggled out the wiener and peed. Pulled the chain, washed my hands in cold water, dried them and waited for the flush to stop before I opened the door. Cast a fleeting glance into the living room, nothing, went into my room, pulled the duvet aside, emptied my pockets of all the sweets, covered them again and went onto the landing.

'Karl Ove, is that you?' dad said from the living room.

'Yes,' I said.

He came out.

'Where have you been?' he said.

'Gamle Tybakken with Geir,' I said.

'What were you doing there?'

His mouth was a straight line. His eyes were cold.

'Nothing much,' I said, so happy my voice held firm. 'Walking around, that was all.'

'Why are you wearing your jacket?'

'I had to go to the loo. I'll take it off now.'

I continued down the stairs. He went back to the living room. I hung up my jacket and quickly returned, unhappy at the thought that the sweets were lying there unprotected. Switched on the small round metal lamp on the desk. The long slim bulb filled the empty space it resided in with its yellow light. Sat down on the bed. Straightened the duvet over the sweets.

What now?

Contrasting feelings coursed through me. One minute I was on the verge of tears, the next my chest was bursting with happiness.

I took out a book about space dad had had as a child and which I had been allowed to borrow the previous time I was ill. It was crammed with drawings of how space travel would be in the future. Astronauts' equipment, the shape of rockets and the surfaces of planets.

Dad strode along the landing.

He opened the door and eyed me.

Without making a move to come in or say anything. I closed

the book and sat up straight. Glanced in the direction of the sweets.

It was impossible to see there was anything underneath the duvet.

'What have you got there?' dad said.

'Where?' I said. 'What do you mean? I haven't got anything.'

'Under the duvet,' dad said.

'I haven't got anything under the duvet!'

He eyed me again.

Then he walked over to the bed and tore the duvet aside.

'You're lying to me, boy!' he said. 'Are you lying to your own father?'

He grabbed my ear and twisted it round.

'I didn't mean to!' I said.

'Where did you get the sweets? Where did you get the money to buy them?'

'An old lady gave it to me!' I said, starting to cry. 'I haven't done anything wrong!'

'An old lady?' dad said. He twisted harder. 'Why would an old lady give you money?'

'Ow! Ow!' I yelled.

'Be quiet!' he said. 'You lied to me, didn't you.'

'Yes, but I didn't mean to!'

'Look at me when I'm talking to you. Did you lie?'

I raised my head and looked at him. His eyes were smouldering with anger.

'Yes,' I said.

'So now you tell me where you got the money from. Do you understand?'

'Yes. I got it from an old lady! We did her a favour!'

'Who?'

'Geir and I and A–'

'You and Geir and who?'

'No one. Just me and Geir.'

'You little liar. Just you come here.'

He twisted my ear round again while pulling my hand and forcing me to stand up. I gasped and sobbed and my insides went hollow.

'Down to my study,' he said, without letting go of my ear.

'I . . . haven't . . . done . . . anything . . . wrong,' I said. 'We . . . were . . . given . . . the money.'

He pushed open the first door so hard that it slammed against the wall. Dragged me in through the second and onto the floor. Then he let go.

'How did you get the money?' he said. 'And don't you tell me any lies!'

'We helped . . . an old lady.'

'To do what?'

'There was . . . a tree. A tree . . . stuck in a stream. We pulled . . . it out.'

'And she gave you money for that?'

'Yes.'

'How much?'

'Five kroner.'

'You're lying, Karl Ove. Where did you get the money from?'

'I AM NOT LYING!' I yelled.

His hand shot out and slapped me on the cheek.

'Do not shout!' he hissed.

He stood up.

'But there is a way to find out,' he said. 'I'll ring the old lady and ask her if it's true.'

He looked me in the eye as he said it.

'Where does she live?'

'In . . . Gamle Ty . . . bakken,' I said.

Dad went to the telephone on his desk, lifted the receiver and dialled a number. Held the receiver to his ear.

'Oh, hello,' he said. 'My name's Knausgaard. I'm ringing about my son. He says he you gave him five kroner today. Is that correct?'

There was a pause.

'You didn't? You didn't have two boys helping you today? You didn't give them five kroner? Oh, yes, I see. I apologise for the intrusion. Thank you very much. Goodbye.'

He cradled the receiver.

I couldn't believe my own ears.

He looked at me.

'She hasn't seen any boys. And she definitely didn't give anyone five kroner.'

'But it's true. We *were* given five kroner.'

He shook his head.

'That's not what she said. So. That's enough lying. Where did you get the money from?'

Another deluge of tears swept through me.

'From . . . the . . . old . . . lady!' I sobbed.

Dad stared at me.

'We're not going to get any further with this,' he said. 'Now you go and throw the sweets in the bin. And you stay in your room for the rest of the evening. Then I'll have a chat with Prestbakmo in a bit.'

'But they're not mine!' I said.

'They're not yours? You've told me *you* were given five kroner? Wasn't it your money after all?'

'It's Geir's as well,' I said. 'I can't throw the sweets away.'

Dad stared at me with his mouth agape and a furious glare.

'You do as I say,' he said at length. 'Now I don't want to hear a single word more from you. Have you got that? You steal, you lie and on top of all that you answer back! So. Up you go.'

With him right behind me, I gathered up all the sweets in my hands, threw them in the kitchen bin and went back to my room.

That autumn and winter we went up to see Anne Lisbet and Solveig as often as we could. We stumbled around playing in the darkness, our waterproofs glistening with rain in the gleam of our torches, which shone narrow tunnels of light into the forest below their houses, we sat in one of their bedrooms drawing and listening to music, we went to the boat factory and the big quay there, up the hill behind, where none of us had been before and we went down into the forest below the bridge next to the immense concrete foundations.

One Saturday we wandered down to the secret refuse tip. They were just as keen as we had been, and Geir and I dragged four chairs and a table, a lamp and a chest of drawers into the trees, we arranged them as if we were in a living room, and it was absolutely fantastic because we were outside in the forest, in the sunlight, yet inside a living room, and we were there with Solveig and Anne Lisbet.

The tingle of excitement I felt when I looked at her never waned, she was so beautiful it hurt. Her thick light blue jacket with the shiny material. The white cap. The rim of wool around the top of her boots. Her face when for some reason she sent us a fierce look. Her smile, as radiant as a billion diamonds.

When the snow began to fall we wandered around searching for suitable places to jump from, slide down or dig holes in. Her hot red cheeks then, the gentle but distinct smell of snow which changed so much according to the temperature, but which was everywhere around us nevertheless; all the possibilities that existed. Once the mist hung between the trees, the air was thick with drizzle and we were wearing waterproof clothing that was so frictionless on the snow that we could slide down it like seals. We climbed to the top of the slope, I lay on my front, Anne Lisbet sat astride me, Solveig astride Geir, and we slid down on our stomachs all the way to the bottom. It was the best day I had ever experienced. We did it again and again. The feeling of her legs clamped round my back, the way she held my shoulders, the howls of delight she gave when we picked up speed, the fantastic somersaults when we reached the bottom, rolling around with our legs and arms entwined. All while the mist hung motionless amid the wet dark green spruce trees, and the drizzle in the air lay like a thin film of skin on our faces.

We discovered lots of new places that winter, such as the deciduous forest below the road which surrounded the whole estate and above the Fina station, two places that had been totally separate in our consciousness but which were now suddenly connected. The old gravel lane that led down there, the last part of which we had joined when we were going to the Fina station, also had a top end, where the children we had never seen lived, they also had a football pitch in the forest, small it was true, but with decent goals. Or the road below Anne Lisbet and Solveig's, where the houses highest up were only a stone's throw away from theirs. Dag Magne, who was in our class, turned out to be Solveig's neighbour. It came as a surprise that their houses were so close to one another, they belonged to two different worlds and there was a belt of forest between them. Presumably it was the forest that had deceived us. It was no more than twenty, perhaps thirty metres wide, but it represented so much more than houses that, emotionally, the distance felt like several hundred metres. This was the same across the whole estate, and not only there, it was like that by the refuse tip too, for if you took the road from Færvik and continued straight on, which very few people did, instead of turning right onto the road to

Hove, you were there. And if you bore right at the end of the long flat stretch, on the road east towards the school, it was only a couple of hundred metres before the refuse tip revealed itself in all its glory between the trees. Areas that had previously been isolated, in their own world, so to speak, were suddenly connected. How many people knew that Lake Tjenna was actually located right by Lake Gjerstad? Lake Gjerstad, which you could walk to from Sandum, on the other side of the island! Or reach via a short cut off the road to school!

Another surprise was that fru Hjellen, our house help, lived with her husband in the house next to Anne Lisbet. They had no children, she was always happy to receive visitors, and I went there both on my own and with the other three. When she cleaned our house I told her all manner of things, even things I didn't tell mum and dad. She taught me how to open the front door with the key I had been given – the trick was to pull it out a *tiny* bit after fully inserting it and *then* turn.

And so it was fru Hjellen I confided in when one of the rocks we regularly dropped on cars from the road below us finally hit one. It was me who dropped it. We were standing by the green fence, Geir had just missed his car, when I picked up a stone and waited for another car to come. The stone was bigger than my hand and so heavy that I pushed it rather than dropped it. There, a car was coming round the bend. Racing across the flat stretch. Now!

The stone flew through the air. The instant it left my hand I knew it was going to hit. However, I had not anticipated the bang on the car roof would be so loud. Nor that the very next second there would be a squeal of brakes and locked tyres screaming across the tarmac.

Geir looked at me with terrified eyes.

'Let's scram!' he said.

He crawled up the rocks, dashed across the road, climbed up the little knoll and was gone.

Absolutely paralysed, I didn't move. I simply couldn't move a muscle. I was too frightened. Even when I heard a car door slamming below, the engine starting and the car heading for where I was standing. I didn't move.

Thirty seconds later the car came up the road. With tears running down my cheeks and my legs trembling so much I could barely stand, I watched it stop on the road three metres above me. The driver didn't open the door and get out; he hurled it open and leaped out, his face red with fury.

'Did you throw that rock?' he yelled, already on his way down the slope.

I nodded.

He grabbed both my arms and shook me.

'You could have killed me, do you understand? If the rock had hit the windscreen! Do you understand! And whatever happens, the car's a WRITE-OFF! Do you know how much it costs to repair a roof? Oh, this is going to cost you a packet!'

He let go of me.

I was crying so much I couldn't see.

'What's your name?' he said.

'Karl Ove,' I said.

'Surname?'

'Knausgaard.'

'Do you live here?'

'No.'

'Where do you live then?'

'Nordåsen Ringvei,' I said.

He straightened up.

'You'll be hearing from me,' he said. 'Or your father will be hearing from me, I should say.'

He took the slope in one stride with his long legs, got into his car, slammed the door hard and drove off with a jerk.

I sat down on the ground sobbing. All hope was gone.

A moment later Geir called from the terrain above. He came sprinting down, bursting with questions about what had happened and what had been said. I knew he was glad it was me who had thrown the rock and that I had given my name. But what he wanted to know most was why I hadn't run. After all, we'd had plenty of time to get away. If I'd run he would never have caught me and never known it was me who had dropped the stone.

'I don't know,' I said, drying my tears. 'But I couldn't. Suddenly I couldn't move.'

'Are you going to tell your mum and dad?' Geir said. 'That'd be best. If you tell them the truth they'll be angry, but it'll be over and done with quickly. If you don't say anything and he rings, it'll be worse.'

'I daren't,' I said. 'I can't tell them.'

'Did you tell him your father's name?'

'No, just mine.'

'But your name's not in the phone book!' he said. 'And he'll have to ring your dad. But you didn't tell him his name!'

'No,' I said with a flicker of hope.

'In that case, definitely don't tell them anything,' Geir said. 'Perhaps nothing will come of it!'

When I got home, fru Hjellen was there. She could see I had been crying and asked me what the matter was. I asked her not to say a word to anyone. She promised. Then I told her. She stroked my cheek and said it would be best if I told my parents. But I didn't dare, I told her, and so we left it at that. Whenever the phone rang in the following days I froze in a fear that was greater than any I had ever experienced. An immense darkness hung over those days. But it was never him on the phone, it was always someone else, and I was beginning to believe that everything would pass and disappear of its own accord.

Then he rang.

The phone rang, dad picked it up downstairs, perhaps three minutes went by before the handset upstairs clicked, which meant he had rung off. He came upstairs, his footsteps firm and laden with determination. On his way to see mum. The voices from the kitchen were loud. I sat in bed crying. A few minutes later my bedroom door opened. Both of them came in. That never happened. Their faces were grave and sombre.

'A man has just called me, Karl Ove,' dad said. 'He told me you dropped a big stone on his car and destroyed the roof. Is that true?'

'Yes,' I said.

'How could you DO such a thing?' he said. 'What's wrong with you? You could have killed him! Don't you understand? Don't you understand how serious this is, Karl Ove?'

'Yes,' I said.

'If the stone had gone through the windscreen,' mum said, 'he could have driven off the road or collided with another car. He could have died.'

'Yes,' I said.

'Now I have to pay for the repairs. Which will run into several thousand kroner. And that's money we don't have!' dad said. 'Where do you think that's going to come from, eh?'

'I don't know,' I said.

'Oh, you accursed boy!' he said, turning away.

'And then you didn't say a word,' mum said. 'It's more than a week since it happened. You have to tell us when this kind of thing happens. Do you understand? Promise me you will.'

'Yes,' I said. 'But I told fru Hjellen.'

'Fru *Hjellen*?' dad said. 'And not us?'

'Yes.'

He looked at me with those cold angry eyes of his.

'Why did you do it?' mum said. 'How could you even think of dropping stones on cars? You must have known it was dangerous?'

'We didn't think we would hit anything,' I said.

'We?' dad said. 'Were there more of you?'

'Geir was with me,' I said. 'But I dropped the stone that hit the car.'

'Looks like I'll have to have a chat with Prestbakmo as well,' dad said, glancing at mum. Then he turned to me.

'You're grounded today and for two more days. No pocket money for this week or the following one. Have you understood?'

'Yes.'

Then they went out.

It had all passed. This too. It had been the darkness between the act and the revelation, when everything appeared normal but wasn't, which had been so terrible. When everything trembled behind the static facade of everyday normality. Once, about a year earlier, a similar situation had made me run away. Then it had been not a rock but a knife that had led to the misfortune. All the other children had been given scout knives, except me. I was too small and too irresponsible. But then one day, in an act that bore some resemblance to a ceremony, dad presented me with a knife. They trusted me, he said. I hid my disappointment that it was a girl's knife he had bought and that the scout in the picture on the sheath wore a skirt not trousers, these were details you could not expect an adult to understand, and I allowed my pleasure at receiving the knife to predominate because now I could cut and carve and chop and throw with the others. All I needed to do was keep the sheath out of their sight. That day I carved a sword with Leif Tore. A long piece of wood I sharpened at the end like a bradawl and a short piece nailed on as a handle. Swords in hand, we roamed the estate. Finding two girls, each with a doll's pram, we sneaked after them for a while before we launched an attack, imagining we were pirates and they were ships, and again and again we ran our swords through the leather hoods of the prams. The girls shouted and screamed, we retreated, they said they would tell on us, we began to worry about what we had done and kept a wary eye on them. First of all they went home, then they came out and started to walk towards Gustavsen's house and ours. Terrified of the consequences, we decided to run away. We climbed the mountain, went into the forest at the top and walked as far as we could, that is, to the cliff above Lake Tjenna. Neither Leif Tore nor I had been there before. It was a long way from home and I thought we could sleep there and leave the following morning. We sat on the edge looking over. The sun hung low in the sky behind us; the countryside that spread out around us was golden in the sunshine. We sat there for half an hour perhaps. Then Leif Tore wanted to go home. He was hungry, he said. I tried to persuade him, we had run away after all, we couldn't go back, but he stuck to his guns, he didn't want to sleep outdoors under any circumstances, so I went back with him. Dad was waiting for me in the garden when I arrived home. He grabbed my arm in an iron grip, dragged me to my room and told me I was grounded. The knife was confiscated, even though that wasn't what I had used but a sword. They didn't understand the difference. Stabbing with a knife was unthinkable. The sword was made of wood, it was what we had used for the attack, and they should have confiscated that. But they took the knife. I heard them talking about it. 'Look,' dad had said. 'Look at the sheath. It's completely ruined.' He was referring to all the holes I had made to hide the fact that the scout was wearing a skirt and not trousers, but he interpreted it as a sign that I was careless and immature. Sitting there in my room, grounded for that night and the following one, I watched Leif Tore playing outside. He had been given a slap around the ear and that was that. Slaps didn't bother him.

But it passed. Everything passed. The girls got new prams, the motorist got a new roof, the grounding came to an end, pocket money was reinstated, the road outside the house was packed with children in the evening, and the forest below was always open, day and night, winter and spring. Anne Lisbet and Solveig didn't come down to us, we always went up to them, and in that way we had two worlds: one outside our houses, where we joined the gatherings of kids every evening, kicking a football, playing in the road, building dens in the forest below, running round and poking our noses in every nook and cranny of the estate, and when the cold came and the water froze, skating on Tjenna, with the wonderful sound of steel blades on ice resounding against the low hills bordering the lake, and every day was filled with such intense pleasure; and another world up there with them, where everything appeared to resemble what we had at home because here too children were throwing themselves into everything you could throw yourself into, here too they kicked a football in the road, played games in the dark, here too they skipped, here too they skated when the water froze and skied when snow fell, yet it was different. The pleasure was somehow elsewhere, not in what we did but those we did it with. So intense was the pleasure that it was often there even when they weren't. One evening we played table tennis in Dag Lothar's garage, one evening we sneaked around a couple of workmen's sheds by a new road in the forest, one evening we sat in Geir's bedroom playing Chinese chequers, one evening I would be getting undressed by my bed and the thought of Anne

Lisbet and her whole being could suddenly strike me with such force that I was left reeling with happiness and longing. Furthermore, it was not just her in those feelings, there was also her beautiful mother and her broad-shouldered father, who was a diver and had a couple of yellow oxygen bottles in the cellar bathroom, her little sister and brother, all the rooms in their house and the pleasant fragrance that filled them. There were all the things she had in her room, so different from those that occupied mine, lots of dolls, dolls' clothes, a lot of pink and frills. And there was what we did together, which her joy and enthusiasm heightened and added gloss to. Especially at school, where we kept to ourselves until a particular situation brought us together, it might be in a circle when we played *Ta den ring og la den vandre* and it was me she gave the ring to, or when it was me she caught while singing the last line of *Bro bro brille* and clasped her arms around or when I chased her in tag and she deliberately slowed down so that I could catch her. Oh, had it been up to me I could have run after Anne Lisbet all my life as long as I was allowed to wrap my arms around her at the end.

Did I know that it couldn't last?

No, I didn't. I thought it would just go on and on for ever. Spring came, and with it a lightness: one day I put on my new trainers, and running in them after months of trudging around in various kinds of boots was like flying. Puffa trousers and jackets, which made all movement so awkward and clumsy, were replaced by light trousers and light jackets. Gloves, scarves and caps were packed away. Skis and skates and sleighs and sledges were put into sheds and garages; bikes and footballs were taken out, and the sun, which for so long had hung low in the sky and whose rays had been for the eyes only, rose higher and higher with every day that passed and was soon so hot that the jackets we put on in the morning were stuffed in our satchels when we returned from school at midday. But during these weeks the most telling sign of spring was the reek of burning garden refuse wafting across the estate. The cool evenings, the bluish darkness, the cold emanating from ditches still littered with the remains of snowdrifts, as hard as ice and studded with grit, the constant buzz of children's voices outside, children running after a football in the road, others cycling up and down ditches or doing wheelies on the pavement, everything bubbled with life and lightness, you had to run, you had to cycle, you had to shout, you had to laugh, all with the pungent yet rich smell of burning spring grass that was suddenly everywhere in your nostrils. Now and then we ran up and watched: the low dense flames like little orange waves, damp almost with the intensity of colour brought out by the evening gloom, tended by a proud mother or father, often with a rake over their shoulder and gloves on their hands, like some kind of lower-middle-class knight. Now and then there were real bonfires they kept watch over, when all the rubbish they had collected in the garden during the winter was burned.

What was it about fire?

It was so alien here, it was so profoundly archaic that nothing about it could be associated with its surroundings: what was fire doing side by side with Gustavsen's caravan? What was fire doing side by side with Anne Lene's toy digger? What was fire doing side by side with Kanestrøm's sodden and faded garden furniture?

In all its various hues of yellow and red it stretched up to the sky, consuming crackling spruce twigs, melting hissing plastic, switching this way, switching that, in totally unpredictable patterns, as beautiful as they were unbelievable, but what were they doing here among us ordinary Norwegians on ordinary evenings in the 1970s?

Another world was revealed with the fire, and departed with it again. This was the world of air and water, earth and rock, sun and stars, the world of clouds and sky, all the old things that were always there and always had been, and which, for that reason, you didn't think about. But the fire *came*, you saw it. And once you had seen it you couldn't help seeing it everywhere, in all the fireplaces and wood-burning stoves, in all the factories and workshops, and in all the cars driving round the roads and in garages or outside houses in the evening, for fire burned there too. Also cars were profoundly archaic. This immense antiquity actually resided in everything, from houses made of brick or wood to the water flowing through the pipes into and out of them, but since everything happens for the first time in every generation, and since this generation had broken with the previous one, this lay right at the back of our consciousness, if it was there at all, for in our heads we were not only modern 1970s people, our surroundings were also modern 1970s surroundings. And our feelings, those which swept through each and every one of us living there on these spring evenings, they were modern feelings, with no other history than our own. And for those of us who were children, that meant no history. Everything was happening for the first time. We never considered the possibility that feelings were also old, perhaps not as old as water or the earth, but as old as humanity. Oh no, why would we? The feelings running through our breasts, which made us shout and scream, laugh and cry, were just part of who we were, more or less like fridges with a light that came on when the door was opened or houses with a doorbell that rang if it was pressed.

Did I really think it would last?

Yes, I did.

But it didn't. One day towards the end of April I told Anne Lisbet we were going to go up to theirs after school, and she said we couldn't come.

'Why not?' I said.

'Someone else is coming,' she said.

'Who?' I said, thinking perhaps it was an uncle or an aunt.

'It's a secret,' she said, smiling her sly smile.

'Someone from the class?' I said. 'Marianne or Sølvi or Unni?'

'It's a secret,' she said. 'You and Geir can't come. Bye!'

I went over to Geir and told him what she had said. We decided to sneak over after school and spy on them. After dropping off our satchels at home we took the other way up, cut through the building site in the forest below, where the foundations for the new houses had already been built, crept through the trees, over the bog and up to the turnaround between their houses.

No one.

Were they indoors?

We couldn't ring the bell of course; we weren't supposed to be there. We walked down. Geir had the brilliant idea of ringing the bell at Vemund's house. He came out and stood in the doorway with that same stupid expression on his round face. Yes, they had gone down the hill some time ago.

Alone?

No, they were with two others.

Who?'

'Fraid he hadn't seen.

Boys or girls?

Boys, he thought. At first he had assumed it was us, as we were here so much, but now he could see of course it must have been someone else!

He laughed. Geir laughed too.

Who could it be?

And what were they doing with them?

'Come on, let's follow them,' I said to Geir.

'But they didn't want us with them,' Geir said. 'Wouldn't it be better to go to Vemund's for a bit?'

I stared at him, my eyes as wide as they could be.

'OK,' he said.

'Don't say anything to the others,' I said to Vemund. He nodded, and then we walked across their property and down to the road.

Where could they be?

For all we knew, they could have gone all the way down to the shop. But something told me they would stay near the house. We joined the road below theirs. Four of them. They should be easy to see and hear.

'Shall we go up?' I said, stopping at the crossroads where one road led up to Dag Magne's and theirs.

Geir shrugged.

We walked up the gentle slope. Dag Magne's house lay in a little dip. There was a garage adjacent to it, full of bikes and tools and car tyres. Under the veranda there was a pile of wood.

Reaching the summit of the slope, we saw Dag Magne in a window looking out at us. To avoid giving the impression that we were on our way to see him we cut across their property without looking at him and down into the forest on the other side. Spring was in the air, the grass which had been white for so long was turning green, but there were no leaves on the trees, so we could see a long way into the young forest.

There. Directly below the slope to Solveig's house I saw something blue and red moving.

'There they are,' Geir said.

We stopped and stood still.

They were laughing and chatting excitedly.

'Can you see who it is?' I whispered.

Geir shook his head.

We went closer. Hiding behind trees as far as we could. When we were about twenty metres away, we crouched down behind a rock.

I poked my head up and watched them.

It was Eivind and Geir B with them.

Eivind and Geir B.

Oh heck, would you believe it! Eivind and Geir B, they were in our class! They were neighbours and best friends, and lived just along from Sverre, who lived just along from Siv, whose house we could see from our road.

What was the difference between them and us?

There was almost no difference!

They were best friends, we were best friends. Eivind was one of the best students in the class; I was one of the best students in the class. Geir B and Geir both just hung out with us two.

But Eivind was better-looking than me. He had curly hair, high cheekbones and narrow eyes. I had protruding teeth and a protruding bum. And he was stronger than me.

Now he was hanging from a dead tree trying to break it. Geir B was on the other side pushing as hard as he could. Anne Lisbet and Solveig stood watching.

They were showing off.

Oh flippin' heck!

What should we do? Go over and act cool? Make a group of six?

I turned to Geir.

'What shall we do?' I whispered.

'I don't know,' he whispered back. 'Beat them up?'

'Ha ha,' I whispered. 'They're stronger than us.'

'We can't stay here all day, anyway,' he whispered.

'Shall we vamoose?'

'Yes, let's hop it.'

As carefully as we had come, we crept off. At the crossroads, Geir asked if I wanted to go up to Vemund's.

'I certainly do not!' I said.

'I'll go then,' he said. 'See you.'

'See you.'

After a few metres I turned and watched him. He had found a twig and was whacking one knee and then the other as he walked on the pavement alongside the wall. I cried almost all the way home and kept to the path past the football pitch so that no one would see.

This happened on a Friday. Early on the Saturday morning I ran up to Geir's, but he was going to Arendal with his parents. Mum and dad were cleaning the house and hoovering, Yngve had caught the bus to Arendal with Steinar, so I was left to my own devices. I went into the bathroom and locked the door, rummaged through the dirty linen basket and found my ugly brown cords, which were filthy round the knees. I put them on, ran into my room and searched for my disgusting yellow jumper, put it on, went downstairs unobserved and into the boiler room, where my rubber boots were, the ugliest footwear I possessed, carried them into the hall and put them on. From the hook I grabbed the thin grey jacket I had been given last spring, too small now and pretty grubby, on top of which the zip didn't work, so I would have to walk with it undone. That suited me fine because the yellow jumper underneath would be visible then.

Dressed like this, in the ugliest clothes I could muster, I set off for the estate where Anne Lisbet lived. With eyes downcast all the while, I wanted people who saw me to realise how upset I was. And if I bumped into Anne Lisbet, which was the object of the exercise, I wanted her to see what she had done. The filthy, ugly clothes I was wearing, the drooping head, all of this was for her benefit, so that she would understand.

I didn't want to ring, or else I would have to talk to her. No, the whole point was that she would happen to catch a glimpse of me and realise for herself how upset I was about what she had done.

When I reached Vemund's house, and there was still no sign of her, I entered the road leading to her house, even though it could ruin my plan, because what was I actually coming here for, if not to meet them?

Meet Bjørn Helge perhaps?

He was a year younger, and the idea of playing with him was inconceivable. Although he played football and was quite grown-up for his age.

I stood for a moment at the turnaround wondering whether to go up to Bjørn Helge's. But just seeing the house where she lived upset me, so after a while I went down into the forest, past the newly blasted building sites. The construction machines and portacabins stood idle, staring ahead through vacant black windows onto the road along the flat land. I looked for a while at the new parish hall that was being built, then at the field where we used to play football and the gate to the path leading to the refuse tip, which was a hundred metres further on. Slowly I began to descend. In the middle of the hill I walked past, hidden behind rocky outcrops and trees, lived Eivind and Geir B. We had been up there a couple of times to play, and in the winter before the snow fell we had taken them to Lake Tjenna and gone skating. Once we had also been to Geir B's birthday party. And once to Sverre's. That time I had lost the ten kroner that had been meant for him, the envelope was empty when I arrived dressed in my Sunday best. I began to cry, it wasn't good, it was not good at all, but there was a reason – ten kroner was a lot of money. His father fortunately went with me to find it, we walked back up the road I had come along, and there, bright blue on the black tarmac, was the ten-krone note. So they could no longer think I had tricked them, taken the money myself and pretended I had lost it.

On a lawn in a garden by the road stood the boy with the long black hair and the Indian features playing keepie uppie.

'Hi,' he said.

'Hi,' I said.

'How many can you do?' he said.

'Four,' I said.

'Ha ha,' he said. 'That's nothing.'

'How many can you do then?'

'Did sixteen not long ago.'

'Show me,' I said.

He killed the ball and placed his foot on top. With one swift flick he sent the ball into the air. One, two, three kick-ups and then the ball was too far from him and the last kick, a wild lunge with his leg, sent the ball into the hedge.

'That was four,' I said.

'It's because you're watching,' he said. 'You make me think about what I'm doing. I'll have another go. Will you wait?'

'Yes.'

This time he got the ball up to knee height, and then it was easy, the ball went from knee to knee five times before he lost control.

'Eight,' I said.

'Yes,' he said. 'But now I'll show you.'

'I've got to run,' I said.

'OK,' he said.

His father, a fat man with glasses and thick grey hair, was in the window watching us. I ran across the road, suddenly realised what clothes I was wearing, slowed down and started to walk with my head bowed again.

When I came down the hill dad was reversing the car out of the drive. He waved me over, leaned across the seat and opened the door.

'Jump in,' he said. 'We're going to town.'

'But my clothes,' I said. 'Can I change first?'

'Nonsense,' he said. 'Jump in, now!'

I pulled the little lever at the side of the seat and was about to push it forward.

'Sit in the front,' he said.

'In the front?' I said.

This never happened.

'Yes,' he said. 'We haven't got all day! Come on now!'

I did as he said. After I had closed the door he put the car in gear and we set off down the hill.

'Your clothes are a bit dirty,' he said, 'but we're only going for a little trip. It won't matter.'

I started fiddling with the seat belt and didn't see a lot until it had clicked into position and we were on Tromøya Bridge.

'I fancied going to the fish market,' he said. 'And the record shop. Do you want to join me?'

'Yes,' I said.

He steered with one hand on the wheel. The other was on the gear stick, a cigarette burning between his fingers. He drove fast as always.

For a long time we said nothing.

On the left was Vindholmen, and the shipyard with the huge cranes like monitor lizards and the fibreglass hall. The car park outside was just under half full. There was an enormous oil platform in the sound. A Condeep platform which was due to be towed out the following week.

After we had driven through the little tunnel and come into the town of Songe, he glanced at me.

'Have you been out with Geir today?' he said.

'No,' I said. 'They're in Arendal.'

'We might bump into them then,' he said.

There was another silence.

It bothered me; he was in such a good mood and didn't deserve to be met with silence. But what could I say?

After a while I thought of something.

'Where are you going to park?'

He shot me a sidelong glance.

'We'll find somewhere,' he said.

'Not in Skytebanen, or what? There's always room on Saturdays.'

'That's the last resort, that is,' he said.

He found a parking spot in Tyholmen. He set off at a fast stride between the tall timber houses, and I had to jog to keep up. I was ashamed of my clothes, I looked such an idiot in them and I kept a close eye on the people we passed to see if they were staring or laughing.

At the fish market dad scanned the glass counters while waiting his turn.

'Let's have some shrimps, shall we, eh, Karl Ove?' he said.

I nodded.

'And perhaps that piece of cod?'

I didn't say anything.

He smiled and looked at me.

'I know you don't like cod, but it's good for you. When you grow up you'll get a taste for it.'

'I doubt that very much,' I said.

I felt like chatting and telling stories, the way I did with mum, but I couldn't even get off the ground with him. However, I was glad he had brought me along and it was important he knew that.

When it was his turn and he pointed out what he wanted to the assistant, one of the other women behind the counter stared at him. Realising that I was watching her, she lowered her gaze and continued to pack the fish on the cutting board in front of her. There was something about dad, in the crowd by the counter, his pointing and talking, that made me think he wanted to dispel from his mind everything that existed around him. Not his appearance, not the face dominated by the beard, not the light blue eyes, not the slightly curled lips, nor his tall slim body, there was something else, something he 'radiated'.

'There we are,' he said as he received his change and held the white bag of fish and shrimps in his hand. 'Let's go then!'

Outside, beneath the grey sky, with people packing all the pavements and pedestrian areas, as always on Saturdays, we walked around Pollen, the central bay area, heading for the record shop, I did a few skips beside him, to show him I was happy. When he looked at me I smiled. The wind coming off the sound ruffled his hair and he patted it back in place.

'Could you carry the bag for me for a bit?' he said inside Musikkhjørnet. I nodded and held it in my hand while he nimbly flicked through the records.

They used to play music when we had gone to bed, especially on Friday and Saturday evenings. Often it was the last thing I heard before I fell asleep. Every now and again he played records when he was alone in his study. Steinar had told me once that he had brought a Pink Floyd LP into the classroom and played it. He had said this with awe in his voice.

'Wouldn't you like to choose a cassette?' dad remarked without taking his eyes off the records he had in front of him.

'But I haven't got a cassette recorder,' I said.

'You can borrow Yngve's,' he said. 'And then we'll see you get one of your own for Christmas. It's good to have a few cassettes lying around then. No point having a recorder without any cassettes!'

Shyly I went over to the cassettes, which were not in boxes like the records but in racks on the wall. One was full of Elvis cassettes. I picked out one with the cover showing him in a leather suit, sitting with a guitar in his lap and smiling.

Dad bought two records, and when he placed them on the counter he told the assistant that I would point out a cassette I wanted. He came over to the rack with a little key in his hand. I indicated the Elvis cassette, he unlocked the glass door, took it out and put it in its own little bag beside dad's big bag.

'Good choice,' dad said as we walked towards the car. 'You know Elvis was number one when I was growing up. Elvis the Pelvis we called him. I still have some of his old records. They're at grandma and grandad's. Perhaps we should bring them back next time we go? So that you can listen to them?'

'Yes, that would be good,' I said. 'Perhaps Yngve would like it too.'

'They must be worth a mint today,' he said. Stopped and took the keys from his pocket. I looked over at the massive oil tankers laid up in Galte Sound, on the Tromøya side of the strait. They were so big that set against the low hills they seemed to come from another world.

Dad opened the door on my side.

'Can I sit at the front on the way home as well?' I said.

'You can. But only today, OK?'

'Yes,' I said.

He put the bags on the back seat and lit a cigarette before strapping himself in, which I had already done, and started the car. On the way home I sat partly looking at the cover of the cassette and partly out of the window. There was a queue of traffic the entire length of Langbrygga, it started moving more freely in the bay around the headland, with Bai Radio and TV on one side and the fish auction hall, with its low white-brick buildings and fluttering flags, on the other. Across the sound and its choppy white-tipped waves lay Skilsø, a collection of timber houses situated along a hill, with a ferry terminal below, beyond which was Pusnes Mekaniske Verksted, marine suppliers, and then it was mostly forest along the coast of the island, while on the mainland, where the road wound up and down, there were houses and jetties all the way to the petrol station, after which came Songe, Vindholmen and the road that led to Tromøya Bridge. All ruffled and tousled, as it were, by the wind from the south. As we drove, the thought of Anne Lisbet crept up on me and darkened my mood. Perhaps it was the Condeep platform that had triggered it because I had been thinking of going with Geir and the girls up to Tromøya Bridge and watching it being towed out to sea. Now I wouldn't. Or would I? She still hadn't been to my room, which I imagined every night before going to sleep, that one day she would be sitting there, on my bed, surrounded by my things, and the thought always set off fireworks of joy in my brain, Anne Lisbet, here, next to me!

Why should Eivind suddenly visit her instead of me? We'd had such fun!

Eivind had to go. We had to get back together.

But how could that be brought about?

Beneath us Tromøya Sound stretched to the east and the west. A double-ender was coming in, approaching land, I saw a figure standing at the stern with the tiller in his hand.

Dad indicated left and slowed down, waited for two passing

cars and then he crossed the road and arrived at the last hill up towards our house. Leif Tore, Rolf, Geir Håkon, Trond, Big Geir, Geir and Kent Arne were playing football in the road. They glanced at us as we passed them and parked in the drive.

I raised a hand to them as I got out.

'Gonna join in?' Kent Arne shouted.

I shook my head.

'I've got to eat.'

As we walked towards the house, out of sight of the boys in the road, dad grabbed my hand.

'Let me have a look,' he said. 'The warts haven't gone yet then?'

'No,' I said.

He let go.

'Do you know how to get rid of them?'

'No.'

'I'll tell you. I have an old method. Come into the kitchen afterwards and I'll tell you. You want to get rid of them, don't you?'

'You bet.'

The first thing I did upstairs was to throw the trousers and the jumper in the dirty linen basket and put on the clothes I was wearing earlier. Then I propped the cassette, face up, against the wall on my desk so that I could see it wherever I was in the room and went to the kitchen, where dad was sitting with a little bowl of shrimps in front of him. Rice pudding was cooking on the stove; mum was in the living room watering the flowers.

'We can just fit this in before we eat,' dad said. 'It's a kind of magic. My grandmother did it for me when I was small. And it worked. My hands were covered with warts. After a few days they were all gone.'

'What did she do?'

'You'll see,' he said. He got up, opened the fridge and took out white wrapping paper which he put on the table and unfolded. There was bacon inside.

'First of all I'm going to grease your fingers with the bacon. And then we'll go into the garden and bury the bacon. Then, in a few days' time, your warts will be gone.'

'Is that true?'

'Yes! That's what's so strange! But they do disappear. Just wait and see! Pass me your paws.'

I gave him one hand. He held it in his, took a rasher of bacon and carefully rubbed it around all the fingers, the palm and the back of my hand.

'Now the other one,' he said. I gave him my other hand and he took another rasher and did the same.

'Have I greased everything now?' he said.

I nodded.

'Let's go outside then. Now you have to carry the bacon and bury it.'

I followed him downstairs, put my boots on without touching them with my hands – I had the rashers of bacon in them – and walked behind him – he was carrying a spade – round the house into the kitchen garden by the fence bordering the forest. He thrust the spade into the ground, pressed with his foot and began to dig. After a few minutes he stopped.

'Drop the bacon in there then,' he said.

I did as he said, he filled in the hole and we left.

'Can I wash my hands now?' I asked.

'Yes, of course,' he said. 'The bacon we buried will remove the warts.'

'How long does it take?'

'We-ell . . . a week or two. It depends on how much you believe.'

*

After dinner I went into the street. No one was playing football any longer, but Geir Håkon, Kent Arne and Leif Tore were still outside, they were running at the wall alongside the road to see how far they could climb before they fell. If they ran fast enough they managed three, perhaps four, steps before gravity took hold and dragged them down. If they got too far up they landed on their backs, so this was an activity that required caution. I was wary at the first attempt, my only attempt in fact, because straight afterwards Geir Håkon was too ambitious and fell in the ditch with a thump, knocking all the air out of his lungs. He filled them again and let out a loud tremulous howl while fighting off tears, which purged us of any desire we had to continue.

Geir Håkon got to his feet, averted his face and, with his back to us, recovered his regular breathing. When he turned everyone could see he had been crying, but no one said a word.

Why not?

If it had been me, they would have said something.

'What shall we do now?' Kent Arne said.

At that moment Kleppe came down the hill on his bike. He was wobbling from side to side, dressed in a black jacket and black cap, his bloated red features sagging and drooping, a bit like the two B-Max bags he had hanging from either side of the handlebars. He was the father of Håvard, a boy living in the house furthest from ours, who was already seventeen, someone we admired but seldom saw. The father, it was rumoured, was a boozer. When he turned into the road where we were I saw my chance. I ran beside him for a little way pretending to be looking inside the bags on the handlebars.

'He's got beer bottles in the bags!' I shouted to the others and stopped.

Kleppe did not so much as send me a glance. But the others laughed.

The next day we sat in Geir's bedroom and wrote a love letter to Anne Lisbet. His parents' house was identical to ours, it had exactly the same rooms facing in exactly the same directions, but it was still unendingly different, because for them functionality reigned supreme, chairs were above all else comfortable to sit in, not attractive to look at, and the vacuumed, almost mathematically scrupulous, cleanliness that characterised our rooms was utterly absent in their house, with tables and the floor strewn with whatever they happened to be using at that moment. In a way their lifestyle was integrated into the house. I suppose ours was too, it was just that ours was different. For Geir's father, sole control of his tools was unthinkable, quite the contrary, part of the point of how he brought up Geir and Gro was to involve them as much as possible in whatever he was doing. They had a workbench downstairs, where they hammered and planed, glued and sanded, and if we felt like making a soap-box cart, for example, or a go-kart, as we called it, he was our first port of call. Their garden wasn't beautiful or symmetrical as ours had become after all the hours dad had spent in it, but more haphazard, created on the functionality principle whereby the compost heap occupied a large space despite its unappealing exterior, and likewise the stark rather weed-like potato plants growing in a big patch behind the house where we had a ruler-straight lawn and curved beds of rhododendrons.

Geir's room was where mine was, his sister, Gro, had her room where Yngve's was, and his parents had theirs between the two, exactly the same as in our house. Geir walked freely from room to room, ran up and down the stairs, and if he felt like a *smørbrød* he helped himself to whatever was in the fridge and made one.

The same applied to me in his house, I could run between their rooms if I wanted or make myself something to eat with Geir. Often we sat in the living room listening to a Knutsen & Ludvigsen record he had, and laughed at it, or at him, because not only did he know all the lyrics, he could also perform them with the same tones and mannerisms. He was hopeless at football, hopeless at all ball games, there was something about his coordination which wasn't quite right, there was something about his enthusiasm which wasn't quite right, he never burned with a passion to play, as I often did, and playing football on a pitch for an entire afternoon but still yearning for more when darkness fell and everyone had left was completely alien to him. He wasn't much good at school either. He was poor at reading, poor with figures, could seldom reproduce anything he had read or heard in the lesson, though he coped well for all that, nothing depended on football or school as far as he was concerned. He was good at imitating people and had started to attract crowds around him at school. He liked that, laughter would egg him on to become more and more adventurous as if it were a kind of fuel, but not even that was important to him. He seemed to have his own small worlds. Such as drawing. He could sit for a whole day in his room drawing. Or building model aeroplanes, which he often did. His laughter was raucous and it could turn hysterical. Perhaps more than anything else, he liked farting; at any rate there was a lot of experimentation and discussion about it.

Having an elder sister was perhaps the reason he wasn't drawn to the girls' world in the same way that I was, not initially anyway. But the idea of a love letter excited him. I would write the letter and he would add a drawing which showed a boy trampling on a heart and two boys standing by watching. Beneath it I wrote in a red felt pen, *Eivind breaking our hearts*. The letter itself consisted of five lines.

Dear Anne Lisbet
Our hearts are broken
Come back to us
Can you hear
We love you so much

We couldn't hand this letter and the drawing to her. For all we knew, she might show them to people, perhaps even people at school, and then we would become a laughing stock. Instead we decided to *show* them to her. With the letter and drawing rolled up like treaties in our hands, we walked to her house. Up along the rock from fru Hjellen's, into her garden, under her window. We threw some gravel up and she appeared. First we held the drawing and the letter up for her to see, then we tore them into pieces and stamped on them, and then we walked off. Now at least she knew how we felt. Now it was up to her.

Geir stopped at the crossroads.

'I'm going up to Vemund's,' he said. 'Coming?'

I shook my head. On the way down I thought I should go and visit a new friend too. Dag Magne perhaps? But that would seem out of character, so I went home instead. Lay down on the bed reading until Yngve came in and asked if I wanted to play football with him in the street. I did. There was nothing I liked more than doing things with Yngve. Indoors we usually played games or listened to music together, whereas outdoors we went our separate ways, him with his friends and me with mine, apart from in the holidays when we went swimming or played football or table tennis or badminton and in cases like now, when he was bored and had no one else to play with other than me.

For more than an hour we kicked a ball to and fro between

us. For a while Yngve took shots at me in goal and I practised goal kicks. Then we did some passing.

As if by a miracle my warts disappeared. They got smaller and smaller, and then, perhaps three weeks later, they had completely gone. My hands were so smooth it was hard to imagine they had ever been any different.

But Anne Lisbet didn't come back. Whereas before she had squealed with pleasure whenever I had taken her cap or pulled her scarf or covered her eyes from behind, now she was irritated or even angry. I felt a stab of pain when I saw her and Solveig going to the bus accompanied by Eivind and Geir B, and every night before I went to sleep I imagined a situation in which I rescued them or somehow stood in a light that enabled her to see the error of her ways and return to me, unless, that is, I wasn't imagining I was dead, and the immense sorrow that would overwhelm her, and the remorse when she realised that what she actually wanted – to be with me – was no longer possible, as I was lying in a coffin bedecked with wreaths and flowers. Death was generally a sweet thought at that time because it was not only Anne Lisbet who would regret what she had done but also dad. Standing by my coffin, weeping for me, the prematurely departed. The whole estate would be there, and all the opinions they had held about me would have to be re-evaluated because now I was gone and the person I had really been would appear in the utmost clarity for the first time. Yes, death was sweet and good and of great comfort. However, even if I was upset about Anne Lisbet, she was still there, I saw her every day at school, and as long as she was at school, there was hope, though precious little. The darkness that thinking about her could generate inside me was therefore of a different order from the other darkness that sometimes came over me, which had a depressing and burdening effect on everything, and which Geir also felt, it transpired. One evening we sat in his room and he asked me what was up with me.

'Nothing much,' I said.

'You're so quiet!' he said.

'Oh, that,' I said. 'I'm just fed up.'

'What about?'

'I don't know. There's no particular reason. I'm just fed up.'

'I feel like that sometimes too,' he said.

'Do you?'

'Yes.'

'You're just fed up for no particular reason?'

'Yes. I'm like that too.'

'I didn't realise,' I said. 'Didn't realise others could feel like that too.'

'That's what we'll have to call it,' he said. '"Like that". We can say it when we're in that mood. "I'm like that today," we can say, and then the other person will understand straight away.'

'That's a good idea,' I said.

There were other new words being added as well; for example, the one Yngve taught me, the real name for fucking, it was 'intercourse', and this knowledge was so shocking that I took Geir to the top of the mountain before I dared tell him. 'It's called *intercourse*,' I told him, 'but don't say you heard it from me! You've got to promise me!' He promised. He was spending more and more time at Vemund's house, and Vemund was coming down to see him now and then. I simply didn't understand that and I told him so. Why do you spend time with Vemund? He's fat and stupid and the worst in the class. He never really gave me a decent answer, just said he liked being there. Why? I said. What do you do that's so fantastic? Well, Geir said, we sit and draw most of the time . . . Even in lessons it was Vemund he turned to when we had to work in pairs, instead of me, which he had done automatically before. I joined him a couple of times at Vemund's, also to be close to Anne Lisbet, but I found what they did boring and when I said so and suggested something else they stuck together and wanted to continue what they were doing. That was fine by me, if he wanted to be with the class dunce, let him. Besides, we were still neighbours, it was still me he came to in the afternoons, and that spring we started going to football together. Almost all the children in our road did. The training sessions were in Hove, and mum and Geir's mum took turns to drive us there. Mum bought me a tracksuit when it started. It was my first, and I had great hopes before the day, imagining a sparkly blue Adidas one, like Yngve's, or even better, a Puma, or at least a Hummel or an Admiral. But the one she bought wasn't a brand name. It was brown with white stripes, and even though I considered the colour ugly, that wasn't the worst thing about it. The worst was that the material wasn't shiny but matt, a bit coarse, and it didn't hang off your body, it clung to you, making my arse stick out even more than usual. When I put on the tracksuit that was all I could think about. Even when I ran onto the pitch and training began, it was all I could think about. My arse is sticking out like a balloon, I would think, running after the ball. My tracksuit is brown and ugly, I would think. I look an idiot in it, I would think. An idiot, an idiot, an idiot.

However, I never said this to mum. I pretended to be happy when I was given it because it had cost a lot of money – she had gone all over Arendal looking for it and if I said I didn't like it, she would first think I was ungrateful and then she would be sad that she had bought the wrong thing. And I did not want that. So I said, how nice. Great. Really. Just what I wanted.

*

The odd thing about the training sessions that spring was that there was such a big difference between the person I was inside and the person I was on the pitch. Inside myself I was full to the brim with thoughts and emotions about scoring and dribbling, about the terrible tracksuit I had and my big arse, and by extension my protruding teeth – whereas on the pitch, running around, I was to all intents and purposes completely invisible. There were so many kids on the field, an enormous melee of arms, legs and heads following the ball like a swarm of mosquitoes, and the coaches didn't know the names of more than a handful of them, the ones from their immediate neighbourhood presumably, their sons and their friends. The first time I stood out from the crowd was an evening when someone had kicked the ball into the forest behind the goal, where it was lost and everyone was ordered over to look for it. Two, perhaps three, minutes of intensive searching followed. No one could find the ball. Then suddenly I saw it in front of me: under a bush, it glowed, white and wonderful, in the dusk. I knew this was my opportunity, I knew I ought to shout, 'Got it!' and carry it with me onto the pitch, so that the rightful credit fell to me, but I didn't dare. Instead I just kicked it onto the field. 'There's the ball!' someone shouted. 'Who found it?' someone else shouted. I emerged from the forest with all the others and said nothing, so it remained a mystery.

The second time was a similar situation, though even more flattering to me. I was running in a pack of players, maybe ten to twelve metres from the goal, the ball landed among us, everything was a vortex of limbs, and when the ball came free, a metre from me, I booted it as hard as I could and it rocketed in by the bottom of the post.

'Goal!' they roared.

'Who scored it?'

I said nothing, did nothing, stood stock-still.

'Who scored? No one?' the coach called. 'No, OK! Let's carry on!'

They might have thought it was an own goal and that was why no one owned up to the shot. Even though I didn't dare say I had scored, it was my very first goal, and the thought of that burned inside me for the rest of the session, and in the car on the way home. The first thing I said when we ran to the car, where mum was waiting, was that I had scored.

'I scored a goal!' I said.

'Oh, lovely!' mum said.

When we returned home and I was sitting at the kitchen table to eat supper, I said it again.

'I scored today!'

'Was it a match?' Yngve said.

'No,' I said. 'We haven't had any matches yet. It was training.'

'Then it means nothing,' he said.

A couple of tears detached themselves and rolled down my cheeks. Dad looked at me with that stern, annoyed expression of his.

'For Christ's sake, you can't cry about THAT!' he said. 'There must be SOMETHING you can take without blubbing!'

By then the tears were in full flow.

Crying so easily was a big problem. I cried every time anyone told me off or corrected me, or when I thought they would. Usually it was dad. He only had to raise his voice to make me cry, even though I knew he hated me doing it. I couldn't help myself. If he raised his voice, and he often did, I began to cry. I seldom cried because of mum. Through the whole of my childhood it had only happened twice. Both times during the spring when I started football training. The first was the most disturbing. I had been down in the forest with a gang of kids, we were standing in a sort of circle, Yngve was there, Edmund from his class was there, as well as Dag Lothar, Steinar, Leif Tore and Rolf. Tongues were going nineteen to the dozen. Gulls were screaming from Ubekilen, the sky was still light, although darkness was creeping across the hill and beneath the trees above the forest floor. The conversation turned to school and teachers, skiving, detentions and having to report to school early. Then it moved to a boy in Yngve's class who was extremely clever. I had just been listening, happy to be with the older boys, but there was a sudden lull in the conversation which I was able to fill.

'I'm the best in my class,' I said. 'At least at reading and writing and natural and social sciences. And local history.'

Yngve stared at me.

'Don't boast, Karl Ove,' he said.

'I'm not boasting. It's true!' I said. 'There is no doubt about it! I learned to read when I was five, before anyone else in the class. Now I can read fluently. Edmund, for example, is four years older than me, and he can't read at all! You said that yourself! That means I'm cleverer than him.'

'Stop that boasting right now,' Yngve said.

'But it's true,' I said. 'Isn't it, Edmund? It's true that you can't read, isn't it? That you have a special teacher? Your sister's in my class. She can't read either. Or only a little. That's not a lie, is it?'

Now something strange happened: Edmund had tears in his eyes. He wrenched himself away and set off up the slope.

'What do you think you're doing?' Yngve hissed at me.

'But it's true,' I said. 'I'm the best in my class and he's the worst in his.'

'Go home,' Yngve said. 'Now. We don't want you here with us.'

'It's not up to you,' I said.

'Shut your mouth and go home!' he snapped, putting his hands on my shoulders and shoving me.

'OK, OK,' I said and set off up the hill. Crossed the road, slipped through the door and took off my outdoor clothes. It was true what I had said, so why had he shoved me?

Tears were in my eyes as I lay on my bed and opened a book. It was unfair, what I had said was true, it was so unfair, so unfair.

Mum came home from work, brewed up some tea and prepared a bite to eat. Yngve was still out, so we ate alone. She asked if I had been crying, I said yes, she asked why, I said Yngve had pushed me, she said she would take the matter up with him. I showed her a letter I had written to grandad, she said he would really like it, gave me an envelope, I put the letter in, she wrote down the name and address and promised to post it the following day. When it was done I went for a lie-down. I heard Yngve come home while I was reading, the footsteps up the staircase and into the kitchen where mum was. Now she would tell him he shouldn't push me and tell me to shut up, I thought, lying there, and I imagined Yngve's bowed head. Then came the sound of their voices and footsteps on the landing, and the door was opened.

I could see at once that mum was angry and sat up.

'Is it true what Yngve has told me?' she said. 'That you made a fool of Edmund because he can't read?'

I nodded.

'Sort of,' I said.

'Don't you understand that Edmund was upset? Don't you understand that you mustn't talk about other people in that way?'

She stepped forward until her face was in front of mine. Her eyes were narrow; her voice was loud and sharp. Yngve stood behind her, watching me.

'Karl Ove, don't you?' she said.

'He cried,' Yngve said. 'And it was you who made him cry. Do you understand?'

And suddenly I did understand. What mum said cast an implacable light over what had happened. *Edmund* was the one she felt sorry for, even though he was four years older. He was upset and it was me who had upset him.

I started crying as I had never done before.

Oh, oh, oh, oh, oh, oh, oh, oh, oh, oh, oh, oh, I sobbed. Oh, oh, oh, oh, oh, oh, oh, oh, oh, oh, oh, oh.

Mum leaned over and stroked my cheek.

'Sorry, Mum,' I wept. 'I'll never do it again. Never ever. I promise you with all my heart.'

The loud sobs and my shouted rather than spoken apologies pacified my mother but not Yngve; several days were to pass before the events receded into the past for him. And that despite Edmund not being central to his life, not one of his best friends, just someone who was in his class. I both understood and I didn't.

The second time mum made me cry was when we went out one evening, she wanted to buy something from the Fina station and preferred to walk there, and I, who loved having her to myself, joined her. I took a torch along, the path was dark, but before we got there I shone the torch through the darkened living-room window of a house we passed.

'Don't do that!' mum hissed. 'There are people living there! You can't invade their privacy like that!'

I shone the torch on the ground at once, and fought back tears for a few seconds, until I had to admit defeat and they streamed out amid great gasps and sobs.

'Was that so upsetting?' mum said, looking at me. 'I had to

tell you. Surely you understand. What you did wasn't very well behaved.'

I started crying not because I had been told off but because *she* had told me off.

But at least she didn't get angry because I was crying.

Outside the house I hardly ever cried. Unless of course I hurt myself, everyone did, no one could restrain the tears then. The fact that no one was exactly beating a path to our door says more about other things over which I had no control. I quarrelled a lot with the others, especially Leif Tore, we disagreed on a wide range of matters, including who gave the orders, and even though we were similar in that neither of us would yield it was still him everyone wanted to play with and not me. As long as there were lots of us, such as when we built dens down in the spruce forest or played football on the field, it wasn't noticeable, it was only when there were three or four of us that it became apparent. Nor was it a problem when I was with older boys, such as Dag Lothar, I just sort of adapted, followed his example without a protest, didn't say a word, and it felt natural, after all he was a year older. Once I pointed out to Geir that Dag Lothar told me what to do, and I told Geir what to do and Geir told Vemund what to do. He went sullen and said I didn't tell him what to do. Yes, I do, I said. I say what we're going to do. But you don't *tell* me what to do, Geir said. What difference does it make? I said. I said Dag Lothar told me what to do. And that you tell Vemund what to do. So what difference does it make if I tell you what to do? Well, it evidently did make a difference. Geir's face went all stiff in the way it did, his body had that mutinous look and soon he was gone. Others got annoyed about even less. Like the time when Geir Håkon, Kent Arne, Leif Tore and I were standing by the road one early afternoon after school, alone on the estate, and a huge lorry drove past with a load of boulders from some blasting work they were doing further up.

'Did you see that?' I said. 'It was a Mercedes!'

I wasn't interested in cars, boats or motorbikes, I knew nothing about them, but as all the others did I had to make an effort now and then, just to show that I too was clued up.

'No, it wasn't,' Geir Håkon said. 'Mercedes don't make lorries.'

'Didn't you see the star then?' I said.

'Are you daft or what? That was not a Mercedes star,' he said.

'Yes, it was,' I said.

Geir Håkon snorted. For a moment his puffy cheeks were even fatter than usual.

'Anyway, Mercedes do make lorries. I've read about it in a book I've got.'

'I'd like to see that book,' Geir Håkon said. 'You're lying through your teeth. You know nothing about lorries.'

'And I suppose you do, just because your dad works on construction machines?' I said.

'Yes, as a matter of fact I do,' he said.

'Oooh,' I said sarcastically. 'You think you know all about slalom skis too just because your dad has bought you a pair. But you can't slalom. You're useless at skiing. So what are you doing with all that gear? If you can't use it. Everyone says you're spoiled. And you are. You get everything you point a finger at.'

'I do not,' he said. 'You're just jealous.'

'Why would I be jealous of you?' I said.

'Give it a rest, Karl Ove,' Kent Arne said.

Geir Håkon had not only averted his face now but his whole body.

'Why should *I* give it a rest, and not Geir Håkon?' I said.

'Because Geir Håkon's right,' Kent Arne said. 'It wasn't a

Mercedes. And he's not the only person who has slalom skis. I've got some too.'

'That's just because your dad's dead,' I said. 'That's why your mother buys you all sorts of things.'

'That's not why,' Kent Arne said. 'It's because she wants me to have them. And we can afford it.'

'But your mother works in a shop,' I said. 'They don't exactly earn a lot of money.'

'Is being a *teacher* any better?' Leif Tore said, who also got his spoke in now. 'Don't you think we've seen the wall at your place? It's full of cracks and falling down because your father didn't know it needed reinforcement. He only used cement! How stupid can you get?'

'And then he reckons he's something special because he's on the council,' Kent Arne said. 'Salutes us with one finger and stuff when he drives past. So you can just shut up.'

'Why should I shut up?'

'Well in fact you don't have to. You can stand here and prattle away as you usually do. We definitely don't want to play with you.'

And then they ran off.

The disagreements never lasted long, a few hours later I was playing with them again if I wanted, but there was something awry, I was finding myself in situations with my back against the wall more and more often, the others were moving away more and more often when I approached, even Geir, in fact, on occasion I realised they were actually hiding from me. On the estate when anyone said something about someone it was immediately repeated by others, and then it suddenly became something everyone said. About me it was said that I always knew best and I was always boasting. But I did know best, I knew much more than the others, so why should I pretend anything else? If I knew something, it was because that was how it *was*. And as far as boasting was concerned, *everyone* boasted, all the time. Dag Lothar, for example, whom everyone liked, didn't he start every other sentence with 'I don't mean to boast but . . .' and go on to tell us about something good he had done or something good someone had said about him?

Yes, he did. So this wasn't about what I did but about the person I was. Why otherwise would Rolf call me 'Mr Pro' when we played football in the road? I hadn't done anything special, had I? You reckon you're so bloody good at football, don't you, he said, eh, Mr Pro? But all I had done was to say what was what, and why shouldn't I if I went on a football course and actually *knew*? We shouldn't run around in a pack, we had to spread out and then pass the ball or dribble, not mill around the way we did.

But I also had the last word that spring. For when the lessons at school were reorganised to make preparations for the end-of-the-year celebrations and Frøken handed out booklets of the play which we were to perform for all the parents on the biggest day of the year, namely the last, who was allocated the principal role but me?

Not Leif Tore, not Geir Håkon, not Trond and not Geir.

But me.

Me, me, me.

None of them would be capable of learning so many lines by heart, it was something only Eivind and I, and perhaps Sverre, of the boys, could do, and the fact that Frøken chose me in the end was by no means fortuitous.

I was so happy when she told me that I didn't know what to do with myself.

Every day of the last week we rehearsed, every day I was the centre of attention in the class, Anne Lisbet's too, and when the final day arrived, in radiant sunshine, all the parents came as well. Dressed in their finest outfits, they sat on chairs by the wall, took photos with their cameras, were hushed when we enthusiastically said our lines and burst into applause at the end.

Then we played recorders, sang, were presented with our grade books, Frøken wished us a good summer and we ran out into the playground and down to the waiting cars.

Grade book in hand, I stood impatiently with Geir in front of mum's Beetle. She strolled along with Martha, they were chatting and laughing and didn't see Geir and me until they were a few metres away.

Mum was wearing beige trousers and a rust-red sweater with the sleeves turned up over her forearms. Her hair hung a long way down her back. On her feet she wore a pair of light brown sandals. She had just turned thirty-two, while Martha, who was wearing a brown dress, was two years older.

They were young women, but we didn't know that.

Mum rummaged through her bag for the car key.

'You were all so good,' Martha said.

'Thank you,' I said.

Geir said nothing, just squinted into the sun.

'Oh, here it is,' mum said at length. She unlocked the car and we got in, adults at the front, children at the back. They both lit up cigarettes. And then we drove home in the sunshine.

That evening I stood in the doorway watching mum drying her hair in their bedroom. Occasionally, when dad wasn't there, I followed her round the house and talked her ears off. Now I was quiet, the whine of the hairdryer made it impossible to speak, instead I watched her as she bent her head and lifted her hair up with a brush in one hand to the dryer in the other. She sent me sporadic glances and smiled. I went into the room. On the little table by the wall there was a letter. I didn't mean to pry, but even at some distance I could see the first name was Sissel, mum's name, and that the full name was longer than mum's, because between Sissel and Knausgaard, which I recognised rather than read, there was a third name. I went closer. 'Sissel Norunn Knausgaard' it said.

Norunn?

Who was that?

'Mum!' I said.

She lowered the hairdryer as though that would make my voice clearer, and looked at me.

'Mum,' I said again. 'What does that envelope say? What kind of name is that?'

She switched off the hairdryer.

'What did you say?'

'What kind of name is that!'

I nodded towards the envelope. She leaned over and took it.

'That's my name.'

'But it says Norunn! Your name's not Norunn!'

'Yes, it is. It's my middle name. Sissel Norunn.'

'Has it always been your name?'

I felt my chest tighten with despair.

'Ye-es. All my life. Didn't you know?'

'No! Why didn't you say?'

Tears were running down my cheeks.

'But darling,' mum said, 'I didn't think it mattered. Sissel is the name I use. Norunn is just a middle name. A kind of extra name.'

I was shaken to the core. Not by the name in itself, but by

the fact that I hadn't known it. That she'd had a name I didn't know.

Was there anything else I didn't know?

A month later, in the middle of the long summer holiday, we drove up to Sørbøvåg by Åfjorden in Ytre Sogn, where my mother's parents lived, and we stayed there for two weeks. I had been looking forward to this so much that on the morning we were due to leave and I was woken at the crack of dawn, there was a tinge of unreality about it. The boot was packed to the gunnels, mum and dad sat in the front, Yngve and I in the back, we would be in the car all day and evening, and even the most familiar sight, the road down to the crossroads and up to Tromøya Bridge, seemed cast in a different light. Now it didn't belong to the house and our existence in it, now it belonged to the great expedition we had set out on, which lent every crag and every rock, every islet and every skerry, excitement and anticipation.

When we came to the crossroads by the bridge I folded my hands as usual and said the short prayer which had worked every time so far:

Dear God,

Please don't let us crash.

Amen

We drove across the mainland, through vast monotonous coniferous forests, past Evje with its long low military barracks and pine plains, past Byglandsfjord and the campsite, up into Setesdalen, with its age-old enclosed fields and farms and the many silversmith signs, along a road which in some places almost seemed to go through people's drives. Slowly buildings disappeared, it was as if the houses lost their hold on us and fell by the wayside one by one, like children fell off the enormous inner tube someone had roped to a boat earlier that summer. As the boat's speed increased only the tube was left. I saw glinting sandbanks along the sides of the river, green-clad hills rising more and more steeply, the occasional enormous bare mountainside in every shade of grey, with some flame-red pine trees on top. I saw rapids and waterfalls, lakes and plains, everything bathed in the glow of the clear bright sun which, as we drove, had risen higher and higher in the sky. The road was narrow, and it gently and unobtrusively followed all the countryside's dips and climbs, curves and bends, with trees like a wall on both sides in some places, towering over everything in others, in sudden and unexpected vantage points.

Sporadically, lay-bys appeared during the journey, small gravelled areas beside the road where families could sit and eat at rough-hewn timber tables, their cars next to them, generally with doors and boot lids open, under the shade of trees, often close to a lake or a river. Everyone had a Thermos on the table, many had a cooler bag, some also a Primus stove. 'Aren't we going to stop for a break soon?' I would ask after seeing such a lay-by because breaks, alongside ferry crossings, belonged to the high points of the journey. We too had a cooler bag in the boot; we too had a Thermos, juice and a little pile of plastic glasses, cups and plates with us. 'Don't pester me,' dad would say then, desperate to cover as many kilometres as he could in one go. That meant that, at the very least, we would have to drive to the end of Setesdalen, past Hovden and Haukeligrend and up Mount Haukeli, before the question of a break even came into consideration. Then we would have to find a suitable place because we would not take the first opportunity, oh no: if the stops were few and far between, then the location of the lay-by had to be something special.

In the uplands the terrain was completely flat. There wasn't a tree or a bush to be seen anywhere. The road continued as straight as a die. Some areas were littered with boulders strewn across the ground, covered with a kind of coating I thought might have been lichen or moss. Others were unbroken rock face, clean, scrubbed. Here and there water sparkled, snow glinted. Dad drove faster as there was such a clear view. At intervals along the roadside we saw tall poles, and Yngve said it was quite incredible, they were markers and so high because the snow in winter could reach up to the top. That was several metres!

The sun shone, the mountain plateau stretched in all directions, and we, we were racing ahead. One lay-by after another was left in our wake until, without warning, dad indicated, braked and pulled in.

It was situated right next to a lake, oval and utterly black. Beyond it the ground rose gently while at the side there was a big snowdrift, bluish in colour and hollow underneath where the water disappeared down an opening.

Around us it was perfectly still. After so many hours with the regular hum of the engine the silence felt artificial, as though it didn't belong to the landscape but to us.

Dad opened the boot, took out the cooler bag and put it on the coarse wooden table, where mum immediately began to unpack it as he fetched the Thermos and the bag with the cups and plates. Yngve and I ran to the water, bent down and dipped a hand in. It was freezing cold!

'What about a swim here then, boys?' dad said.

'Oh no, it's freezing!' I said.

'Sissies,' he said.

'But it's freeezing!' I said.

'Yes, I'm sure it is. I was only joking. We haven't time for a swim anyway.'

Yngve and I walked over to the snowdrift. It was so solid we couldn't make snowballs from it, as we had hoped. And walking across the top, with the water underneath, wouldn't be on the cards if mum and dad were there.

I broke off a clump and threw it into the lake, where it bobbed up and down like a mini-iceberg. Now at least, when we were home, I could say we had thrown snowballs in the middle of July.

'Come and eat,' mum called.

We sat down. We each had a packed lunch. Three slices of bread with boiled egg on top. In addition, there was a packet of biscuits on the table. In our glasses there was juice. The plastic gave it a different taste, but I liked it, it reminded me of the trips we used to have when we picked berries and went on camping holidays. We didn't have that many, there had been basically only one, last summer when we went to Sweden with grandma and grandad. A car raced up from behind me, it was as though the sound vibrated as it increased in volume, then after a kind of boom it went quieter again until it was gone. Steam rose from mum and dad's coffee. A car towing a caravan came from the other direction. I watched it as I finished my juice. It was creeping along. Then it indicated. As it pulled over into the lay-by dad turned.

'What's that idiot doing?' he said. 'There's only one table here. Can't he see?'

He turned back, put his coffee cup down and took the fox-emblazoned pouch of tobacco from his breast pocket.

The car with the caravan stopped only a few metres from us. The door opened and a fat man dressed in a pair of beige shorts and a yellow T-shirt, with a brown bucket hat, emerged. He opened the door of the caravan and disappeared inside as a woman came out of the other car door. She was also fat and wore light grey elasticated trousers with a crease and a woollen sweater. From her mouth hung an unlit cigarette, her hair was big and grey and yellow and over her eyes she wore a pair of large glasses with tinted lenses. She went to stand by the lake, lit her cigarette and gazed across as she smoked.

I started on the last slice of bread.

The man re-emerged with a camping table in his hands. He erected it between the car and our table. Dad turned again.

'Haven't they got any manners?' he said. 'We're sitting here eating and he's intruding.'

'It doesn't matter,' mum said. 'It's beautiful here.'

'It *was* beautiful here,' dad said. 'Until that fathead came.'

'He can hear you,' mum said.

The man put a clinking cooler bag down beside the table. The woman went over to him.

'They're Germans,' dad said. 'They don't understand. We can say whatever we like.'

He took a last swig from his cup and jumped to his feet.

'Well, we'd better be moving on.'

'The boys haven't finished eating yet,' mum said. 'We're not in *such* a hurry, are we?'

'In fact, we are,' dad said. 'Eat up, come on. Be quick about it.'

He flicked the half-smoked cigarette to the ground, took the glasses and cups to the lake, rinsed them and put them in the bag with the plates and Thermos. Zipped up the top of the cooler bag and put everything in the boot. The man and woman said something I didn't understand as they stared up the gentle slope on the other side of the lake. He was pointing. Something was moving in the distance. Mum scrunched up the greaseproof paper from the *smørbrød*, put it in a bag and got up.

'Let's go then,' she said. 'We'll have to eat the biscuits the next time we stop.'

That was what I had feared.

Dad pushed the seat forward for me and I got in. After the fresh air outside, the smell of smoke inside hit you. Yngve clambered in through the other door. He wrinkled his nose.

'I don't think the car sickness tablets are working any more,' he said.

'Say if you feel sick,' mum said.

'It would help if you didn't smoke all the time,' he said.

'That's enough of that, boy,' dad said. 'Don't whinge. We're on holiday.'

Slowly the car pulled out onto the road. I glanced across, past the lake, up to the spot where the man had been pointing. There was something there. A grey patch in all the green, moving slowly. What on earth could it be?'

I nudged Yngve and pointed through the window when I had his attention.

'What's that?' I said.

'Reindeer maybe,' he said. 'We saw them last year as well. Don't you remember?'

'Oh yes,' I said. 'But they were much closer. These ones are so small they're like mice!'

Then we sank into the trance-like state car travel can induce. We crossed the rest of the mountain range, descended into Røldal and drove on to Odda, the dirty little town at the end of Hardangerfjord, which despite its run-down polluted appearance still shared some of the magic the far end of the mountains evoked, so dizzyingly and at bottom incomprehensibly different from the world we had left only a few hours earlier. While Sørland for the most part consisted of low crags and knolls, small bedraggled forests with a wide-ranging selection of trees standing side by side in countryside that was both wide open and restricted, and while on the island where I lived the tallest mountain was no more than a hundred and twenty metres high, this countryside here, which you always stumbled on, was remarkable for its *immense* mountains, so dominating in their purity and simplicity that all other details of the surroundings were forced to adjust to them, they disappeared, utterly and completely: who cared about a birch tree, however tall, when it stood beneath one of these endlessly beautiful and eternally immutable mountains? The most conspicuous difference, however, was not the dimensions but the colours, which seemed deeper here – nowhere is the colour green so deep as in Vestland or so clear – even the sky, even its blue was deeper and clearer than the blue of the sky where I came from. The sides of the valley were green and cultivated, in the spring and early summer the blossoming fruit trees a Japanese white, the mountain peaks a hazy blue, snow-tipped here and there, and, oh, between the ridges, which rose in a long line on both sides, lay the fjord itself, greenish in some places, bluish in others, gleaming in the sun everywhere, as deep as the mountains were high.

To travel in a car through this landscape was always overwhelming because nothing of what you had seen so far prepared you for what was waiting here. And then, as we drove along the northern side of the fjord, all the other unfamiliar features appeared, like the electric fences, like the red barns, like the old white timber houses, like the cows grazing, like the long rows of hay-drying racks scattered across the sides of the valley. Tractors, forage harvesters, manure cellars, long brown boots on doorsteps, shady farmyard trees, horses, shops in the basements of normal houses. Children selling wild cherries or strawberries from small stands with handwritten signs along the road. Life here was different from life at home: I could see a stooped old woman wearing a flowery dress and a neckerchief, you didn't see that where I came from, or a stooped old man in blue overalls and a black peaked cap in some field or along some gravel track. But however much of an impression the places here made on me, the unusual names they bore played a part of course – Tyssedal, Espe, Hovland, Sekse, Børve, Opedal, Ullensvang, Lofthus and Kinsarvik, which because of the strange sound was my favourite: all right, *vik* was an inlet, but a kinsar, what on earth was *that*? – and however bright the colours and however different the myriad of details, an atmosphere of extravagance also hung over these regions, not over the people and their activities but over the space they moved in, it seemed much too big for them; perhaps it was the flood of sunlight that did it, perhaps the blueness of the vast sky or perhaps the range of mountains stretching up into it, or else it was simply the fact that we were only passing through, we didn't stop anywhere, apart from at the bus shelter where Yngve staggered out to throw up, we didn't know anyone here and were in no way connected with what we saw. For when we did finally reach Kinsarvik and left the car, which dad had parked in the ferry queue, this sense of extravagance was no longer noticeable; on the contrary, everything seemed nice and cosy here with the sound of car radios, doors being opened and closed, people stretching, walking to and fro, children quietly kicking a ball about next to the queue or doing what Yngve and I were doing, walking to the kiosk at the end to see whether there was anything we could spend some of our holiday money on.

An ice cream?

Oh yes.

Yngve bought an ice cream in a boat-shaped wafer, I bought a tub with a little red spatula and we ambled over to the quay with them in our hands. We sat on a brick wall and looked down at the water and the seaweed lying in wet greasy clusters against the rocks. In the distance we saw the ferry arriving. The air smelled of salty water, seaweed, grass and exhaust fumes, and the sun burned our faces.

'Are you still feeling sick?' I said.

He shook his head.

'Shame we forgot the football,' he said. 'But they've probably got one in Våjen.'

He said Våjen the way grandma did.

'Yes,' I said, squinting into the sun. 'Do you think we'll get on this one?'

'Don't know. Hope so.'

I dangled my legs. Loosened a big chunk with the spatula and put it in my mouth. It was so big and cold that I had to jiggle it to and fro with my tongue to prevent the icy texture from becoming intolerable. While doing this, I turned and glanced at our car. Dad was sitting with the door open and one leg on the ground, smoking. The sun glinted on his sunglasses. Mum was standing beside him with a punnet of wild cherries on the roof and helping herself every now and then.

'What shall we do tomorrow?' I said.

'I'm going to be with grandad in the cowshed anyway. He said he would teach me everything so that I can take over one day.'

'Do you think it's possible to swim there now?'

'Are you out of your mind?' he said. 'It's as cold in the fjord as it was in the mountain lake.'

'Why is that?'

'It's so far north of course!'

Some of the cars started their engines. The bow doors of the ferry opened. Yngve got up and walked towards the car. I ate my ice cream as quickly as possible and followed him.

After the ferry trip to Kvanndal the next high point of the journey was climbing Vikafjellet. The steep narrow road wound upwards, round and round, round and round, so steep in some places I was frightened the car would tip over and fall backwards.

'There are probably quite a few tourists who get a bit of a shock here,' dad said as we drove up and I sat trembling and peering down at the precipice beneath us. 'They use the brakes to slow down, you see. That could be fatal.'

'What do we use?' I said.

'We use the gears,' he said.

We weren't tourists, we knew what was what, we weren't the motorists you saw behind clouds of steam issuing from an open bonnet at the roadside. But immediately afterwards things almost did go wrong, because at the next hairpin bend we met a car towing a caravan, we were only a few metres away from a collision, but dad jumped on the brakes and the other car did the same. Dad reversed down until the road was wide enough for both of us. The other driver waved to us as he passed.

'Did you know him, Dad?' I said.

In the mirror I saw he was smiling.

'No, I didn't know him. He waved to thank me for making room for him.'

Then it was on to the next mountain, and down to the next fjord. The mountains here were as high as by Hardangerfjord, but they were gentler in a way, not as steep, and the fjord here was wider, at some junctures almost like a lake. What's the problem? the Hardangerfjord mountains said. Take it easy, these mountains said. Everything's hunky-dory.

'Shall we take it in turns to sleep?' Yngve said.

'Fine by me,' I said.

'Great,' he said. 'Me first then?'

'OK,' I said. And he laid his head on my lap and closed his eyes. It was good to have him sleeping there, his head was nice and warm, and it was as though something was going on in two places at once, the countryside outside the window, which was changing constantly and I never took my eyes off it, and Yngve's head asleep on my lap.

When we parked in the queue for the next ferry, he woke up. We stood on the deck and enjoyed the wind blowing into our faces. Half an hour later we were back in the car and it was my turn to rest my head on Yngve's lap.

I woke up and knew we were getting close. The nearer we got to the sea, the lower the uplands and the denser the vegetation, but of course nowhere near Sørland's scrubbed-clean terrain and gnarled qualities. None of the roads here had stuck in my mind; I looked out of the window without connecting what I saw with anything until I suddenly recognised Lihesten, the vertical drop that plunged several hundred metres on the other side of the fjord from my grandparents' house. We'd had the mountain in front of us for ages, but it was unrecognisable from all other angles except the one we had now, as we approached it from the side. The excitement constricted my chest. We were there! Oh, yes, there's the waterfall! There's the chapel! There's the hotel! There's the Salbu sign! And there's the house! Grandma and grandad's house!

Dad slowed down and turned into the shingle track. It led first past the neighbour, and then through the gate, with the shed on the right, up the last steep incline to the front of the house. I opened the door almost before the car had stopped and jumped out. On the other side of the enclosed field I saw grandad. He was standing by the beehives in his bee-keeper outfit. White overalls, white hat with a long white veil around his head. All his movements were slow, including the hand he raised to greet us. It was as if he was submerged beneath water or on an alien planet with different gravity. I lifted my hand and waved, then I ran into the house. Grandma was in the kitchen.

'We almost crashed into a car on Vikafjellet! We were climbing like this,' I said, depicting the gradient on the yellow vinyl tablecloth with my finger while she smiled at me with her warm dark eyes.

'And then a car with a caravan came. Like this . . .'

'I'm glad you got here safe and sound,' she said. Mum came in through the other door. In the hall I could hear what must have been dad carrying in all the baggage. Where was Yngve? Had he gone over to grandad? With all the bees buzzing around?

I dashed out onto the drive. Nope. Yngve was helping dad to unload the car. Grandad was still there in his white spacesuit. With infinite patience he lifted some frames from the hive. The sun had gone from the farm, but was shining on the spruces growing on the slope behind the mere. A light wind blew past the house, rustling the treetops above me. Kjartan walked over from the cowshed. He was wearing overalls and boots. Longish black hair, square glasses.

'Good evening,' he said, stopping by the car.

'Oh, hi, Kjartan,' dad said.

'Good trip?' Kjartan said.

'Yes, it was fine.'

Kjartan was ten years younger than mum, so in his early twenties that summer. There was something stern, almost angry about him, and even though I had never experienced his anger, I was still afraid of him. He was the only one of the children to live at home: Kjellaug lived in Kristiansand with her husband Magne and their two children, Jon Olav and Ann Kristin, who would soon be coming here, while the next youngest, Ingunn, was a student and lived in Olso with Mård and their two-year-old daughter, Yngvild. Kjartan and grandma quarrelled a lot, he was not as she would have liked her only son to be, I gathered. The idea was that he would take over the smallholding when the time came. Now he was training to become a pipe fitter on ships and planning to work at a yard somewhere in their county of Hordaland. But the most important thing to know about Kjartan, which was frequently mentioned when talk turned to him, was that he was a communist. A fervent communist. When he discussed politics with mum and dad, which he was wont to do on their visits, for some reason their conversations always ended up there, and his somewhat shy evasive eyes changed and became fiery. At home when the subject of Kjartan came up, dad tended to laugh at him, mostly to tease mum, who was not exactly a communist, but who nonetheless disagreed with dad on most matters concerning politics. Dad was a teacher and voted for Venstre, a centre party.

'I'd better take this off and have a shower so I don't smell of cowshed, now that we have such refined company,' Kjartan said. 'I think there is food for you in there.'

Even outside I could hear the stairs creak when he went up to the bathroom on the first floor. How the stairs creaked here!

And indeed a table had been set for us in the living room. There was a pile of still-hot pancakes and a dish of griddle cakes, as well as bread and various spreads. Mum shuttled to and fro between living room and kitchen. Although she had left home when she was sixteen, married dad, given birth to Yngve when she was twenty and lived with her own family ever since, she merged into the household effortlessly as soon as she arrived. Even the way she spoke changed and became much more like the way her parents spoke. With dad it was the opposite: he was always lost in the background. When he was talking to grandad, who loved chatting and had a story for every occasion, often from his own experience, there was something formal about dad that made him so alien but which I still recognised, it was the manner he adopted when he spoke to other parents and colleagues. Grandad wasn't polite in that way, he was completely and utterly himself, so why would dad sit there nodding and saying, I see, oh yes, really, mhm, mhm? Mum was different here too, she laughed and chatted more, and these changes amounted to a plus for us, not to say an enormous plus: dad was in the background, mum was livelier and there were no house rules, and unlike where we came from here we could do as we liked. If one of us knocked over a glass of milk it wasn't a catastrophe, grandma and grandad understood that accidents can happen, we could even put our feet on the table here, well, if dad wasn't in the room at that point, of course, and we could sit on the brown sofa with orange and beige stripes, as slumped as we wanted, even lie on it if we felt like it. And all the work they did, we did too on our own minor scale. We were not unwanted. On the contrary, it was expected of us that we would help as far as we could. Rake the mown hay on the field, lay it on the drying rack, collect the eggs, shovel muck into the cellar, set the table for meals and pick redcurrants, blackcurrants and gooseberries when they were ripe. The doors here were open and people came in without even knocking, they just shouted from the hallway and were suddenly in the living room, made themselves at home and drank coffee with grandad, who didn't bat an eyelid, just started chatting as though their conversation had only been interrupted for a few seconds. These people who came were strange, one in particular, a fat-bellied sloppily dressed and slightly malodorous man with a high voice who used to wobble up the hill on his moped in the evening. His accent was so broad I barely understood half of what he said. Grandad's face lit up when he came, but whether that was because he liked him all that much was hard to say as his face lit up whenever anyone came. I was sure he liked us although I doubted whether the thought had ever struck him; we existed, that was enough for him. For grandma it must have been different, at least it appeared so from the interest she showed when we talked.

Mum stood staring at the table, probably to check that everything was there. Grandma took the coffee pot off the stove in the kitchen and the steadily increasing noise of the whistle died with a little sigh. Dad deposited the luggage in the room above our heads. Grandad came into the hall after hanging up his bee-keeper outfit in the basement.

'The Norwegian population is going through a growth spurt, I see!' he said when he saw us. He came over and patted me on the head as though I were some kind of dog. Then he patted Yngve's head and sat down as grandma came in from the kitchen carrying the coffee pot, and dad and Kjartan both came down the stairs.

Grandad was small, his face was round and apart from a thin wreath of white hair around his head he was bald. The corners of his mouth were often stained with tobacco juice. The eyes behind his glasses were sharp, but were totally transformed once he had removed them and then they were like two small children who had just woken up.

'Looks like I came at just the right moment,' he said, putting a slice of bread on his plate.

'We heard you in the basement,' mum said. 'Nothing to do with luck.'

She turned to me.

'Do you remember the time we heard you in the hall ten minutes *before* you arrived?'

I nodded. Dad and Kjartan sat down on opposite sides of the table. Grandma went to pour coffee into the cups.

Grandad, who was spreading butter over the bread with his knife, looked up.

'You heard him *before* he came?'

'Yes, strange, isn't it?' mum said.

'That's a *vardøger*, that is. A kind of guardian angel,' grandad said. 'It means you'll have a long life.'

'Is that what it means?' mum said with a laugh.

'Yes,' grandad said.

'Surely you don't believe that, do you?' dad said.

'Did you two hear him when he wasn't there?' grandad said. 'That's what's remarkable. Is it so remarkable that it has some significance?'

'Hm,' Kjartan said. 'You've become superstitious in your old age, Johannes.'

I looked at grandma. Her hands were trembling, and as she went to pour the pot was moving up and down so much it was only with the greatest effort of will that she managed to direct the jet from the spout into the cup without spilling the coffee. Mum looked at her too, and was on the point of getting up, presumably to take over, only to lean back and reach for the bread basket instead. It was both painful to watch grandma because she was so slow – in fact some coffee did end up in a saucer – and also unheard of that she, an adult, was unable to manage such a simple task as pouring coffee without spilling it, and the strangeness of seeing someone with hands shaking non-stop, with a mind of their own, it seemed, meant that I couldn't take my eyes off her.

Mum placed her hand on mine.

'Wouldn't you like a griddle cake?' she said.

I nodded. She reached for one and put it on my plate. I spread a thick layer of butter on it and sprinkled sugar. Mum lifted the jug of milk and filled my glass. The milk came straight from the cowshed; it was warm and yellowish with tiny lumps floating round. I looked at mum. Why had she filled my glass? I couldn't drink that milk, it was disgusting, it had come straight from the cow, and not just any cow but one standing outside and pissing and shitting.

I ate the griddle cake and took another while dad asked grandad some questions, which he answered in his own time. Kjartan sighed louder than he would have done if he had been alone. Either he had heard all this before or he didn't like what he heard.

'We were thinking of going up Lihesten this year,' dad said.

'Is that so?' grandad said. 'Well, it's a good idea. Yes, it's nice there. You can see over seven parishes from the top.'

'We're looking forward to it,' dad said while mum and grandma were talking about an oak and a holly tree they had brought from Tromøya the previous year and were now growing here.

I decided I would go and have a look at them.

Dad's glare stopped me in my tracks.

'Aren't you going to drink your milk, Karl Ove?' he said. 'It's straight from the cow, you know. You won't get better milk anywhere.'

'I know,' I said.

As I didn't make a move to drink it, he fastened his eyes onto mine.

'Drink the milk, boy,' he said.

'But it's warm,' I said. 'And there are lumps in it.'

'Now you're offending your grandparents,' dad said. 'You have to eat and drink whatever you're served. And that's that.'

'The boy's used to pasteurised milk,' Kjartan said. 'From a carton in the fridge. They sell it in the shop here too. Of course he can have some of that! We can buy it tomorrow. He's not used to milk straight from the cow.'

'That seems unnecessary,' dad said. 'The milk here is just as good. If not better. What nonsense to buy milk just because he's pampered.'

'I like pasteurised milk best myself,' Kjartan said. 'I agree wholeheartedly with your son.'

'Right,' dad said. 'Just so long as you're not taking the side of the underdog as usual. But this is more about manners.'

Kjartan smiled and studied the table. I put the glass of milk to my mouth, stopped breathing through my nose, tried to think about something other than the white lumps and drank it all in four long swigs.

'See,' dad said. 'It was good, wasn't it?'

'Yes,' I said.

After the meal we asked if we were allowed to go for a little walk even though it was late. We were. On with our shoes, into the yard and down the road to the barn. The dusk was tenuous and hung like a spider's web all around us. The shapes were intact; the colours were absent or had gone grey. Yngve undid the catch of the cowshed door and pushed. The door was stuck and he had to put all his weight behind it to open up. Inside it was dark. Dim light from the dirty peepholes above the stalls made it possible for us to glimpse contours. The cows, lying in their stalls, stirred when they heard us. One turned its head.

'There, there, cows.'

It was nice and warm inside. The small calf, which was isolated in a kind of pen on the other side of the muck channel, was stamping around. We leaned over towards it. It looked at us with frightened eyes. Yngve patted it.

'There, there, little calf,' he said.

It wasn't only the door which was overgrown; all the walls and the floor and the windows were as well, as though the room had sunk at some point and was now submerged beneath water.

Yngve opened the barn door. We climbed into the hay that was lying there, clambered up onto the barn bridge and opened the door to the small henhouse. The floor was covered with sawdust and feathers. The chickens sat motionless on the roosts staring straight ahead.

'Doesn't look like there are any eggs,' Yngve said. 'Shall we go up and have a look at the minks as well?'

I nodded. When he pushed the tall barn door to, a white cat shot past us like an arrow and disappeared under the bridge. We went down and called it, knowing it was hiding somewhere, and in the end we gave up and headed for the three mink huts which stood to the far west of the property, right by the forest. The acrid smell that met us as we approached was almost unbearable and I started breathing through my mouth.

There was a rustling and a banging in all the cages as we stopped in front of them.

How unpleasant it was.

It was darker here by the forest. The minks' claws clinked against the metal of the cages as they paced back and forth. We went up close to one. The black animal shrank as far back as it could, turned its head and hissed at us. Its teeth shone. Its eyes were black like black stones and when, twenty minutes later, I was lying on the bed in our room on the first floor, alongside Yngve, who had his head on the pillow at the other end and was reading a football magazine, it was them I was thinking of. Of them moving to and fro in the cages all night while we slept. Suddenly voices were raised in the living room beneath us. It was mum and dad talking with Kjartan. Raised voices didn't mean anything worrying; on the contrary, there was something reassuring about them. They wanted something, and they wanted it so much it couldn't be whispered or mumbled, it had to be shouted.

*

The next morning grandad came in and asked if we would like to help pull up the fishing nets. We did, and a few minutes later we followed him down the path to the fjord, carrying an empty white tub between us.

The boat was moored to a red float in the water. The mist was so dense it seemed to be hovering in the air. Grandad pulled the boat ashore, we jumped on board, and after he had shoved off with an oar against the bottom Yngve sat down on the thwart by the oarlocks and began to row. Grandad sat at the stern directing him whenever necessary; I sat in the bow looking into the mist. Lihesten, on the other side, was almost completely lost from view, visible only as something hard and grey in all the moist haze.

'It's very unusual for there to be mist here,' grandad said. 'And especially at this time of year.'

'Have you been to the top of Lihesten, Grandad?' Yngve said.

'Oh yes, you bet I have,' grandad said. 'Many times. But it's a few years now since the last time.'

He sat forward with his arms resting on his thighs.

'Once I went there as part of a rescue mission. It was Norway's first real plane crash. Have you heard about it?'

'No,' Yngve said.

'It was misty, like now. The plane flew straight into Lihesten. We heard the bang, you see. We didn't know what it was though. But then the plane was reported missing, and the local police chief needed men to go up with him. So I went.'

'Did you find it?' I said.

'Yes, but there were no survivors. I saw the captain's head. That's a sight I'll never forget. His hair was perfect! Combed back. Not a strand out of place. Yes, I'll never forget that.'

'Where did it crash? Into the wall of the mountain?' Yngve said.

'No, we can't see it from here. But there's a pinnacle on the plateau. It crashed there. We had to climb up to the wreck. Bit to port!'

Yngve's eyes narrowed, presumably trying to work out which side port was.

'That's it, yes,' grandad said. 'You're a good oarsman, Yngve! Well, it was a big affair at that time. It was in all the papers. And there was lots of talk about it on the radio.'

In front of us the float above the net shone red through all the grey.

'Grab it, will you, Karl Ove!' grandad said. I leaned over with a pounding heart and caught it in both hands. But it was slippery and I lost hold at once.

'Scoop your hands underneath,' grandad said. 'Let's try again! Row back a bit. That's it, yes.'

This time I managed to bring it on board. Yngve drew in the oars. Grandad began to drag in the net. The fish were revealed first as small twinkling lights deep in the black depths, then they grew in size and clarity until a moment later they were dragged wriggling over the side. They were so shiny and clean with grey-brown or bluish markings on their spines, their yellow eyes, pale red mouths and razor-sharp fins and tails. I held one of them in my hands, where it writhed with such force it was hard to imagine it could be the fish I saw lying still on the boards at my feet the very next moment.

Grandad patiently extricated them from the mesh of the net and threw them into the tub. We had twenty. Mostly saithe but also the odd cod and pollock, plus two mackerel.

When Yngve began to row back I suddenly heard a simultaneous low *whoosh* and splash, not unlike the noise yachts make when they travel at speed, and I turned my head. Perhaps thirty metres away I could see dark dorsal fins moving through the water.

I was scared.

'What's that?' Yngve said, raising the oars. 'Over there.'

'Where?' grandad said. 'Oh! Porpoises. They've been here a few days now. It's quite rare, but not so unusual. Have a good look at them. Seeing porpoises is a good omen, you know.'

'Is it?' I said.

'Oh yes,' he said.

Grandad gutted the fish over the sink in the basement, which was more like a grotto than a room in the house. The concrete floor was often wet and slippery, the ceiling was so low that dad couldn't stand up straight – not a problem for grandad as he was quite small – and the shelves on the walls were crammed with all sorts of objects and tools that had accumulated over their many years there. When he had finished, and the fish that only a few hours earlier had been alive and wriggling were in the freezer wrapped in plastic, we helped him to clean the net, standing in the rain on the grass by the shed, until mum called us in for dinner.

After eating they usually had a nap. Dad, restless already after just one day, beckoned to me from the hall.

'Join me for a walk,' he said.

I put on my boots and waterproof jacket and followed him across the fields. He walked with long strides and appeared to assimilate the countryside in long panoramic sweeps of his eyes. The mist hung over the spruce forest in front of us. The water in the lake shone black between the tree trunks. A tractor came down the road on the other side.

'Are you enjoying yourself here?' dad said.

'Ye-es,' I said, unsure where this was leading.

He stopped.

'Could you imagine living here?'

'Ye-es,' I said.

'We might take over the farm here one day. Would you like that?'

'Living here?'

'Yes. When the time comes, it's a real possibility.'

I thought Kjartan would take over the farm, but I didn't say so, it would have ruined a wonderful moment for him.

'Come on, let's have a look around,' he said, striding out again.

Live there?

Oh, that was certainly a novel idea. It was impossible to visualise dad there, in that house, surrounded by those things. Dad drying hay? Dad mowing hay and putting it in the silo? Dad spreading muck on the fields? Dad sitting in his chair in the living room listening to the weather forecast?

Even though history didn't exist for me when I went there as a child and everything belonged to the moment, I could still feel its presence. Grandad had lived there all his life, and in some way or other that influenced the image I had of him. But if there was one image or notion that embodied grandad, it was not everything he had done in his life, of that I knew very little, and the little I did know, I had nothing to compare it with, no, the one thing that embodied grandad was the little two-stroke tractor he used for a multitude of purposes. That tractor was the very essence of grandad. It was red and a bit rusty, needed to be kick-started and had a small gear stick, a column with a black ball on top, on one hand lever, while the accelerator was on the other. He used it for mowing, walking behind it while an enormous scissor-like attachment on the front cut down the grass in its path. And he used it to transport heavy items; then he put a trailer on the back with a green seat, from which he steered what all of a sudden had become a lorry-like vehicle.

There was little I rated higher than being with him then, sitting on the back and chugging towards the two shops in Vågen, for example, where he would collect cans of formic acid or sacks of feed or artificial manure. The vehicle was so slow you could walk beside it, but that didn't matter, speed wasn't of any consequence, all the rest was: the rattle of the engine, the exhaust fumes which smelled so good and wafted across the road as we drove, the feeling of freedom on the trailer, being able to hang over one side, then the other, all the things there were to see on the journey, including grandad's slight figure and his peaked cap in front of me, and getting out at the shop, where the Bergen boat docked and being able to walk around, often with an ice cream in our hands while grandad did whatever he had to do.

They also had a handcart with which they used to transport heavy items over short distances, such as the milk canisters which were trundled down to the milk ramp by the road for collection. The cart was made of metal and the wheels were as big as those on a bike. Other things no one else had at home were: scythes, the three big ones with wooden shafts and the small ones that you had to bend down to use, and the big whetstone outside the shed, where they were sharpened; the pitchforks with their three long thin prongs. The flat heavy shovels used to toss cow muck into the cellar, which was beneath a hatch in the floor of the cowshed. The electric fence, which Yngve tricked me into pissing on for the first and last time. The hay racks, these strange, extended, timid creatures standing outside all farms waiting for alms, unless you saw them from a distance or in the darkness, in which case they looked more like military units lined up ready for battle. The large round griddle grandma cooked her cakes on. The black waffle maker. The filters and the flat metal filtering devices used for the milk, and even the milk canisters with their plump bodies and short headless necks, the way they stopped their flustered mumbling and chattering when filled to the top with milk and how they were then placed on the cart and trundled down to the ramp, side by side, suddenly solemn and dignified – that is, if one of them didn't gaily rock to and fro whenever the wheel hit a pothole in the road. And, oh, grandad standing by the cowshed and singing the cows inside every afternoon.

'Come by here, my cows!' he sang. 'Kum by ya! Kum by ya!'

How could I tell my friends at home about all this when they asked where we had been and what we had done on holiday? It was impossible, and it was supposed to be impossible, there was a Chinese wall between the two worlds, both in my mind and the world outside.

In the two weeks we were there the unfamiliar became familiar and homely, while home, after a long day of travelling by car, had become unfamiliar, or had been lowered into the pool of unfamiliarity, for as we drove down the hill after Tromøya Bridge and turned into the last stretch up to the house, brown with red frames, surrounded by a lawn parched and scorched, the dark windows staring at us through sorrowful eyes, it was as if I both recognised it yet didn't, because although my gaze was accustomed to all it saw, it put up some resistance, a bit like a pair of new trainers can, lying there, gleaming in their un-used-ness and, as it were, refusing to adapt to their latest surroundings, insisting on their distinctive character, until the resistance has been worn down over a few weeks and they are just one pair among many. Some of this feeling of newness was conferred on the estate when we arrived, it had been stirred up, so to speak, and wasn't to settle for quite a few days.

Dad parked and switched off the engine. A little white kitten lay sleeping on mum's lap. It had miaowed and squealed in the cage all morning, and when it was finally let out it had run around the back seat and on the ledge under the rear window until mum caught it and at last it fell asleep and was quiet. It had completely red eyes, and although its coat was big and furry, underneath it was tiny. Especially the head, I thought as I was patting it and felt the small cranium in my hand, but also the neck. It was so thin.

'Where's Whitie going to live?' I said.

'Oh, what a name,' dad said, opening the door and getting out.

'We'll have to give it a room in the cellar,' mum said, lifting the kitten to her bosom with one hand and opening the door with the other.

Dad pulled the seat forward and I stepped out onto the shingle, my legs like jelly. Yngve got out on the opposite side, and together we followed dad to the house. He unlocked the door and went into the laundry room, where he opened the hatch and poked the hosepipe through. He screwed the other end to the tap, and then he walked out with the sprinkler in his hand while mum, Yngve and I went into the cellar storeroom, where the kitten, who was still sleeping, was given a basket with a blanket in, a bowl of water and a bowl containing some pieces of sausage from the fridge, and then we put a low plastic tray of sand in the corner.

'Now we'll close all the doors except this one,' mum said. 'So he can't run away when he wakes up.'

While the thin jets of water from the sprinkler rotated around the lawn and dad carried in the baggage from the car below us, Yngve, mum and I sat having supper in the kitchen. It was Sunday, all the shops were closed and so mum had brought a loaf and some butter, meat and cheese from Sørbøvåg. We drank tea; I had it with milk and three spoonfuls of sugar.

Suddenly we heard the kitten squeaking from the hall. We got up, all of us, and went out. He was at the top of the stairs. On seeing us, he ran down again. We followed. Mum called him. He shot across the floor, darted past us, bounded up the stairs and into the living room, where he hid. For several minutes we went around searching and calling until Yngve found him. He was in the narrow gap between the bookcase and the wall, impossible to reach unless you moved the whole bookcase.

Mum went downstairs to fetch the bowls of food and water, put them beside the bookcase and said he would come out when he wanted them. When I went in next morning he still hadn't moved. In the evening he came out and ate something, then he disappeared again. He stayed there for three days. But when he did eventually come out it was for good. He was still a bit jittery at first, but he got more and more used to us and after a week he was running around and playing and jumping onto our laps and purred whenever we stroked him. Every evening he stood in front of the TV smacking whatever appeared on the screen with his paw. He was particularly interested in football. He ignored all the players, he only had eyes for the ball, which he watched with the utmost attention. Now and then he padded behind the TV set to look for it.

When school started again, he began to cough. It was comical, it sounded as if there was a person downstairs in the cellar. Slowly and imperceptibly, the mornings became cooler until one day there was a thin glassy layer of ice on the puddles in the road, which had melted after a few hours, but nevertheless autumn was at the door. The leaves on the trees straddling the hill above our house turned yellow and red and spiralled down from the branches when the wind gusted in. Mum was unwell and in bed when I left for school in the morning and returned some hours later. I went in to talk to her and she could barely raise her head. At the same time Whitie fell ill: he lay in his basket coughing. At school I kept wondering how he was and on my return the first thing I did was to go into the cellar storeroom. If only he would get well soon! But the opposite happened, he got worse and, one day when I ran in to see him, he wasn't in his basket but in the corner, on the concrete floor, writhing to and fro and wheezing. I placed my hand on him, but he kept on writhing.

'Mum! Mum!' I shouted. 'He's dying! He's dying!'

I flew up the stairs and wrenched open the door to her room. She turned sleepily to me with a smile.

'You've got to ring for a vet!' I shouted. 'Right now! It's urgent!' She sat up gingerly.

'What's going on?' she said.

'Whitie's dying! He's writhing around on the floor. He's in such pain! You've got to ring for a vet! At once!'

'But we can't, Karl Ove,' mum said. 'I don't think anything will help. And I'm ill . . .'

'You've got to ring now!' I shouted. 'Mum, Mum, he's dying! Don't you understand?'

'I can't, don't you understand? I'm sorry. It's no good.'

'But Whitie's DYING!'

She gently shook her head.

'But Mum!'

She sighed.

'He was probably already ill when we took him with us. He's an albino as well. They're often a bit weaker. There's nothing we can do. Nothing.'

I looked at her with my eyes full of tears. Then I slammed the door and ran down to the cellar. He was lying on his side, pulling himself along by his claws on the floor and wheezing. Spasms shook through him. I bent down and patted him. Then I ran out, down into the forest, right down to the water. Up again on the other side. Crying non-stop. When our house came into sight again I ran as fast as I could, I had to try and persuade her again. She wasn't a vet, what did she know about what they could or couldn't do? I opened the door and paused. Inside the house there was silence. Carefully I crept into the storeroom. He was back in his basket, lying still, with his head rolled back.

'Mum!' I yelled. 'Come here!'

I dashed up the stairs and opened the door to her room again.

'He's not moving,' I said. 'Could you check to see if he's dead? Or if he's recovered.'

'Do you think you can wait until your father comes?' she said. 'He won't be long.'

'No!' I said.

Mum stared at me.

'OK, I can do it,' she said. She lifted the duvet, placed her feet on the ground and stood up, all at the same slow speed. She was wearing a white nightdress. Her hair was in a mess, her face pale and softer than when she was well. She steadied herself with one hand against the wardrobe. I ran downstairs and waited for her outside the storeroom. I didn't want to be inside on my own.

She leaned forward and felt the kitten.

'I'm sorry,' she said. 'But I think he's dead.'

She looked at me and got up. I put my arms around her.

'He won't be in any more pain,' she said.

'No,' I said.

I wasn't crying.

'Shall we bury him straight away?' I said.

'It's best to wait until dad and Yngve come home, don't you think?'

'Yes,' I said.

And so we did. While mum was in bed dad carried the kitten to a corner of the garden, followed by Yngve and me, dug a hole in the ground, put the kitten in and shovelled earth over it. He wouldn't hear of a cross.

*

There are two pictures of the kitten. In one he's standing in front of the television with a raised paw, trying to catch a swimmer. In the other he's lying on the sofa beside Yngve and me. He has a blue bow tie around his neck.

Who put the bow tie on?

It must have been mum. That was the sort of thing she would do, I know that, but during the months I have been writing this, in the spate of memories about events and people who have been roused to life, she is almost completely absent, it is as if she hadn't been there, indeed as if she were one of the false memories you have, one you have been told, not one you have experienced.

How can that be?

For if there was someone there, at the bottom of the well that is my childhood, it was her, my mother, mum. She was the one who made all our meals and gathered us around her in the kitchen every evening. She was the one who went shopping, knitted or sewed our clothes; she was the one who repaired them when they fell apart. She was the one who supplied the plaster when we had fallen and grazed our knees; she was the one who drove me to hospital when I broke my collarbone, and to the doctor's when I, somewhat less heroically, had scabies. She was the one who was out of her mind with worry when a young girl died from meningitis and at the same time I got a cold and a bit of a stiff neck. I was bundled straight into the car, off to Kokkeplassen, her foot flat on the accelerator, concern flashing from her eyes. She was the one who read to us, she was the one who washed our hair when we were in the bath and she was the one who laid out our pyjamas afterwards. She was the one who drove us to football training in the evening, the one who went to parents' meetings and sat with other parents at our end-of-term parties and took pictures of us. She was the one who stuck the photos in our albums afterwards. She was the one who baked cakes for our birthdays and cakes for Christmas and buns for Shrovetide.

All the things mothers do for their sons, she did for us. If I was ill and in bed with a temperature she was the one who came in with a cold compress and placed it on my forehead, she was the one who put the thermometer up my backside to take my temperature, she was the one who came in with water, juice, grapes, biscuits, and she was the one who got up in the night and came in wearing her nightdress to see how I was.

She was always there, I know she was, but I just can't remember it.

I have no memories of her reading to me and I can't remember her putting a single plaster on my knees or being present at a single end-of-term event.

How can that be?

She saved me because if she hadn't been there I would have grown up alone with dad, and sooner or later I would have taken my life, one way or another. But she was there, dad's darkness had a counterbalance, I am alive and the fact that I do not live my life to the full has nothing to do with the balance of my childhood. I am alive, I have my own children and with them I have tried to achieve only one aim: that they shouldn't be afraid of their father.

They aren't. I know that.

When I enter a room, they don't cringe, they don't look down at the floor, they don't dart off as soon as they glimpse an opportunity, no, if they look at me, it is not a look of indifference, and if there is anyone I am happy to be ignored by it is them. If there is anyone I am happy to be taken for granted by, it is them. And should they have completely forgotten I was there when they turn forty themselves, I will thank them and take a bow and accept the bouquets.

Dad knew what the situation was. Lack of self-knowledge was not one of his failings. One evening at the beginning of the 1980s he said to Prestbakmo that it was mum who had saved his children. The question is whether it was enough. The question is whether she was not responsible for exposing us to him for so many years, a man we were afraid of, always, at all times. The question is whether it is enough to be a counterbalance to the darkness.

She made a decision: she stayed with him, she must have had her reasons.

The same applies to him. He also made a decision, he also stayed. Throughout the 1970s and the beginning of the 1980s this is the way they lived, side by side, in the house in Tybakken, with their two children, their two cars and their two jobs. They had a life outside the house, a life in the house in the way they were to each other and a life in the house in the way they were to us. We, as children, were like dogs in a crowd of people, only interested in other dogs or doggy things, we were never aware of what else was happening, over our heads. I had a vague sense of who dad was outside the house, for something seeped down, even to me, but it never made any sense. He was always well turned out, I was aware of that, but not what significance it carried, only when I was older and met some of his former pupils could I see him in that role. A young, slim, well-dressed teacher stepping out of his Opel Ascona, walking with determined strides up to the staffroom, putting down his briefcase full of papers, pouring a cup of coffee, exchanging a few words with colleagues, going to his class when the bell rang, hanging his brown cord jacket on the chair and scanning the class, who sat quietly looking at him. He had a well-groomed black beard, sparkling blue eyes and a handsome face. The boys in the class feared him; he was strict and tolerated no nonsense. The girls in the class were in love with him because he was young, had a strong aura and looked nothing like any of the other teachers. He liked teaching and he was good at it, he held his classes in a spell when he spoke about subjects that engaged him. Obstfelder was his favourite. But he also liked Kinck and, of the contemporary writers, Bjørneboe.

He was very correct in his dealings with colleagues, but also kept his distance. The distance lay in his attire; many of the other teachers would wear smocks and jeans or the same suit for months on end. The distance lay in the impartiality he exhibited. The distance lay in his body language, his posture, his aura.

He always knew more about them than they knew about him. It was a rule in his life, which applied to everyone, even his parents and brothers. Or perhaps especially to them.

When he came home from school he went into his study and prepared the evening meetings; he was a Venstre representative on the council, as well as sitting on several committees, and at one point he was a possible Storting candidate for his party, according to him. But what he said wasn't always true, he was notorious for manipulating the truth in the circles in which he moved, although not in his work at school or in politics, where he was proper and seemly. He was also a member of a philately club in Grimstad and showed his collection at a variety of exhibitions. In the summer he devoted himself to the garden, where he was also ambitious and a perfectionist, if such is conceivable in a garden around a house on an estate in the 70s. He had inherited his interest in everything that grew from his mother, and that was perhaps what they spoke about most: various plants, bushes and trees and the experiences they'd had with them. Sun, soil, moisture, acidity levels. Grafting, pruning, watering. With no friends, his social intercourse took place in the staffroom and the family. He visited his parents, brothers, uncles and aunts frequently and received frequent visits from them. With them he used a tone of voice that was unfamiliar to Yngve and me, and we therefore viewed it with suspicion.

Mum's life differed in many ways from his. She had lots of friends, mostly because of her job, but also in other places, not least among the neighbours. With them she would sit and chat, or 'prattle' as dad would say, and smoke and eat the cakes they had baked – if, that is, they weren't knitting in the thick cloud of tobacco smoke that hung in so many living rooms in the 70s. She had an interest in politics, was in favour of a strong state, a well-developed health system and equal rights for all, and was probably committed to women's liberation and the peace movement, was against capitalism and the growing materialism, and sympathised with Erik Dammann's *The Future in our Hands* movement; in short she was on the left. She said she had hibernated during her twenties, everything was about her job, her children and making ends meet, the budget was tight, you had to fight to keep to it, although in her early thirties she focused on herself and the society she was living in. While dad rarely read anything other than what he had to, she was genuinely interested in literature. She was an idealist, he was a pragmatist; she was contemplative, he was practical.

They brought us up together even if I never experienced my

upbringing as such; I always drew a strict distinction between them and perceived them as two utterly separate beings. But for them it must have been different. In the evenings when we were asleep they sat up talking about the neighbours, colleagues, us the children, unless they were discussing politics or literature. Once in a while they went on holiday alone, to London, to the Rhine Valley or into the mountains, while Yngve and I were with either mum's or dad's parents. They were more equal than the parents of my friends as far as chores in the house were concerned: dad cleaned and cooked, which none of the other fathers did, not to mention all the food gathering they did at that time, all the fish he caught on the far side of the island and the hundreds of kilos of berries we picked on trips to the mainland in late summer and autumn, which afterwards they converted into juice and jam and poured into bottles and jars to stand on the shelves in the cellar all winter, glowing dimly in the light from the little window at the top of the wall. Raspberries, blackberries, blueberries, cowberries and cloud-berries, which would excite dad so much he would shout out if he found any. Sloes for wine. In addition, they would pay to pick fruit from gardens on Tromøya, and it was from there we had apples, pears and plums. Then there was the cherry tree belonging to dad's Uncle Alf in Kristiansand and of course both grandmothers had fruit trees. Our days were structured and clear: on Sundays it was lunch with dessert, on weekdays it was generally a variety of shapes and kinds of fish. We always knew when we had school on the following day, how many lessons we had in which subjects, and not even the course of the evening was without a framework, as it was seasonally determined: if there was snow or ice on the ground, then it was skiing and skating. If the water temperature rose above fifteen degrees, well then swimming was the order of the day, come rain come shine. The sole really unpredictable factor in this life, from autumn to winter, spring to summer, from one school year to the next, was dad. I was so frightened of him that even with the greatest effort of will I am unable to re-create the fear; the feelings I had for him I have never felt since, nor indeed anything close.

His footsteps on the stairs – was he coming to see me?

The wild glare in his eyes. The tightness around his mouth. The lips that parted involuntarily. And then his voice.

Sitting here now, hearing it in my inner ear, I almost start crying.

His fury struck like a wave, it washed through the rooms, lashed at me, lashed and lashed and lashed at me, and then it retreated. Then it could be quiet for several weeks. However, it wasn't quiet, for it could just as easily come in two minutes as two days. There was no warning. Suddenly, there he was, furious. Whether he hit me or not made no difference, it was equally awful if he twisted my ear or squeezed my arm or dragged me somewhere to see what I had done, it wasn't the pain I was afraid of, it was him, his voice, his face, his body, the fury it emitted, that was what I was afraid of, and the terror never let up, it was there for every single day of my entire childhood.

After the confrontations I wanted to die. Dying was one of the best, most enjoyable fantasies I had. He would have fun then. He would be standing there thinking about what he had done. He would be feeling remorse then. Oh, what remorse he would feel! I visualised him standing there and wringing his hands in despair with his head turned to heaven in front of the tiny coffin where I lay, with my prominent teeth, no longer able to pronounce my 'r's.

What sweetness there was in that image! It almost put me in a good mood again. And that was how my childhood was: the distance between good and evil was so much shorter than it is now as an adult. All you had to do was stick your head out of the door and something absolutely fantastic happened. Just walking up to B-Max and waiting for the bus was an event, even though it had been repeated almost every day for many years. Why? I have no idea. But when everything glinted with moisture in the mist and your boots were wet from the slush on the road, and the snow in the forest was white and sunken, and we stood in a gang chatting or playing, or we ran after girls to trip them up, pinch their woolly hats or simply throw them into a snow-drift, and I felt one of them against me as I squeezed my arms around their waists as tight as I could, perhaps Marianne, perhaps Siv, perhaps Marian, because they were the girls I prized and thought about most, all my nerves were a-quiver, my chest bubbled with joy – and why? Oh, because of the wet snow. Because of the wet down jackets. Because of the many good-looking girls. Because of the bus rattling along with chains on its tyres. Because of the condensation on the windows when we went inside, because of the screaming and shouting, because Anne Lisbet was there, as happy and lovely, as dark-haired and red-mouthed, as she had ever been. Every day was a party, in the sense that everything that happened pulsated with excitement and nothing was predictable. Nor was it over when the bus came, it had only just begun, for the whole school day stretched out before us, with the transformation we went through when our wet clothes were hanging on hooks and we shuffled into the classroom on stockinged feet, with red cheeks and messy hair, wet at the tips because it had been outside the hat. The tingling in your body as the break beckoned, and we ran up the stairs, through the corridors, down the outside steps, across the playground, down the slope and onto the pitch. And afterwards, going home, playing music, reading, perhaps putting on skis and racing down the steep hill to Ubekilen, where the others always were, and all this at the intensity that only exists in childhood, standing at the bottom, back up herringbone style, racing down, until the darkness was so dense we could hardly see a hand in front of our faces and hung over our ski sticks chatting about everything and nothing.

The glimpse of ice on the bay covered by a shallow layer of water. The lights from the houses on the estate, which formed a kind of cupola over the forest above us. All the sounds the darkness amplified whenever someone shifted weight and the blue mini-skis scraped against each other or cut into the soft snow. The car that came down the narrow gravelled road, it was a Beetle, belonging to the people who lived there, the light shining a path across the ground, making everything spookily visible for a moment or two and then the darkness closing around us again.

Childhood consisted of an infinity of such moments, all equally compact. Some of them could raise me to dizzying heights, like the evening I got together with Tone and half ran, half slid down the hill, which must have just been cleared by the snowplough, judging by the shiny surface, and when I arrived at the dark patch between the roads outside our house, I lay down in the snow on my back and looked up at the dense, clammy and lightless night above me and was utterly happy.

Others could open a void beneath me, like the evening mum told us she was going to start studying the following year. We were at the table eating supper when she told us.

'The school's in Oslo,' she said. 'It's just for one year. I'll come home every Friday and I'll be here all weekend. Then I'll go back on the Monday. So that's three days here and four there.'

'Are we going to be alone here with dad?' Yngve said.

'Yes. It'll be fine. You'll see a bit more of each other.'

'Why are you going to go to school?' I said. 'You're an adult.'

'There's something called further education,' she said. 'I'm going to learn more about my profession. It's very exciting, you know.'

'I don't want you to go,' I said.

'It's just for a year,' she said. 'And I'll be here for three days a week. And all the holidays. I'm going to have long holidays.'

'I still don't want you to go,' I said.

'I understand,' mum said. 'But it'll be fine. Dad wants to spend time with you. And next year it will be the other way around. Dad will do a further education course and I'll be at home.'

I took the last mouthful of tea, closed my mouth and let it seep through, as I blocked the many wet black tea leaves at the bottom with my lips.

I half-rose and lifted the heavy teapot over to the cup with both hands, poured and put it back. The tea was almost black, it had been brewing for so long. I added a generous portion of milk and three large spoonfuls of sugar.

'Sugar in tea,' Yngve said.

'And?' I said.

At that moment there was the sound of footsteps on the stairs.

Oh, and I had filled the cup to the brim! I would have to sit there until it was drunk. But Yngve had no such reservations; he stood up and was gone.

Dad walked past with sombre step. He switched on the television and sat down on a chair.

'Would you like some supper?' mum said.

'No,' he said.

I poured in more milk to make the tea colder and drank it up in three long swigs.

'Thank you, Mum!' I said, getting up.

'Pleasure,' mum said.

*

The news was shocking, but I wasn't shocked as I went to my room afterwards, it was April now and the course she was doing didn't start until August. That was four months away and for a child four months is an eternity. Mum's further education course belonged to the future in the same vague way that my next school did or confirmation or my eighteenth birthday. We were in mid-childhood and time was suspended there. That is, the moments raced along at breakneck speed while the days that contained them passed almost unnoticed. Even when the last day of school arrived and we were no longer in the third class I didn't think that soon she would be off. Wasn't there the whole of the long summer holiday to go yet? It was only when she was in her bedroom taking out her clothes and a suitcase lay open on the floor that I realised. At the same time there were so many other things going on, the next day school would be starting again, when we, the fourth class, would definitively belong to the oldest children. We would have a new classroom, and more importantly, a new class teacher. Inside my room there was a new satchel, in the wardrobe there were new clothes. The thought of all this made my stomach tingle, and although I was sad watching her pack I was no sadder than I usually was when she went to work.

She stopped packing and looked at me.

'I'll be back on Thursday,' she said. 'It's only four days.'

'I know,' I said. 'Have you got everything?'

'You know what, I think I have,' she said. 'Would you mind helping me with the suitcase? Put your knee there so that I can close it properly?'

I nodded and did as she asked.

Dad came up the stairs.

'Are you ready?' he said with a nod at the suitcase. 'I'll take it.'

Mum gave me a hug and then she followed him downstairs.

I watched them from the bathroom window. As she got into the green Beetle it was exactly like any afternoon when she had to go to work – apart from the suitcase in the boot, that is. I waved, she waved back, started the engine, reversed up the incline, put the car in first gear and it beetled down the hill the way it always did and was gone.

What would happen now?

What would the days be like now?

It was mum who bound us all together, it was mum who was at the centre of Yngve's and my life, we knew that, dad knew that, but perhaps she didn't. How else could she leave us like this?

Knives and forks clinking on plates, elbows moving, heads held stiff, straight backs. No one saying a word. That is us three, a father and two sons, sitting and eating. Around us, on all sides, it is the 70s.

The silence grows. And we notice it, all three of us, the silence is not the kind that can ease, it is the kind that lasts a lifetime. Well of course you can say something inside it, you can talk, but the silence doesn't stop for that reason.

Dad put the bone on the plate with the potato skin and took another chop. Yngve and I were given only one each.

Yngve had finished.

'Thank you, Dad,' he said.

'There's dessert,' dad said.

'Don't want any,' Yngve said. 'Thanks, anyway.'

'Why don't you want any?' dad said. 'It's pineapple and cream. You like it.'

'It gives me so many spots,' Yngve said.

'I see,' dad said. 'You can leave the table.'

He looked at me as though Yngve didn't exist when he got up.

'But you want some, don't you, Karl Ove?'

'You bet,' I said. 'It's my favourite.'

'Good,' he said.

I sat looking out of the window waiting for him to finish. Listening to the music from Yngve's room. A crowd of children had collected in the road, they put two rocks on the ground as a goal, immediately afterwards there was the sound of heavy thuds as boots hit an under-inflated ball and of low shouts, which always increase in volume when football is played, whatever form it takes.

At last dad got up, took the plates and scraped them clean over the bin. He put a bowl of pineapple and cream in front of me and one in front of himself.

We finished the dessert without saying a word.

'Thanks, Dad,' I said, getting up. Dad said nothing, but got up as well, filled the coffee pot with water and took a packet of coffee from the cupboard.

Then he turned.

'Karl Ove?' he said.

'Yes,' I said.

'Now don't you tease Yngve about his spots, do you understand what I'm saying? I don't ever want to hear a word about it again.'

'OK,' I said and stood waiting to see if there was more to come.

Dad turned and cut off the corner of the coffee packet, and I went into Yngve's room, where he was playing his electric guitar, a black Les Paul copy I had been so surprised to hear the first time, as I was convinced not a sound would come from it without an amplifier. But it did, a low plunking sound, he was sitting there and playing with a face full of spots.

'Shall we play something?' I said.

'I already am,' he said.

'A game, you chump,' I said.

'Fifty-two-card pick-up?' he said.

'Ha ha,' I said. 'You can only do that once and I've already done it. Can you teach me a chord?'

'Not now. Another time.'

'Please.'

'One then,' he said. 'Sit here.'

I sat down beside him on the bed. He put the guitar in my lap. Placed three fingers on the finger board.

'That's an E,' he said and took his hand away.

I put my fingers where he'd had his.

'Good,' he said. 'Now strum.'

I strummed, but not all the strings made a sound.

'You have to press harder,' he said. 'And you have to watch your other fingers don't catch the free strings.'

'OK,' I said and tried again.

'That was good,' he said. 'That's the way. Now you can do E.'

I passed him the guitar and got up.

'Do you remember which strings are which then?' he said.

'EADGBE,' I said.

'Correct,' he said. 'Now all you need is a band.'

'But then I would have to borrow your guitar,' I said.

'You can't have it.'

I said nothing because things could change so quickly.

'When do you start tomorrow?' I said instead.

'First lesson,' he said. 'And you?'

'No, at eleven, I think.'

'Think?'

'Know. Dad?'

'First lesson, dead sure.'

That was good news. I would be alone for a few hours.

I turned and went into my room. The new satchel was by the desk leg. The square blue one I'd had for years had become too small and childish. The one I had now was dark green and made of some synthetic material that smelled wonderful.

I sniffed at it for a while. Then I put on *Sgt. Pepper's Lonely Hearts Club Band* and lay back on my bed staring at the ceiling.

Getting so much better all the time!
It's getting better all the time!
Better, better, better!
It's getting better all the time!
Better, better, better!
Getting so much better all the time!

The music lifted me at once, I beat the air with one hand and rocked my head backwards and forwards, happy to the core. *Bettåh, bettåh, bettåh!* I sang. *Bettåh, bettåh, bettåh!*

There was the school building, black, with all its many windows glinting, as we stormed off the bus. We were among the older pupils now and knew both how to behave and what to expect. While the new kids, hair combed and smartly dressed, stood with their parents listening to the head teacher's welcome talk by the flagpole, we swaggered around and spat or leaned against the wall of the wet-weather shed talking about what we had done that summer. Three cows on a farm was no longer good enough, but even if our only holiday trip had been to Sørbøvåg, where I had stayed with Jon Olav and the others, alone for a week, I definitely had something to offer because there had been a girl there, my second cousin, whose name was Merete, she had blonde hair and lived outside Oslo. I went out with her, I said, and although that was not quite as impressive as Liseberg in Gothenburg, northern Europe's biggest funfair, it was better than nothing.

Some of the girls unfurled their skipping elastic from what were to me hidden places and started jumping.

No, *dancing*.

We managed to persuade them to play the high jump instead, so that we could join in without losing face in front of the other boys. Two of the girls held the elastic between them, and then, one after the other, we ran towards it, launched both legs and brought our feet down on it to land on the other side.

It was a pleasure to watch the girls as they took off, legs first, in their elegant controlled fashion.

Whoosh, you heard, and then they were safely on the other side.

Then the height was raised until there was only one person left.

I hoped it would be me because Anne Lisbet had joined us now as well, but it was, as so often before, Marianne.

Tap, tap, tap, you heard as she ran forward, *whoosh*, you heard when she jumped, and then she was over.

She smiled shyly, swept her shoulder-length blonde hair to one side with a finger, and I wondered if she would be the one I fell in love with this year.

Probably not. She was in my class.

Perhaps it would be someone in the A class?

Or, hey, future of dreams, perhaps someone from *another* school?

After we had been given the timetable and some new books in the first lesson we had to tell the class what we had done over the summer, one after the other. In the second lesson we had to hold an election for the new school council. I had been the class rep with Siv in the previous year and I thought being re-elected would be a formality until Eivind put up his hand and said he would also like to stand as a candidate. There were six names to choose from. Eivind's involvement led to my breaking the unwritten rule that you never, under any circumstances, voted for yourself. I thought the election might be touch and go, so one vote could be decisive. I considered the chances of anyone finding out that I had voted for myself unlikely in the extreme. After all, it was a secret ballot, and the only person who would see what we wrote as well as our handwriting, and could therefore expose me, was Frøken, and she wouldn't say anything.

How cruelly mistaken I was.

I wrote KARL OVE in capital letters on the little scrap of paper, folded it and gave it to Frøken when she came round with a hat. On the board she wrote the names of the six candidates, and then she called on Sølvi, of all people, to read out the ballot slips. Every time Sølvi read out a name she put a cross by the appropriate person on the board.

It was taking time for my votes to start coming in. At first Eivind got most of the boys' votes. Then I realised to my horror that there were no more votes. I hadn't received a single one! How was that possible?

But there. At last.

'Karl Ove,' Sølvi said, and Frøken put a cross beside my name.

'Eivind,' Sølvi said.

'Eivind.'

'Eivind.'

'And that must be it, isn't it? Now let's see. The class reps on the council this year are therefore Eivind and Marianne!'

I looked down at the desk in front of me.

One vote.

How was that possible?

And, to cap it all off, the one vote was my own.

But I was the best student in the class! At least in Norwegian! And natural and social sciences! And in maths I was the second best, or perhaps the third. But, altogether, who could be better than me?

OK, Eivind won. But one vote? How was that possible?

Hadn't anyone voted for me?

There had to be a mistake somewhere.

No one?

When I opened our front door dad was standing inside.

I gave a start of surprise.

How had he managed that?

Had he been waiting for me?

'You've got to go to B-Max for me,' he said. 'Look.'

He passed me a shopping list and a hundred-krone note.

'I want all the change back, OK?'

'Yes,' I said, put down my satchel and ran into the road.

If there was one area in this world where I was meticulous it was with dad's change. When B-Max had just opened Yngve returned home with less change than there should have been. Dad gave him the beating of his life. And that was no small matter because Yngve had been on the receiving end of quite a few beatings. Many more than me. Yes, I got off lightly with everything. Even my bedtimes were lenient compared with his.

I looked at the list.

1 kilo of potatoes
1 packet of rissoles

2 onions
Coffee (for boiling)
1 tin of pineapple slices
¼ kilo of whipping cream
1 kilo of oranges

Pineapple? Were we going to have dessert again? On a Monday?

I put all the items in a basket, stood flicking through some magazines on the shelf by the counter, paid, put the change in my pocket and ran home with the heavy bag hanging from my hand.

I passed it to dad upstairs in the kitchen with the change, which he pocketed while I waited for him to say I could go. But he didn't.

'Sit!' he said, pointing to the chair.

I sat.

'Straighten your back, boy!' he said.

I straightened my back.

He took the potatoes, which were covered in soil, from the bag and started peeling them.

What was it he wanted?

'Well?' he said, turning to look at me while his hands worked under the water from the tap.

I looked at him in surprise.

'What did Frøken have to say?' he said.

'Frøken?'

'Yes, *Fwøken*. Didn't she have anything to say to all of you on your first day?'

'Yes, she did, she welcomed us back. Then we were given our timetable and some books.'

'What's your timetable like then?' he said, walking over to the cupboard by the stove and taking out a saucepan.

'Shall I go and get it?'

'No, no. You must remember some of it, don't you? Did it look good?'

'Yes,' I said. 'Great.'

'That's good,' he said.

That evening I realised what mum's absence meant.

The rooms were lifeless.

Dad sat downstairs in his study, and the living room and kitchen were 'out there', dead. I tiptoed towards them, and the feeling that came over me when I was alone in the forest, when the forest was sufficient unto itself and it didn't want to incorporate me, re-emerged here as well.

The rooms were only rooms, a gaping space I entered.

But not my room, thank goodness. It wrapped itself around me, soft and friendly as it had always been.

The next day Sverre and Geir Håkon came over to me in B-Max. Several kids from the class were standing around us.

'Who did you vote for yesterday, Karl Ove?' Geir Håkon said.

'It's a secret,' I said.

'You voted for yourself. You got only one vote, and that was the one you gave yourself.'

'No, it wasn't,' I said.

'Yes, it was,' Sverre said. 'We've asked everyone in the class. No one voted for you. So you're the only one left. You voted for yourself.'

'No,' I said. 'That's not true. I didn't vote for myself.'

'Who did then?'

'I don't know.'

'But we've asked everyone. No one voted for you. You voted for yourself. Come on, admit it.'

'No,' I said. 'It's not true.'

'But we've asked everyone. There's only you left.'

'Then someone's lying.'

'Why would anyone lie?'

'How should I know?'

'You're the one who's lying. You voted for yourself.'

'No, I did not.'

The rumour spread through the school, but I denied everything. And kept denying it. Everyone knew what had happened, but as long as I didn't admit it, they couldn't be *absolutely* sure. They thought it was typical of me. I thought I *was* someone. But I didn't think that. A person who votes for himself is a nobody. The fact that I never went scrumping, never did any shoplifting, never fired a catapult at birds or a pea-shooter loaded with cherry stones at cars or passers-by and never joined in when others locked the gym teacher behind the garage door in the equipment room or when others put drawing pins on the supply teachers' chairs or dunked their sponges until they were sopping wet, plus the fact that I told them they shouldn't do these things, told them it was wrong, did not do a great deal for my reputation either. I knew, however, that I was right and what the others were doing was wrong. Occasionally I would pray to God to forgive them. If they swore, for example. Then a prayer might come into my mind. *Dear God, Forgive Leif Tore for swearing. He didn't mean to.* I said things like: heck, blast, golly, gosh, crikey, cripes, crumbs, sugar, fudge, blimey, bother and yikes. But despite this, despite not swearing, not lying, except in self-defence, not stealing or vandalising or playing up teachers, despite being interested in clothes and my appearance and always wanting to be right and the best, which meant my general reputation was poor and I was not someone others said they liked, I wasn't shunned or avoided, and if I was, by Leif Tore and Geir

Håkon for instance, there were always boys I could turn to. Such as Dag Lothar. Or Dag Magne. And when all the children got together in big groups no one was rejected, everyone was accepted, including me.

Of course, it was easier to be at home reading.

Nor did it do much for my reputation that I was a Christian. Actually, that was mum's fault. One day, the year before, she had banned the reading of comics. I had come home early from school, run up the stairs, happy and excited as dad was still at work.

'Are you hungry?' she said, sitting on a chair in the living room with a book in her lap and looking at me.

'Yes,' I said.

She got up and went into the kitchen, where she took a loaf from the bread bin.

The rain outside was like stripes in the air. Some stragglers were coming down the road from the bus, heads bowed beneath the hoods of their waterproofs.

'I was looking at some of your comics today,' mum said, cutting a slice of bread. 'What *do* you read? I'm aghast.'

'Aghast?' I said. 'What does that mean?'

She put a slice on the plate in front of me, opened the fridge and took out some mild white cheese and margarine.

'What you read is absolutely awful! It's just violence! People shooting one another and laughing! You're too young to read stuff like this.'

'But everyone does,' I said.

'That's no argument,' she said. 'It doesn't mean *you* have to.'

'But I like it!' I said, spreading the margarine with my knife.

'Yes, that's what's so bad about it!' she said, sitting down. 'That kind of magazine gives a terrible view of humanity. Especially of women. Do you understand? I don't want your attitudes to be shaped by that.'

'By the killing?'

'For example.'

'But it's not meant seriously!' I said.

Mum sighed. 'You know Ingunn's writing a university thesis about the violence in comics, don't you?'

'No,' I said.

'It's not good for you,' she said. 'Simple as that. At least you understand. That it's not good for you.'

'So am I not allowed?'

'No.'

'Eh?'

'It's for your own good,' she said.

'I'm not allowed? But Mum, Mum . . . Never?'

'You'll have to read Donald Duck.'

'DONALD DUCK?' I yelled. '*No one* reads DONALD DUCK!'

I burst into tears and ran to my room.

Mum followed me, sat on the edge of the bed and stroked my back.

'You can read books,' she said. 'That's much better. You can go to the library, you and me and Yngve. To Arendal, once a week. Then you can borrow as many books as you like.'

'But I don't want to read books,' I said. 'I want to read comics!'

'Karl Ove,' she said, 'my mind is made up.'

'But *dad* reads comics!'

'He's an adult,' she said. 'It's not the same.'

'So no more comics *ever* again?'

'I have to work this evening. But tomorrow we can go to the library,' she said and got up. 'Shall we leave it at that?'

I didn't answer, and she left.

*

She must have stumbled on a comic in the *Kamp* series or *Vi Vinner*, which were about war, in which all the Germans, or Fritz or Sauerkraut or whatever they were called, were killed with a smile on their lips, and the pages were littered with *Donnerwetters* and *Dummkopfs* or whatever they shouted to one another in the heat of battle, or she could have found *Agent X9* or *Serie Spesial*, where most of the women wore bikinis and often not even that. It was just great to see Modesty Blaise undressing, though only when I was alone, normally nudity was incredibly embarrassing. Every time *Agaton Sax* was on children's TV I blushed if mum and dad were there because in the intro he was ogling a naked woman through binoculars. Sometimes there was actually some bonking in the cartoons or films on TV, and if it took place when I was allowed to watch, it all became unbearable. There we were, the whole family, mum, dad and their two sons watching TV, and then a couple screwed in the middle of our living room, where did you look?

Oh that was dreadful.

But I kept the comics in my room; mum had never so much as cast a glance at them.

Now, out of the blue, I wasn't allowed to read them.

How unfair was that?

I cried, I was incensed, I went to see her again and said she had no right to ban them knowing that the battle was lost, she had made up her mind and if I didn't stop protesting she would just tell dad, after which further resistance would be hopeless.

The comics I had borrowed were returned; the others were thrown away. The next day we went to the library, we were each given a membership card and then it was done: from this moment on books held sway. Every Wednesday I came down the steps outside Arendal Library with a carrier bag full of books in each hand. I went with mum and Yngve, who had likewise borrowed vast quantities, then it was back to the car, go home, lie down on my bed, read almost every evening, all Saturday and all Sunday, a pattern broken only by shorter or longer sorties outside, all depending on what was going on, and when the week was up it was back to the library with the two bags of finished books and two new bags. I read all the series they had, I liked Pocomoto best, the little boy who grew up in the Wild West, but also Jan, and the Hardy Boys of course, and the Bobbsey Twins and Nancy Drew, the Girl Detective. I liked the Famous Five series and I ploughed through some books about real people, reading about Henry Ford and Thomas Alva Edison, Benjamin Franklin and Franklin D. Roosevelt, Winston Churchill, John F. Kennedy, David Livingstone and Louis Armstrong, always with tears in my eyes over the last pages, because, naturally enough, they all died. I finished the *Vi Var Med* series, about all the known and unknown expeditions of discovery in the world, I read books about sailing ships and space travel, Yngve got me into books by von Däniken, who thought that all the great civilisations had come about as a result of encounters with extraterrestrial creatures, and books about the Apollo programme, starting with the astronauts' fighter-plane pasts and their attempts to set speed records. I also read all dad's old Gyldendal books for boys, of which the one that made the greatest impression was probably *Over Kjølen i Kano*, where a father goes on a camping trip with two boys and sees a great auk everyone thought was extinct. I also read a book about a boy who was picked up by a zeppelin in England during the years between the wars, I read Jules Verne's many books, my favourites being *Twenty Thousand Leagues under the Sea* and *Around the World in Eighty Days*, also one called *The Lottery Ticket* about a poor family in Telemark who won a fortune in a lottery. I read *The Count of Monte Cristo* and *The Three Musketeers*, *Twenty Years After* and *The Black Tulip*. I read *Little Lord Fauntleroy*,

I read *Oliver Twist* and *David Copperfield*, I read *Nobody's Boy* and *Treasure Island* and *The Children of the New Forest*, which I loved and read again and again as I had been given it and didn't borrow it. I read *Mutiny on the Bounty*, Jack London's books and books about the sons of Bedouins and turtle hunters, stowaways and race-car drivers, I read a series about a Swede who was a drummer boy in the American Civil War, I read books about boys who played football and I followed them season after season, and I read the more social issue-style books that Yngve brought home, about girls who got pregnant and were going to have a baby, or who ended up on skid row and started taking drugs, it made no difference to me, I read everything, absolutely everything. At the annual flea market in Hove I found a whole series of the Rocambole books which I bought and devoured. A series about a girl called Ida was another I read even though there must have been all of fourteen titles. I read all dad's old copies of *Detektivmagasinet*, and bought books about Knut Gribb, the Oslo detective, when I had enough money. I read about Christopher Columbus and Magellan, about Vasco da Gama and about Amundsen and Nansen. I read *A Thousand and One Nights* and Norwegian folk tales, which Yngve and I were given one Christmas by grandma and grandad. I read about King Arthur and the Knights of the Round Table. I read about Robin Hood, Little John and Maid Marian, I read about Peter Pan and about poor boys who swapped their lives for those of rich men's sons. I read about boys who participated in sabotage operations during the German occupation of Denmark, and about boys who rescued someone from an avalanche. I read about a strange little man who lived on a beach and survived on what he could salvage from shipwrecks, and about young English boys who were cadets on naval vessels and Marco Polo's adventures at the court of Genghis Khan. Book after book, bag after bag, week after week, month after month. From everything I read I learned that you had to have courage, that courage was perhaps the supreme attribute, that you have to be honest and sincere in all your dealings and that you must never let others down. In addition, that you must never give in, never give up, because if you have been resolute, upright, brave and honest, however lonely it has made you and however alone you stand, in the end you are rewarded. I thought a lot about that, it was one of the thoughts I embraced when I was alone, that one day I would be back here and be someone. That I would be someone big whom everyone in Tybakken would be forced, whether they liked it or not, to admire. It wouldn't come any day soon, I knew that, for it wasn't respect I won when Asgeir made a derogatory comment about me and a girl I liked, and I went for him and he simply forced me to the ground, straddled me and started prodding my chest and cheeks, laughing and jeering. I happened to have a yellow Fox in my mouth and I tried to spit it out at him, to no avail, which was underhand, everyone knew that, but the sticky yellow mess went all over my face. You smell of piss, you shit, I said to him, and it was true, he did. And, if that wasn't enough, he had two sets of teeth, just like a shark, one row inside the other, and I pointed this repugnant sight out to the crowd milling around, not that it helped, I was on my back, vanquished, utterly powerless. You couldn't get further from the ideals I had acquired through reading – which in fact were also valid among children, there were many of the same concepts of honour, although that precise word was not used, but that was what it was about. I was weak, slow, cowardly; not strong, quick, courageous. What good was it that, unlike them, I had been in contact with the ideals, that I knew them inside out, better than any of them ever would, when I couldn't live up to them? When I cried for no reason? It felt unjust that I, of all people, who knew so much about heroic bravery, should be saddled with such frailties. But then there were books about frailties as well, and one of them carried me on a wave that would last several months.

One autumn I fell ill, during the day I lay in bed and was bored and one morning before going to work dad brought me some books. He'd had them in the cellar, they were from his childhood in the 1950s and I was free to borrow them. A handful had been published by a Christian company and for some reason they were the ones that made the strongest impression on me, one of them indelibly. It was about a boy whose father had died and who stayed at home to look after his sick mother; they lived in poverty and were completely dependent on the boy's efforts to make ends meet. He was confronted by a group, or a gang more like, of boys. Not only did they hound and beat up this boy who was so different from them, they swore and stole as well and the inequity of this gang's successes, in the light of the constant setbacks suffered by the honest, loving and upright protagonist, was almost impossible to bear. I cried at the unfairness of it, I cried at the evil of it, and the dynamics of a situation whereby good was suppressed and the pressures of injustice were approaching bursting point shook me to the core of my soul and made me decide to become a good person. From then on I would perform good deeds, help where I could and never do anything wrong. I began to call myself a Christian. I was nine years old, there was no one else in my close vicinity who called themselves a Christian, neither mum nor dad nor the parents of any of the other kids – apart from Øyvind Sundt's parents, who warned him off Coke and sweets and watching TV and going to the cinema – and of course no young people, so it was a fairly solitary undertaking I initiated in Tybakken at the end of the 1970s. I began to pray to God last thing at night and first thing in the morning. When in the autumn the others gathered to go apple scrumping down in Gamle Tybakken I told them not to go, I told them stealing was wrong. I never said this to all of them at once, I didn't dare, I was well aware of the difference between group reactions, when everyone incited each other to do something or other, and individual reactions, when each person was forced to confront an issue head on with no hiding place in a deindividuated crowd, so that was what I did, I went to those I knew best, my peers, and said to each one that apple scrumping was wrong, think about it, you don't have to do it. But I didn't want to be alone, so I accompanied them, stopped by the gate and watched them sneak across the age-old fields in the dusk, walked beside them as they scoffed apples on the way back, their winter jackets bulging with fruit, and if anyone offered me anything I always refused, because dealing was no better than stealing.

When one Easter I made a new friend while visiting my grandparents in Sørbøvåg, I implored him again and again to stop swearing. I can remember how afraid I was that he would disobey my instructions when he came in with me and said hello to grandma and grandad, and how many times I had told him to promise not to swear. Afterwards he avoided me and I coped with this by thinking that I had done the right thing. I offered my seat to elderly people on the bus, asked if I could carry something for them when they came out of supermarkets, never held on to the back of cars, never broke anything, never fired a catapult at birds, looked where I walked so as not to tread on ants or beetles, and even when I picked flowers in the spring with Geir or anyone else to give to mum or dad, my heart sank at the thought of the lives I was taking.

In winter after snowfalls I wanted to help old people shovel it away. On one such day – it was a Monday after school and it had snowed heavily all night – I tried to persuade Geir to come with me to clear someone's drive. It was only by hinting that the old man would probably give us a tip for helping him out that I managed to get him to join me. Dad had just bought a new snow shovel, the type called the Sørland shovel, red, shiny and attractive, and as he had cleaned our drive that morning I assumed he wouldn't need it any more that day, so I went off with it, side by side with Geir, who was pushing their green Sørland shovel in front of him. The house I had chosen was on the bend and, when we rang, the face of the old man opening the door lit up when he realised that we weren't there to throw snowballs at his house, which many did, but to help him clear his drive. It was heavy work but fun; we dug a channel along which we could push the snow over the edge into the ditch, we tipped it here and it rushed down like mini-avalanches. The sky was a leaden grey, the snow so wet that water ran from it if you packed it together. From Torungen we heard the blare of the foghorn. Children raced downhill on sledges or skis, cars going up the hill on their way home from work skidded and spun. It took us an hour to finish the drive. We went to the front door and told the old man, he thanked us and then he closed the door. Geir sent me an accusatory look.

'Weren't we supposed to get money for this?' he said.

'Ye-es. Actually we were. But it's not my fault he didn't give us any . . .'

'Have we done all this for nothing?'

'Looks like it,' I said. 'Doesn't matter. Come on, let's go.'

He followed me, grumbling. As we reached the road in front of our house I saw dad standing in the doorway. My heart felt as though it had stopped beating. My stomach contracted and I could hardly breathe. His eyes were wild.

'Now you come here this minute!' he shouted when I was

in the drive. I fixed my eyes on the ground over the last few steps.

'Look at me!' he said.

I raised my head.

He slapped my face.

I gasped.

Then he grabbed the lapels of my jacket and pressed me against the wall.

'Did you take my Sørland shovel?' he said. 'It's brand new! And it's mine! Don't touch my things! Do you understand? You didn't ask me for permission! I thought it had been stolen!'

I was crying and sobbing so much I barely heard what he said. He grabbed my jacket again, pushed me through the door and sent me flying into the wall on the other side.

'Don't you ever do that again! Never! Go up to your room and stay there until I tell you otherwise! Have you understood?'

'Yes, Dad,' I said.

He slammed his study door and I began to remove my outdoor clothes. My hands were shaking. I took off my mittens and hat, I wriggled out of my boots, then the Puffa pants, then the jacket, then the thick jumper. In my room I lay down on my bed. Everything inside me was red raw. I sobbed and tears streamed down over my pillow as a fearful anger took hold of me, tore me this way and that, I didn't know what to do with it. I hated him and I had to get my revenge. I would get my revenge. He'd soon see. I would crush him. Crush him.

Then it struck me: what would a nice boy do? What would a true Christian do?

He would forgive.

Once the thought was there, a warmth spread through me.

I would forgive him.

It was a big thought.

And it made me a big person.

But only when I was alone. When I was in the same room as him it was as though he swallowed up everything inside me, there was only him left, I couldn't think about anything else.

The first day alone with dad was to form a pattern for all the other days of the year to follow. Breakfast buttered and ready on the table, packed lunch in the fridge, off shopping when I came home, sitting and answering questions while he cooked, interspersed with little jibes followed by the constant *Straighten your back, boy* – sometimes I had to stay there until he had finished, sometimes he could suddenly say *Off you go*, as though he did actually understand what a torment I found these half-hour sessions where I was supposed to keep him company – then we ate and for the rest of the evening I was alone with Yngve upstairs, or outdoors, while he was either at meetings or working in his study. Once a week we went to Stoa after school to do a big shop. In the evenings he would sometimes watch TV with us. We gave him nothing: we sat stiff-backed, without moving and without speaking. If he asked us something we answered in monosyllables.

Gradually he began to turn away from Yngve and spend more and more time with me. I never dared to be as sullen and tight-lipped as my brother.

But it didn't always work.

His footsteps on the stairs, they were an ominous sign. If I was playing music I kept it down low. If I was reading on my bed I sat up so as not to seem too casual.

Was he coming here?

He was.

The door opened, there he stood.

It was eight o'clock; he hadn't been upstairs since the meal at four.

His eyes took in the room. And stopped at the desk.

'What have you got there?' he said. Came in, lifted the pack of cards. 'Shall we play?'

'Yes, if you like,' I said, putting down my book.

He sat beside me on the bed.

'I'll teach you a new game,' he said. Lifted the pack and threw all the cards around the room.

'Fifty-two-card pick-up, it's called,' he said. 'Away you go. Pick them up!'

I had thought he really wanted to play cards and was so disappointed he was only messing around and I had to go down on my knees and pick up all the cards while he sat on the bed laughing that I muttered an expletive.

I would never have said it if I had been thinking.

But I hadn't been, and it slipped out.

'Bloomin' heck!' I said. 'Why did you do that?'

He stiffened. Grabbed my ear and stood up as he twisted.

'Are you swearing at your own father?' he said and twisted harder and harder until I burst into tears.

'Now you pick the cards up, boy!' he said, keeping hold of my ear while I bent down and started picking up the cards.

Once it was done he let go and left. When it was time for supper he was in his study and when we went into the kitchen he had prepared everything.

The next day he didn't call me in while he was cooking, as he usually did. A call from the kitchen only came when the food was ready. We sat down, helped ourselves without a word, whale steak with gravy and onions and potatoes, we ate in total silence, thanked him and got down from the table. Dad washed up, ate an orange in the living room, I could tell by the aroma, and drank a cup of coffee, I could hear from the hiss of the coffee pot, went down to his study, where he played some music before putting on his coat, going to the car and driving off.

As the drone of the car faded down the hill I opened the door and went into the living room. Draped myself over the brown leather chair and put my feet on the table. Got up, went into the kitchen, opened the fridge and looked inside: two plates of sandwiches, ready made, that was our supper. Opened the cupboard next to it, took out the box of raisins, filled my hand and tossed them into my mouth with one hand while flattening the level of the raisins in the box with the other. Munching, I walked into the living room and switched on the TV. At half past six there was a repeat of *Blind Passasjer*. It was a series about a spaceship, unbelievably scary, broadcast on Friday night, and we weren't allowed to watch, but neither mum nor dad knew anything about the repeats, which to our great good fortune were on when they weren't here.

Yngve came in and reclined on the sofa.

'What are you eating?' he said.

'Raisins,' I said.

'I want some too,' he said.

'Don't take too many,' I said as he got up, 'or dad'll notice.'

'All right,' Yngve said. He opened the cupboard door.

'Do you want some almonds as well?' he called.

'Yes, please,' I said. 'But not many.'

The street lamp outside shone orange in the darkness. The tarmac beneath glistened the same colour. And some of the spruce tree behind it. But the forest behind that was as dark as the grave. From the steepest part of the hill came the whine of a moped.

'There you go,' Yngve said, releasing some almonds into my palm. I could clearly recognise his odour. It was acrid yet faint, almost metallic. Not his sweat, that smelled different, but his skin. It smelled of metal. When we wrestled I could smell it, when he tickled me I could smell it, and sometimes when he was lying down and reading, for example, I could put my nose to his arm and breathe in the smell. I loved him, I loved Yngve.

Five minutes before *Blind Passasjer* started, Yngve got up.

'Let's lock the front door,' he said. 'And then let's switch off all the lights to make it scary.'

'No!' I said. 'Don't do that!'

Yngve laughed.

'Are you scared already?'

I got up and stood in his way. He fastened his arms around me, lifted me up and sat me back down and continued towards the stairs.

'Don't!' I said. 'Please!'

He laughed again.

'I'm going downstairs now to lock the door,' he said from the stairs.

I ran after him.

'I mean it, Yngve,' I said.

'I know you do,' he said. Locked the door and stood by it. 'But I'm in charge when we're on our own.'

He switched off the light.

In the murk, illuminated only by the light from the adjacent room, there was something satanic about his smile. I ran upstairs and sat in the chair. Listened to him switching off light after light. The hall, the lamp over the living-room table, the ceiling lamp in the kitchen. Then the four small wall lamps above the sofa and, lastly, the lamp on top of the television. Apart from the faint shimmer from the outside lamp and the blue flickering glow from the screen it was completely dark when the episode began. It was scary right from the opening scene, a man was standing and swinging a scythe somewhere, and then he turned, and his face wasn't a face but a mask. I felt a tingle at the very tips of my fingers and toes and my innards were taut with fear. But I watched, I had to watch. When it was over, half an hour later, Yngve got up behind me.

'Don't say anything,' I pleaded. 'Don't do anything!'

'Do you know what, Karl Ove?' he said.

'Oh no!' I said.

'I'm not who you think I am,' he said, coming towards me.

'Yes, you are!' I said.

'I'm not Yngve,' he said. 'I am another.'

'No, you're not!' I said. 'You're Yngve! Tell me you're Yngve.'

'I'm a cyborg,' he said. 'And this . . .' He stretched out his hand and lifted his jumper. 'This is not flesh and blood. This is metal and cables. It looks like flesh and blood, but it isn't. I am not a human being.'

'Yes, you are!' I said, starting to cry. 'You are Yngve! Yngve! Say you're Yngve!'

'Now you will come down to the cellar with me,' he said. 'Heh heh heh . . .'

'YNGVE!' I screamed.

He smiled at me.

'I'm only joking,' he said. 'You didn't seriously think I was a cyborg, did you?'

'Don't do that,' I said. 'Switch the light on right now.'

He took a step towards me.

'NO!' I shouted.

'OK, OK,' he laughed. 'Let's switch on the light then. Shall we eat now or what? Are you hungry?'

'Switch on the light first,' I said.

He switched on the wall lights and the lamp on the TV, where the news had already started. Then we went into the kitchen and had our supper. Yngve made us some tea, which was fine as long as we made sure to clear up after us, it must have been inconceivable for dad that we could actually use the stove and boil water when he wasn't here. Afterwards we unpacked our football game on the living-room table, with the door to his room open and my favourite Queen record – *A Night at the Opera* – playing.

When we heard dad's car outside we hurriedly cleared the table and went into our separate rooms. Sometimes he summoned Yngve if we had been alone and asked what we had been doing and how it had been, but this evening he walked straight into the living room and sat down in front of the television.

It was actually a relief that he kept his distance the way he did, but there was more to it than that, I had a sense he didn't want things to be like this, it was as though the air in the house was weighed down with this feeling, a demand no one could fulfil.

When he came up to us next time it was dreadful. I had been under the weather, I had a cold and a temperature which had risen dramatically in the last hour, and I was sitting in Yngve's bed, leaning against the wall and reading one of his magazines. He was doing his homework at the desk and the Boomtown Rats were playing on the turntable.

Bang, the door opened, and there was dad looking at us.

He was in a good mood, his eyes beaming with energy.

'You're playing music,' he said. 'It sounds good. What's their name?'

'The Boomtown Rats,' Yngve said.

Dad translated the name into Norwegian. 'Do you remember how you laughed when I said Crystal Palace was Krystallpalasset? You didn't believe me!'

He smiled and came into the room.

'Do you like the music too, Karl Ove?' he said.

I nodded.

'Come on. Let's dance,' he said.

'I'm ill, Dad. I think I've got a temperature. I don't feel like it.'

'Course you do,' dad said, grabbing my hands, dragging me to my feet and swinging me round.

'Stop it, Dad!' I said. 'I'm ill! I don't want to dance!'

But he carried on, swung me round, faster and faster, wilder and wilder. It was unbearable and I was on the point of throwing up.

'PACK IT IN, DAD!' I shouted in the end. 'PACK IT IN!'

He stopped as quickly as he had started, threw me down on the bed and left.

Every Friday mum came home, I would always be close at hand so that I could be with her first, because if I was first dad couldn't send me to my room, which he could do if they were sitting and talking. By the time she left again on Sunday night or Monday morning it was as if dad had come closer to us, or at least me, for again he called me to the kitchen to tell him what had happened during the day while he cooked. We ate in silence and after washing up he disappeared down to his study without fail. Occasionally he came to watch TV with us, but usually he was downstairs until supper, and so it was as if Yngve and I were on our own at home. Not that I spent my time much differently from how I would have done if he hadn't been there. Mostly I lay on my bed reading. As mum no longer drove us regularly to the library, and I had read all the books in the school library, I started on mum and dad's shelves. I read Agatha Christie and I read Stendhal, *Le Rouge et Le Noir*, I read a book of French short stories, I read a book by Jon Michelet and I read a biography of

Tolstoy. I started writing a book myself, it was going to be about a sailing ship, but after I had written the first ten pages, which consisted largely of listing all the people on board, what kinds of provisions they had and what cargo they were carrying, Yngve said no one wrote books about sailing ships nowadays, they did when sailing ships existed, now people write about what it's like to be alive today, and so I stopped. I also compiled a newspaper that autumn, in triplicate, which I put in three post boxes, one for Karlsen, one for Gustavsen and one for Prestbakmo, but I never heard any more, they just seemed to disappear into a void, as if they had never existed.

I lived one life indoors and another outdoors, as it had always been and as I suppose it was for all children; in front of the TV on Saturday night, surrounded by their parents and brothers and sisters they were probably very different, much gentler and more accepting than when I saw them down in the forest, where freedom was total and nothing prevented them from following their smallest inclinations. The difference was particularly pronounced in the autumn. In the spring and summer so much of life was lived outdoors, the degree of contact between a child's life and an adult's life was changed, but when autumn came and the nights drew in so early it was as if the ties were cut and we slipped into our own worlds as soon as the front door closed behind us. The brief, dark, cold evenings were laden with all the excitement that exists in the unseen and the hidden. The autumn was darkness, earth, water and hollow spaces. It was breathing, laughter, torchlight, dens, bonfires and a flock of children drifting here and there. And not least the bedrooms afterwards. Even though I never got permission to have anyone at home and none of the children on the estate had ever been to my bedroom, I was always allowed to go to theirs. To some occasionally, to others often. That autumn it was the turn of Dag Lothar's bedroom. Red-faced after running through the darkness, we would sit in his room and play Monopoly while listening to one of his two Beatles albums, the red one or the blue one, on the cassette recorder. I liked the red one better, with their first songs, they were simple and happy, we would sing along loudly with the chorus, almost shouting, in English, not bothering too much about the semantics, only the sound, although the blue one was played more and more as we began to enjoy the sombre, more unfamiliar tones on it.

These evenings are among the happiest in my life. It is strange because there was nothing exceptional about them, we did what all young people did, sat playing games, listening to music, chattering away about whatever came into our heads.

But I liked the smell in their house, I liked being there. I liked the darkness we had just come from, which lent everything an unaccustomed quality, especially when it was damp and you could feel it in your whole body, not only see it with your eyes. I liked the light from the street lamps. I liked the atmosphere that arose when there were lots of us together, the voices in the night, the bodies moving around me. I liked the sound of the foghorn from the open sea. My thinking on these evenings: anything can happen. I liked just dashing around, coming across the unexpected – objects, features, situations. The huts that had been erected in the forest above the pontoons, they were empty in the evening, the windows were lit and we peered in. Were they porn mags lying there? Yes, they were. No one dared to smash a window and go in and take them, but now all of a sudden it was a possibility, and we knew someone would do it soon, perhaps even we would. This was a time when one morning there could be a centrefold from a porn magazine lying in the road outside the house. This was a time when you could find porn mags in the ditches, in fields and under bridges. Who had left them there we had no idea, they were scattered as if by God's hand, a part of nature like wood anemones, catkins, swollen streams or rain-smooth rocks. And the elements marked them too: they were either spongy with moisture or bone dry or the paper had cracked after having dried out again, often they were sun-faded, soil-stained and discoloured.

A thrill went through me when I thought about the magazines. It had nothing to do with the way we talked about them – we talked tough, we laughed and ogled them greedily – but the thrill lay somewhere else, so deep that rational thought never reached it.

There were many youths on the estate you could imagine would have pornographic magazines at home, and they were without exception the same ones you could imagine buying a moped when the time came, starting to smoke and skiving from school, in short, the ones who hung out at the Fina station. The bad boys. So within me there were two incompatible entities. The magazines belonged to the bad, but what they filled me with, the intense thrill that forced me to gulp again and again, was also something I desired with a wild urgency. I went weak at the knees when I got to see one of the naked women. It was fantastic, it was terrible, it was the world opening and hell revealing itself, the light shining and the darkness falling, we just wanted to stand there flicking through the pages, we could have stood there for all eternity, beneath the heavy boughs of the spruce trees, with the aroma of damp earth and wet mountain, leering at the pictures. It was as though these women rose from the bog, straight up from the autumn-yellow grass, or at least were closely related to it. Parts of the pictures were often obliterated, but we saw enough of both the soft and the hard to know with certainty that these feelings existed and never left us, and every rumour of the existence of a magazine was always followed up at once.

Geir was one of the keenest in this regard. Already in the second class he had borrowed a copy of his father's *Vi Menn* and we sat down in the forest to study the topless women while, to ward against any suspicions, we talked in high-pitched voices about what Donald and Dolly were doing as though we were reading cartoon strips.

Now there were porn mags in the huts.

We circled them, but the doors were locked and we didn't have the nerve to smash the glass, undo the catch on the windows and steal the magazines.

But the desire was aroused and it cast around in other directions. The clumps of trees around the car wreck in the forest?

The ditch behind the bus stop by B-Max?

The trees under the bridge?

The refuse tip, of bloomin' course! There had to be some there, didn't there? Hundreds? Thousands?

Sunday morning, the end of September, dad fishing in his boat, mum in the living room, Yngve on his bike somewhere on the east of the island and me out of the door and across the wet shingle, wearing my beige jacket and my blue jeans, on my way up to Geir's, butterflies in my stomach, we were finally going to the refuse tip. The sun was shining, but it had rained early in the morning and the tarmac was still black and wet in those places the sun didn't reach, such as in the shade under the spruce trees outside our house.

Geir was standing in front of our house, ready, when I arrived, and we sprinted off. Up the hill, over the long plain where there were boats under tarpaulins in front gardens, mostly plastic boats but also some small dinghies, and one cabin cruiser, renowned far and wide. The lawns were brown, the trees behind the houses orange and red, the sky was blue. We had taken off our jackets and knotted them around our waists. Walked up past Ketil's house, onto the gravel road and through the gate that marked the end of the road and the start of the path. On the other side of the field was the new parish hall, where Ten Sing, with all the blonde girls, rehearsed and had their meetings.

The stream alongside the path was full, cool green water, flowing lazily down the gentle slope. It got its colour from the heather, the grass and the plants the water flowed and lay across. Only minor ripples on the surface revealed that it was moving. Where the hill became steeper and the stream fell with a roar we began to run. The white stones littering the path were a matt grey in the shadow, a gleaming yellow in the sun. Ahead of us someone was walking uphill and we slowed down. It was an elderly couple. She had grey hair and a cardigan; he had a cord jacket with leather patches on the elbows and a stick in his hand. His mouth was open and his jaw trembled.

We turned and looked after them.

'That was Thommesen, that was,' Geir said.

We hadn't seen him since he had us in the second class.

'I thought he'd died ages ago!' I said.

We took the old short cut through the forest and emerged on the edge above the refuse tip. The mountain of white plastic bags and black bin bags glinted in the full sun. A dozen or so seagulls were screaming and flapping their wings. We clambered down the slope and wove our way between all the objects, which in some places were stacked high, perhaps four times higher than us, and in others lay strewn around with nothing on top. We were looking for bags and cardboard boxes, and there was no shortage of them, also containing magazines – weeklies that the elderly read – *Hjemmet* and *Allers* and *Norsk Ukeblad* – weeklies for girls – *Starlet* and *Det Nye* and *Romantikk* – piles of newspapers, mostly *Verdens Gang* and *Agderposten*, but also *Vårt Land* and *Aftenposten* and *Dagbladet*; we found *A-Magasinet* and *Kvinner og Klær*, horsey magazines for girls, *Donald Duck* comics and a fat *Fantomet* album from the late 60s that I immediately put to one side, a *Tempo* album as well, some *Kaptein Miki* comics and one *Agent X9* paperback, which I was pretty pleased with, but it didn't alter the fact that what we were searching for, magazines like *Alle Menn*, *Lek*, *Coctail* and *Aktuell Report*, and perhaps even a few foreign magazines, because there were quite a few Danish ones in circulation, one called *Weekend Sex*, for example, and some Swedish and English ones, were nowhere to be found. We didn't find a single porn magazine! What was going on? Had someone beaten us to it? They had to be here!

After an hour's searching we gave up and flopped down in the heather to read the normal magazines we had found. Perhaps because I'd had my mind set on something quite different and had felt the expectation all day, I wasn't really happy about just sitting there. Something was missing, and I got up, paced between the trees, looked down at the stream, perhaps a wade in the water was what was required?

'Shall we go for a wade?' I called.

'Can do. Just got to read this first,' Geir said without looking up from his magazine.

I went over to the two bags of bottles we had found. Most of them were the long brown ones with the yellow Arendals Bryggeri label, but there was also the odd dumpy green Heineken bottle. I took one of them out. There was a bit of earth and grass stuck to the outside, and I wondered if it had been lying on the edge of a lawn for a while and had been picked up when the garden was being prepared for winter.

The lust was still there in my stomach.

I rotated the bottle in my hand. The dark green glass lit up in the sun.

'Do you reckon it's possible to stick your willy in this?' I said.

Geir rested the magazine on his lap.

'Ye-eah,' he said. 'If the neck's not too narrow. Are you going to try?'

'Yes,' I said. 'Are you?'

He got up and came over. Took a bottle.

'Think anyone can see us here?' he said.

'No, are you crazy?' I said. 'We're right in the middle of the forest. But we could move over there, to be on the safe side.'

We walked towards the trunk of a large pine tree. I undid my belt and dropped my trousers to my knees, took out my willy with one hand and held the bottle in the other. I pressed my willy into the top, the glass neck was cold and hard against my soft warm skin, and actually too narrow, but with a bit of humping and pumping and wriggling, it slipped inside. A tingle ran down my back as my willy throbbed and the bottle seemed to tighten around it, harder and harder.

'I can't get it in,' Geir said. 'It won't go.'

'I've done it!' I said. 'Look!'

I turned to him.

'But I can't budge it,' I said. 'There's no room. It's stuck!'

To show how stuck it was, I let go of the bottle. It hung between my legs.

'Ha ha ha,' Geir laughed.

I was about to pull my willy out when I felt a sharp pain shoot up.

'Ow. Ow, ow, ow, fudge!'

'What's the matter?' Geir said.

'Ow! Ow! Oh FUCK!'

It was a stabbing pain, as if from a knife or a jagged piece of glass. I pulled as hard as I could and got my willy out of the bottle.

On the tip of it there was a black beetle.

'OH! FUCK! FUCK! FUCK!' I howled. I gripped the beetle or whatever it was, it was black with big claws, pulled it off and hurled it as far as I could while running to and fro and waving my arms.

'What's the matter?' Geir said. 'What's the matter? What's the matter, Karl Ove?'

'A beetle. It was biting my willy!'

At first he stared at me, slack-jawed. Then he burst into laughter. It was exactly his kind of humour. He fell about in the heather laughing.

'Don't tell anyone!' I said, doing up my belt. 'Have you got that?'

'Yeah-heh-heh-heh!' Geir said. 'Ha ha ha ha!'

Three times I made him promise he wouldn't tell anyone as we walked uphill, each carrying a bag and with the sun beating down on our necks. I also said a short prayer to apologise for my swearing.

'Shall we go down and get the deposit on the bottles at Fina now?' Geir said.

'Do they take beer bottles there?' I said.

'Oh, that's right,' Geir said. 'We'd better hide them then.'

We walked back across the field, jumped over the stream, and there, on the other side, in a clump of trees below the chapel, we left the bags of bottles. Pulled up some ferns and tufts of grass and covered them as well as we were able, glanced around to make sure no one was nearby, then calmly moved away, knowing that if you ran you drew attention to yourself, up the road next to the chapel, which we then started to follow.

Outside the cellar door of the house where he lived stood Ketil, his bike turned upside down in front of him. He was revolving the rear wheel with a pedal in one hand while lubricating the chain with a small plastic bottle of oil he was holding in the other. His smooth black hair hung down in front of his face.

'Hi,' he said.

'Hi,' we said.

'Where've you been?'

'To the dump.'

'What were you doing there?'

'Searching for porn mags,' Geir said. I sent him a glare. What was he doing? This was a secret!

'Did you find any?' Ketil said, smiling at us.

Geir shook his head.

'I've got a pile of them in my room,' he said. 'Would you like to borrow them?'

'Oh yes!' Geir said.

'Is that true?' I said.

He nodded.

'Do you want them now?'

'I've got to go home and eat,' I said.

'Me too,' Geir said. 'But we can take them with us and hide them in the forest.'

Ketil shook his head.

'No chance. Then they would be ruined. You'll have to take them home. But that's OK. I can deliver them this afternoon.'

'That's great. But then we'll have to meet you outside. No ringing the bell. Agreed?'

'Oh?' he said, smiling with narrowed eyes. 'Are you frightened I'll show the mags to your dad, or what?'

'No, but . . . he asks a lot of questions. And you haven't been there before.'

'Fine,' he said. 'Be outside at five and I'll be there. OK?'

'That's when the football's on,' I said.

'Six then. And don't tell me you want to watch children's TV!'

'OK. Six.'

Mum was sitting in the kitchen reading a book with the radio on and rice boiling on the stove. The whole of one side of the pan was white with milk and in the area between the hotplates there was also milk and rice, almost dried up from the heat, so I could see it had boiled over.

'Hi,' I said.

She put the book down.

'Hi,' she said. 'Where have you been?'

'Mm,' I said. 'Around and about. We found some bottles and we're going to get the money back on Monday.'

'Nice,' she said.

'Are you going to make pizza this evening?' I said.

She smiled.

'That's what I'd planned.'

'Great!' I said.

'Have you started the book you got?'

I nodded. 'I started yesterday. It seems really good. I'm going to go to my room and read some now in fact.'

'You do that,' she said. 'Food'll be ready in a quarter of an hour.'

She always brought something when she came on Fridays, and this time it had been a book. *A Wizard of Earthsea*, written by someone called Ursula K. Le Guin, and already after the first few pages I knew that this was an absolutely fantastic book. Yet I didn't settle down with the book without some hesitation, because mum was at home and I wanted to be with her as much as possible. On the other hand, she was here and almost all the qualities her presence brought to my life were in place, not least the fact that dad never did anything nasty when she was here, never had one of his furious outbursts, always controlled himself, even though I was lying on my bed and she was in the kitchen.

I watched the English Football League match with Yngve and dad. He had bought toffees as usual, and both Yngve and I had been given a pools coupon with eight rows of twelve matches each. I got five correct results, which the others laughed at because that was less than half and I might just as well have rolled a dice. Dad said it was as hard to get five as it was ten. But whereas those who got ten right were sent money by Norsk Tipping, those who got five had to pay money to them, he said. Yngve got seven right and dad got ten, but unfortunately this time there was no payout for ten.

By the time all the results were in it was two minutes to six. Outside, Ketil came whizzing down the hill on his bike with a bulging plastic bag strapped to the luggage rack. I jumped up and said I had to go.

'What are you going to do now?' dad said. 'Children's TV is starting.'

'I'm not in the mood for it,' I said. 'And I'm meeting Geir.'

'Meeting, eh?' dad said. 'Well, that's fine. Just make sure you're back home by eight.'

'Are you going out?' mum said from the doorway. 'And there was me thinking you could help me make the pizza.'

'I'd love to, but I've arranged to meet someone,' I said.

'Our son has started making arrangements,' dad said. 'Are you sure it's Geir? Not a little sweetheart?'

'Yes, I'm absolutely sure about that,' I said.

'Be back home by eight then,' mum said.

Dad stood up.

'Soon we'll be all alone in the evenings, Sissel,' he said, hauling his trousers up by the belt loops and running a hand through his hair. I was already on my way down the landing and didn't hear what she answered. My throat was thick with excitement, my whole body tingling. In the hall I put on my trainers – if we were lucky the forest would be dry now – the blue jumper and the blue quilted waistcoat mum had made for me, opened the door and rushed out to meet Ketil, who was sitting on his bike with one foot on the pedal and one on the ground, and Geir, who was standing next to him. Both glanced towards me.

'Let's go to the boathouse,' I said. 'No one will see us there.'

'OK,' Ketil said. 'I'll cycle round. See you down there.'

Geir and I ran down the slope and onto the path, jumped over the stream and scurried down the hill, which seemed to vibrate beneath our feet, crossed the field, the gravel road and only slowed down when we reached the grassy incline at the same time as Ketil hove into view at the top of the hill, beside the old white house.

Ketil was two years older than us and kept himself very much to himself, at least that was how it appeared to us. The high cheekbones, the narrow eyes and the gleaming black hair made him look like an Indian and caused a stir among the girls. It wasn't long since that had started. From one day to the next Ketil became the one they talked about and looked at, suddenly you heard his name all over the place, and the strange thing about this was not the way that he suddenly existed now, having existed before in a kind of vale of shadows, but that there was a certain pride in the girls who talked about him and eyed him, as if it was *them* who became interesting by making such an unexpected selection, almost more interesting than he was. For he just carried on with his life, cycling round, one day here, one day there, invariably alone and always friendly to us.

He kicked down the stand on his bike, an orange DBS racer with drop handlebars and the tape hanging off one end, lifted the spring flap on the luggage rack, took the bag and strolled over to where we were lying in the grass, each with a sprig of grass in our mouths.

'It's porn time!' he said, grabbing the bag from the bottom and spilling the magazines over the ground.

The sun was low in the sky over the ridge behind us, and his shadow stretched a long way across the ground. From the islet in the bay came the sound of screeching gulls. Feeling weak all over, I took a magazine and rolled onto my stomach. Even though I looked at the pictures one at a time, and focused on one part, such as the breasts, which I only needed to catch a glimpse of to feel an electric shock of excitement shoot through me, or such as the legs and the wild thrill aroused by the sight of the slit between them, more or less open, more or less pink and glistening, often accompanied by a finger or two nearby, or near the mouth, which was often open, often contorted into a grimace, or such as the buttocks, sometimes so wonderfully round that I couldn't lie still, this wasn't about the parts in themselves, this was more like bathing in the totality, a kind of sea to which there was no beginning and no end, a sea in which, from the first moment, from the first picture, you always found yourself in the middle.

'Can you see a big mons anywhere, Geir?' I said.

He shook his head. 'But there's one here with enormous tits. Do you want to see?'

I nodded, and he held up the magazine for me.

Ketil sat some metres from us, with his legs crossed and a magazine in his hands. But after only a few minutes he threw it down and got to his feet.

'I've looked at them so many times,' he said. 'I'll have to get some new ones.'

'Where did you get them?' I said, gazing up at him and shielding my eyes from the sun.

'I bought them.'

'BOUGHT THEM?' I said.

'Yes.'

'But they're old, aren't they?'

'They're used, you chump. There's a hairdressing salon in town that also sells old magazines. They've got loads of porn mags.'

'Are *you* allowed to buy them?'

'Obviously,' he said.

I stared at him for a few seconds. Was he pulling my leg?

Didn't look like it.

I flicked through. There were photos of two girls on a tennis court. They wore short skirts, one light blue, the other white, white shirts, a sweat band over their wrists, white socks and white trainers. Each was holding a racquet. Surely they weren't going to . . . ?

I flicked on.

One was lying on the grass and had opened her shirt so you could see her breasts. Her head was back. Was she wearing any knickers?

Nope.

Soon they were both naked, on their knees by the net, with their bottoms in the air. It was fantastic. Fantastic. Fantastic.

'Look, Geir,' I said. 'Two playing tennis!'

He glanced at me and nodded, too absorbed in his own pictures to waste any time.

Ketil had walked down to the old tumbledown pontoon, where he stood skimming stones he must have found on the beach nearby. The water was like a mirror, and every time a stone hit the water, small circular ripples spread outwards.

I had flicked through three or four magazines when he reappeared in front of us. I looked up at him.

'It feels good to lie on your stomach and read them,' I said.

'Ha ha ha! So you like rubbing yourself, do you?' he said.

'Yes,' I said.

'I can imagine,' he said. 'But I've got to be off now. Keep the mags if you like. I'm sick of them.'

'Can we *have* them?' Geir said.

'Be my guest.'

He kicked the bike stand, raised a hand to say goodbye and set off up the hill with one hand in the middle of the handlebars. It looked as if he was leading an animal.

It was so obvious to us both that Geir would have to hide the magazines in his room that we didn't even talk about it when we parted outside our house an hour later.

Mum's pizzas had thick bases that rose around the edges, making the filling of minced meat, tomato, onions, mushrooms, peppers and cheese look like a plain surrounded by long ranges of mountains on all sides. We were sitting at the living-room table, as always on Saturday evenings. We had never eaten in front of the television; that belonged to the realm of the unimaginable. Dad cut a piece for me and put it on my plate, I poured myself a glass of Coke from the litre bottle where the words Coca-Cola were printed in white on the greenish glass, not on a red label, which you also saw. Pepsi-Cola wasn't sold in Sørland, I had drunk it only at the Norway Cup, and apart from the Metro and the breakfast where we could help ourselves to as many bowls of cornflakes as we wanted, that had been one of the tournament's biggest attractions.

When the pizza was finished, dad asked if we fancied playing a new game.

We did.

Mum cleared the table; dad fetched a pad of paper and four pens from his study.

'Would you like to join in, Sissel?' he shouted to mum, who had started washing up.

'Love to,' mum said and joined us. She had soap lather on one arm and her temple. 'What are we going to play? Yatzy?'

'No,' dad said. 'We each have a piece of paper and we write down six headings: country, town, river, sea, lake and mountain. One column for each. Then we choose a letter and the aim of the game is to jot down as many names as we can that begin with the respective letter in three minutes.'

We hadn't played this one before. But it seemed like fun.

'Is there a prize?' Yngve said.

Dad smiled.

'Only the honour. Whoever wins becomes the family champion.'

'You start,' mum said. 'I'll put some tea on for us.'

'We can do a trial run,' dad said. 'Then we can play properly when you're back.'

He looked at us.

'M,' he said. 'So, the letter M. Are you with me?'

'Yes,' Yngve said, and was already writing, with one arm shielding his work.

'Yes,' I said.

Mont Blanc, I wrote under mountain. Mandal, Morristown, Mjøndalen, Molde, Malmö, Metropolis and Munich under town. I couldn't think of any seas, or rivers. Next was countries. Were there any countries beginning with an M? I went through all the countries I could think of. But no. Moelven. Was that a river? Mo in Rana, that was a town anyway. Midwest? Oh yes, Mississippi!

'Time's up,' dad said.

A quick glance at their pieces of paper was enough to confirm that they had beaten me.

'You read yours out, Karl Ove,' dad said.

When I got to Morristown both dad and Yngve were laughing.

'Don't laugh at me!' I said.

'Morristown only exists in *The Phantom*,' Yngve said. 'Did you think it really existed?'

'Yes? And why not? Sala works in the UN Building in New York, and that exists, doesn't it. Why shouldn't Morristown?'

'Good answer, Karl Ove,' dad said. 'You get half a point for that.'

I pulled a face at Yngve, who smirked back.

'Tea's up,' mum said. We went into the kitchen and took a cup. I added milk and sugar.

'OK, let's play properly now,' dad said. 'We'll do three letters. That's probably as much as we can manage before bedtime.'

Mum knew almost as few names as I did, it turned out. Or else she wasn't concentrating as much as Yngve or dad. However, it was good for me; it was us two against the other two.

After dad had counted the points from the first round, she said she had changed her name.

'I've gone back to my old maiden name. So now I'm Hatløy and not Knausgaard any more.'

My body ran cold.

'You're not called Knausgaard any more?' I said, staring at her with my mouth open. 'But you're our mother!'

She smiled.

'Yes, of course I am! I always will be!'

'But why? Why aren't you going to have the same name as us?'

'I was born Sissel Hatløy, as you know. That's my name. Knausgaard is dad's name. And your names!'

'Are you getting divorced?'

Mum and dad smiled.

'No, we're not getting divorced,' mum said. 'We're just going to have different names.'

'But a rather stupid consequence of this,' dad said, 'is that we can't meet grandma and grandad from now on. My parents don't like your mother changing her name, so they don't want to see us any more.'

I gaped at him.

'What about at Christmas?' I said.

Dad shook his head.

I started crying.

'This is nothing to cry about, Karl Ove,' dad said. 'It'll pass. They're just angry now. And then it'll pass.'

I scraped my chair back, got up and ran to my room. After closing my door I heard someone follow. I lay down on the bed and bored my head into the pillow while sobbing loudly with tears flowing as they had never flowed before.

'But, Karl Ove,' dad said behind me. He sat on the edge of the bed. 'Don't get so upset. Is it that much fun with grandma and grandad?'

'Yes!' I shouted into the pillow. My whole body was contorted in convulsive sobs.

'But if they don't want to meet your own mother. It's not much fun meeting them then, is it? Surely you understand, don't you? They don't want to see us.'

'Why should she change her name?' I shouted.

'It's her real name,' dad said. 'It's what she wants. And neither you nor I nor grandma nor grandad can deny her that right. Can we?'

He placed his hand on my shoulder for a fleeting moment. Then he stood up and left the room.

When the tears had dried up I picked up the book mum had bought me and carried on reading. At the back of my mind I was aware that Yngve had gone to bed, that the sliding door was closed, that they were playing music in the living room, but without a scrap of it sticking. From the first sentence I plunged headlong into the story and fell deeper and deeper. The main character was Ged, a boy who lived on an island and had special gifts, and when this was discovered he was sent to a school for wizards. There it came out that his gifts were extra-special, and once when he had to perform for the others, in an act of excessive arrogance, he opened the door to the other world, the underworld, the kingdom of death, and a shadow stole out. Ged was dying, he was weak, with failing powers, for many years afterwards, marked for life, and the shadow pursued him. He fled from it, hid in some obscure place somewhere in the world, abandoned all his ambitions knowing that what he had done, the simple wizardry tricks, were just empty gestures and pretence, that there was another, a more profound kind of magic woven into all existence, and it was to maintain the balance here that was the wizards' real responsibility. All objects and all creatures had a name corresponding to their essence, and only by knowing the objects' and creatures' real names could they be controlled. Ged could do that, but he didn't reveal that he could, because every spell, every act of wizardry, affected the balance, something else could happen somewhere else, which could not be foreseen. The villagers where he had settled thought therefore that he was a poor wizard; after all he wouldn't perform even the simplest tricks with which every village wizard plied his trade. He was young, serious, there was a large scar across his face, he was sensitive to cold, but when the chips were down, when he really had to use his gifts, he did. Once there was a child dying. He followed it into the kingdom of death and brought it back, even though he should not have done, even though it was dangerous, for if there was one balance that should not be upset, it was that between life and death. But he did it and almost died in the process. The villagers saw for the first time who he was. And the shadow which he had released from beyond, who all this time had been flitting around the world after him, saw him, because whenever he used his powers, it noticed and came closer. He had to leave. And he did, in a boat on the sea between islands to the furthest shore. The shadow came closer and closer. After several confrontations, with Ged near to death, came the final showdown. All the while he had been trying to find the name of the shadow. He had scoured reference works about creatures from the oldest times, asked other, cleverer wizards, but in vain, the creature was unknown, nameless. Then he knew. On the sea, alone in a boat, with the shadow getting closer and closer, he knew. The shadow was called Ged. The shadow had his name. The shadow was himself.

When I turned off the light, after reading the last page, it was nearly twelve o'clock and my eyes were full of tears.

He was the shadow!

At least once, often twice, a week during that autumn and winter I was on my own in the house. Dad was at meetings, Yngve was at rehearsals with the school band or training with the volleyball or football teams, or at his friends' houses. I liked being at home on my own, it was a wonderful feeling not to have someone telling me what to do, yet I didn't like it that much either because the nights were drawing in and the reflection from the windows of my figure wandering around was extremely unpleasant to see, it smacked of death and the dead.

I knew this was not how it was, but what good did this knowledge do?

It was especially spooky when I was engrossed in what I was reading because it was as if I wasn't attached *anywhere* when I lifted my head from my page and got up. All alone, that was the feeling I had, I was absolutely alone, isolated by the darkness which rose like a wall outside.

Oh, I could always run the bath if I had enough time before dad returned – he didn't like me having a bath at all hours, once a week was enough according to him and he kept a beady eye on this, like everything else I did. But if I took a liberty now and ran the bath, got in, switched on my cassette recorder and let the hot water wash over my body, I could see myself from the outside, my mouth *agape*, as it were, as though my head were a skull. I sang, the voice rebounded, I submerged my head and was terrified: I couldn't see anything! Someone could sneak up on me! Was anyone there? The two, three, four seconds I had been underwater represented a hole in time, and someone might have sneaked in through that hole. Perhaps not into the bathroom, no, there was no one there, but they could have sneaked into the house.

The best I could do in this situation was to switch off the kitchen light or my bedroom light and look out because outside, when there was no reflection from the windows, there were the other houses, there were the other families and sometimes the other children too. Nothing made you feel more secure than that.

On one such evening I was kneeling on a kitchen stool in the darkness and staring out, it was snowing and a gale was blowing. The wind was howling across the landscape, rushing down the chimney and the roof gutters were rattling. It was pitch black outside under the yellow glow from the street lamps, there wasn't a soul, only gusting snow.

A car drove up. It turned into Nordåsenringvei, coming towards our house. Was it coming here?

It was. It came into our drive and parked.

Who could it be?

I ran out of the kitchen, down the stairs and into the porch.

There I stopped.

Surely no one was coming to visit us?

Who could it be?

I was frightened.

Went to the door and pressed my nose against the wavy glass. I didn't need to open the door; I could stand there and see if I recognised the late-night visitor.

The car door opened and a figure *fell* out!

The figure was moving *on all fours*!

Oh no! Oh no!

Swaying from side to side like a bear, it came towards me. It stopped by the bell and rose onto two legs!

I backed away.

What sort of creature was this?

Ding dong, the bell went.

The figure dropped to all fours again.

The abominable snowman? Lightfoot?

But here? In Tybakken?

The figure raised itself again, rang the bell and fell back onto all fours.

My heart was pounding.

But then I twigged.

Oh, of course.

It was the local council man, the one who was paralysed.

It had to be.

The abominable snowman didn't drive a car, did he.

I opened the door as the figure was starting to crawl away. It turned.

It *was* him.

'Hello,' he said. 'Is your father at home?'

I shook my head.

'No,' I said. 'He's at a meeting.'

The man, who had a beard and glasses and a bit of saliva at the corners of his mouth, and who often drove around with youngsters in his especially designed car, sighed.

'Say hello and tell him I was here,' he said.

'OK,' I said.

He dragged himself to the car using his arms, opened the door and lifted himself up into the seat. I watched him through widened eyes. In the car his slow helpless movements were transformed, he revved the engine and reversed up the incline at speed, shot down the road and was gone.

I closed the door and went to my room. No sooner was I lying on the bed when the door downstairs opened.

From the sounds I worked out that it was Yngve.

'Are you here?' he shouted up the stairs. I got up and went out.

'I'm so hungry,' he said. 'Shall we have supper now?'

'It's only just gone eight,' I said.

'The earlier, the better,' he said. 'Then I can make some tea for us. I'm absolutely ravenous.'

'Call me when the tea's ready,' I said.

A quarter of an hour later we were at the table eating bread, each with a big mug of tea in front of us.

'Was there a car here this evening?' Yngve said.

I nodded. 'The paralysed bloke on the council.'

'What did he want?'

'How should I know?'

Yngve looked at me.

'Someone was talking about you today,' he said.

My blood ran cold.

'Oh?' I said.

'Yes, Ellen.'

'What did she say?'

'She said you had a funny walk.'

'She didn't!'

'Yes, she did. And it's true, isn't it. You do have a funny walk. Hasn't it ever struck you?'

'I do NOT!' I shouted.

'Oh yes, you do,' Yngve said. 'Little shrimp can't even walk properly.'

He got up and walked across the kitchen floor, falling forward with every step. I watched him with tears in my eyes.

'There's nothing wrong with my walk,' I said.

'Ellen said it, not me,' he said and sat down. 'They talk about you, you know. You're a bit odd.'

'I AM NOT!' I shouted, throwing my bread at him as hard as I could. He moved his head to one side, and it hit the stove with a soft *splat*.

'Is Karlikins in a temper now?' he said.

I stood up with my mug in my hand. When Yngve saw that he got up too. I hurled the hot tea at him. It hit him in the stomach.

'You're so sweet when you're angry, Karl Ove,' he said. 'Poor little shrimp. Shall I teach you how to walk then? I'm good at walking, you know.'

My eyes were filled with tears, but that wasn't why I couldn't see anything, it was because I was seething with anger inside and the red mist had descended.

I flew at him and punched him with all my strength in the stomach. He grabbed my arms and twisted me round, I tried to wriggle loose, he held me tight, I kicked out, he pulled me harder to him, I tried to bite him on the hand and he pushed me away.

'Now, now,' he said.

I flew at him again, intent only on punching him in the face, smashing his nose, and if there had been a knife there I wouldn't have hesitated to plunge it into his stomach, but he knew all that, it had happened many times before, so he did what he always did, held me tight and squeezed while calling me a little shrimp and saying I was so sweet when I was angry until I tried to bite him and he couldn't keep my head at a distance and he pushed me away. This time I didn't go for him again; instead I ran out of the kitchen. On the living-room table there was a fruit bowl from which I took an orange and I flung it at the floor with all my might. It split open and a thin jet of orange juice spurted up and sprayed the wallpaper.

Yngve stood in the doorway watching.

'What have you done?' he said.

I looked at him. Then I saw the line of juice on the wallpaper.

'You'd better wash it off, you idiot,' I said.

'It won't wash off,' he said. 'The stain will just get bigger. Dad will be livid when he sees that. Why did you do it?'

'He might not see it,' I said.

Yngve just gawped at me.

'Well, we can hope,' he said, bending down and taking the orange into the kitchen. From the rustling noises that followed I gathered he was putting it at the very bottom of the rubbish bin. He came back with a cloth and wiped the floor.

I was trembling so much I could barely stand upright.

The juice ran in a thin line and I couldn't imagine how dad could avoid seeing it when he came home.

Yngve washed the kettle and the two cups. Threw away the bread, picked up the crumbs. I sat in the chair by the dining table with my head in my hands.

Yngve stopped near me.

'Sorry,' he said. 'I didn't mean to make you cry.'

'Yes, you did.'

'It's just that you get so angry,' he said. 'Surely you can see that it's tempting? I *have* said sorry.'

'It's not that,' I said.

'What is it then?'

'My funny walk.'

'Come on,' he said. 'Everyone walks in a different way. The main thing is to move forward. I was only kidding, wasn't I. I wanted to make you angry. And I succeeded. The way you walk is no stranger than anyone else's.'

'Sure?'

'Sure as eggs are eggs.'

When dad came home I was in bed. In the darkness I lay listening to his footsteps. They didn't stop on the landing as I had expected but continued into the kitchen. He fiddled around in there for a while before coming out again. And he didn't stop on the landing this time either.

He hadn't seen anything.

We were saved.

The next evening I went to the swimming course with Geir. We caught the bus from Holtet to the bus station in Arendal and walked up the hills to Stintahallen, each carrying a bag over our shoulders. In my bag I had some dark blue Arena swimming trunks, a white Speedo cap with the Norwegian flag on the side, a pair of Speedo goggles, a bar of soap and a towel. We had been members of Arendal Swimming Club since the previous winter. We could barely swim then, just getting from one end of the pool to the other was an enormous effort bordering on the impossible, but since it was actually expected of us as an absolute minimum in a swimming club, and the coach, a man with tattoos on his arms who wore clogs, followed us along the side of the pool shouting, it took us a surprisingly short time to get by without any problems. We weren't good, at least not if you compared us to the older boys, who sometimes walked around inside with their long-limbed, slim yet muscular bodies and who *powered* through the water with open mouths and bug-eye goggles. In comparison to them we were more like tadpoles, I sometimes mused, splashing and straining and just as likely to swim sideways as forward. But even though we gradually improved and could soon swim a thousand metres in the course of a training session, it wasn't thanks to my progress that I continued, I knew I would never be a competitive swimmer because when the competitions came and I gave everything it was never enough, I couldn't even overtake Geir – no, it was all the rest I liked, starting the moment we clambered onto the bus and continuing through the evening darkness on the road to Arendal, the deserted town we passed through, the shops we always stopped outside on our way to the course, and inside the hall, this large public building with its strange mixture of inside and outside, which we were funnelled through from standing at the entrance wrapped up in winter clothes to standing almost naked, fifteen minutes later, wearing only a strip of cloth at the edge of the pool, after having passed through the minor ritual of undressing, showering and dressing, and then throwing ourselves into the wonderfully transparent cold water that smelled of chlorine. That was what I liked. The sounds echoing around the pool, the night outside the windows, the coral-jewel partition between lanes, the diving boards, the thirty-minute-long hot showers we had afterwards. Then the process was reversed and we went from being pale, fragile, semi-naked boys with big heads to once again standing fully clothed in the winter outside, with wet hair under our hats and the smell of chlorine on our skin, our limbs deliciously tired.

I also liked the feeling of being enclosed inside myself when I put on my swimming cap and goggles, not least during competitions, when I had a whole lane of my own waiting for me beneath the starting blocks, but often the thoughts waiting there, in swimming's astronaut-like loneliness, became chaotic and I sometimes also panicked. There could be water in the goggles, it slopped against my eyes, making them sting and preventing me from seeing, which of course upset the purity of my thoughts. I could swallow water and I could make a mess of the turn, which left me so breathless that I swallowed more water. And I could see that the swimmers in the adjacent lanes were already way ahead, which I was told by the voice inside me intent on winning, and I started a discussion with it. But even though this inner dialogue, which carried on calmly while I was swimming and fighting for all I was worth and was therefore lent an almost panic-stricken aura, a bit like a military HQ deep in an underground bunker with officers speaking in controlled tones while the battles raged overhead, had the effect of me increasing the tempo, and for a few seconds I really gave it my all, it didn't help in the slightest, Geir was ahead of me and would remain so, and I could not understand that, I was obviously better than him, I knew so much more than him, also about the will to win. Nevertheless, he was the one to touch the pool wall *then*, and I touched it . . . .

. . . .

then.

When the coach blew his whistle and the session was over for another week, it was not without some relief that I put my hands on the edge of the pool and heaved myself up, to run with Geir across the tiled floor into the shower, where the pace seemed to be slower, at least our pace was lowered as we took off our caps and trunks and entered the showers, to feel with closed eyes the heat spreading through our bodies, no longer needing to say or do anything, not even having to bother to laugh as one of the men on his way into the pool, which was now open for all-comers, began to sing. There was something dreamlike about the atmosphere inside, the white bodies that appeared in the doorway and stood under the showers with slow introspective movements, the sound of water beating against the tiles and mingling with the muffled noise from outside, the steam saturating the air, the hollow resonance of voices whenever anyone spoke.

Normally we stood around long after those we had trained with had gone, Geir with his face to the wall, me with my face to the room to hide my backside. I snatched occasional glances at him when he wasn't paying attention. He had thinner arms than me, yet he was stronger. I was a little taller than him, yet he was faster. That wasn't why he swam faster than me though. It was because he wanted it more. It was different with his drawings, they were just something he could do, it was in him, it had always been there. Apart from people, he could reproduce everything in precise detail. Houses, cars, boats, trees, tanks, planes, rockets. It was a mystery how he could do it. He never copied, as I did, his mother never let him use either a ruler or a rubber. Now and then his Norwegian could throw up oddities, such as *fantisere* and *firkanti* instead of *fantasere* and *firkantet*, and *en appelsin* instead of *et appelsin*, and even though I corrected him every time, he continued to say them as though these terms were a feature of him that was as permanent as the colour of his eyes or the set of his teeth.

Then he noticed my glance and his eyes met mine. With a smile on his lips he stretched up and pressed the palm of his hand against the shower head, stopping the jet; and the water appeared to bulge beneath it. He laughed and turned to me. I held my hands out. My fingertips were red and swollen from the water.

'They look like raisins,' I said.

He examined his.

'Mine too,' he said. 'Imagine if your whole body had gone like that when we were swimming!'

'My ball bag always goes all wrinkly,' I said.

We bent forward and peered down. I ran a finger slowly over the hard yet sensitive folds of skin and a tingle went through me.

'Stroking it feels nice,' I said.

Geir looked around. Then he turned off the shower, went to the row of hooks and began to dry himself. I grabbed a bar of soap and squeezed hard. It skidded along the floor of the room, hit the wall in the corner and finished up over one of the grids. I turned off the shower and was about to follow Geir when I suddenly couldn't bear the thought of the soap lying there in the middle of the floor. I picked it up and threw it in the bin by the wall. I pressed my face against the dry material of the towel.

'Imagine what it will be like when we've got pubes,' Geir said, walking with his legs wide apart.

I laughed.

'Imagine what it will be like if they're really long!' I said.

'Right down to your knees!'

'Then we'd have to comb them!'

'Or make a pony tail!'

'Or go to the hairdresser's! I'd just like a trim round my dick, please!'

'Oh yes. And how would you like it, sir?'

'Crew cut, please!'

At that moment the door opened and we stopped laughing. A fat elderly man with sad eyes came in, and the vacuum the laughter had left in us was soon filled with giggles as he first nodded to us and then turned away in embarrassment to remove his trunks. As we grabbed our swimming things and were leaving the shower room, Geir said loudly, 'I bet he's got a whopper!'

'Or a teeny-weeny one!' I said, just as loudly, and then we slammed the door behind us and ran into the changing room. We sat laughing, wondering whether he had heard us or not, until the normally quiet atmosphere also affected us and we sluggishly began to pack our gear and get dressed. The only sounds you could hear inside were feet on lino, rustling noises as legs were slipped into trousers, arms into jackets, the metallic clink as lockers were opened or closed, someone sighing to himself, perhaps drained by the heat in the sauna.

I took my bag from the locker and put my swimming things inside. First, the goggles, which I held in my hand and examined for a second, because they were new and filled me with such pleasure that they were mine. Next, trunks, cap and towel and, last of all, the soap case. With its gently rounded lines, greenish colour and faint aroma of perfume, the case belonged to another world from the rest of my swimming equipment, intimately connected with mum and the items in her wardrobe: earrings, rings, flasks, buckles, brooches, scarves and veils. She herself was unaware there was such a world, she had to be, otherwise she would never have bought me a woman's bathing cap that time. Because a woman's cap belongs to that world. And if there was one thing everyone knew it was that one world should never be associated with the other.

Beside me Geir was almost ready. I stood up, pulled on my underpants, took my long johns and put one leg in, followed by the other. Then I pulled them up tight to my waist before turning and starting to search through my clothes for my socks. I found only one and searched through the pile again.

It wasn't there.

I looked in the locker.

Nothing, empty.

Oh no!

No, no, no.

I frantically went through my clothes again, shook item after item in the air, hoping desperately to see it drop out onto the floor in front of me.

But it wasn't there.

'What's up?' Geir said. He was sitting, fully clothed, on the opposite bench watching me.

'I can't find my other sock,' I said. 'Can you see it?'

He leaned forward and looked under the bench.

'It's not there,' he said.

Oh no!

'But it's got to be somewhere,' I said. 'Can you help me look? Please!'

I could hear my voice quivering. But Geir didn't let on that he had noticed, if indeed he had heard anything at all. He leaned over and looked under all the benches while I walked towards the showers in case it had got caught up in my towel and dropped out. It wasn't there either. Perhaps, inadvertently, I had packed it in my bag with the other swimming things?

I hurried back and emptied the contents of my bag on the floor.

But no. No sock.

'It wasn't anywhere there?' I said.

'No,' Geir said. 'But we have to get going, Karl Ove. The bus is leaving soon.'

'I have to find the sock first.'

'Well, it's not here, is it. We've looked *everywhere*. Can't you just go without it?'

I didn't answer. Once again I shook all the clothes, crouched down and scanned the floor under the benches; once again I went into the shower room.

'We've got to go now,' Geir said. He held his watch in front of me. 'They'll be angry if I miss the bus.'

'Can you search while I get dressed?' I said.

He nodded and half-heartedly wandered round examining the floor. I put on my T-shirt and jumper.

On the top shelf perhaps?

I stood on the bench and peered along.

Nothing.

I put on my trousers and quilted trousers, zipped up my jacket and sat down to tie my laces.

'We've *got* to go now,' Geir said.

'I'm getting there,' I said. 'You wait outside.'

After he had left I hurried back into the shower room. I looked in the refuse bin, ran my hand along the window sills and even opened the door to the pool.

But no.

Geir was standing by the hill when I went out. He started running down before I had even caught up with him.

'Wait for meee!' I cried. But he showed no signs of stopping, he didn't even turn, and I sprinted off after him. Down into the darkness, past the grey trees, into the light on the road below. For every step I took the bare foot rubbed against the coarse leather of my boot. *I've lost my sock*, a voice inside me said. *I've lost my sock. I've lost my sock.* A ticking started in my head. It happened now and again when I was running, my head ticked, somewhere inside my left temple, *tick tick*, it went, but although it was alarming, sounding as if something had come loose or perhaps it was rubbing against something else, I couldn't tell anyone, they would just say I had a screw loose and laugh.

Tick, tick, tick

Tick, tick, tick

I ran behind Geir all the way down to the sweet shop where we went; the bag of sweets we came out with was always the high point of these trips. Geir was waiting outside, impatiently shifting from one foot to the other. I stopped in front of him. As a result of the snowploughs' work we were standing half a metre higher than usual, and the new angle changed our view of the sweet shop. It had a cellar-like feel to it, and this feel transformed everything, at a glance I saw the shelves were only 'shelves', that the goods were 'goods' displayed in a very ordinary room in a house, in short that the shop was a 'shop', although I didn't articulate this to myself, it was just an idea that struck me and disappeared as quickly as it had come.

Geir opened the door and went in.

I followed.

'Are we very short of time?' I said.

'Yes,' he said. 'It goes in eleven minutes.'

In the back room the assistant put her newspaper down, came into the shop and stood behind the counter with a bored, even slightly disdainful expression on her face. She was old and repulsive; there were three long grey hairs growing out of a mole on her chin.

The whole of one wall was covered with pipes and pipe cleaners, cigarette-rolling machines and papers, tobacco pouches and cigarette packets, cigar boxes and snuff tins of various shapes and colours, all with different writing and small stylised images of dogs, foxes, horses, sailing ships, racing cars, black men smiling, sailors smoking and women in casual poses. The sweets shelves, which we were both looking at now, covered the whole of the second wall. Unlike the tobacco products, the sweets had no packaging; chocolates, sweets and wine gums were in transparent plastic jars and represented themselves, with no pictures between them and us: what you saw was what you got. The black ones tasted of salt or liquorice, the yellow ones of lemon, the orange ones of orange, the red ones of strawberry, the brown ones of chocolate. The small square pieces of chocolate with the hard surface, called *Rekrutt*, were filled with hard caramel, just as the shape promised; the heart-shaped chocolates, for their part, were filled with a soft jelly-like mass tasting of apricot, also as expected. The colour codes applied to the sweets and the wine gums, with a few exceptions, which on these evenings we tried to narrow down. Some black sweets could taste dark green while some dark green sweets tasted green in a throat-pastille or eucalyptus kind of way – in other words lighter – and not a sweet-type green, which you would imagine from the colour. And then there were the black sweets which actually tasted like the King of Denmark aniseed sweets, an orangey-brown. The strange thing was that it was never the other way around, there were no orangey-brown King of Denmark sweets that tasted black, nor had we ever come across any eucalyptus-green sweets that tasted sweet-type green or black.

'What would you like?' the assistant said.

Geir had put the money he would spend on the glass counter and leaned forward to see the range of sweets better, the signs of time pressure evident on his face.

'Errr . . . ' he said.

'Hurry up!' I said.

Then it all came out in a rush.

'Three of those, three of those and three of those, and four of those and one of those and one of those,' he said, pointing to the various jars.

'Three of . . . ?' the assistant said, opening an empty paper bag and turning to the stand.

'The green sweets. Oh, make that four. And then three of the red and white ones. You know, the polka dots . . . and then *five* babies' dummies . . .'

When we emerged from the shop, each with a small bag in hand, there were just four minutes to go before the bus left. But that was enough time, we told each other, running down the stairs. The steps, covered with hard-trodden snow and ice, were slippery, so we had to hold on to the banisters, which was at odds with the speed we were after. Beneath us lay the town, the white streets appearing almost yellow in the reflection from the lamps, the bus station, where the buses skidded in and out like sledges in the snow, and the tall church with the red tiles and green spire. The black sky arched above everything, strewn with twinkling stars. When there were only ten to fifteen steps left Geir let go of the banister and set off at a sprint. After a couple of strides he lost his balance and his only chance of staying upright was to run as fast as he could. He swept down the hill at a blistering pace. Then he changed tactics and decided to slide instead, but his upper body had more momentum, he was pitched forward and plunged headlong into the drift beside the road. It had all happened so fast that I didn't start laughing until he was lying in the snow.

'Ha ha ha!'

He didn't move.

Was he seriously hurt?

I walked as briskly as I could over the last stretch and stopped beside him. At first he breathed in short sob-like bursts. Then came a long hollow groan.

'*Shit*,' he whispered, holding his chest. '*Shit. Shit. Shit*.'

'I wish you wouldn't swear,' I said.

He sent me a brief withering glare.

'Did you hurt yourself?' I said.

He groaned again.

'Did it knock the breath out of you?'

He nodded and sat up and started breathing normally again. He had tears in his eyes.

'We've missed the bus now anyway,' I said.

'It knocked the breath out of me,' he said. 'I'm not crying.'

He held his side as he struggled to his feet with a grimace.

'Can you walk?' I asked.

'Yep,' he said.

From the entrance of the Arena Shopping Centre we saw our bus depart, turn onto the road and disappear around the street corner. The next bus would be in half an hour.

We sat down inside the bus station, on a bench beside a photo machine, and ate our sweets. There weren't many people around. Two youths buying hamburgers and chips while their car idled outside, a drunk sitting on the floor with his head down, asleep, and a friend of the girl working in the kiosk.

Geir put one of the red and white sweets in his mouth.

'What colour does it taste of?' I said.

He looked at me with raised eyebrows.

'Red and white of course!' he said. 'It was a red and white sweet.'

'It doesn't necessarily follow,' I said. 'Suppose I ate it and it tasted green.'

'What are you talking about now?' he said.

'Suppose it tasted of jam, for example,' I said.

'Jam?'

'Don't you understand anything?' I said. 'We can't know if sweets taste the same as the colour!'

But he didn't understand. I wasn't absolutely sure I even understood myself. But Dag Lothar and I had once put a sweet shaped like a black bolt in our mouths, exchanged glances and said, both at the same time, it tastes *green*! And later that autumn we'd had visitors, grandma, grandad, Gunnar, dad's uncle Alf and his wife Sølvi had been staying at ours, we ate shrimps, crab and a lobster which dad had caught in the net only a few days before, and while we were eating Sølvi looked at dad and said, 'Imagine you catching this lobster yourself. It tasted *delicious*.'

'It really was delicious,' grandma said.

'Nothing tastes as good as lobster,' dad said. 'But we can't know if it tastes the same for all of us.'

Sølvi stared at him.

'What do you mean by that?'

'I know how it tastes to *me*,' dad said. 'But I have no idea how it tastes to you.'

'It tastes of lobster of course!' Sølvi said.

Everyone laughed.

I didn't understand what they were laughing about. What they said was right. But I laughed too.

'But how can you know that lobster tastes the same to me as it does to you?' dad asked. 'For all you know, it could taste like jam to me.'

Sølvi was about to say something but held back, looking down at the lobster, then up at dad. She shook her head.

'I don't understand,' she said. 'The lobster's there. And it tastes of *lobster*. Not jam!'

The others laughed again. I knew dad was right, but I didn't know exactly why. For a long time I sat musing. It was as if I was constantly on the point of understanding, but then as I was beginning to comprehend, it slipped from my grasp. The thought was too big for me.

But it had been even bigger for Geir, I remembered, and looked up as the door opened. It was Stig. His face lit up when he saw us and he came over.

'Hi,' he said.

'Hi,' Geir said.

'Hi,' I said.

'Missed the bus, did you?' he said, sitting down beside us. Geir nodded.

'Do you want one?' he said, holding out the bag to him. Stig smiled and chose a baby's dummy. So I had to offer him one afterwards as well. Why on earth had Geir done that? We didn't exactly have a lot of sweets.

Stig was in the class above ours and did gymnastics training in Arendal three times a week. He competed at national level, but there wasn't a touch of arrogance about him, as there was with Snorre, who swam for the national squad and wanted nothing to do with us. Stig was nice, one of the nicest boys I knew in fact. When the bus came he sat in the seat in front of Geir and me. By the end of Langbrygga the conversation had petered out, he turned round and sat like that for the rest of the journey. Geir and I were quiet too, and the thought of the missing sock returned with renewed vigour.

Oh no, oh no.

What was going to happen?

What was going to happen?

Oh no oh no oh no.

No, no, no!

Perhaps he had noticed that we were late. Perhaps he would be standing there waiting. On the other hand, he might not be, he might be busy with something else, in which case I was safe; if I could get from the hall to the boiler room unnoticed everything would be fine because I had my other socks there and I could change into them.

The bus drove onto Tromøya Bridge and was buffeted by the wind. The windows vibrated. Geir, who always wanted to be the first to pull the bell cord, reached up and rang even though we were the only passengers to get off here. The bus stop was right at the bottom of the hill, and I always felt guilty when I alighted here because the bus would have to set off again and wouldn't be able to pick up speed until it had passed the brow of the hill a few hundred metres further on. Sometimes this feeling was so strong in me that I didn't get off until the next stop, up by B-Max, especially when I was on my own. Even now, with thoughts of the sock burning in my consciousness, I felt a little pang as Geir pulled the cord and the bus braked with a sigh of irritation to drop us off.

We stood by the drifts of snow and waited until the bus had pulled out again. Stig raised his hand to say goodbye. Then we crossed the road and walked up the path to the estate.

Usually I would kick my boots against the doorstep a couple of times to shake the snow off and then brush my trousers with the broom leaning against the wall for that very purpose, but this time I skipped the kicks, fearing he might hear, just brushed my trousers and cautiously opened the door, sidled in and closed it behind me.

But that was enough. From inside, I heard his study door open, and then the door to the porch.

He stood in front of me.

'You're late,' he said.

'Yes, I'm sorry,' I said. 'But Geir fell and hurt himself on the road, so we missed the bus.'

I started undoing the boot with a sock in.

He didn't show any sign of wanting to leave.

I pulled the boot off and placed it by the wall.

Looked up at him.

'What is it?' he said.

'Nothing,' I said.

My heart was pounding in my ears. Getting up and walking with one boot on across the floor was obviously not an option. Standing still and waiting for him to leave was not an option either, because he wasn't going anywhere.

Slowly I began to untie my laces. While doing so I had a brainwave. I unwound my scarf, placed it beside my boot and, after undoing the laces, I pulled it off, took the scarf and casually tried to cover my naked foot.

Then, with the scarf half-covering my foot, I stood up.

'Where's your sock?' dad said.

I looked down at my foot. Glanced at him.

'I couldn't find it,' I said, my eyes downcast again.

'Have you *lost* it?' he said.

'Yes,' I said.

The next instant he was up close to me, grabbing my arms in an iron grip and pinning me to the wall.

'Have you LOST your sock?'

'Yes!' I shouted.

He shook me. Then let me go.

'How old are you now? And how much money do you think we've got? Do you think we can afford to lose items of clothing?'

'No,' I said to the floor, my eyes full of tears. He held my ear and twisted it.

'You young brat!' he said. 'Keep an eye on your things!'

'Mm,' I said.

'You can't go to the swimming pool any more. Is that understood?'

'Eh?'

'YOU CAN'T GO TO THE SWIMMING POOL ANY MORE!' he said.

'But . . .' I sobbed.

'NO IFS OR BUTS!'

He let go of my ear and marched to the door. Turned to me.

'You're not old enough. You've shown that tonight. You can't go there again. This was the last time. Have you got that?'

'Yes,' I said.

'Right. Up to your room with you. There'll be no supper for you. You can go straight to bed.'

The following week I didn't go swimming, but I missed it so much that the next week I acted as if nothing had happened, packed my things and caught the bus with Geir and Dag Lothar. My fears trickled through at various points, but something inside me said I would be fine, and I was as well, on my return everything was as normal, and so it stayed, he never said another word about my not being able to continue the course.

At the start of December, three days before my birthday and two days before mum came home again, I was sitting on the toilet having a dump when the familiar sound of dad's car turning and parking in the drive was not followed by the equally familiar sound of a door being opened and closed but the doorbell ringing.

What could this be?

I hurriedly wiped my arse, pulled the chain, yanked up my trousers, opened the window above the bathtub and poked my head out.

Dad was standing beneath me wearing a new anorak. On his legs he wore knee-length breeches and long blue socks, and on his feet a pair of blue and white boots, all equally new.

'Come on!' he said. 'We're going skiing!'

I got dressed in a flash and went outside, where he was tying my skis and sticks to the roof rack beside a pair of brand new long wooden Splitkein skis.

'Have you bought yourself some skis?' I said.

'Yes,' he said. 'Isn't it great? So we can go skiing together.'

'OK,' I said. 'Where are we going then?'

'Let's go to the west of the island,' he said. 'To Hove.'

'Are there pistes there?'

'There? Oh yes!' he said. 'They've got the best.'

I doubted it but didn't say anything, got in the car beside him, how unfamiliar he looked in his new clothes, and then we left for Hove. Not a word was said until he parked and we got out.

'Here we are!' he said.

He had driven through Hove Holiday Centre, which consisted of a large number of red houses and huts originating from the last war, most probably built by the Germans, like the firing range which, I had heard rumoured, had been an aerodrome, like the concrete gun emplacements towering above the sea-smoothed rocks and the pebble beaches close to the edge of the forest and the fascinating low bunkers among the trees, where we used to play on the roofs and in the rooms when we were here in the afternoon on 17 May celebration days, he had driven past all this, along a narrow road into the forest which came to an end by a small sand quarry, where he stopped and parked.

After taking the skis off the roof, he came over with a little case full of ski-waxing equipment he had also bought, and we waxed the skis with blue Swix, which, after reading the back of one of the tubes, he said had to be the best. Apparently unfamiliar with bindings, it took him a bit longer to put on his skis than it did me. Then he put his hands through the loops on the poles. But he didn't do it from underneath so that the loop wouldn't slip off even if you lost hold of the pole. No, he put his hands straight through.

That was how small children who knew no better held them.

It hurt me to watch, but I couldn't say anything. Instead I took my hands out and then threaded them through again so that, if he was paying attention, he could see how it was done.

But he wasn't watching me; he was looking up at the little ridge of hills above the sand quarry.

'Let's get going then!' he said.

Although I had never seen him ski before, I could never have dreamed in my wildest imagination that he couldn't ski. But he couldn't. He didn't glide with the skis, he walked as he normally walked without skis, taking short plodding steps which on top of everything else were unsteady, which meant that every so often he had to stop and poke his poles into the snow so as not to topple over.

I thought perhaps this was just the beginning and soon he would find his rhythm and glide as he should glide along the piste. But when we reached the ridge, where the sea was visible between the trees, grey with frothy white-flecked waves, and started to follow the ski tracks he was still walking in the same way.

Occasionally he would turn and smile at me.

I felt so sorry for him I could have shouted out aloud as I skied.

Poor dad. Poor, poor dad.

At the same time I was embarrassed, my own father couldn't ski, and I stayed some distance behind him so that potential passers-by wouldn't associate me with him. He was just someone out ahead, a tourist, I was on my own, this was where I came from, I knew how to ski.

The piste wound back into the forest, but if the view of the sea was gone its sounds lingered between the trees, rising and falling, and the aroma of salt water and rotten seaweed was everywhere, it blended with the forest's other faintly wintry smells, of which the snow's curious mixture of raw and gentle was perhaps the most obvious.

He stopped and hung on his ski poles. I came alongside him. A ship was moving on the horizon. The sky above us was light grey. A pale greyish-yellow glow above the two lighthouses on Torungen revealed where the sun was.

He looked at me.

'Skis running well?' he said.

'Pretty well,' I said. 'How about you?'

'Yes,' he said. 'Let's go on, shall we? It'll soon be time to head for home. We have to make dinner as well. So, away you go!'

'Don't you want to go first?'

'No, you head off. I'll follow.'

The new arrangement turned everything in my head upside down. If he was behind me he would see how I, someone who knew how to ski, skied and realise how clumsy his own style was. I saw every single pole plant through his eyes. They cut through my consciousness like knives. After only a few metres I slowed down, I began to ski in a slower, more staccato style, not unlike his, just not as clumsy, so that he would understand what I was doing, and that was even worse. Beneath us the white frothy breakers washed lazily onto the pebble beach. On the rocks, in some places, the wind whirled snow into the air. A seagull floated past, its wings unmoving. We were approaching the car, and on the last little slope I had an idea, I changed the tempo, and went as fast as I could for a few metres, then pretended to lose my balance and threw myself into the snow beside the piste. I got up as quickly as possible and was brushing my trousers down as he whistled past.

'It's all about staying on your feet,' he said.

We drove home in silence, and I was relieved when we finally turned into our drive and the skiing trip was definitively over.

Standing in the hall and taking off our skiing gear, we didn't say anything either. But then, as he opened the door to the staircase, he turned to me.

'Come and keep me company while I'm cooking,' he said.

I nodded and followed him up.

In the living room he stopped and looked at the wall.

'What on earth . . .' he said. 'Have you noticed this before?'

I had forgotten all about the streak of orange juice. My surprise as I shook my head must have had a dash of authenticity about it because his attention wandered as he bent down and ran his finger over the thin line of orange. Even his imagination would hardly stretch far enough to guess it was caused by my flinging an orange at the floor just there, on the landing outside the kitchen.

He straightened up and walked into the kitchen. I sat down on the stool as usual, he took a packet of pollock from the fridge, placed it on the worktop, fetched flour, salt and pepper from the cupboard, sprinkled it on a plate and began to turn the soft slippery fillets in the mixture.

'Tomorrow after school we'll go to Arendal and buy you a birthday present,' he said without looking at me.

'Shall I go with you? Isn't it supposed to be a secret?' I said.

'Well, you know what you want, don't you?' he said. 'Football kit, isn't it?'

'Yes.'

'You can try it on and then we'll know if it fits,' he said, pushing a knob of butter from the knife into the frying pan with his finger.

What I wanted was Liverpool colours. But when we went to the Intersport shop they didn't have Liverpool kit on the stand.

'Can't we ask one of the people working here? Perhaps they've got some in stock?'

'If it's not hanging up, they haven't got it,' dad said. 'Take one of the others.'

'But I support Liverpool.'

'Take Everton then,' he said. 'It's the same town.'

I looked at the Everton shirt. Blue with white shorts. Umbro.

I looked at dad. He seemed impatient, his eyes were wandering.

I put on the shirt over my jumper and held the shorts in front of me.

'Well, it looks good,' I said.

'Let's take it then,' dad said, grabbing the shirt and shorts and going to pay. They wrapped them up while he counted the notes in his fat wallet, combed his hair back with his hand and looked into the street outside, which was crowded with shoppers now, three weeks before Christmas.

On my birthday I woke up very early. The parcel containing the football strip was in my wardrobe. I couldn't wait to try it on. Tore off the paper, took out the kit, pressed it against my nose, was there any better smell than new clothes? I put on the glistening shorts, then the shirt, which was rougher, a bit uneven against my skin, and the white socks. Then I went into the bathroom to look at myself.

Turned from side to side.

It looked good.

It wasn't Liverpool, but it looked good, and they were from the same city.

Suddenly dad swung open the bathroom door.

'What are you up to, boy?' he said.

He eyed me.

'Have you opened your present!' he shouted. 'On your own?'

He grabbed my arm and hauled me into my bedroom.

'Now you wrap it up again!' he said. 'NOW!'

I cried and took off the kit, tried to fold it as well as I could, placed it in the paper and stuck it together with a bit of the tape that was still sticky.

Dad oversaw everything. As soon as I had finished, he snatched the parcel out of my hands and left.

'Actually I should have taken it off you,' he said. 'But now I'll keep it until we give you the rest of your presents. It is your birthday, after all.'

As I knew what I was getting and I had even tried the kit on in the shop, I had been sure it was the *day* that was important and that on the *day* I could wear it. I hadn't seen it as one of the presents I would be given when we ate the birthday cake in the afternoon. It was impossible to make him understand. But I was right, he wasn't. The kit was mine when all was said and done! On this day it became mine!

I lay in bed crying until the others got up. Mum was in high spirits and wished me a happy birthday when I went into the kitchen, she had baked fresh rolls the evening before, which she was warming up in the oven, and she was boiling some eggs, but I didn't care, my hatred for dad cast a cloud over everything.

In the afternoon we ate cake and drank pop. I had never been allowed to invite friends on my birthday, and nor was I on this one. I was sullen and surly, I ate the cake without a word, and when dad put the presents in front of me with a smile that showed no insight into what had happened that morning, as though it *were* possible to start afresh, I looked down and unwrapped the Everton kit without showing any sign of pleasure.

'How nice,' mum said. 'Are you going to try it on?'

'No,' I said. 'I tried it on in the shop. Fits perfectly.'

'Put it on,' dad said. 'So mum and Yngve can see.'

'No,' I said.

He eyed me.

I took the kit to the bathroom, changed and went back in.

'Excellent,' dad said. 'I bet you'll be the coolest on the pitch this winter.'

'Can I take it off now?' I said.

'Wait till we've finished with the presents,' dad said. 'Here's one from me.'

He passed me a small square packet that *had* to be a cassette.

I opened it.

It was the new Wings cassette. *Back to the Egg*.

I looked at him. He looked out of the window.

'Do you like it?' he said.

'Oh yes,' I said. 'It's the new Wings cassette! I'll play it now!'

'Hang on a moment,' he said. 'You've got a couple of presents left.'

'Here's a tiny one from me,' mum said.

It was big but light. What could it be?

'Just something for your room,' she said.

I unwrapped it. It was a stool. Four wooden legs and a kind of net seat between them.

'A stool of the more fragrant kind,' Yngve said.

'Thanks, Mum,' I said. 'It'll be good for when I read!'

'And here's one from me,' Yngve said.

'Oh yes?' I said. 'I wonder what you've come up with this time?'

It was a book on how to play the guitar.

I looked at him with moist eyes.

'Thank you very much,' I said.

'It's got scales, solos, everything,' he said. 'Very simple. There's a black dot for where you have to press. Even you can follow that.'

For the rest of the day I listened to *Back to the Egg*.

Yngve came in and said that John Bonham, the drummer in Led Zeppelin, was on one of the tracks. And he had read in the newspaper that a Norwegian priest spoke at the beginning of one of the songs. It had to be at the start of the LP, we worked out, 'Reception', where there was a recording off the radio.

'There!' Yngve said. 'Play it again!'

And then I heard it too.

'*Men la oss nå prøve å se dette I lys av Det nye testamentet,*' a faint grating old man's voice said.

The thought that neither Paul McCartney, Linda McCartney, Denny Laine, Steve Holly nor Laurence Juber had a clue what was being said there, but that Yngve and I did, as we were Norwegian, sent my senses into free fall.

As always, dad was kind all Christmas, even in the morning. As New Year's Eve approached and the shops finally opened for a few hours, mum drove to Arendal to buy some food and fireworks. She must have intimated that perhaps it wasn't necessary to spend hundreds of kroner on rockets, as dad always did, at any rate, she it was who had the responsibility for buying fireworks while dad kept well in the background.

It wasn't a great success.

Dad usually showed us the rockets he had bought and said,

well, this year we were going to knock Gustavsen into a cocked hat, for instance, or there were going to be a few really big bangs this year! When New Year's Eve came we would see him standing outside on the shimmering snow astutely and meticulously arranging the launch site. With a strand of hair hanging down over his face, which his beard almost blotted out in the darkness, he would set up the clothes stand in the snow and line the biggest rockets up against it, and place the others in a whole battery of bottles and hollow objects. Once the preparations had been made, he would wait until half past eleven. Then he would call us outside and the New Year was brought in with several salvos. He started small, with a few little firecrackers or sparklers that Yngve and I were allocated, and then he gradually stepped up the power until the biggest rocket was launched at twelve. Afterwards he would declare that there had been lots of wonderful rockets this year but we, as usual, had had the best. That of course was open to debate because we were not the only ones to invest money in fireworks, Gustavsen and Karlsen did too.

But this New Year's Eve dad, the King of Fireworks, had abdicated.

I pondered quite a bit on the cause. Whatever it was, I suspected that the consequences would be of major significance. No, it wasn't a suspicion, I *knew*.

When it was a few minutes after half past eleven and mum said perhaps it was time to go out and light the rocket, my jaw dropped.

'*The* rocket?' I said. 'Have we only got one? One rocket?'

'Yes,' mum said. 'Surely that's enough? It's a big one. They said in the shop it was the biggest and best they had.'

Dad smirked to himself. He went out after Yngve and me, stood beside us on the terrace at the back of the house where the launch was to take place.

The rocket really was big, she was right about that.

She put it in a bottle, but the bottle was too small, and both the bottle and rocket tipped over. She stood it up and looked around. Her light-coloured leather coat was open, the zips in her high boots were undone, making them seem as if they were unfolding as she moved like two exotic plants. Around her neck she had wound her thick rust-brown scarf.

'We could do with something bigger to put this rocket in,' she said.

Dad said nothing.

'Dad normally uses the clothes horse,' Yngve said.

'That's true!' mum said.

The clothes horse, which was only used in the summer, was made of wood and leaned against the wall. Mum fetched it and set it up in the snow. She crouched down and positioned the rocket against it, but, seeing at once that it wouldn't work, she stood up with the rocket in her hand. Around us fireworks were going off everywhere. The sky was lit with explosions, which we sensed rather than saw because it was overcast and misty, so of the showers of stars and all the colours and patterns not much more than flashes of light were to be seen.

'What about if you lay it on its side,' Yngve said. 'Dad usually does that.'

Mum did as he suggested.

'It's twelve o'clock now,' dad said. 'Aren't you going to light our rocket soon?'

'Yes,' mum said. She took a lighter from her pocket, crouched down, shielded the tiny flame with her hand and averted her whole body, ready to run. The second the fuse was lit she dashed towards us.

'Happy New Year!' she said.

'Happy New Year,' Yngve said.

I said nothing because the rocket, which the burning fuse had reached now, sounded as if it was going to fizzle out. Then the flame died and the hiss stopped.

'Oh no,' I said. 'It didn't work! It was a dud! And we've only got one. Why did you buy only one? How could you do that?'

'That was New Year's Eve then,' dad said. 'Perhaps I should sort out the fireworks next year?'

I had never felt so sorry for mum as I did then, when we left the rocket and went into the warm, surrounded by neighbours' exultant shouts and explosions. What hurt most was that she had done the best she could. She couldn't do any better.

One afternoon two weeks later I was down by Lake Tjenna and my legs were absolutely freezing. Framlaget, the Socialist Party's children's organisation, which I and almost all the other kids on the estate were in, had arranged a ski race. There were numbers on chests and medals for everyone, but above all it was numbingly cold standing there and waiting your turn. And when my turn did come, my skis were slippery, I could never really get a decent speed going and I finished way down the results list. As soon as I had passed the line and received my medal I set off for home. The darkness hung between the branches, the cold chafed at my toes, the skis kept slipping and sliding, I couldn't even manage the steepest hill using the herringbone technique and had to ascend sideways. But at last the road was there with its illuminated street lamps like a luminous ribbon in the dusk, and our house was on the other side. I staggered across and into the drive, undid my skis and leaned them against the house, opened the door and stopped.

What was that smell?

Grandma?

Was *grandma* here?

No, out of the question, that was impossible.

Perhaps dad had been to Kristiansand and had brought the fragrance back with him?

No, for Pete's sake, there was someone talking in the kitchen!

I had my boots off in a flash, registered that my socks were wet so I couldn't walk in them, they would leave marks, and I jogged through the hall into the boiler room, where there was a fresh pair hanging from a line, put them on, strode up the stairs as fast as I dared, stopped.

The fragrance was stronger here. There was no doubt: grandma was here.

'Is that you, champ?' dad said.

'Yes,' I said.

'Come in here a moment!' he said.

I went into the kitchen.

There was grandma!

I ran over and hugged her.

She laughed and ruffled my hair.

'How big you've grown!' she said.

'What are you doing here?' I said. 'Where's the car? Where's grandad?'

'I caught the bus,' she said.

'The bus?' I said.

'Yes. My son is alone with his children, I thought, so I can go and give him a bit of a hand. I've already made some dinner for you, as you can see.'

'How long are you staying?'

She laughed.

'Well, I'm catching the bus back tomorrow, I think. Someone has to look after grandad as well. I can't leave him alone for too long.'

'No,' I said, hugging her again.

'Now, now,' dad said. 'You go to your room for a while and I'll call you when the food's ready.'

'But he must have his present first,' grandma said.

'Thank you for my Christmas present, by the way,' I said. 'It was brilliant.'

Grandma leaned forward, lifted her bag and took out a little packet, which she passed to me.

I tore off the paper.

It was an IK Start mug.

It was white, with the Kristiansand club logo on one side and a football player in a yellow shirt and black shorts on the other.

'Wow, a Start mug!' I said and gave her another hug.

It was strange having grandma there. I had hardly ever seen her without grandad, and hardly ever on her own with dad. They sat chatting in the kitchen; I could hear them through the door, which I had left ajar. There were intermittent pauses when one of them got up to do something. Then they chatted a bit more, grandma laughed and told a story and dad mumbled. He called us, we ate, he was quite different from how he normally was, coming closer to us and then distancing himself all the time. Sometimes he was completely in tune with what grandma was saying, then he would be gone, looking elsewhere or getting up to do something, then he would look at her again and smile and make a comment which would make her laugh, and then he was gone again.

She left the following evening. She gave Yngve and me a hug, then dad drove her to the bus station in Arendal. I put on *Rubber Soul* and lay down with a biography of Madame Curie. When the second song came, 'Norwegian Wood', I took my eyes off the book and gazed at the ceiling as the mood of the music in some incomprehensible way got into me and raised me to where it was. It was a fantastic feeling. Not only because it was beautiful, there was something else present which had nothing to do with the room I lay in or the world I was surrounded by.

I once had a girl, or should I say, she once had me?
She showed me her room, isn't it good, Norwegian wood?

Fantastic, fantastic.

Then I went on reading about Madame Curie until ten and I switched off the light. As I drifted into sleep, as whatever existed in my room was somehow diluted with images, where they came from I had no idea, but I accepted them nonetheless, the door was suddenly thrust open and the light switched on.

It was dad.

'How many apples have you had today?' he said.

'One,' I said.

'Are you sure? Grandma said she gave you one.'

'Really?'

'But you had one after dinner too. Do you remember?'

'Oh yes! I'd forgotten that one!' I said.

Dad switched off the light and closed the door without another word.

The next day after dinner he called me. I went into the kitchen.

'Sit down,' he said. 'Here's an apple.'

'Thanks,' I said.

He handed me an apple.

'Sit here and eat it,' he said.

I glanced up at him. He met my gaze, his eyes were serious, and I looked down, started to eat the apple. Once it was finished, he handed me another.

Where had he got it from? Had he got a bag behind his back or what?

'Have another,' he said.

'Thanks,' I said. 'But I only eat one a day.'

'You had two yesterday, didn't you?'

I nodded, took it and ate it.

He handed me another.

'Here's another,' he said. 'This is your lucky day.'

'I'm full,' I said.

'Eat your apple.'

I ate it. It took me longer than the first two. The bite-sized chunks seemed to be lying on top of the food from dinner; it was as though I could feel the cold apple flesh down below.

Dad handed me another.

'I don't want it,' I said.

'There were no limits yesterday,' he said. 'Have you forgotten? You must have had two apples because you wanted them. Today you can have as many as you want. Eat.'

I shook my head.

He leaned down. His eyes were cold.

'Eat your apple. Now.'

I started eating. Whenever I swallowed my stomach contracted and I had to swallow several times not to throw up.

He was standing behind me, there was no way I could trick him. I cried and swallowed, swallowed and cried. In the end, I couldn't go on.

'I'm so full!' I said. 'I simply can't eat any more!'

'Eat up,' dad said. 'You like apples so much.'

I tried a couple more bites, but it was no good.

'I can't,' I said.

He looked at me. Then he took the half-eaten apple and threw it in the bin in the cupboard under the sink.

'You can go to your room,' he said. 'Now I hope that has taught you a lesson.'

Inside my room there was only one thing I longed for, and that was to grow up. To have total control over my own life. I hated dad, but I was in his hands, I couldn't escape his power. It was impossible to exact my revenge on him. Except in the much-acclaimed mind and imagination, there I was able to crush him. I could grow there, outgrow him, place my hands on his cheeks and squeeze until his lips formed the stupid pout he made to imitate me, because of my protruding teeth. There, I could punch him on the nose so hard that it broke and blood streamed from it. Or, even better, so that the bone was forced back into his brain and he died. I could hurl him against the wall or throw him down the stairs. I could grab him by the neck and smash his face against the table. That was how I would think, but the instant I was in the same room as he was, everything crumbled, he was my father, a grown man, so much bigger than me that everything had to bend to his will. He bent my will as if it were nothing.

That must have been why, unwittingly of course, I was converting the inside of my room into an enormous outside. When I read, and for a while I did hardly anything else, it was always the world outside I moved in as I lay still on my bed, and not just the world that existed in the here and now, with all its foreign countries and foreigners, but also the one that had been, from Stokke's Bjørneklo, the Stone Age boy, to the one in the future, such as in Jules Verne's books. And then there was the music. It too opened my room with its moods and the strong emotions it evoked in me, which had nothing to do with those I normally felt in life. Mostly I listened to the Beatles and Wings, but also to Yngve's music, which for a long time was bands and solo artists like Gary Glitter, Mud, Slade, the Sweet, Rainbow, Status Quo, Rush, Led Zeppelin and Queen, but who in the course of his secondary school education changed as other, quite different, music began to sneak its way between all these old cassettes and records, like the Jam and a single by the Stranglers, called 'No More Heroes', an LP by the Boomtown Rats and one by the Clash, a cassette by Sham 69 and Kraftwerk, as well as the songs he recorded off the only radio music programme there was, *Pop Spesial*. He started to have friends who were interested in the same music and also played the guitar. One of them was called Bård Torstensen, and one day at the beginning of May when dad was out for a few hours and so the house was left unguarded, he joined Yngve in his room. They sat playing guitars and listening to records. After a while there was a knock at my door, it was Yngve, there was something he wanted to show Bård. I was reclining on the bed reading and got up when they came in.

'Look,' Yngve said, going over to the Elvis poster I had on the wall over the desk. 'Can you guess what's on the back?'

Bård shook his head.

Yngve loosened the drawing pins, took the poster down and turned it round.

'Look,' he said. 'Johnny Rotten! But he prefers Elvis!'

Both of them laughed.

'Can I buy it off you?' Bård said.

I shook my head.

'It's mine.'

'But you've got it up the wrong way round!' Bård said, laughing again.

'I haven't,' I said. 'That is Elvis, you know!'

'Elvis is the past!' Bård said.

'No, he isn't. Not Elvis Costello,' Yngve said.

'That's true,' Bård said.

After they had gone I looked at the two pictures for a while.

The one called Johnny Rotten was ugly. Elvis was good-looking. Why should I swap the ugly one for the good-looking one?

Outdoors we did what we always do every spring: cut branches off the birch trees, tie bottles on to the stumps left behind, collect them the next day, full of light-coloured viscous sap, and drink it. We cut branches off the willow trees and made flutes from the bark. We picked large bunches of white wood-anemones and gave them to our mothers. Well, we were too big for the latter really, but it was a gesture, it was us being good. Then one morning, when we had only three hours, I dragged Geir with me into the forest, I knew a place where there were so many anemones that from a distance they looked like snow on the ground. Not without some self-torment though, for flowers were living beings, picking them was killing them, but the cause was good, with their help I could spread happiness. The light fell in shafts through the branches, the bog was a luminous green and we each picked an enormous bunch, which we ran home with.

When I arrived dad was at home. He was in the laundry room at the bottom of the house. He turned to me, anger in every movement.

'I picked you some flowers,' I said.

He reached out with his hand, took them and threw them in the large sink.

'Little girls pick flowers,' he said.

He was right. And he was probably ashamed of me. Once some of his colleagues had come home and they had seen me on the stairs, with my blond hair quite long, because it was winter, and I was wearing red long johns.

'What a nice girl you've got,' one of them said.

'It's a boy,' dad answered. He had smiled, but I knew him well enough to know the comment had not gladdened his heart.

There was my interest in clothes, my crying if I didn't get the shoes I wanted, my crying if it was too cold when we were in the boat on the sea, indeed my crying if he raised his voice in situations when it would have been absolutely normal to raise your voice, was it so strange for him to think: what kind of son have I got here?

I was a mummy's boy, he was constantly telling me. I was as well. I longed for her. And no one was happier when she moved back for good at the end of the month.

When summer was over and I was about to start the fifth class it was dad's turn. He was going all the way to Bergen, to stay at something called the Fantoft Student Town, to major in Nordic literature and become a senior teacher.

'I'm afraid I won't be able to come home every weekend,' he said during dinner just before leaving. 'Perhaps no more than once a month.'

'That's a shame,' I said.

I went out to the drive to see him off. He put his suitcases in the boot, and then he got in on the passenger side because mum was driving him to the airport.

It was one of the strangest sights I had seen.

Dad didn't look right in a VW Beetle, he didn't. And if he was going to sit in one, it definitely shouldn't be as a passenger, it verged on the grotesque, especially when mum got in beside him and started the engine, turned her head and reversed.

Dad wasn't a passenger; that much was obvious.

I waved, dad raised a hand and they were gone.

What should I do now?

Go into the workshop room, hammer and saw, chop and cut for all I was worth?

Go into the kitchen and make waffles? Fry an egg? Brew up some tea?

Sit with my feet on the table?

No, I knew what.

Go into Yngve's room, take out one of his records and put it on full volume.

I chose *Play* by Magazine.

Turned up the volume almost full blast, opened the door and went into the living room.

The bass was making the walls vibrate. Music was *belting* out of the room. I closed my eyes and I swayed back and forth to the rhythm. After doing that for a while I went into the kitchen, took the bar of cooking chocolate and ate it. The music was booming out around me, but I wasn't inside it, it was more like part of the house, the dining-room table or the pictures on the wall. Then I started swaying to and fro again and it was as though I was devouring the music and had it inside me. Especially when I closed my eyes.

Someone downstairs was calling me.

I opened my eyes and gasped.

Had they forgotten something and come back?

I dashed into the bedroom and turned the volume right down.

'What *are* you doing?' Yngve called from downstairs.

Oh. What a relief.

'Nothing,' I said. 'I borrowed one of your records.'

He came up the stairs. Followed by another boy. I hadn't seen him before. Perhaps someone from volleyball?

'Have you gone completely nuts?' Yngve said. 'You can *burst* the speakers. They're probably ruined now. You bloody idiot!'

'I didn't know,' I said. 'Sorry. A thousand times sorry.'

The other boy smiled.

'This is Trond,' Yngve said. 'And this is my stupid little brother.'

'Hi, little brother,' Trond said.

'Hi,' I said.

Yngve went into his room, turned up the volume and placed his head against the speakers.

'You haven't burst them, fortunately,' he said, straightening up. 'You were lucky. You'd have bought me some new ones otherwise. I would have personally made sure you did.'

He looked at me.

'Have they been gone long?'

I shrugged.

'Half an hour,' I said.

Yngve closed his bedroom door, and I hung around in the living room for a while until I spotted Marianne and Solveig outside. They were pushing a pram. I went out and ran after them.

'Let's walk together, shall we?' I said.

'All right,' they said. 'Where are you going?'

'Up.'

'Who are you going to see?'

I shrugged. 'Whose is the baby?'

'The Leonardsens'.'

'How much are you getting?'

'Five kroner.'

'Are you saving up for something?'

'Nothing special. A jacket maybe.'

'I'm going to buy a new jacket too,' I said. 'A black Matinique. Have you seen it?'

'No.'

'The sleeves are long and they're made of a different material from the rest. Sort of wavy. And it's got a little flap down the middle covering the zip. What kind of jacket are you going to get?'

Marianne shrugged.

'A coat, I was thinking.'

'A coat? A light colour?'

'Perhaps. Quite short.'

'You're the only boy who talks about clothes,' Solveig said.

'I know,' I said. And it was something I had discovered recently. It was so difficult to talk to girls. Once you had taken their hats or shouted a few bad words after them that was where it usually ended. Well, you could talk to them about homework. But nothing else. Then I suddenly realised. Clothes, that was what they were interested in. All you had to do was chat away.

As we got closer to B-Max, I said bye and ran down the slope to the play area, which was deserted, then up the grass slope to the old car wreck, which was deserted, then over to the football pitch, which was deserted, and over the fence to Prestbakmo's and the front of the house, where I rang the bell. But Geir was having dinner, and afterwards he was going up to Vemund's.

Oh, yes.

The road too was deserted. It was Sunday, dinner time, kids were eating or they were out visiting or they were on a trip with their parents.

Then I had a sudden brainwave: Yngve had a friend with him! Perhaps I could join them?

I ran down the hill, but their bikes had gone, they must have already left.

What could I do?

It was cloudy and not very warm. There probably wasn't anyone at the Rock.

Slowly I started walking down to the pontoons. Probably no one there either, but if nothing else I could look at the various boats and breathe in the distinctive smell of fibreglass and wood, petrol and salt water.

No, a whole crowd was there.

I mingled with them unobtrusively. Some of them had boats, they were sitting on board and spitting into the water while listening to those on the pontoon who didn't have a boat but had come to be close to those who did. I stood with them although I had no dreams of ever owning a boat, it was so unrealistic that I might just as well have dreamed about waking up in the Viking age the next morning, as a boy had done in one of the books I was reading. No, if I dreamed about anything, it was a pair of new white trainers with the light blue Nike logo, like the ones Yngve had, or new light blue Levi jeans, or a light blue Catalina jacket. Or a new pair of Puma football boots, an Admiral tracksuit or a pair of Umbro shorts. Or Speedo trunks. I thought a lot about the black and white Adidas Olympia trainers. Then there was a pair of shin pads with instep protection I wanted, and a Puma bag, and for winter Atomic slalom skis and Dynastar slalom poles. I wanted slalom pants and a genuine down jacket. Splitkein fibreglass skis, new Rottefella bindings. And light-coloured Sami reindeer-hide boots, the ones with the little curled-up toe. I wanted a new white shirt and a red college sweater. I had mentally chosen white rubber boots instead of the dark blue ones I had now. I would also have liked a pink coral necklace I had seen, white at a pinch.

Boats, mopeds and cars interested me less. But as I couldn't say this to anyone I had a few favourite brands among them too. Boat: ten-footer With Dromedille with a five-horsepower Yamaha engine. Moped: Suzuki. Car: BMW. These choices had a lot to do with the unusual letters. Y, Z, W. For the same reason I was drawn to Wolverhampton Wanderers, it was the first football team I supported, and even after Liverpool took over that role, my heart still beat for Wolves, who else when their ground was called Molineux and their logo was a wolf's head on an orange background?

Trousers, jackets, sweaters, shoes and sports gear were on my mind a lot because I wanted to look good and I wanted to win. When John McEnroe, whom I rated as perhaps the all-time greatest, when he got that dangerous glint in his eye after an umpire's decision, when he glared up at the umpire while bouncing the ball on the court before serving, I thought desperately, no, don't do it, don't do it, it won't help, you can't afford to lose the point, don't do it! – and could barely watch when he did it anyway and started to swear at the umpire, perhaps even sling his racquet to the ground so hard it bounced up several metres. I identified with him to such a degree that I cried every time he lost, and couldn't bear to be indoors, but had to go out onto the road, where I sat on the concrete barriers mourning the defeat, my cheeks wet with tears. The same applied to Liverpool. A defeat in the FA Cup Final drove me outside onto the road with my face streaming. In that team I liked Emlyn Hughes best, he was the one I supported, but I liked the others too, of course, especially Ray Clemence and Kevin Keegan, before he went to Hamburg and Newcastle. In one of Yngve's football magazines I had read a comparison of Kevin Keegan and his replacement, Kenny Dalglish. They were compared point by point, and even though they had their own strengths and weaknesses, they came out of it fairly even. But one thing that had been written left a searing mark on me. The article said that Kevin Keegan was an extrovert while Kenny Dalglish was an introvert.

Just seeing the word *introvert* threw me into despair.

Was I an introvert?

Wasn't I?

Didn't I cry more than I laughed? Didn't I spend all my time reading in my room?

That was introverted behaviour, wasn't it?

Introvert, introvert, I didn't want to be an introvert.

That was the last thing I wanted to be, there could be nothing worse.

But I was an introvert, and the insight grew like a kind of mental cancer within me.

Kenny Dalglish kept himself to himself.

Oh, so did I! But I didn't want that. I wanted to be an extrovert! An extrovert!

An hour later, after I had taken the road through the forest and climbed a tree to find out how far I could see, I ran onto the road the moment mum's Beetle came up the hill. I waved, but she didn't see me and I ran as fast as I could after the car, up the hill, across the short flat stretch and into the drive, where she got out of the car, hitched her bag over her shoulder and shut the door.

'Hi,' she said. 'Would you like to help me bake some bread?' That might have been the year dad lost his grip on us.

Many years later he was to say Bergen was where he started drinking.

It came up casually, I was visiting him one summer at the beginning of the 90s, he was drunk and I said I was going to move to Iceland that winter, and he said, Iceland, I've been there, to Reykjavik.

'Have you now?' I said. 'When would that have been?'

'It was when I was living in Bergen, you remember,' he said. 'I had a girlfriend there, she was Icelandic and we went to Reykjavik together.'

'While you were with mum?'

'Yes. I was thirty-five and living in a student residence.'

'You don't have to make an excuse. You can do what you like.'

'Yes, I can. Thank you, son.'

None of this came to our ears at the time of course and we didn't have the experience to imagine it either. All that counted for me was that he wasn't at home. But even though the house opened up, and for the first time in my life I could do what I wanted, in a strange way he was still there, the thought of him went through me like a lightning strike if I brought dirt in with me to the hall or if I dropped crumbs on the table while eating or even if juice ran down my chin while eating a pear. Can't you even eat a pear without making a mess, boy, I could hear him saying. And if I did well in a test it was to him I wanted to bring the news, not mum, that wasn't the same. However, what was happening outside was slowly changing character, it was becoming both better and worse, it was as though the gentle world of the child, where the blows that fell were muted and somehow untargeted, in the sense that they were intended for everything and nothing, became sharper and clearer, any doubt was removed, it is *you* and what *you* say that we dislike, and this was a red line, while something else opened and this something else had nothing to do with me personally, although perhaps it affected me to an even greater degree, because I was a part of it, and that part had *nothing* to do with my family, it belonged to *us*, to those of us who were out there. I was tremendously attracted by almost all the girls that autumn as I started the fifth class, but I didn't perceive them as radically different, I had something inside me that enabled me to approach them. I had no idea this was a huge blunder, indeed, the biggest blunder a boy can commit.

We had an older woman teacher that year, her name was fru Høst, she taught us a range of subjects and she liked to set up role plays. Often she chose little events for dramatisation, and I always volunteered, it was my favourite activity, everyone looked at me and I could be someone else. I had a special talent for acting girls' parts. I was good at it. I flicked my hair behind my ears, pouted a little, swung my hips as I walked and spoke in a slightly more affected voice than normal. Fru Høst sometimes laughed so much tears were rolling down her cheeks.

One evening I was hanging out with Sverre, who also liked role plays and was also a good student and bore a strong enough resemblance to me for two stand-in teachers to think, independently of each other, that we were twins, and I suggested going to visit fru Høst. She lived three kilometres or so east of the estate.

'Good idea,' Sverre said. 'But my bike's got a flat. And it's a bit of a slog on foot.'

'Let's hitch,' I said.

'OK.'

We walked down to the crossroads and stood by the kerb. I had hitch-hiked quite a lot the previous year, mostly with Dag Magne, to Hove or up to Roligheden or some of the other places we found appealing, and we had never stood there for more than an hour without getting a lift.

This evening the first car stopped.

There were two youths inside.

We got in. They were playing loud music; the windows were vibrating from the bass. The driver turned to us.

'And where are you going?'

We told him, he put the car in gear and drove off so fast we were pinned back against the seat.

'Who lives out there then?'

'Fru Høst,' Sverre said. 'She's our teacher at school.'

'Aha!' the one in the passenger seat said. 'You're going there to cause some mischief. We did that too, when we were younger. Went to the teachers' places and tormented the hell out of them.'

'Well, we're not going to do that exactly,' I said. 'We're just going to visit her.'

He turned and looked at me.

'Visit her? Why? Something to do with homework or what?'

'No-o,' I said. 'We just felt like it.'

He turned back. They were silent for the rest of the journey. Braked sharply at the crossroads.

'Out you jump, lads,' the driver said.

I had a bit of a bad conscience, knowing we had disappointed them, but lying wasn't an option. So I thanked them as warmly as I could.

They raced off into the darkness with the bass pounding.

Sverre and I trudged up the shingle driveway. Large leafy trees with outstretched branches on both sides. We had never been to her house, but we knew where it was.

There were two cars outside and all the windows were lit.

I rang the bell.

'Well, I never,' fru Høst said in surprise, opening the door.

'We thought we would visit you,' I said.

'Can we come in?' Sverre said.

She hesitated.

'I'm afraid I've got visitors here. It's not such a convenient time. But have you come all this way just to visit me?'

'Yes.'

'Come on in then! You can stay for half an hour if you like. In fact, I have some biscuits. And some juice!'

We went in.

The living room was full of adults. Fru Høst introduced us, we sat down at the table, on stools, and she gave us a plate with three biscuits on and a glass of juice.

She said we were her favourite pupils and we were such good actors.

'Could they perform something for us now?' someone asked.

Fru Høst glanced at us.

'Could do,' I said. 'OK with you?'

'Of course,' Sverre said.

I tucked my hair behind my ears, pouted and we were off, improvising, and it made everyone there laugh. After the performance we bowed, slightly flushed but happy to hear the applause.

I repeated the success at the fancy dress party just before Christmas when both Dag Magne and I dressed up as women, complete with make-up, dress and handbag, and my impersonation was so good that no one recognised me, not even Dag Lothar, who I was standing next to for at least five minutes before he suddenly realised who the stranger really was.

Although I wasn't ashamed about dressing up as a girl, nor about discussing girlish things with them, I also actually went out with some of them. The best was Mariann, it lasted two weeks, we went skating together, she sat on my lap and kissed me, I went to her birthday party, the only boy, and she sat on my lap and I held her while she chatted to her friends, we snogged there too, but in the end I couldn't be bothered any more – she was without doubt one of the best-looking girls at school, although not at the absolute top – and perhaps I also felt a little sorry for her because she lived alone with her mother and sister and they were quite poor, for example, she almost never had any new clothes, her mother did the best she could with old ones and hand-me-downs, so I felt an emptiness when I was in her room and claustrophobia when we kissed, I just wanted to leave as soon as possible, and in the end I persuaded Dag Magne to tell her it was over. That same day I made a terrible mistake, she was running behind me in the wet-weather shelter, and as a purely reflex action I stuck my foot out, she tripped and hit her face on the tarmac, there was blood and she cried, but that wasn't the worst, the worst was the ensuing fury she poured over me, which the other girls united behind as they gathered round to help her. It would be wrong to say that I was popular for the next few weeks. That I hadn't meant anything by it, that I had only done it for fun, didn't get much of a sympathetic response. At times it was as though the girls really hated me, considered me some sort of scum; at others it was the opposite, not only did they want to talk to me but at the class parties we had begun to arrange, in one another's houses and at school, they also wanted to dance with me. My attitude to them was also ambivalent, at least as far as the girls in my class were concerned. On the one hand, I knew them so well that after close on five years at school I was completely indifferent towards them; on the other hand, they had started changing, the bulges under their sweaters were growing, their hips were widening and they were behaving differently, they had risen above us, suddenly when they looked at boys, they were from two or three classes up. With our high-pitched voices, more or less furtive glances as we admired all the attributes they now possessed, we were no more than air to them. But even though they were so important, they knew nothing about the world they were moving towards. What did they know about men and women and desire? Had they read Wilbur Smith, in which women were taken by force under stormy skies? Had they read Ken Follett, in which a man shaves a woman's pussy while she lies in a foam-filled bathtub with her eyes closed? Had they read *Insect Summer* by Knut Faldbakken, the passage that I knew by heart, when he takes her panties off in the hay? Had they ever got their hands on a porn magazine? And what did they know about music? They liked what everyone liked, the Kids and all the other crap on the hit lists, it meant nothing to them, not really, they had no idea what music was or what it could be. They could barely dress, they turned up at school wearing the strangest combinations of clothes and didn't realise. And then they were looking down on me? I had read Wilbur Smith and Ken Follett and Knut Faldbakken, I had been flicking through porn mags for years, I listened to bands who really counted and I knew how to dress. So was I supposed to be inferior to them?

To demonstrate the true state of affairs I pulled off a little coup in the music lesson. Every Friday we had something we called Class Top of the Pops. Six pupils brought along a song which everyone voted on afterwards. Mine always came last, whatever I played. Led Zeppelin, Queen, Wings, the Beatles, the Police, the Jam, Skids – the result was the same, one or two votes, last. I knew they were voting against me and not the music. They weren't really listening to the music. This irritated me beyond endurance. I complained to Yngve and he not only understood how irritating it was, because he disliked hit list music too, but he also came up with a way to trick them. The Kids' second record hadn't been released yet. One Friday I took with me the Aller Værste!'s first LP, *Materialtretthet,* which Yngve had bought a few days before, and said that I had an advance copy of the Kids' new record. The music teacher was in on my ruse and played the first song off the LP, which was still in a white inside sleeve because, as I told them, the record was so new that the cover hadn't been designed yet. For them the Aller Værste! was the worst of the lot, the last time I had played a song by them, the single 'Rene Hender', they had shouted *Rene Hender! Rene Hender!* after me for several days, but when the opening notes of the band's first song sounded in the classroom it was to mumbles of appreciation and mounting enthusiasm, which culminated when the vote was taken and it transpired that the

Aller Værste!, under the pseudonym of the Kids, had won hands down. How the triumph shone in my eyes as I was able to stand up and say that they had *not* voted for the Kids but for the Aller Værste! I said this proved that they weren't interested in the music, there were other issues determining their votes. How angry they were! But there was nothing they could say. I had fooled them too well for that.

Of course I never heard the last of it. I was conceited, I thought I was the big I am, I always had to like weird things, not what everyone else liked. That wasn't true though, in fact I liked good music and not bad music, surely that wasn't my fault? – and I learned more and more about it, thanks to Yngve and his music magazines, which I ploughed through, and to the records he played me. Bands like Magazine, the Cure, the Stranglers, Simple Minds, Elvis Costello, Skids, Stiff Little Fingers, XTC, the Norwegian groups Kjøtt, Blaupunkt, the Aller Værste!, the Cut, Stavangerensemblet, DePress, Betong Hysteria, Hærværk. He also taught me more and more chords on the guitar, and when he wasn't at home I stood playing by myself with the black Gibson plectrum in my hand and the black Fender strap over my shoulder. To be on the safe side, I also bought a teach-yourself-drums book, carved two sticks, placed some books around me in a circle on the floor, the one on the left was the hi-hat, the one next to it the snare drum and the three books above them the tomtoms. The only person on my wavelength was Dag Magne, with whom I was spending more and more time. We were mostly up at his, playing records and trying to copy the songs on his twelve-string guitar, but he also came down to ours, where we read magazines because mum's ban was no longer absolute, while listening to my cassettes and talking about girls or the band we were going to start, especially what we were going to call it. He wanted it to be Dag Magne's Anonymous Disciples; I wanted it to be Blood Clot. Both were equally good, we agreed, and we didn't need to make a decision until the time was ripe and we were on performing on a stage.

In this way winter passed, with the first class parties, where we played postman's knock and danced slows, round and round on the floor holding some of the girls we had been in the same class with for five years and knew better than our sisters, and my head almost exploded when I held Anne Lisbet's body so close to mine. The fragrance of her hair, the sparkling eyes that were bursting with life. And, oh, the little breasts under the thin white blouse.

Wasn't that a FANTASTIC feeling?

It was completely new, unknown for all these years, but now I knew it, now I wanted to go there again.

Winter passed, spring came, with its light, which every day held the passage to night open for a little longer, and with its cold rain causing the snow to slump and dwindle. One of these March mornings, oppressed by the darkness and the rain, I went into the kitchen to have breakfast as usual. Mum had already left, she was on the early shift. She had forgotten to switch off the radio. Even in my room I had gathered that something had happened in the night because the voices on the radio – I could hear the resonance but not the words – sounded unusually dramatic. I buttered a piece of bread, added a slice of salami and poured milk into a glass. There had been an accident in the North Sea, an oil platform had capsized and turned upside down. Raindrops slid slowly down the outside of the windows. The faint thrum of the rain on the roof surrounded the house like a membrane. The gutters were running. Up at Gustavsen's a car was started, the headlights were switched on. It was a catastrophe, a number of people were missing, no one knew how many. When I arrived at B-Max half an hour later, my trousers tucked into my boots and my waterproof hood tied tightly around my face, no one spoke of anything else. Everyone knew someone who knew someone who had a father or a brother working on that particular platform. Alexander Kielland it was called, and apparently one leg had given way. Was it a hundred-year wave that had caused it? A bomb? A construction fault?

In the first lesson the teacher talked about the accident, even though it was a mathematics class. I wondered what grandad would be saying now. He always told us we should find a job in oil. Oil was the future. But other signals were coming in from elsewhere: an item on the news had opened with a forecast that the oil reserves would soon be running out, it was happening faster than anyone would have believed, within a mere twenty-five years it would all be gone. I was fascinated by the year that was quoted, 2004, because it was so far into the future, and actually unreal, but treated here as a sober reality, different in kind from the one you met in science fiction books and magazines, and hence shocking: would 2004 ever *really* arrive? In *our* lifetimes? At the same time I was also unnerved by the doom and gloom in these men's voices warning of terrible things to come and despondent that something was going to come to an end. I didn't like that; I wanted everything to last and go on for ever. All ends were frightening. Therefore I hoped that Jimmy Carter would get a second term and that Odvar Nordli and the Socialist Party would win the next election. I liked Jimmy Carter. I liked Odvar Nordli even though he was always so drained and exhausted. I didn't like Mogens Glistrup or Olof Palme, there was something smarmy about them, about their lips and eyes. Einar Førde and Reuilf Steen also had it, though not so much. But I liked Hanna Kvanmo. Not Golda Meir and not Menachem

Begin, despite the Camp David Agreement. It was hard to judge Anwar Sadat. The same applied to Brezhnev, on quite a different scale though. When I saw him standing there in his fur coat and hat, with the bushy eyebrows above the narrow Mongolian eyes in his expressionless face, mechanically waving to the parade below, as one artillery rocket after the other rolled past, surrounded by thousands of identical goose-stepping soldiers, I didn't see him as human, he was something else, impossible to relate to.

Did I like Per Kleppe?

Yes, in a way, I certainly hoped with a passion that Kleppe's anti-inflation packages would work.

I liked Hans Hammond Rossbach, but I considered Trygve Bratteli a bit odd with that low, whispering voice of his and his strange 'r's, the narrow shoulders and the big skull-like head with the thick black eyebrows.

The accident in the North Sea was the main topic of conversation for a quarter of an hour, then the lesson proceeded as usual, that is, we worked on sums in our books while the teacher walked between the rows of desks helping whoever needed it as the hand of darkness outside released its grip on the morning and it slowly became lighter. In the break someone said there might be air pockets inside the platform where you could survive for several days. Others said no parents from our school had been on board, but the father of a pupil at Roligheden was missing. It was hard to know where all the rumours were coming from, or how true they were. In the next lesson we had Norwegian. When Frøken sat down at her desk I put up my hand.

'Yes, Karl Ove?'

'Have you corrected our essays?'

'You'll have to wait and see,' she said.

But she must have done because the next thing she did was to go through some words and rules on the blackboard, which presumably were examples of the mistakes we had made in the essays we had handed in the Thursday before.

Yes indeed. The big pile of exercise books was taken from her bag and put on the desk.

'There were lots of excellent essays this time,' she said. 'I could have read out all of them, but there wasn't enough time, so I chose four. This doesn't necessarily mean they are the best, as you know. Everyone in the class writes good essays.'

I stared at the pile to see if I could recognise mine. It wasn't the one on top, that was for sure.

Anne Lisbet put up her hand.

She was wearing a white sweater. It suited her so well. Her black hair and her black eyes went well with white, and her red lips and the redness in her cheeks, which always flushed when she came into the warm, did too.

'Yes?' Frøken said.

'Can we knit while you read?' Anne Lisbet said.

'Yes, I don't have a problem with that,' Frøken said.

Four of the girls leaned forward and took out some knitting from their satchels.

'Can we do our homework as well?' Geir Håkon said.

Someone giggled.

'Put your hand up like everyone else, Geir Håkon,' Frøken said. 'But the answer is, of course, no.'

Geir Håkon smiled, blushing, not because he had been put in his place but because he had ventured to speak. He was always pink-faced when he spoke in class.

Frøken began to read. The first was not mine. But there were three left, I thought, stretching my legs out under the desk. I liked the first lessons when it was dark outside and it was like we were sitting in a bright capsule, all of us with slightly messy hair and sleepy eyes and these soft-focus movements that the day seemed to sharpen until everyone was running around shouting over one another with wide-open eyes and flapping limbs.

The second essay wasn't mine either. Nor the third.

I peered up uneasily as she lifted the fourth book. That wasn't mine, was it?

Oh. She wasn't going to read it.

Something inside me slumped with disappointment. While something else soared. My essay was the best, I knew that, and she knew that. Yet she hadn't read it the previous time, nor this. What was the point of writing well if that was what happened? The next time I would write as badly as I could.

Finally she put the wretched essay down.

I put up my hand.

'Why didn't you read mine?' I said. 'Was it no good?'

Her eyes narrowed for a second, then opened and she smiled.

'I have received twenty-five essays. I can't read all of them out. Surely you can understand that? Your essays are in fact among those I read out most often. This time it was someone else's turn.'

She clapped her hands again.

'And they were really fantastic this time. What imagination you have! I really enjoyed all of them.'

She nodded to Geir B, who jumped to his feet and went to the desk. He was the class monitor and had to hand out the essays. I scanned mine. About a mistake a page. At the end she had written, 'Imaginative and elegant, Karl Ove, but perhaps the story finished a little abruptly? Very few mistakes, but you have to work on your writing more!'

We had had to write about something in the future. I had

written about a journey in space. That is, I had spent so much time describing the various training programmes the astronauts went through that ten pages were already covered before the day of the launch, so after some deliberation I decided the trip would be cancelled at the last moment because of a fault and the astronauts would go home with their work left undone.

Somewhere in the essay I had written *Hotel*, and she had added an extra 'l' in her red looped script. I put up my hand and she came over.

'*Hotell* is spelt with one "l". I know that. I saw it in a book, so I'm absolutely sure.'

She leaned over. Soap fragrance rose from her hands, and from her neck a faint scent of a summery perfume.

'Ah, well, in one way you're right. "Hotel" with one "l" is English. There are two "l"s in Norwegian.'

'Hotel Phønix has one "l",' I said. 'And that's in Norway. And on top of that, it's in Arendal!'

'You're right.'

'So it's not a mistake after all?'

'No. Let's say that, shall we? And it was a good essay, Karl Ove.'

She straightened up and went back to her desk. Her words were warming, even though they were only meant for my ears.

Outside, the rain and the wind continued. The trees beyond the school grounds swayed and creaked, and when we went into the gym at the end of the break the wind was gusting against the external walls with such force that it sounded like waves hitting them. The ventilation grilles howled and wheezed as though the building were alive, a huge beast full of rooms, corridors and shafts that had settled here beside the school, and in its despondency sang lonely laments. Or perhaps it was the sounds that were alive, I wondered, sitting on the bench in the changing room and undressing. They rose and fell, whirled around for a while, drifting here, drifting there, as if in the middle of a game. I stood up, naked, took my towel and went into the shower, which was already hot with the steam. I found a place among the throng of pale, almost marble-white boys' bodies, and was engulfed by the hot water that first hit the top of my head and then ran in steady streams down my face and chest, neck and back. My hair stuck to my forehead and I closed my eyes. That was when someone shouted.

'Tor's got a hard-on! Tor's got a hard-on!'

I opened my eyes and looked over at Sverre, the boy who had shouted. He was pointing across the narrow room to where Tor was standing, with his arms down by his sides, his dick in the air and a smile on his face.

Tor had the biggest dick in the class, well perhaps in the whole school. It dangled between his legs like a classic pork sausage and it was no secret because he always wore tight trousers and he placed it at an angle, pointing upwards, so that everyone could see. Yes, it was big. But now, in its erect state, it was enormous.

'Jumpin' Jehoshaphat,' Geir Håkon shouted.

Everyone looked at Tor, there was a sudden excitement in the atmosphere and it was obvious something had to be done. Such an extraordinary circumstance could not be allowed to go to waste.

'Let's take him to fru Hensel!' Sverre shouted. 'Come on, quick, before it's too late!'

Fru Hensel was our gym teacher. She came from Germany, spoke broken Norwegian, was strict, neat and prim, which was emphasised by her narrow glasses and her tightly pinned-up hair. She was meticulous yet distant, in sum what we called snooty. As a teacher she was a nightmare because she had a predilection for gym apparatus and hardly ever let us play football. When Sverre suggested taking Tor to her – she was tidying up in the gymnasium, still with her whistle around her neck, wearing her blue tunic and white tights – we all knew it was perfect.

'No,' Tor said. 'Don't do that!'

Sverre and Geir went over and grabbed him by the arms.

'Come on!' Sverre shouted. 'We need a couple more of you!'

Dag Magne went over, and with Geir B they grabbed Tor's legs and lifted him. Tor protested and writhed as they carried him out of the shower, but rather half-heartedly. The rest of us followed. And it was quite a sight. Tor, stark naked with an enormous stiffy, carried by four boys, also naked, followed by a procession of more naked boys, through the changing room and into the large cold gymnasium, where fru Hensel, who was around thirty years old, turned to us from the stage at the far end.

'What do you want?' she said.

Those carrying Tor *ran* over with him. Once in front of fru Hensel, they straightened him up as though he were a statue to be examined, left him like that for five seconds or so, then laid him down and charged back to the changing room.

Fru Hensel said nothing other than *No, no, boys, this is really not on* and she did nothing. There were no screams, no howls, no bulging eyes and no gaping mouth, as perhaps we had hoped. Nevertheless, it had been a success. We had shown her Tor's massive hard-on.

In the changing room afterwards we discussed what would happen now. Few believed there would be any consequences, for the simple reason that it would be embarrassing for her to take the matter any further. We were wrong. It turned into a big affair, the headmaster came to the class, the four boys who had carried Tor were given detention and the rest of us a lecture we would never forget. The only person to come out of this with their honour intact was Tor, who now emerged as a victim – the headmaster, the class teacher and fru Hensel regarded the incident as a case of bullying – and a winner, for now everyone knew, including the girls, this sensational detail of his physique without his having to lift a finger.

That night I posed naked in front of the mirror for a long time.

It was easier said than done. The only full-length mirror we had was in the hall by the stairs. I couldn't exactly stand there naked even if there was no one in the house because someone could come in at any moment and even if I reacted quickly they would still see my arse beating a swift retreat up the stairs.

No, it had to be the bathroom mirror.

But it was designed solely for faces. If you got up close and had your legs as far back as possible you could catch a glimpse of your body but from such a bizarre angle that it told you nothing.

So I waited until mum had finished washing up after dinner and sat down in the living room with the newspaper and a cup of coffee. Then I went into the kitchen and fetched a chair. If she asked what I was doing with it, I could say I was going to put the cassette recorder on it while I was in the bath. If she asked why it couldn't be on the floor as usual, I could say I had heard water and electricity were dangerous if they came into contact, and water often slopped on the floor when I had a bath.

But she didn't ask.

I locked the door, undressed, placed the chair by the wall and clambered up.

First I looked at the front of my body.

My dick wasn't like Tor's, not at all. More like a little cork. Or a kind of spring because it quivered when you flicked it lightly.

I put it in my hand. How big was it?

Then I turned and looked at it from the side. Actually it seemed a bit bigger then.

Anyway, it looked like all the dicks in our class, apart from Tor's, didn't it?

I fared worse with my arms. They were so thin. And my chest was thin. I had a sudden image of it from a Norway Cup photo and the way it tapered the closer it came to my head. And that was definitely not how it was meant to be. I was supposed to do press-ups in training, but I always cheated because in reality, and only I knew this, I couldn't do a *single* one.

I climbed down from the chair, ran the water into the bath and while it splashed out from the tiny mouth under the miniature iron girder construction which the two eyes, one red and one blue, rested on, I hurried into my bedroom, fetched the cassette recorder, inserted *Outlandos d'Amour*, which for me was bath music, put it on the chair, pressed play and carefully stepped into the bathtub. The hot water stung my skin so much it was impossible to sit. But I managed. I sat, got up, sat, got up, sat, got up until my skin was used to the temperature and I could lie there letting the heat wash over me while the music poured from the little recorder and I sang 'So Lonely' by the Police at the top of my voice, dreaming about becoming famous and what all the girls I knew would say then.

I caught every little nuance in Sting's voice, even the whimper at the end. Now and then I banged my fists on the edge of the bath in my enthusiasm. When the song had finished I dried my hands on a towel, turned the cassette over and wound forward to 'Masoko Tanga', another favourite of mine.

Oh, Masoko Tanga!

Afterwards I stood in front of the wardrobe in my bedroom looking for clothes to wear. There were still some hours of the evening left.

It had to be the light blue shirt with the white buttons and the dark blue Levis.

'When are we going to buy clothes for the seventeenth of May?' I said to mum, stopping in front of her in the living room.

'It's only the end of March now,' she said. 'We've got plenty of time.'

'Perhaps it would be cheaper now?' I said.

'We'll have to see,' she said. 'We haven't got much money now either, you know, as dad is studying.'

'But we've got a bit?' I said.

She smiled.

'Of course you'll have new clothes for the seventeenth.'

'And shoes.'

'And shoes.'

The seventeenth of May was still the high point of spring for us, as Christmas was of the winter. At school we sang '*Vi Ere En Nasjon Vi Med*', '*Norge I Rødt*', '*Hvitt og Blått*' and '*Ja, Vi Elsker*', we learned about Henrik Wergeland and what happened at Eidsvoll in 1814. At home ribbons and flags were taken out and all the flutes and blowing instruments we could find. On the day itself flags were hoisted on all the masts, and from very early morning families came out of their houses wearing traditional costume, dresses or suits covered with capes or coats, as it was cold or raining, children with flags in their hands, now and then an instrument case, for quite a few of my neighbours played in a marching band and they wore a uniform instead of their finery, which they changed into later. The uniform of the Tromøya School band consisted of a mustard-yellow jacket and black trousers with a white line down the sides and a black Foreign Legion-style kepi on top. Their chests were festooned with medals acquired at the innumerable gatherings they had attended. Then car after car left front drives, onto the road and into Arendal, where you had to park well outside the centre because people were trickling in from every direction and the streets were packed with crowds lining the long street along which the procession would pass. And the procession, that was us. We assembled in Tyholmen, beneath the standard of Sandnes School, which we were proud to walk behind in an almost endlessly long line consisting not only of all Arendal's schools but all the schools in the district. Then we walked in two lines up and down the streets, in a sea of people, which you had to keep a constant eye on, because your parents, whom you had to wave to and who had to take a photo of you, could be anywhere.

That day, 17 May 1980, was different from all the other Constitution Days I had experienced. It was raining when we got up, and I was upset about that because I had to wear a waterproof anorak and trousers over my new clothes. I had been given light blue Levis, a pair of white Tretorn tennis shoes and a greyish-white waist-length jacket. I was especially pleased with the jeans. Outside the houses up the hill there were sporadic protracted laments from the instruments the children were carrying. Car doors slammed, shouts carried across garden paths, the atmosphere was feverish but expectant. As we approached the assembly area in Tyholmen, with the skies opening in unfailingly regular bursts of drizzle, it became clear that we would be walking side by side with a class from Roligheden School. I played football with some of them, but I had never seen many of their faces.

A girl turned.

She had wavy blonde hair, large blue eyes and she smiled at me.

I didn't smile back, but I held her gaze and then she turned forward.

The procession began to move. Somewhere far ahead a band was playing. One of our teachers began to sing and we joined in. After marching for perhaps twenty minutes many began to find their patience waning, especially the boys, we started laughing and fooling around, and when some boys used the flag to lift girls' skirts, and the idea caught on, I made my way towards the blonde girl, along with Dag Magne, fortunately, so that I was part of something and not just on my own. I put the flag under the pleat of her skirt and lifted, she spun on her heel, held it down with one hand and shouted *Don't you dare, don't you dare.* But the eyes that looked at me were smiling.

I did it to some other girls as well, until it would no longer be suspicious if I approached her again.

'Don't do that!' she said this time, and ran ahead, away from me. 'Don't be so childish!'

Was she really angry?

Seconds passed. Then she turned and smiled. Briefly, but it was enough, she wasn't angry, she didn't think I was childish.

But wasn't that an Østland accent?

Was she not from here? Was she only visiting?

Then I would never see her again.

No, no, no. Relax. Visitors wouldn't be allowed in the school procession!

I suddenly noticed the flag I was holding and raised it. Last seventeenth of May dad was annoyed I had let the flag droop as I passed them.

Dag Magne beamed his broadest smile. A camera flashed. His

parents were in the front row. They were unlike their normal selves, their Sunday best looked unfamiliar on them.

I observed the girl again.

She wasn't very tall and she was wearing a pink jacket, a light blue skirt and thin white stockings. Her blonde hair was wavy, her nose small, her mouth large and she had a little cleft in her chin.

I felt pains in my stomach.

When she spun round to stop her skirt being lifted I had seen that she had big breasts, her jacket had been open and the white sweater beneath insubstantial.

Oh, dear God, please let me go out with her.

'Hi, Karl Ove!' mum shouted from somewhere. I scanned the lines of people. There they were, on the other side of the street from Hotel Phønix. Mum waved and lifted her camera to her eye, dad sent me a nod.

On our way back to the centre she turned and looked at me again. Straight afterwards the procession broke up and she was lost in the madding crowd.

I didn't even know her name.

After the school procession in Arendal everyone drove back home to the estate, where clothes were changed, food was eaten and perhaps also TV broadcasts of the children's processions around the country were watched before everyone piled into their cars, rather more informally dressed, and headed for Hove, where the climax of the celebrations would take place. Here there were stalls selling hot dogs, ice cream and pop, stalls where you could buy a lottery ticket and play tombola, organised games and a huge crowd of children with ten-krone notes burning holes in their pockets, running here and buying a hot dog, running there and jumping in a sack race, with ketchup on their sleeves and ice cream smeared around their mouths and a bottle of Coke with a straw in their hands. We hadn't quite outgrown that, but the speed with which we did everything had perhaps dropped, compared with the previous year. For my part, I searched for the girl in the procession all afternoon, if I caught sight of a pink jacket or a blue skirt my heart almost stopped beating, but it was never her, she wasn't there. Even if I knew which class she was in and even if I played football with two boys who were in the same class as her, I couldn't ask them, they would realise straight away what was going through my mind and wouldn't hesitate for a moment, they would spread it far and wide. However, sooner or later I would see her again, that much I did know, Tromøya was not that big.

Dad moved back home two weeks later, proud to have finished his studies in a matter of months. He had sold his stamp collection, he had given up his political commitments, the garden was immaculate, he was so on top of his teaching it was boring. What he was doing was applying for new jobs. And if he got one, we would move. He hoped the coming year as a bog-standard *ungdomskole* teacher would be his last.

He bought himself a boat at the beginning of the summer, a Rana Fisk 17 with a twenty-five horsepower outboard motor. Mum, Yngve and I were standing on the pontoons when he came back from Arendal for the first time. He was standing behind the wheel as the boat skimmed across the water and although he didn't smile or wave to us I could see he felt proud.

He eased back on the throttle and the prow of the boat sank, but not enough for him to be able to turn into our berth as he had planned, the boat overshot and bumped into the pontoon. He reversed, put the engine into gear and glided in.

Threw the mooring rope to mum, who didn't quite know what to do with it.

'Does it go well?' I said.

'Yes, it certainly does,' he said. 'You saw, didn't you?'

He jumped ashore with a red petrol canister in his hand. Secured the tarpaulin, stood for a moment inspecting the boat, then we got into the car and drove up towards home, with dad at the wheel even though it was mum's car.

When the school year began I had to join him casting nets in the afternoons and pulling them up at the crack of dawn. We gulped down a couple of pieces of bread, our faces drawn with tiredness, and then we went into the darkness. He started the car and drove down to the pontoons, which lay quiet and deserted, undid the green tarpaulin on the boat, put the red canister of petrol in its place, loosened the mooring ropes, got the engine going and carefully reversed out. I sat at the front, behind the windshield, shoulders hunched, arms close to my body and hands in my pockets because it was cold, and even though the boat was faster than the old double-ender, the trip to the far side of the island still took over half an hour. Dad stood at the wheel concentrating on steering through the narrow passage between the shore and the island of Gjerstadholmen, where there was some sunken rock he had run onto earlier that summer. As we emerged into Tromøya Sound he sat down and we ploughed across, with the waves thumping against the underside of the plastic propeller and spray hurtling through the air. He usually set the nets quite close to the shore and it was my job to sit in the bow and grab the floats to which they were attached. It was difficult, they were slippery, and if I didn't succeed the first time dad told me to get my act together, all I had to do was pick them up. My hands were already freezing, the water was obviously ice cold, and out here, in open sea, there was always a wind blowing early in the morning. Dad's hair was in wild disarray, his eyes flashed with annoyance as he reversed and steered into the wind again, and if I didn't grab the float this time, he would shout at me and I would start to cry, and then he would become even more angry and perhaps stomp forward to grab it himself, while telling me to take the wheel, steer into the bloody wind, he would say, *into the wind*, I told you, you idiot! Can't you do anything! Steering's not so easy, I said, and he replied, it's not *steewing*, it's *steering*! RRR. STEERING! I was crying and I was frozen and dad leaned over the railing and pulled the float on board. Then, as we rocked on the waves, with the dawn light a stripe on the horizon, and he pulled up the net, the glow of fury in his eyes gradually abated and he would try to mitigate the effect of his outburst, but it was too late, the cold was as deep in my soul as it was in my hands, I hated him as you can only hate your father, and on the way back, with the fish still squirming in the white tub, not a word passed between us. While he gutted the fish in the utility room I packed my satchel and left for the day, which for my classmates had only just begun but which for me had already lasted several hours.

That same autumn our band finally became a reality. The name I chose won the day, it was to be Blood Clot we wrote on our jackets and satchels, and we practised in the basement of the new chapel. Dag Magne had arranged it, his mother did the cleaning for a doctor who was also on the church committee. He was also the only one of us who could play or evince anything that was redolent of musical talent. He played the guitar and sang, I played the guitar, Kent Arne played the bass his mother had bought for him, Dag Lothar played the drums. At the end-of-term Christmas party we were lined up to play in the gymnasium. Yngve had taught me the chords for *'Forelska I Lærer'n'*, the Kids' big hit, 'In Love with the Teacher', and even though playing that song of all songs was like sucking up, at least for me, it was the easiest song Yngve knew, and probably the only song in existence that was simple enough for us to play. Although the band came apart at the seams in the process, everyone played at their own tempo and Kent Arne started tuning his bass in the middle, and although most of the audience was critical, even the fourth years ventured a few remarks, and rightly so as we couldn't play, the feeling among us afterwards, standing in the school playground, dressed in ripped jeans and denim jackets, and with scarves around our necks, could not be surpassed. We were in the sixth class, would soon be in the *ungdomskole* and we were in a *band*. The fact that the band split up straight afterwards, as neither Dag Lothar nor Kent Arne wanted to continue, was a setback, but Dag Magne and I carried on as a duo for as long as it lasted, recording songs in his house, listening to music, dreaming of a breakthrough, for example at the locally famous Saga Nights, which would be in Arendal during the summer and at which new bands were allowed to play. I went up to see Håvard, who played in the town's only punk band, was five years older than us and lived by Tromøya Bridge, and asked him if he could help us to get in. He couldn't promise anything, but he would put in a good word and we would have to wait and see.

That spring, at a school parents' evening, we performed two songs, Dag Magne on guitar and me on snare drum, first of all one I had written myself, *'Tramp på en Soss'*, 'Stamp on a Snob', and then Åge Aleksandersen's *'Ramp'*, 'Riff-Raff'. Before we played I gave a little introductory talk about punk to the parents.

'In recent years a completely new form of music has sprung

up in the English working classes,' I explained. 'Some of you may have heard about it. It's called punk. Those who play punk are not great musicians but rebels who want to revolt against society. They wear leather jackets and studded belts and they've got safety pins everywhere. You could say the safety pin is their symbol.'

I gazed enthusiastically across the assembly of hairdressers, secretaries, nurses, cleaners and housewives. I was twelve years old, and before every Christmas and summer for the last five years they had seen me standing on the stage, either as Joseph in the Nativity play or the mayor in *Borgmester I Byen*, and now here I was again, this time as a spokesman for punk and a member of Blood Clot.

'We're going to give you a taste of this type of music. We'll begin with a song we wrote ourselves. It's entitled "*Tramp på en soss*".'

Then Dag Magne, who had been standing beside me with his twelve-string guitar over his shoulder, started to play while I sang and hit the snare drum when the whim took me.

Our next performance was in a lesson. We played the same two songs. After we had finished most of the class whistled and the teacher, the red-bearded Finsådal, went over to Dag Magne and said his guitar-playing was beginning to take off.

That hurt.

In response, in the deepest secrecy I sent a letter to NRK, who broadcast a programme where children could perform with their idols, and I wrote that I would like to play '*Ramp*' with Åge Aleksandersen.

For a long time I lived in hope, but no answer ever came, and slowly the dream of overnight fame as a pop star faded while another appeared: our football coach, Øyvind, gathered us together at the end of a training session and said that we might be playing the pre-match game before IK Start versus Mjøndalen. For me who, the year before, had been at the League Cup Final in Kristiansand Stadium and had seen Start win the match in the dying seconds, who had charged onto the pitch with several hundred others, stood under the building where the changing rooms were, singing and cheering and paying tribute to the players and even getting my hands on Svein Mathiesen's shirt, only to have it ripped from my grasp by a grown man with piggy eyes a second later, for me, who every alternate Sunday over many years had been to all the home games and whose Uncle Gunnar actually knew Svein Mathiesen enough to get an autograph for Yngve, for me, playing at Kristiansand Stadium, with the opportunity to be seen not only by the whole of the immense crowd but also by the players themselves, this was charged with enormous significance. The team I played for was one of the region's best, we won most matches by several goals and had won the league every single year I had been involved, and I always thought my being one of the worst players in the team, slow and without much skill, was a temporary state of affairs, *actually* I was good, *actually* I could do everything as well as the others, it was just a question of time before it would become evident. I felt like this because *in my mind* I could knock in goals from every conceivable and inconceivable angle, like John, and steam past whoever was on the wing, like Hans Christian. All I needed to do was align my actions with my thoughts, making them one and the same, and then it was done. Why couldn't that happen during a pre-match game at Kristiansand Stadium just as easily as at a training session in Hove? Was it not the case that I always got *better* over the weeks in the autumn? In fact, from out of nowhere could I not actually ghost past one player after the other?

Yes, that was how it was. It was all in my head. And despite the fact that I still hadn't shown any of what I hoped for, strangely enough I still had a regular spot in the midfield. Early that spring we had played our first practice match on the shale pitch outside the new Tromøya Sports Hall above Roligheden School, and when I was brought off at some point during the second half, my eyes were full of tears as I left the pitch. Even though I was looking down, the trainer realised and ran after me as I headed for the changing room. I should have stayed to see the rest of the match, but partly I was so disappointed to have been taken off that I couldn't be bothered, and partly I didn't want anyone else to see me crying.

'What's up, Karl Ove?' he said.

'Nothing,' I said.

'Is it because you were taken off? Everyone has to have a go, you know. It doesn't mean you've been dropped from the team. It doesn't. It was just for today. It's a practice match.'

I smiled through my tears.

'It's nothing,' I said. 'It's OK.'

'Sure?'

'Yes,' I said, feeling fresh tears building up.

'Good,' he said.

After that I wondered perhaps if I would be allowed to play because he was sorry for me, or he didn't want to repeat the experience. It wasn't a pleasant thought, but actually being in the team meant a great deal to me, my shortcomings notwithstanding.

We trained and played home games at Kjenna, a ground immediately below the big estate in Brattekleiv, and most of the boys I played with came from there.

That was where I saw her again.

The beginning of June, blue sky, not a cloud in sight. We played between cones placed in the middle of one half of the pitch because around the goals and in the centre circle the grass was already cut up and the soil eroded, and even though the sun was low and the shadows from the trees stretched across the pitch it was so hot that sweat ran down my face and neck as we ran around after the ball. Birds sang in the trees on both sides of the pitch, gulls screamed, the occasional car roared past, somewhere in the distance the drone of a lawnmower rose and fell, and down by the makeshift changing rooms came squeals and laughter, a group of children in the hot brown water of the Tjenna, all while we panted and puffed and kicked and the ball thudded between us. I was in the best team this season, playing with boys a year older than me, whereas, because of how my birthday fell, I would be doing the same next year as last year, playing with boys a year younger. We were on top of the league by some distance, and in a month's time we would be off to the Norway Cup again, not without some hope of going all the way and playing the final in Ullevål Stadium. I had white Umbro shorts and a pair of Le Coq Sportif boots which I polished after every session and could still turn round in my hand and admire with immense pleasure and satisfaction.

This evening four girls jumped off their bikes at the end of the pitch, pressed down the kickstands and strolled laughing and chatting over to the side by the rocks, where they sat down to watch us. Girls did sometimes come and watch us like this, but I had never seen her there before. For it was her, there was no doubt. This time she was wearing blue jeans and a white T-shirt.

For the rest of the session my awareness of her never left me for a moment. Everything I did, I did for her. When we had finished playing, done our stretching exercises and the

XL1 bottles had been passed around I sat down on the grass below them with Lars and Hans Christian. They shouted some insults up to them and received laughter and more insults in return.

'Do you know them?' I said as warily as I could.

'Yes,' said Lars, bored.

'Are they in your class?'

'Yes. Kajsa and Sunnva. The others are in HC's class.'

So she was called either Kajsa or Sunnva.

I leaned back with my hands behind my head on the grass and my eyes squinting into the rays of the orange sun. One of the others ducked the whole of his head into a bucket of water by the touchline. He straightened up and tossed his head. The drops of water formed a glittering arc in the air for a brief instant before dissipating. With prong-like fingers he ploughed both hands through his wet hair.

'I've seen one of them before,' I said. 'The one on the far right. What's her name?'

'Kajsa?'

'Oh, is it now?'

Lars glanced at me. He had curly hair, freckles and a slightly cheeky expression, but his eyes were warm and always had a glint.

'We're neighbours,' he said. 'I've known her since I learned to walk. Are you interested?'

'No-oo,' I said.

Lars bored a rigid finger in my chest a few times.

'Ye-es,' he said with a grin. 'Shall I introduce you?'

'Introduce?' I said, my mouth suddenly dry.

'Isn't that what it's called, you who knows everything?'

'Yes, I suppose it is. No. Not now. That is, not at all. I'm not interested. I was just wondering. I thought I had seen her before.'

'Kajsa's nice, she is,' Lars said. Then he whispered, 'And she's got big breasts.'

'Yes,' I said. I turned without thinking and looked at her. Lars laughed and got up. She looked at me.

She looked at me!

I got up as well, and followed Lars down to the changing rooms.

'Can I have some?' I said.

He threw me the XL1 bottle, I leaned back and squirted the greenish liquid through the long narrow plastic tube and down my throat.

'Are you going for a shower?' he said.

'No, I've got to go home,' I said.

'Perhaps Kajsa will be in the showers too,' he said.

'You don't say,' I said. He eyed me. I shook my head. He smiled. Behind us the others straggled in. In the changing room I just put on my T-shirt, tracksuit top and shoes, then I placed my bag on the luggage rack of my bike and cycled home along the old gravel road through the forest, where the air soon cooled in places the sun hadn't been shining for a while, and I had to close my mouth because these cool grey pockets buzzed with large swarms of insects. The sun shone on the ridge close by, still bare after a fire the previous year, before it disappeared where the hills began and tall dense spruce trees lined both sides of the road like a wall. My bike was the same one I'd had since I was small, a DBS kombi, with the seat and the handlebars raised as far as they would go, which made it look like a kind of mutant, a bike's first clumsy transition from a bike. I sang at the top of my voice as I raced between all the bumps and potholes and sometimes skidded sideways with a static rear wheel. Sang and hummed and imitated the opening track on the *Abbey Road* LP, 'Come Together', or at least how it sounded to my ears. Well, I knew it wasn't exactly what they sang, juju eyeballs, but what did it matter as I whizzed down the hill in the forest, absolutely throbbing with happiness? Down at the crossroads I braked in front of a car, then picked up speed and pedalled as hard as I could up the gravel on the other side. I swallowed a midge or two and tried in vain to cough them up, crossed the main road at the top of Speedmannsbakken, and followed the cycle path down to the Fina station, where a gang of kids was sitting at the tables outside and not, as in winter, in the café. Their bikes and mopeds were parked a little way from them. I wasn't frightened of going in there any more, the worst that could happen was that someone might make a comment, but I still didn't like it, so when I passed them it was on the other side of the road. There were three from my class with them this evening, John and I also saw Tor and Unni, and then Mariann from the parallel class. I had been out with her. No one took any notice of me, if indeed they saw me at all.

The quickest way to cycle home was along the main road, but I jumped off on the way up to the path and began to push my bike uphill. As soon as the trees closed off the view of the main road behind me the scenery became rural and I liked the change enough to relish the extra minutes it took.

Then it was all forest, not a house or a road to be seen, there were trees everywhere, tall broad-crowned deciduous trees, crammed with green leaves, full of chattering birds. The path, which was no more than beaten earth and bare rock face, was crossed in several places by huge roots resembling prehistoric animals. The grass growing alongside the bed of a stream was thick and lush, in the wilderness at the bottom there were fallen trees with smooth trunks, and many plants covered the bed between the dry lifeless branches, which had been there for as long as I could remember, and behind them there was a ridge of stumps between the long grass and the new trees that had shot up. Walking down the first hundred metres of the path, you could imagine the forest was deep, indeed endlessly deep, and full of mystery. It wasn't hard to dismiss the thought that between the branches in autumn and winter you could glimpse the long rocky slope down from the road which went around the estate or glimpse the orange roof of one of the houses. The problem is not so much that the world limits your imagination as your imagination limits the world. But this time I was not outside to play but to surround myself with nature and to cultivate the feeling of liberation Kajsa's gaze had given me.

Kajsa, her name was Kajsa!

With my bike bumping along beside me, I trudged up the hill, across the gentle slope, then jumped on my bike again when I emerged on the road just below the parish hall. Outside Ketil's house the road teemed with children playing football. His father sat in a camping chair on the terrace wearing shorts, with his belly bulging out of an open short-sleeved shirt. Smoke wafted over from a barbecue not far away from him.

Oh, the smell!

On the other side Tom was washing his car. He was wearing large pilot glasses and denim shorts with long frayed threads hanging down his thighs, otherwise nothing. I recognised the music blaring out through the open doors, which made the car look like a small, plump aeroplane, it was Dr Hook. Then I reached the hill and saw the distant blue of Tromøya Sound behind the green trees, and the white gas holders on the other side. The wind forced tears from my eyes as I hurtled downhill. Another crowd of children was playing football on the road outside our house. Marianne's little brother, Geir Håkon's little brother, Bente's little brother and Jan Atle's little brother. They said hello, I didn't say hello back, I jumped off my bike and trundled it down there, where there were two cars. There was Anne Mai's big Citroën and Dagny's 2CV. I had completely forgotten they were coming, and a little shiver of pleasure went through me when I saw them.

They were sitting in the living room with mum. She had baked a cake, perhaps there was a third left, and she had made coffee. Now they were chatting, wreathed in clouds of smoke. I said hello, they asked how I was, I said fine, I had been at football training, had the school holiday started, they asked, I answered yes and it was wonderful. Anne Mai took out a packet of Freia Ms.

'I suppose you're too old for these now?'

'Not for Ms,' I said. 'You're never too old for them, are you?'

I took the bag and had turned to go into the kitchen when Anne Mai said, 'What on earth's that on your back? Trauma?'

She laughed.

'His football team's called Trauma,' mum said.

'Trauma!' Dagny said. Now all three of them were laughing.

'What's wrong with it?' I said.

'That's what we work with, you know. It's when something terrible happens. You can have trauma. It was quite funny to see it on your back.'

'Oh,' I said. 'But that's not what it means. It comes from Thruma, the old name for Tromøya. From Viking times.'

They were still laughing when I went to my room. I put the Specials on the cassette recorder and lay down to read while the last rays of sun were shining on the wall beyond the bed, and the estate outside was slowly draining of noise.

Kajsa was constantly on my mind over the following weeks. I had two recurrent images of her. In one she was turning to me, with her blonde hair and blue eyes, wearing the pink and light blue clothes of the seventeenth of May. In the second she was lying naked in front of me in a field. The latter I saw every night before I went to sleep. The thought of her big white breasts with the pink nipples made my body ache. I lay writhing while imagining various indistinct but intense things I did with her. The second image aroused something else in me, and at other moments in time: jumping from a cliff on the island, floating in the air, with the sun on my face, I caught a glimpse of her and a wild cheer broke free from my innards more or less at the same instant as my feet hit the surface and my body plunged into the bluish-green seawater, breaking my fall of several metres, and, surrounded by a rush of bubbles and with the taste of salt on my lips, I headed for the surface again with slow arm movements and a quiver of happiness in my chest. Or at the dinner table, while I was peeling the skin off a piece of cod, for example, or chewing a mouthful of hashed lung, which had such an unpleasant consistency, it swelled and filled my mouth at first, but when I chewed, my teeth went right through the mass, which only resisted at the last, when it stuck to my gums, then the image of her could suddenly appear and she was so radiant that everything else was pushed into the shadows. But I didn't see her at all in reality. The distance as the crow flew between our two estates could have been only a few kilometres, but the social distance was greater and could not be covered by either bike or bus. Kajsa was a dream, an image in my head, a star in the firmament.

Then something happened.

We were playing a match on the Kjenna pitch, the spring season was actually over, but a game had been cancelled and moved forward, so there we were, running around the grass in the heat with the usual ten to fifteen spectators, when from the corner of my eye I espied three figures walking along the touch-line, and I knew at once it was her. For the rest of the match I watched the spectators standing on the slope as much as the ball.

After the match a girl came over to me.

'Can I have a word with you?' she said.

'Yes, of course,' I said.

A hope so wild it made me smile was lit inside me.

'Do you know who Kajsa is?' she said.

I reddened and looked down.

'Yes,' I said.

'She wants me to ask you a question,' she said.

'Pardon,' I said.

A wave of heat surged up inside me, as though my chest were filling with blood.

'Kajsa was wondering if you would like to go out with her,' she said. 'Would you?'

'Yes,' I said.

'Great,' she said. 'I'll tell her.'

She made a move to leave.

'Where is she?' I said.

She turned.

'She's waiting over by the changing room,' she said. 'Will we see you there afterwards?'

'Yes,' I said. 'That's fine.'

As she went away I looked down at the ground for a second.

Thank God, I said to myself. Because now it had happened. Now I was going out with Kajsa!

Was it true?

Was I really going out with Kajsa?

With *Kajsa*.

Dazed, I began to walk along the touchline. Suddenly it struck me that I had a big problem. She was there and waiting for me. I would have to speak to her. We would have to do something together. What would it be?

On my way into the changing room I could either pretend I didn't see her or just flash a fleeting smile because I had to go in and change. But when I had to go out again . . .

It was a mild evening, the air smelled of grass and was filled with birdsong, we had won and the voices rising from the changing room were cock-a-hoop. Kajsa was standing in the road nearby with two other girls. She was holding her bike and glanced at me when I looked over. She smiled. I smiled back.

'Hi,' I said.

'Hi,' she said.

'I'll just get changed,' I said. 'Be out afterwards.'

She nodded.

In the shed-like changing room I undressed as slowly as possible while feverishly trying to find a way to extricate myself with honour. To go off with her, unprepared, was inconceivable, it would never work. So I had to find a convincing excuse.

Homework? I wondered, loosening a shin pad, slippery with sweat on the inside. No, that would give a bad impression of me.

I put one shin pad in the bag and took off the other, staring at the lake through the small window. Unwound the bandage from my foot and rolled it up. The first boys had already gone out. 'Bloody hell, are you crazy or what?' John said to Jostein, who was smacking John's face with a goalie's glove. 'Pack it in, you bastard,' John shouted. I'm going out with Kajsa, I felt like saying, but I didn't of course. Got up and put on my light blue jeans instead.

'What posh pants,' Jostein said.

'You're the one with posh pants,' I said.

'These?' he said, motioning towards his red and black striped trousers.

'Yes,' I said.

'They're punk trousers, you prat,' he said.

'They're not,' I said. 'They're from Intermezzo, and that is definitely a posh shop.'

'Is the belt posh too?' he said.

'No,' I said. 'It's a punk belt.'

'Good,' he said. 'But your pants are definitely bloody posh.'

'I am not bloody posh,' I said.

'But you are a bit of a jessie,' John piped up.

A jessie? What did that mean?

'Ha ha ha!' Jostein laughed. 'Come on, jessie!'

'What did you say, you bloody daddy's boy,' I said.

'Is it my fault my father has a lot of money?' he said.

'No,' I said, zipping up the blue-and-white Puma top. 'Bye,' I said.

'Bye,' they said, and I went out to Kajsa without having prepared anything.

'Hi,' I said, stopping in front of them, with my hands round the handlebars.

'You were so good, all of you,' Kajsa said.

She was wearing a white T-shirt. Her breasts bulged beneath it. Levi 501s with a red plastic belt. White socks. White Nike trainers with a light blue logo.

I swallowed.

'Do you think so?' I said.

She nodded. 'Are you coming back with us?'

'In fact, I don't have a lot of time this evening.'

'Oh yes?'

'Yes. I really have to be going now.'

'Oh, that's a shame,' she said, meeting my eyes. 'What have you got to do?'

'I promised I would help my father with something. A wall he was building. But can't we meet tomorrow?'

'Of course.'

'Where then?'

'I can go to yours after school.'

'Do you know where I live?'

'Tybakken, isn't it?'

'Yes, it is.'

I swung a leg over my bike.

'Bye!' I said.

'Bye!' she said. 'See you tomorrow!'

I cycled off, casually to the observer, until I was out of sight, then I stood on the pedals, leaned forward and began to pump like a wild man. It was absolutely fantastic and absolutely awful. Go to yours, she had said. She had known where I lived. And she wanted to be with me. Not only that. We were *going out*. I was going out with Kajsa! Oh, everything I wanted was now within reach! Though not yet. What would I talk to her about? What would we do?

When I turned into our drive half an hour later, mum was sitting on the terrace behind the house reading the newspaper with a cup of coffee on the camping table in front of her. I went over and sat down.

'Where's dad?' I said.

'He's gone fishing,' she said. 'How was the match?'

'Good,' I said. 'We won.'

Brief silence.

'Has something happened?' mum said, looking at me.

'No,' I said.

'Something on your mind?'

'No, not really,' I said.

She sent me a smile and went on reading the newspaper. The sound of a radio wafted over from Prestbakmo's. I looked up. Martha was sitting, like mum, in a camping chair with a newspaper spread out in front of her. Nearby, next to the stone wall facing the forest, Prestbakmo himself was bent over a bed in the vegetable garden with a trowel in his hand. Then a movement on the path made me turn my head. It was Freddie, I saw at once, he was an albino and his white hair was unmistakable. He was in the fourth class and had an archery bow on his back.

I looked at mum again.

'Do you know what a jessie is, Mum?' I said.

She lowered the newspaper.

'A jessie?' she said.

'Yes.'

'No, not really. But it is a girl's name.'

'So, like a girl?'

'I suppose so. Why do you ask? Have you been called a *jessie*?'

'No, not at all. I just heard it after the match today. Someone else was called it. I just hadn't heard it before.'

She glanced at me. I could see she was on the point of saying something, and I got up.

'Oh well,' I said. 'Better bring my football gear in.'

After supper I went into Yngve's room and told him what had happened.

'I got together with Kajsa this evening,' I said.

He looked up from the school books spread over his desk and smiled.

'Kajsa? I haven't heard her name before. Who's she?'

'She's at Roligheden. In the sixth class. She looks really good.'

'I don't doubt that,' Yngve said. 'Congratulations.'

'Thanks,' I said. 'But there's just one thing . . . I need some advice . . .'

'Oh yes?'

'I don't know . . . Well, I don't know her at all. I don't know . . . What shall we do? She's coming here tomorrow, you see. I don't even know what to say!'

'It'll be fine,' Yngve said. 'Just don't think about it, and it'll be fine. You can always snog instead of speaking!'

'Ha ha.'

'It'll be fine, Karl Ove. Relax.'

'Do you think so?'

'Goes without saying.'

'OK,' I said. 'What are you doing?'

'Homework. Chemistry. And then geography.'

'I'm looking forward to starting at *gymnas*,' I said.

'Lots of reading to do,' Yngve said.

'Yes,' I said. 'All the same.'

Yngve turned back to his book and I went to my room. Yngve had just finished the first year at *gymnas* and I understood he wanted to do social studies while dad wanted him to do natural sciences, so that was what he had to do. It was a bit odd because dad's subjects were Norwegian and English.

I put on *McCartney II* and lay down on the bed wondering what I could say and do the next day. Every so often I had an attack of the shivers. Fancy me actually going out with her! Perhaps she was lying in bed, in her room, in her house, thinking about me at this very minute? Perhaps she had gone to bed, perhaps she was wearing only panties in bed? I rolled over onto my stomach and rubbed my groin against the mattress while singing

'Temporary Secretary' and thinking about all that lay in store for me.

She arrived an hour after we'd had dinner. I had been walking to and fro by the windows facing the road and was as prepared as I could be. Nevertheless, it was a shock to see her cycling up the hill. For a few seconds I was unable to breathe normally. Kent Arne, Geir Håkon, Leif Tore and Øyvind were outside, hanging over the handlebars of their bikes, and when they all turned to look at her a rush of pride surged through me. No one had ever seen a more attractive girl in Tybakken. And it was me she had come to see.

I put on my shoes and jacket and went out.

She had stopped by them and was chatting.

I grabbed my bike and pushed it over.

'She was asking where you lived, Karl Ove!' Geir Håkon said.

'Oh yes?' I said to him. Meeting Kajsa's gaze. 'Hi,' I said. 'You found your way here?'

'Yes, it was no problem,' she said. 'I didn't know exactly which house it was, but . . .'

'Shall we go?' I said.

'All right,' she said.

I mounted my bike. She mounted hers.

'See you!' I said to the four boys. I turned to her. 'We can go up there.'

'Fine,' she said.

I knew they were watching us and that they were more than ordinarily envious of me. How on earth had he done it? they were thinking. Where had he met her? And how in the name of all things living and moving had he managed to land her?

After we had cycled part of the way up, Kajsa got off her bike.

I did the same. A wind rose through the forest, rustling the leaves beside us and then it dropped. The sound of tyres on tarmac. Trouser legs rubbing against each other. The cork heels of her sandals on the road.

I waited for her to come alongside.

'That's a nice jacket,' I said. 'Where did you get it?'

'Thank you,' she said. 'At Bajazzo's in Kristiansand.'

'Oh,' I said.

We reached the crossroads with Elgstien. Her breasts were swaying; my eyes were permanently drawn to them. Did she notice?

'We can go over to the shop and see if anyone's there,' I said.

'Mm,' she said.

Was she regretting this already?

Should I kiss her now? Would that be right?

We were at the top of the hill and I swung a leg over the bike saddle. Waited until her feet were on the pedals, then I set off. Another gust of wind blew past us. I cycled with one hand and half-turned to her.

'Do you know Lars?' I said.

'Lars, yes,' she said. 'We're neighbours. And we're in the same class. Do you know him? Of course you do. You're in the same team.'

'Yes,' I said. 'Did you watch the whole match last night?'

'Yes. You're a very good team!'

I didn't answer. I put my other hand on the handlebars and freewheeled down the little hill to B-Max. It was closed and there was no one around.

'Doesn't seem to be anyone here,' I said. 'Shall we go to yours?'

'All right,' she said.

I decided I would kiss her if a glimmer of a chance arose. And definitely hold her hand. Something had to happen. After all we were girlfriend and boyfriend now.

Kajsa was my girlfriend!

But no chance arose. We cycled along the old gravel road up to Kjenna, which was deserted, up the hills to her house and stopped outside. We hadn't exchanged many sentences on the way, but enough to know it hadn't been a disaster.

'Mum and dad are at home,' she said. 'So you can't come in.'

Did that mean I could when they weren't?

'OK,' I said. 'But it's late. Perhaps I should be getting back.'

'Yes, it's quite a long way!' she said.

'Shall we meet again tomorrow?' I said.

'I can't,' she said. 'We're going out in the boat.'

'On Thursday then?'

'Yes. Will you come up here?'

'Yes, of course.'

The bikes were between us all the time. It wasn't possible to lean over and kiss her. And perhaps she wouldn't have wanted it either, right in front of her house.

I got back on my bike.

'I'll be off then,' I said. 'See you!'

'Bye,' she said.

And I cycled off as fast as I could.

Well, it could have been worse. I hadn't got very far, but nothing had been ruined for ever. It couldn't continue like this, I realised, we couldn't just talk, if we did, everything would wither and die. I had to kiss her; we had to do what proper boyfriends and girlfriends did. But how to make the move? I had snogged Mariann, but I hadn't been that keen on her, it hadn't been a problem, I had just put my arms around her, pulled her to me and kissed her. I had just taken her hand when we walked side by side. I couldn't do that with Kajsa though, couldn't just put my arms around her, out of the blue.

Imagine if she didn't want it! Imagine if I couldn't pull the move off! It had to happen, and it would have to happen next time, that much was certain. And in a suitable place where no one could see us.

Thank God for the boat trip. It gave me two whole days to plan.

As I was about to fall asleep I remembered we had football training on Thursday. That meant I would have to ring and tell her. All next day I dreaded it. Our telephone at home was in the hall, everyone could hear what was said unless I closed the sliding door, but that was bound to arouse their curiosity, so the best would be to ring from a telephone box. There was one by the bus stop opposite the Fina station and I cycled down as late as I could, to be precise a little after eight. If there was nothing special on, I had to be home by half past eight, because I had to be in bed by half nine on weekdays, the rule was still inflexible, even though everyone I knew stayed up later.

Having parked my bike outside, I searched for their home number in the telephone directory. What I was going to say had been reverberating around my head.

I dialled the whole number, apart from the last digit, very quickly. Then I waited a few seconds to get my breathing under control and dialled the last digit.

'Pedersen,' a woman's voice said.

'May I speak to Kajsa please?' I said hurriedly.

'Who's calling?'

'Karl Ove,' I said.

'Just a moment.'

There was a pause. I heard footsteps fading into the distance, voices. A bus came down the hill and slowly pulled into the bus stop. I pressed the receiver tighter against my ear.

'Hello?' said Kajsa.

'Is that Kajsa?' I said.

'Yes,' she said.

'This is Karl Ove,' I said.

'I could hear that!' she said.

'Hi,' I said.

'Hi,' she said.

'I have to go to football tomorrow,' I said. 'So I can't make it to yours as we agreed.'

'Then I'll see you down there. You'll be at Kjenna, won't you?'

'Yes.'

Pause.

'Was it nice?' I said.

'Was what nice?'

'The boat trip? Was it nice?'

'Yes.'

Pause.

'See you tomorrow then!' I said.

'Yes. Bye,' she said.

'Bye.'

I put down the receiver and my eyes were met by those of an old teacher in his forties who worked with dad; he was on the bus and looked away when I saw him. I opened the dusty door and went out. The air was warm and full of the fumes from the idling bus engine. A family with two children was sitting outside the Fina station and eating ice cream. As I cycled by, John came out of the door. He was holding a helmet in one hand. Bare chest, clogs on his feet.

'Hi, Karl Ove!' he called.

'Hi,' I shouted back.

He put on his helmet, it was black with a black visor, and he got on the back of a motorbike. The driver started it up with two hefty kicks. Afterwards they roared up the hill behind me. John waved an arm in the air as they raced past. My forehead was soaked with sweat. I ran my hand through my hair. My hand was sweaty too. But my hair was fine; I had washed it the night before so that it would be perfect for the following day and the date with Kajsa. At the bus stop on the crest of the hill, outside B-Max, I stopped. Rested my foot against the kerb.

Suddenly I knew how I would do it.

Only a few weeks ago I had been here, surrounded by a whole crowd of people, with Tor the centre of attention. He had built his own bicycle, mounted a motorbike saddle and an enormous new cogwheel at the front. He was doing wheelies to and fro, spitting great gobbets of saliva across the tarmac. Merethe, his girlfriend, was also there. I had just been hanging out with Dag Magne, and we had bumped into them and stayed there. Tor cycled over to Merethe and kissed her. Then he took a watch from his inside pocket, it was on a chain, glanced at it and said, 'Shall we see how long we can snog, eh?' Merethe nodded, and then they leaned towards each other and kissed. You could see their tongues working in each other's mouths. She had her eyes closed and her arms around him; he stood with his hands in his pockets and his eyes open. Everyone was watching them. After ten minutes he held up his watch and straightened his back. Wiped his mouth with the back of his hand. 'Ten minutes,' he said.

That was how to do it. I would take off my watch and ask if we could see how long we could kiss. And then all we had to do was kiss.

I pushed off with my foot and cycled down to Holtet. It was important to find a suitable place. In the forest, of course, but where? Up at hers? No, I didn't know my way around there. It should be somewhere near here.

Perhaps not too close to either of us.

We were meeting at hers.

But of course. Oh yes. In the forest, by the path up from Fina. Under the trees there. That was perfect. No one would see us. The ground was soft. And the light was so wonderful as it fell between the treetops.

So as not to be the very first to arrive at football training the next afternoon, I pushed my bike up all the hills, not that it made much difference because when I saw the pitch in front of me it was deserted, covered with clicking, murmuring jets spraying water around, each at its own rhythm. Christian and Hans Christian were sitting on the gate by the entrance squinting at me in the sunshine.

'No one got a ball?' I said.

They shook their heads.

'Is it true you're going out with Kajsa?' Christian said.

'Yes,' I said, biting my lip to stop myself smiling.

'Pretty, she is,' he said.

Christian had never gone out with any girls, he wasn't the type. But at the Norway Cup the previous summer he had bought a porn magazine from the kiosk outside the school the evening we arrived. Unfortunately for him his father, who coached the juniors, found him lying in his sleeping bag ogling the hypnotic pictures. With everyone in the team watching, he had to go and throw the magazine in the bin and apologise to his father.

'Ye-es,' I said.

Soon after, Øyvind came with the balls and keys, and we ran out between the sprinklers to the goal furthest away and we began to take shots while Øyvind switched off the water and moved the sprinklers from the pitch. When everyone was there we ran around the pitch a couple of times, did some stretching exercises and practised some set pieces before playing seven against seven on half of the pitch. Kajsa didn't come until close to the end, with the three girls she had been with before. She waved to me; I waved back.

'Concentrate, Karl Ove!' Øyvind shouted. 'Training first, girls later!'

After the session I dipped my head in the bucket of water on the touchline and tried to act as normal. But it wasn't easy; the knowledge that she was up there, and not just her but also her friends, looking at me, was burned into my consciousness.

Then she came down.

'Are you going to get changed?' she said.

I nodded.

'I'll come with you. I've got something to tell you afterwards.'

Tell me? Was she going to finish it?

I started walking. She stretched out her hand. It brushed against mine. Had it been by chance? Or could I hold it?

I looked at her.

She smiled at me.

I grabbed her hand in one swift movement.

Someone was whispering behind us. I turned. It was Lars and John. They were rolling their eyes. I smiled. She gently squeezed my hand.

The walk across the pitch had never been as long as it was this evening. Holding her hand was almost more than I could bear; all the time I felt an urge to withdraw my hand to bring this unbearable happiness to an end.

'Hurry up then,' she said when we were there.

'OK,' I said.

On the bench I leaned back against the wall. My heart was

pounding and pounding. Then I pulled myself together, threw on my clothes and left. They were standing on the road beneath the pitch with their bikes. I went over and stood beside Kajsa. She looked happy. Stroked a strand of hair from her face with her small hand. Her nails were painted in a semi-transparent pink varnish. Her friends got on their bikes as if at a signal and cycled off.

'This Saturday I'll be at home without my parents,' she said. 'I've told mum that Sunnva's coming. So she's going to make a pizza and buy Coke for us. But Sunnva isn't coming. Would you like to come?'

I swallowed.

'Yes,' I said.

Some of the other boys in the team cheered us from the shed. Kajsa stood with one hand on the handlebars and the other down by her side.

'Shall we go?' I said.

'Let's,' she said.

'Down?' I said.

She nodded and we got on our bikes. We pedalled along the shaded gravel road, me in front, Kajsa right behind. At the crest of the long hill I braked so that we could race down side by side. The sun lit up the ridge beyond. The insects swarming in the air were like glitter someone had scattered. Halfway down there was an old forest track to the right and it suddenly struck me that it might lead to a suitable place, so with the wind streaming through our hair I shouted to Kajsa that we would go up there, she nodded, we turned off and must have gone ten metres before our bikes slowed down and we dismounted. She said nothing, I said nothing, we walked up the grassy track strewn with bark and bits of tree. Reaching the top and looking into the forest I could see it wasn't suitable. The ground was covered with tree stumps, and where they stopped the spruces were so close together it was like a wall.

'No,' I said. 'That's no good. Let's go on.'

Kajsa still said nothing, just got on her bike as well and free-wheeled down, standing on the pedals and braking harder than me.

No, the path above the Fina station was the place to be.

The thought sent a wave of terror through me. It was like having climbed up a rock too high and looking down at the water, knowing you either had to conquer your fear and dive or chicken out.

Did she know what was going to happen?

I sneaked a glance at her.

Oh, the ripple of her breasts.

Oh, oh, oh.

But her face was serious. What did that mean?

We jumped off our bikes and walked up the hill to the main road, beneath the deep shadows from the trees whose tops stretched far above us. We hadn't said a word since we were in Kjenna. If I said something now it had to be important, it couldn't be some triviality.

Her trousers were cotton, a pastel green colour and secured around the waist by a rope belt. They hung loose over her thighs but were tighter around the groin and across the bottom. On her chest she was wearing a T-shirt with a thin cardigan over, which was white with a hint of yellow. Her sandalled feet were bare. Her toenails were painted with the same varnish as her fingers. She had a chain around one ankle.

She looked fantastic.

When we came to the main road and only a long hill down and a long hill up separated us from what was to happen, what I most wanted to do was cycle off and leave her. Just step on the pedals and cycle out of her life. And then why stop at that? I could cycle from our house. Tybakken, Tromøya, Aust-Agder, Norway, Europe, I could leave everything behind me. I would be called the Cycling Dutchman. Damned for ever to cycle around the world, with a ghostly light from the lamp on my handlebars illuminating the country roads.

'Where are we going actually?' she said as we sped down the hill.

'I know somewhere nice,' I said. 'It's not far.'

She didn't say anything. We cycled past the Fina station, I pointed up the hill between the trees, again she jumped off as soon as the road became steeper. A thin layer of sweat glistened on her forehead. We walked past the old white house and the old red barn. The sky was clear and blue. The sun hung over the ridges to the west, a silent blaze. Its light gave the leaves on the trees in front of us an intense glow. The air was filled with birdsong. I was close to throwing up. We entered the path. Light filtered down between the treetops, as I had imagined it. It was refracted in a similar way to the way it was refracted underwater. Pillars of light sloped into the ground.

I stopped.

'We can put our bikes here,' I said.

We did. Both of us kicked out the stands and stood our bikes upright. I started walking. She followed. I looked for a suitable place to lie down. Grass or moss. Our footsteps sounded unnaturally loud. I didn't dare look at her. But she was right behind me. There. There was a good spot.

'We can lie down here,' I said. Without looking at her I sat down. After some hesitation she sat down next to me. I put my hand in my pocket and located my watch. I took it out and held it in my open palm in front of her.

'Shall we time how long we can kiss?' I said.

'What!' she said.

'I've got a watch,' I said. 'Tor managed ten minutes. We can beat that.'

I put the watch down on the ground, it was eighteen minutes to eight, I noted, placed my hands on her shoulders and gently leaned her back while pressing my lips against hers. When we were both lying down I inserted my tongue in her mouth, it met hers, pointed and soft like a little animal, and I began to move my tongue round and round inside. I had my hands alongside my body, I wasn't touching her with anything except my lips and my tongue. Our bodies lay like two small boats laid up on land beneath the treetops. I concentrated on getting my tongue to go round as smoothly as possible while the thought of her breasts, which were so close to me, and her thighs, which were so close to me, and what was between her thighs, under her trousers, under her knickers, was seared into my consciousness. But I didn't dare touch her. She lay with her eyes closed rotating her tongue around mine, I had my eyes open, groped for the watch, found it and held it within reach. Three minutes so far. Some saliva ran down from the corner of her mouth. She wriggled. I pressed my groin against the ground letting my tongue go round and round, round and round. This wasn't as good as I had imagined, in fact it was quite strenuous. Some dry leaves crunched beneath her head as she shifted position. Our mouths were full of thick saliva. Seven minutes now. Four left. Mmm, she said, but this was not a sound of pleasure, there was something wrong, she stirred, but I didn't let go, she moved her head while I continued to rotate my tongue. She opened her eyes, but didn't look at me, they were staring up at the sky above us. Nine minutes. The root of my tongue ached. More saliva from the corners of our mouths. My dental brace occasionally knocked against her teeth. Actually we didn't need to continue for more than ten minutes and one second to beat Tor's record. And that was now. We had beaten him now. But we could beat him by a large margin. Fifteen minutes, that ought to be possible. Five left then. But my tongue ached, it seemed to be swelling, and the saliva, which you didn't notice much when it was hot, left you with a slight feeling of revulsion when it ran down your chin, not quite so hot. Twelve minutes. Isn't that enough? Enough now? No, a bit more. A bit more, a bit more.

At exactly three minutes to eight I took my head away. She got up and wiped her mouth with her hand without looking at me.

'We did fifteen minutes!' I said, getting up. 'We beat him by five minutes!'

Our bikes gleamed at the far end of the path. We walked towards them. She brushed leaves and twigs off her trousers and cardigan.

'Hang on,' I said. 'There's something on your back as well.'

She stopped and I picked off bits and pieces that had got caught in her cardigan.

'There we are,' I said.

'I'd better go home now,' she said as we reached the bikes.

'Me too,' I said, pointing upwards. 'There's a short cut through the forest.'

'Bye,' she said, getting on her bike and freewheeling down the bumpy path.

'Bye,' I said, grabbing the handlebars and walking up.

That night I lay fantasising about her breasts, milky-white and large, and all the things we could have done on the forest floor, until I fell asleep. I had to ring her because we hadn't arranged when I should go to hers on Saturday, but I put off doing it all the next day and also part of the Saturday until there was no avoiding it and at two o'clock I jumped on my bike and pedalled down to the telephone box again. There was another problem as well, which was that I had to be home by half past eight, which was not at all in tune with the life I was leading now. I couldn't leave hers at eight because I had to go home to bed, what would she think of me? I hinted to mum that I had something important to do that evening; couldn't I come home at half past nine, or even at ten? She wanted to know what and I said I couldn't tell her. If you can't tell me, you can't have permission, she said. We have to know where you are and what you are doing. Then perhaps you can have permission. You do understand, don't you? Yes, I did understand and I was prepared to toe the line and tell her about Kajsa. But first I had to get in touch with her.

The sky was overcast and the grey matt cloud cover seemed to suck the colours out of the countryside. The road was grey, the rocks in the ditch were grey, even the leaves on the trees had a weft of matt grey in their greenness. Also the heat from the previous days had gone. It wasn't cold, it was maybe sixteen or seventeen degrees, but enough for me to button up to the neck as I cycled down. My jacket ballooned out in the air. Two vehicles were at the bus stop, which in fact was a mini bus station, with buses often parked there all night. Now they were standing there, engines idling, ready to proceed on their way, one to the other side of the island, the other to Arendal, and the two drivers had parked so that they could chat to each other through the open windows.

I stood my bike behind the green hat-shaped fibreglass shelter. A stream flowed nearby, through branches and bushes and litter, mostly sweet papers, probably from the Fina station; I could see Caramello, Hobby, Nero, Bravo and a blue Hubba Bubba wrapper, but there were also some shiny bottles without labels, some newspapers and there was a cardboard box full of assorted junk. I took the money from my pocket, went into the box and placed it on top of the machine, ready. Dialled the number in the directory as various jokes went through my head. Why are there so many Hansens in the phone book? They've all got phones. Followed by: Why haven't the Chinese got a phone book. Too many Wings and Wongs, and you might wing a wong number. Operator, operator, call me an ambulance. OK, you're an ambulance. With my finger under the number and the receiver in my hand I stood for a long time staring through the dusty glass without quite registering what I saw until I plucked up the courage, put the phone to my ear and dialled.

'Hello?' a voice said.

It was Kajsa's!

'Hi,' I said. 'This is Karl Ove. Is that Kajsa?'

'Yes,' she said. 'Hi.'

'We forgot to talk about when I should come,' I said. 'Is there any particular time that would be suitable? It makes no difference to me.'

'Errrm,' she said. 'Well, in fact, it's all off.'

'Off,' I said. 'Can't you make it? Aren't your parents going out after all?'

'What I mean to say is,' she started. 'Erm . . . erm . . . I can't . . . well, go out with you any longer.'

What?

Was she finishing it?

But . . . we'd only been going out for five days!

'Hello?' she said.

'Is it over?' I said.

'Yes,' she said. 'It's over.'

I said nothing. I could hear her breathing at the other end. Tears were running down my cheeks. A long time passed.

'Bye then,' she said suddenly.

'Bye,' I said, and put down the phone and went to the bus stop. My eyes were blinded by tears. I wiped them with the back of my hand, sniffed, got on my bike and began to pedal homewards. I barely saw the road in front of me. Why had she done that? Why? Now that things had started to click? On the day we were going to be alone in her house? She liked me a few days ago, so why didn't she like me now? Was it because we hadn't talked much?

And she was so good-looking. She was so unbelievably good-looking.

Bloody hell.

Bloodyfuckinghell.

Bloodyfuckingcuntinghell.

When I got to B-Max I dried my tears on the sleeves of my jacket, it was Saturday just before closing time, the car park was full of cars and people with shopping bags and kids, loads of kids. But if they saw my tears, could they have been caused by the wind? I was cycling after all.

I plodded up the little hill before the flat stretch. Completely empty neutral spaces were developing inside me, ten seconds could pass without my thinking a single thought, without knowing that I even existed, and then the image of Kajsa was suddenly there, it was over, and a sob shook through me, impossible to stop.

I locked my bike and put it in its place outside the house, stood still inside the house listening to hear where the others were, now was not the time to bump into anyone, and when it sounded as if the coast was clear I went upstairs and into the bathroom, where I washed my face carefully before going into my room and sitting down on the bed.

After a while I got up and went to Yngve's room. He was on his bed playing the guitar and glanced up when I entered.

'What's up? Have you been crying?' he said. 'Is it Kajsa? Has she finished it?'

I nodded and started crying again.

'Now, now, Karl Ove,' he said. 'It'll soon pass. There are many girls out there waiting. The world is full of girls! Forget her. It's no big deal.'

'Yes, it is,' I said. 'We only went out for five days. And she's so good-looking. She's the only one I want to be with. No one else. And today of all days. When we were going to be alone at her place.'

'Hang about,' he said, getting up. 'I'll play a song for you. It might help.'

'What kind of song?' I said, sitting down on the chair.

'Hang on,' he said, flicking through a pile of singles on the shelf. 'This one,' he said, holding up one of the Aller Værste!'s. '"No Way Back".'

'Oh, that one.'

'Listen to the lyrics,' he said, removing the single from the sleeve, placing the plastic centre in the middle of the deck, then the single, lifting up the stylus and putting it down on the first groove, which was already whizzing round. After a second's scratching the energetic drums pumped into life, then came the bass, the guitar and the Farfisa organ with the rest, followed by the jangling, unbelievably exciting guitar riff and then the voice of the singer with the Stavanger accent:

I'm not lying when I say I knew
That me and you were already through
I saw you were trying to hide it
Until the sensi thin condom split

Long-term plans and our shared visions
Blown to bits in one minute flat
You gave me a hug; I wanted to give you more
But you certainly put paid to that

'Listen now!' Yngve said.

All things pass – all things must decay
You go to sleep; you wake up to a new day
No way back now, nothing to thank you for
Nuthin' to say, there's your coat, there's the door

'Yes,' I said.

We were on the point of going banal
I heard myself speaking and got irritated
We had one too many and went sentimental
But the words were still infected
You broke my heart and gave me the clap
I still haven't finished the penicillin rap
Why must we bang our heads against the same old wall
When we know deep down we hate it all

All things pass – all things must decay
You go to sleep; you wake up to a new day
No way back now, nothing to thank you for
Nuthin' to say, there's your coat, there's the door

'All things pass,' Yngve said when the song was over and the stylus had returned to its little rest. 'All things must decay. You go to sleep; you wake up to a new day.'

'I understand what you're saying,' I said.

'Did it help?'

'Yes, a bit. Could you play it again?'

Fortunately mum and dad didn't notice that I had been crying when we were having dinner. Afterwards, too restless to stay inside, I went out, and as the road was empty and the children I knew best were on holiday I ambled down to the pontoons. There was a whole crowd standing around Jørn's boat, which was brand new. Lots of people had a new boat that spring, both Geir Håkon and Kent Arne had one, a GH 10 and a With Dromedille respectively, a ten-footer as well, both with five-horsepower Yamaha outboard motors.

I walked over to them.

'Here's our jessie,' Jørn said as I stopped.

That word again.

They laughed, from which I concluded it wasn't well meant.

'Hi,' I said.

Jørn started the engine after a few tugs on the cord.

'Come here, Karl Ove,' he said.

'No,' I said. 'Not likely.'

'I want to show you something,' he said, looking at his little brother. 'You reverse when I tell you, right.'

His little brother nodded.

'Come on,' he said, moving to the bow.

I took a few hesitant steps forward. When I was on the edge of the pontoon he threw himself around my legs.

'Reverse!' he shouted to his brother.

The boat reversed, I went into a crouch, my legs were pulled away from beneath me, I fell and was dragged over the edge because Jørn didn't let go and the boat continued to reverse. I made a grab for the edge and clung on by my fingers. Jørn's brother accelerated, the engine revved, and I hung there with my legs on board the boat, my body over the water and my hands on the pontoon. I shouted to them to stop. I started to cry. The bystanders smiled and looked on calmly at what was happening.

'That's enough!' Jørn shouted.

The whole incident had lasted perhaps a minute. Jørn's brother revved forward, Jørn let go of my legs and I climbed up and walked off as quickly as I could, crying. The tears didn't stop until I was up by the rock face, where I sat down in the hot, perfectly still air saturated with the aromas of the sun-warmed rocks, dry grass and wild flowers.

I mulled over whether I should ring Kajsa and ask her why she had finished with me, so that I could learn from it for the next time, but it was too complicated, I could hear it all now, her hesitation and my groping for words, and for what, it was over, she didn't want to be with me, simple as that.

Still weak at the knees and shaking, I got up and walked home. Washed my face slowly in cold water in the bathroom, drew the curtains, didn't want anything from outside to slip in, put on Motörhead, *Ace of Spades*, but it felt wrong, so I took it off and put on the new solo record by Paul McCartney instead and started a Desmond Bagley book I had bought with my own money called *The Vivero Letter*. I had read it before, but it was about the pyramids in South America, the enormous underwater grottos where the protagonists dived in search of a hoard of gold others were also after . . .

When I sat down to have supper mum looked at me and smiled.

'It might be time for you to start wearing a deodorant, Karl Ove?' she said. 'I can buy you one tomorrow.'

'Deodorant?' I repeated stupidly.

'Yes, don't you think so? You'll be starting at the new school soon and so on.'

'You do pong, in fact,' Yngve said. 'No girls like that, you know.'

Was that *why*?

But when I asked Yngve about it afterwards, he smiled and said he doubted it was that simple.

The next morning dad came in and told me I couldn't spend the whole summer on my bed reading, I had to get out. Why don't you go for a swim? he said.

I closed my book without a word and walked past him without a second glance.

I sat on the concrete barriers for a few minutes throwing pebbles into the road. But I couldn't stay there, everyone would see that I had nothing to do and nobody to be with, so I trudged down towards the big cherry tree at the edge of the forest by the road, where Kristen's field started, to see if the cherries were ripe enough to eat yet. Who owned this tree was unclear, some said it was a wild cherry, others said it belonged to Kristen, but we had still stripped it every summer since we were old enough to climb, and no one had complained so far. Knowing every branch, I climbed almost to the top and along a branch until it began to bend. The berries weren't quite ripe yet, the skin was hard and green on one side, but the other exhibited a faint redness, and that was enough for me to bite into their skins, chew and swallow and spit the stones as far as I could afterwards.

Sitting there, I saw Jørn come cycling towards me. He was holding a canister of petrol on the luggage rack with one hand and steering with the other. When he spotted me he braked gently and stopped.

'Karl Ove!' he shouted.

I climbed down as fast as I could. It took roughly the same time to clamber down as it took him to get off his bike and come to the tree because by the time I was on the ground he was only a few metres from me. Our eyes met, then I hared off up towards the forest.

'I only wanted to say I was sorry!' he said. 'About yesterday! I heard you blubbing.'

I didn't turn.

'I didn't mean it!' he said. 'Come back down so that we can shake hands on it!'

Ha ha, I thought, and stumbled on up between thickets and bushes until I was at the top and could watch him amble back to his bike, get on and continue on his wobbly way down to the boats. Then I went back down. But the hard bitter cherries had lost their fascination, so I gave up on the tree and instead mooched off in the hope that someone would appear on the road after a while. Sometimes people came out if they saw you from a window, so I went for a walk up the hill, staring into the gardens on both sides as I went. Not a soul anywhere. People were in their boats or they had driven to bathing spots on the far side of the island or they were at work. Tove Karlsen's husband was lying on a sunbed in the middle of their yellowing lawn with a radio beside him. Fru Jacobsen, the mother of Geir, Trond and Wenche, was sitting under a parasol on the veranda smoking. On her head she was wearing a white bucket hat. She had covered the rest of her body in light, white clothes. Her two-year-old son was sitting on the ground beside her; I glimpsed him between the bars of his play pen. Behind me someone called my name. I turned. It was Geir; he sprinted up with his palms facing inwards.

He stopped in front of me.

'Where's Vemund?' I said.

'On holiday,' Geir said. 'They left today. Are you coming in the boat?'

'All right,' I said. 'Where are we going then?'

Geir shrugged.

'Gjerstadsholmen. Or one of the small islands beside it?'

'OK.'

Geir only had a rowing boat, so the radius of his activities was much more limited than that of the other boat owners. Nevertheless, it took us out to the islets and on occasion we had rowed several kilometres along the coast of the island. He wasn't allowed to row in Tromøya Sound.

We scrambled on board, I pushed off, he positioned the oars in the rowlocks, applied force with his feet and rowed so hard, with his oars so deep, that a grimace distorted his entire face.

'Ugh,' he groaned at every pull. 'Ugh. Ugh.'

We glided along the light blue surface of the sea, which was sporadically ruffled by gusting shoreward winds. The waves further out in the sound had white tips.

Geir turned and located the little island, adjusted his course with one oar and then resumed his grunts while I hung my hand in the water and rested my eyes on the little there was of a wake.

As we approached, I stood up, leaped ashore and pulled the boat into a tiny inlet. I didn't know how to tie any knots, so it was Geir who tethered the rope to one of the metal rods that appeared to be fixed to every single little crag in the archipelago.

'Shall we have a swim?' he said.

'Fine by me,' I said.

On the side facing Tromøya Sound a rock rose from the sea into a two-metre-high pinnacle from which we jumped and dived. It was cold in the wind but warm in the water, so we swam for almost an hour before getting out and lying on the cliff to dry.

When we had dressed, Geir took a lighter from his pocket and showed it to me.

'Where did you get hold of that?' I said.

'It was in the cabin,' he said.

'Shall we set light to something?'

'Yes, well, that was the idea.'

Grass grew in all the cracks on the rock face, and in the middle of the islet there was a grass plain.

Geir crouched down, cupped his hand around the lighter and set fire to a little tuft. It caught at once with a clear transparent flame.

'Can I have a go?' I said.

Geir stood up, swept his stiff fringe to one side and passed me the lighter.

'Hey!' I said. 'Watch out! It's spreading!'

Geir laughed and stamped on the fire. It was as good as out when flames suddenly flared up further away, where he had already put it out.

'Did you see that?' he said. 'It started all on its own!'

He stamped it out, and I walked over to the plain and lit the grass there. At that moment a strong wind gusted in. The fire burst into a blanket of flames.

'Give me a hand,' I said. 'There's so much to put out.'

We jumped and stamped for all we were worth, and the fire was extinguished.

'Give me the lighter,' Geir said.

I passed it to him.

'Let's light the grass in lots of places at once,' he said.

'OK,' I said.

He lit it where he was, passed me the lighter, I ran to the other side and lit it there, ran over to where he had moved and he lit it there.

'Can you hear it crackling?' he said.

It was indeed. The fire crackled and spat as it slowly ate its way across. Where I had lit the grass the fire resembled a snake.

Another rush of wind blew in off the sea.

'Ooooh dear!' Geir said as the flames rose and took a substantial chomp out of the middle of the grass.

He started stamping like a wild man. But suddenly it didn't help.

'Give me a hand,' he said.

I heard a growing panic in his voice.

I started stamping as well. Another blast of wind, and now some of the flames were up to our knees.

'Oh, no!' I shouted. 'It's burning like hell over there too!'

'Take your jumper off! We'll put it out with our jumpers. I saw them do it in a film once!'

We took off our jumpers and began to beat the ground with them. The wind continued to whip up the flames, which spread even further with every gust.

Now the grass was well alight.

We stamped and beat at the flames like crazy men, but it was no use.

'It's no good,' Geir shouted. 'We won't be able to put this out.'

'No,' I said. 'It's just getting worse and worse!'

'What shall we do?'

'I don't know. Can we use the bailer, do you think?' I said.

'The bailer? Are you completely stupid or what?'

'No, I am not stupid,' I said. 'It was just a suggestion.'

Oh no. The fire was burning out of control. I could feel the heat from several metres away.

'Let's get out of here,' Geir said. 'Come on!'

And so, as the flames danced and crackled across the grass

with ever greater ferocity, we shoved out the boat. Geir got behind the oars and began to row, even harder than before.

'Bloody hell,' he kept saying. 'What a fire! What a fire!'

'Yes,' I said. 'Who would have thought it?'

'Not me anyhow.'

'Nor me. Hope no one sees it.'

'Makes no difference,' Geir said. 'The important thing is that no one saw *us*.'

On reaching land we dragged the boat deep into the forest to hide any possible traces. There was soot on our T-shirts; we dipped them in the water and wrung them out, and for safety's sake we removed our shorts and rinsed them as well. If anyone asked we would say we had been swimming in our shorts and our T-shirts had fallen in the sea. Then we dived in to get rid of the smell of fire and walked home.

From a distance I could see there was no one in the front garden. I stopped in the hall: not a sound. Slipped into the boiler room, hung up the T-shirt and went up to my room bare-chested, took another T-shirt from the wardrobe and changed my shorts.

From the window in Yngve's room I saw dad lying on the sunbed on the lawn. He could lie in the sun for hours without moving, like a lizard. And the tan he had bore witness to it. The sound of a radio drifted over from somewhere; mum must have been sitting on the terrace under the living-room window.

An hour later she came into my room with some deodorant for me. MUM for Men, it was called. It was a glass bottle, blue, and smelled sweet and good. I thought: for men. I was a man. Or a youth at least. I would be starting a new school in a few weeks and would use the deodorant.

She explained I should rub it in under my arms after washing, but always after washing, never without, otherwise the smell would be worse.

After she had gone I did as she said, inhaled the new aroma for a while, then resumed the book I was reading, it was *Dracula*, my all-time favourite, I was reading it for the second time, but it was just as exciting now.

'Supper's up!' mum called from the kitchen, I laid it aside and went in.

Dad was sitting in his place, dark-skinned and dark-eyed. Mum poured boiling water in the teapot and set it down on the table between us.

'Martha has invited us to their cabin today,' she said.

'Out of the question,' dad said. 'Did she say anything else?'

Mum shook her head.

'Nothing special.'

I looked down at the table and ate as fast as I could without giving the appearance of haste.

An engine was started up nearby, it coughed a couple of times, then died. Dad got up to look out of the window.

'Isn't Gustavsen on holiday?' he said.

No one answered; he looked at me.

'Yes,' I said. 'But not Rolf or Leif Tore. They're the only ones at home.'

The car was started again. This time the engine was revved hard. Then it was put into first gear, and the drone rose and sank and stuttered.

'Someone's driving their car anyway,' dad said.

I stood up to see.

'Sit down!' said dad.

I sat down.

'What's going on?' mum said.

'The brats are taking their parents' car without asking.'

He turned and looked at mum.

'Isn't that incredible?' he said.

Jerking and stuttering, the drone went up the hill.

'Have they *no* control over their kids?' he said. 'Leif Tore is in *Karl Ove's* class. And he goes and steals his parents' *car*?'

I gulped down the last bit of bread, poured a drop of milk in my tea to cool it enough to drink. Got up.

'Thanks, Mum,' I said.

'Pleasure,' mum said. 'Are you going to bed?'

'Think so,' I said.

'Goodnight then.'

'Goodnight.'

He came in before I switched off the light.

'Sit up,' he said.

I sat up.

He fixed me with a long stare.

'I hear you've been smoking, Karl Ove,' he said.

'What?' I said. 'I have not! I promise you. I'm telling the truth.'

'That's not what I've heard. I've heard you've been smoking.'

I glanced up and met his eye.

'Have you?' he said.

I looked down. 'No,' I said.

There it was, his hand around my ear.

'You have,' he said, twisting it. 'Haven't you?'

'Noooo!' I yelled.

He let go.

'Rolf told me you had,' he said. 'Are you telling me Rolf was lying?'

'Yes, he *must* have been,' I said. 'Because I have never smoked.'

'Why would Rolf lie?'

'I don't know,' I said.

'And why are you crying? If you have a clear conscience? I know you, Karl Ove. I know you've been smoking. But you won't do it again. So that'll have to do this time.'

He turned and left as darkly as when he came.

I dried my eyes with the duvet cover and lay staring at the ceiling, suddenly wide awake. I had never smoked.

But he had known I had done something.

How did he know?

How *could* he have known?

The next day we were unable to keep away and rowed past the islet.

'It's all black!' Geir said, resting on the oars.

We laughed so much we almost fell in the water.

Even if, on the outside, this summer was like all previous summers – we went to Sørbøvåg, we went to grandma and grandad's cabin and for the rest of the time I hung around the estate and headed off with anyone who was around, if I wasn't on my own and reading – on the inside it was quite different, for what awaited me, when it was over, was not a new school year like all the other new school years, no, at the end-of-term party in June the head teacher had made a speech, and he had done this because we were leaving Sandnes *Barne*skole, our time there was past; after the summer holiday we would be starting the seventh year at Roligheden *Ungdoms*skole. We were no longer children, but youths.

I worked in a market garden all July, standing in the fields from dawn under the burning hot sun picking or packing strawberries, thinning carrots, sitting on a knoll eating my packed lunch as fast as I could in the middle of the day so that I could cycle to Lake Gjerstad and have a swim before work resumed. Everything I earned I would use for pocket money during the Norway Cup. For the week the tournament lasted mum and dad went walking in the mountains. There was a heatwave that summer, we played one of the matches on shale, it was so hot I collapsed and was taken to a kind of field hospital on the plain, where I came round that night; someone was playing Roxy Music's 'More Than This' in the distance, I looked up at the tent ceiling and was as happy as I had ever been for some reason I did not comprehend but acknowledged.

Could it have been because I had hung around with Kjell during those days, sung Police songs on the Metro so loud the walls reverberated, chatted up girls and bought loads of band badges from a street vendor, including ones of the Specials and the Clash, as well as a pair of black sunglasses I wore every waking hour?

Yes, it certainly could. Kjell was one year older and the most popular boy with the girls in the school. His mother was Brazilian, but he was not only brown-eyed, black-haired and attractive, he was also tough and someone everyone respected. So it was an enormous boost that he didn't seem to mind me, it elevated me at once to somewhere higher than Tybakken and the kids there. They didn't want to have anything to do with me, but Kjell did, so what did it matter? I also went with Lars to Oslo, which was more than I could really have hoped for.

This was possibly why I was so incredibly happy there. But it may have been that song by Roxy Music, 'More Than This'. The song was so captivating and so beautiful, and around me in that pale bluish summer night lay a whole capital, not only crowded with people of whom I knew nothing, but also record shops with hundreds, perhaps even thousands, of good bands on their shelves. Concert venues where the bands I had only read about actually played. The traffic hummed in the distance, everywhere there was the sound of voices and laughter, and Brian Ferry sang *More than this – there is nothing. More than this – there is nothing.*

Late one evening in mid-August we all went to the island of Torungen, south of Hisøya, to go crabbing. Dad had bought a powerful underwater torch and had brought along a rake, as well as a diving mask, flippers and an empty white tub. A whole colony of gulls took off when we went ashore, flew above our heads screaming, some diving so close they almost brushed us, it was intense and frightening, but it eased as we moved to the far side of the island and the night-black sea lay still before us. Mum lit a fire, dad undressed, put on the flippers and glided into the water with a torch in his hand, slipped on the mask and swam under the surface. The water cascaded off the snorkel as he re-emerged.

'None there,' he said. 'Let's try a bit further up.'

Yngve and I walked slowly along the smooth rocks. The gulls were still screaming behind us. Mum was preparing food.

There he was, coming up again, this time with a big crab with splayed claws in one hand.

'Bring the tub!' he said. Yngve went down to the water's edge, dad put the crab in and swam off again.

I was a bit embarrassed, that wasn't how you should catch crabs, you did it with a rake on land and a torch. On the other hand, there was no one else on the island but us.

Afterwards, with the tub brim-full of crawling crustaceans, dad sat down and warmed himself by the fire while we grilled sausages and drank pop. On the way down to the boat, after he had extinguished the fire with a bucket of seawater and a hiss, I discovered a dead gull lying in a hollow in the rock face. I felt it.

It was warm. A quiver went through its leg and I was startled. Wasn't it dead? I leaned forward and poked a finger in its white breast. No reaction. I stood up. Its lying there was spooky. Not so much because it was dead but because its colours and lines seemed almost obscenely precise to me. The orange beak, the black and yellow eyes, the large wings. And its feet, scaly and reptilian.

'What have you found?' dad said from behind me.

I turned and he shone the torch on my face. I raised a hand in defence.

'A dead seagull,' I said.

He lowered the torch.

'Let me see,' he said. 'Where is it?'

'There,' I said, pointing.

The next instant it was the focus of the light, as if it was on an operating table. Its eyes flashed in the reflection.

'There may be some chicks in distress somewhere,' dad said.

'Do you think so?' I said.

'Yes, they still have chicks in the nests. That was why they were so angry at us. Come on.'

Back towards the glittering lights of Arendal, through Tromøya Sound to the quay, with the constant clicking of the crabs and the ghostly rattle from the two full tubs. Dad boiled them as soon as he got home, and there was a sense of liberation at witnessing the pitilessness of the operation: they were taken from the tubs alive, they were dropped into the boiling water alive, and, dead, they floated round slowly on their backs in their bone-white and leaf-brown shells.

Two days after our nocturnal trip dad was transferred to Kristiansand. He had been offered a job at a *gymnas* in Vennesla, it was too far to commute, so he had rented a flat in a block in

Slettheia. He took all the things he needed in three loads using a hired trailer, and from then on he turned up at home every weekend, and after a while barely that. The idea was that he would look for a house in the Kristiansand area and we would move there the following summer.

It was a great relief when he left. And an incredible stroke of luck that he would change his job the precise autumn I started at the school where he had been employed for thirteen years. If he had been working there I would have felt his eyes on me the whole time and hardly dared to lift a finger without first considering the consequences. That was how it had been for Yngve. But that was not how it would be for me.

The first days at my new school reminded me of those we had experienced when we started the first class six years earlier. All the teachers were new and unfamiliar, all the buildings were new and unfamiliar, and apart from those in our class, all the other pupils were new and unfamiliar. Here, other rules and codes held sway, here other rumours and stories circulated, here the atmosphere was quite different. No one played at this school. No one did French skipping, no one did any skipping, no one played ball, no one played tag or any of the games we played in the playground. The sole exception was football, which was played here just as in our first school. No, what kids did in the break here, in the new school, was lounge about. The smokers lounged about in a corner on their own by the wet-weather shelter, chatting and laughing and flicking their lighters and smoking their cigarettes, some of them in leather jackets, some in denim jackets, almost all with a moped of some description because a vehicle was part of the life they led. Rumours circulated about some of them, that they had been involved in burglaries, for example, that they had turned up at school drunk, or even that they had tried drugs, which of course they didn't deny, but nor did they confirm it, they were somehow surrounded by an air of mystery and evil, and who else but John should stand side by side with them on the very first normal school day, laughing his gruff laugh? All of those standing there despised bookish learning, hated school, most were good with their hands and already wanted to be out in the world of work in the eighth year, and they were given permission, all lost causes were given permission, the school was only too happy to get rid of them. But, the cigarette hanging from the corner of the mouth aside, in practice they behaved no differently from any of the other pupils because they hung around in gangs as well and chatted and laughed. The girls stood in groups, the boys in other groups. Sometimes the boys baited the girls and there could be a bit of running to and fro and jeering, and on rare occasions fights broke out between two boys, which attracted everyone in the playground to them, like swimmers on a tidal wave, it was impossible to resist.

It took us several weeks to adjust to our new school life. Everything had to be tested. We had to explore the teachers' limits and preferences. We had to explore the boundaries. Of what went inside the classroom walls and what went outside.

For natural sciences we had Larsen, the teacher who had come to school drunk, he always looked as if he had spent the night on the sofa in his clothes and had just been woken, whatever time of day we had him, he was always a bit torpid and unfocused, but he loved experiments, smoke and bangs, so we liked his lessons. For music we had Konrad, he was in charge of the youth club, he wore blouse-like shirts under a black waistcoat, had glasses, a round face, a moustache and a little bald patch, was jovial and youthful, so he was on Christian-name terms with all of us; for maths we had Yngve's previous form teacher, Vestad, a ruddy-faced bald man with glasses and gimlet eyes; for domestic science we had Hansen, a bespectacled, grey-haired, strict, missionary-type Frøken who seemed to be genuinely interested in teaching us to fry fishcakes and boil potatoes: for English, Norwegian, RI and social sciences we had our form teacher, Kolloen, a tall thin man in his late twenties with pointed features and very little patience, who generally kept a distance from us but who could show flashes of empathy and sympathy.

These teachers not only made general comments and evaluations, as the teachers at our first school had done, no, here they gave us grades for everything we did. This created a very new tension in the class, for now we were all given an idea of everyone's strengths and weaknesses in black and white. It was impossible to keep your grades secret, or it *was* possible, but it was regarded as bad form. I averaged around a B or B+ and on rare occasions achieved an A or dropped to a C, but if I didn't keep the grades quiet inside the classroom, I began to tone them down outside as in recent months I had begun to detect signs that it was not cool to be good at school, that an A, despite what one might assume, was indicative of a character flaw, a deficiency, and not the opposite, which originally it had been meant to express. My status had long been on the wane, now I tried to reverse the process and re-establish a good reputation without this being so clearly defined; of course it was all based on hunches and intuition according to the social codes people confronted everywhere. In this task I had a huge advantage, namely football, where I had met many of the boys in the eighth and ninth classes, among whom there were four or five who were really respected by both boys and girls. I was the only person in my class who could go over to the gang Ronny was in, for example, or Geir Helge, or Kjell, or all of them at once, without them staring at me with eyebrows raised or starting to harass me. They were none too keen on me, I didn't get a lot from them, but that wasn't the main point, the main point was that I could actually stand there and be seen standing there. Geir and Geir Håkon and Leif Tore had gone overnight from being little nabobs to becoming little idiots, here they were nobody, here they had to build themselves up anew, and God knows whether they would manage that in the course of the three years they had. I didn't look their way any longer, except in class, which no longer counted.

During the first weeks of school Lars became my new best friend. He was in the parallel class and as such represented something new: he lived in Brattekleiv, where we from Tybakken seldom went, and he played football. He was sociable, knew a lot of people and got on well with everyone. He had curly auburn hair, was permanently in a good mood, had a loud, ringing, confident laugh and teased everyone, but rarely in a malicious way. His father was a former European skating champion, had participated in various world championships and Olympic tournaments, among them Squaw Valley, their basement was full of cups, medals, diplomas and a large, dried-up and faded laurel wreath. He was a friendly and considerate though firm man, married to a Dane, who couldn't do enough for those around her.

With Lars as a friend everything that Tybakken could throw at me bounced off. At the same time I had changed, it happened almost from one day to the next, I was no longer interested in good deeds, quite the contrary, I started swearing, I went apple scrumping, I threw stones at street lamps and shed windows, I was prone to answering back in lessons and I stopped praying to God. The freedom there was in that! I loved scrumping, and the greater the risk the better. Stopping my bike by the kerb in the morning on the way to school, sprinting into a garden and helping myself to five or ten apples in broad daylight and then just straddling my bike and continuing on my way as though nothing had happened gave me a good feeling I hadn't known before and hadn't even known existed. One of the gardens I passed was newly established, and in the middle there was a little apple tree with a single apple on it, and it didn't require much imagination to see that the apple had special significance for the father who had planted the tree that spring and for his two children who were looking forward to the day the apple, which for them must have been *the* apple, became ripe. It was their apple which I saw dangling there every morning on the way to school and which in the end I snaffled.

Not in the evening when it was dark and the odds of doing it unseen were good, no, I did it in the morning on the way to school, just dropped the bike, climbed over the fence, walked across the lawn, snatched the apple and sank my teeth into it as I was walking back. A world had opened. I wasn't stealing from shops yet, but it was on my mind, I was considering the possibility. At home, however, the only way I had changed was that I behaved more freely, was happier, chatted more, which mum didn't appear to find unusual since a lack of liberty was strongly associated with dad's presence and his anger only found its most extreme expression when we were alone with him. With mum and Yngve I had always been like that. With mum I had always talked about everything, that is, seldom about things directly concerning the world outside, I spoke more about things that I was thinking at any given point, all kinds of ideas and notions, but these days I was beginning to become aware of what I said and what I didn't say to her, for I understood that it was important that one world had to be light and clean and exclude any of the other world's many long shadows.

This autumn both these worlds opened, but it was no mechanical garage door being raised, this was a living organic process governed by a muscle: every Friday when dad came home the world closed around me again, the old patterns were resumed and I stayed there as little as possible. But whereas the world at home was familiar and always the same, the world outside was completely unpredictable, or, to be precise, what happened, happened clearly and unequivocally and without any ambivalence, it was the causes of these events that were so murkily unclear.

Every Friday there was a youth club meeting in the school's old gymnasium. It was open to all the pupils in the school. For a couple of years it had been a mythological place for me, as fascinating as it was unattainable. I had seen Yngve dress with meticulous care before going there, even with a neckerchief once; I knew they had dancing there, table tennis and carrom, sold Coke and hot dogs, sometimes showed films, held concerts and put on special events. There was quite a lot of talk about us being allowed to enter this miraculous place one day, mostly by the girls, for in some strange way they were the ones who identified with it most closely, as though it were primarily for them but only now and then for us boys.

The first time I cycled there it felt as though I was being initiated into a rite of passage. The evening air was cool, up the hill towards the school I passed some year-seven girls, all of them had made a special effort with their appearances, none looked as they did every day. I parked the bike outside, ambled past the crowd of kids smoking, bought an admission ticket and entered the dark converted gymnasium with kaleidoscopic spotlights, flashing disco balls and music pounding out from two enormous loudspeakers. I looked around. There were lots of year-eight and year-nine girls there, none of whom dignified me with a glance, of course, but most people were year sevens like myself. We were the only ones for whom the club had novelty value.

The dance floor was empty. Most of the girls were sitting at tables by the wall; most of the boys were hanging out in other rooms, where the table tennis and carrom tables were, or outside the exit where kids always gathered with mopeds during the evening. Many of these belonged to boys who had left school, but not so long ago that they had stopped keeping an eye on the girls.

But I wasn't there to play table tennis or hang around the car park with a Coke in my hand. I liked music, I liked girls and I liked dancing.

I didn't dare dance on my own on an empty floor. But when a couple of girls I was friends with tentatively began to dance and two more joined them, I also ventured out.

Captivated by the rhythm and the pleasurable awareness that I was so visible, I danced away. One song, two songs and then I went to find someone I knew. Bought a Coke and sat down with Lars and Erik.

My whole being, with my liking for clothes, my long eyelashes and soft cheeks, my know-all attitude and poorly concealed academic prowess, was fertile and ready ground for a pre-puberty catastrophe. My behaviour on these evenings didn't exactly improve matters. But of that I knew nothing. I saw nothing from the outside, I experienced everything from the inside, where all that counted was the seductive pumping rhythm of 'Funkytown', the Bee Gees' strange falsetto singing, Springsteen's catchy 'Hungry Heart', the glittering darkness, all the girls moving around inside it, with their breasts and thighs, mouths and eyes, the exciting aromas of perfume and sweat, that was what this was about. I could return home after these Friday evenings with my head totally in a spin, normality cast under some mysterious spell and suddenly appearing in a murky light, unclear in a shadowy way, but endlessly rich and alluring, full of hope and possibilities. Because, hey, this was the gym we were talking about! This was Sølvi, Hege, Unni and Marianne! Geir Håkon, Leif Tore, Trond and Sverre! This was hot dogs and ketchup and mustard! The tables and chairs were the same ones as in our classrooms. The bars on the walls, the ones we had in gym lessons. But they were of no significance when the darkness came and the flashing lights filled it, when everything was sucked into the dark circle of magic, so full of promise, when everything was dusky eyes and lovely soft bodies, pounding hearts and jangling nerves. I left the youth club after the first Friday in a daze, I arrived there on the next, tense and full of expectancy.

What was brilliant about the place was that it made it easier for you to approach girls. Usually they were out of reach, in recent months the majority had a blasé, world-weary air about them, they sat there in the sun chatting or knitting during the breaks with their cassette recorders on, most of what we did was childish, they were impossible to get through to. Even though I tried, because I still spoke their language, it never led to anything. As soon as the bell rang we went our separate ways.

But at the youth club it was different, there you could go straight up to a girl and ask her to dance. As long as you didn't set your sights too high and approach the most attractive year nine with boys buzzing round her, it always went well, they said yes and all you had to do was step onto the floor, press yourself against her warm soft body and sway from side to side until the song had finished. The hope was that it would develop into something more, perhaps being followed by stolen glances and tiny mischievous smiles, but even if it didn't, these moments had value in themselves, not least because of all the promises they bore of a future paradise in complete nakedness. All the girls I had gone out with so far, Anne Lisbet, Tone, Mariann and Kajsa, went to the school and were at the youth club, but even though I could still feel a stab in the heart when I saw them with boys, they were dead to me, history, from them I wanted nothing except that they shouldn't say anything to others about the person I had been. Especially in Kajsa's case. I realised that what had happened in the forest was ridiculous, I had behaved like a complete clod, I was deeply ashamed and had decided long ago that I would never tell *anyone*, not even Lars. Especially not Lars. But she had no reason to feel ashamed, and I kept a bit of an eye on her when she was in the vicinity, to see whether she would lean forward and whisper, and everyone would look at me. It didn't happen. Instead the body blows came from other, unexpected sources. Right from the fourth class I'd had my eye on Lise in the parallel class, she was good-looking and I liked watching her, the way she smiled, what she wore, the sharpness in her character, she was one of those who would say if she didn't agree, she was fearless, but her facial expressions were gentle, and when we started the seventh class her figure was beautifully rounded. More and more my eyes were drawn to her. She was Mariann's best friend, and after the arguments since I had finished it with her had subsided Mariann and I would often sit together and chat or walk together back from school, and it was on one of those occasions she repeated something Lise had said about me that day.

I had gone into the old gymnasium, which during the day was used as a dining hall where we could tuck into our lunch boxes in the breaks. I had gone in, and when Lise, who was sitting at a very full table, saw me coming she had said, 'Yuk, he's so revolting! I get the heebie-jeebies whenever I see him!'

'Well, I don't agree,' Mariann added after she had told me. 'I don't think you're a jessie either.'

'Jessie?' I said.

'Yes, that's what everyone says.'

'What?'

'Didn't you know?'

'No.'

And as if there had been some secret pact not to call me a jessie to my face before I had been properly but discreetly informed, after the conversation with Mariann it began to be used against me, spreading with the speed of sound. Suddenly I was the jessie. Everyone called me that. The girls in the class, the girls from other classes, some of the boys in the class, boys from other classes, in fact even in the football team they would call me that. One day John turned to me in training and said, 'You're such a bloody jessie, you are.' Even younger children, fourth years on the estate, had picked it up and would shout it after me. 'Jessie, jessie, jessie,' I heard all around me. A sentence had been passed, and it could not have been worse. If I was arguing with someone, for example Kristin Tamara, she swept away all the arguments and crushed me totally by just saying, 'You're such a jessie. You jessie. Hey, jessie! Come here, jessie.' This got me down, I thought of almost nothing else, it was like a black wall in my consciousness and impossible to escape. It was the worst; there was nothing I could do.

It wasn't as if I could behave in a less effeminate way for a couple of days and then everyone would say, 'Oh, you aren't a jessie after all!' No, this went deeper, and it would be there for ever. They had something on me and they used it for all it was worth. Apart from Lars, he just said I shouldn't take any notice, and for that I was grateful, one of my first thoughts when this all started was that Lars would no longer want to be seen with me, suddenly he had a lot to lose. But it didn't bother him. Neither Geir nor Dag Magne nor Dag Lothar said it. And of course none of the teachers or parents. But everyone else did. The term undermined any other qualities I had, it made no difference what I could or couldn't do, I was a jessie.

In a biology lesson, as we were about to focus on human reproduction, as fru Sørsdal called it, Jostein from the parallel class, our goalkeeper, came into the classroom and sat down at a free table. At first he wasn't noticed, the lesson began, fru Sørsdal talked about homosexuality, and Jostein said, Karl Ove knows all about that! He's one himself, isn't he! You should ask *him* to tell *you*. The laughter that followed was desultory, he had gone too far and was at once ejected, but a seed was sown. Was I perhaps homosexual as well? Was that what was wrong with me? I began to ponder on that. I was a jessie, perhaps even a homo, and, if so, all hope was lost. Then there would be nothing to live for. Dark times, they had never been as dark as now.

I said nothing to mum of course, but after a few weeks I plucked up courage and told Yngve. He was on his way up the hill to the shop when I caught him.

'Are you in a hurry or what?' I said.

'Pretty much,' he said. 'What's the matter?'

'I've got a problem,' I said.

'Oh yes?' he said.

'They're calling me names,' I said.

He glanced at me as though he didn't really want to know.

'What names?'

'Yeah . . .' I said. 'Well, it's . . .'

He stopped.

'*What* are they calling you? Tell me!'

'Well, they call me a jessie,' I said. 'I'm the jessie.'

Yngve laughed.

How could he *laugh*?

'That's no big deal, Karl Ove,' he said.

'Jesus Christ,' I said. 'Of course it is! Don't you understand?'

'Think about David Bowie,' he said. 'He's androgynous. It's a good thing in rock, you see. David Sylvian as well.'

'Androgynous?' I said, so disappointed that he hadn't understood a thing.

'Yes, ambiguous sexual identity. Bit woman, bit man.'

He looked at me.

'It'll pass, Karl Ove.'

'Doesn't seem like it,' I said, turning and walking back home while Yngve continued up the hill.

I was right, it never stopped, but somehow I became accustomed to it, that was how it was, I was the jessie, and even if thoughts about it tormented me in a way I had not experienced before, and the shadows it cast were long, there was enough happening around me, most of such an intensity it nullified everything else.

We drifted around, that was what we did. Actually I always had done, but whereas the point for Geir and me during all these years had been to seek out secret places, places for ourselves, the opposite was now the case, with Lars we sought places where something might happen. We hitch-hiked everywhere, to Hove if there was something going on there, over to Skilsø, to the east of the island, hanging around outside B-Max in the hope that something might happen, someone might come, hanging out around the Fina station, drifting around town, cycling up to the new sports hall even though we weren't going to do any training, up to the parish hall where Ten Sing had their rehearsals, because at the sports hall there were girls, at Ten Sing there were girls, and that was all we talked and thought about. Girls, girls, girls. Who had big breasts and who had small ones. Who might become attractive and who was attractive. Who had the nicest bum. Who had the best legs. Who had the nicest eyes. Who we might have a chance with. Who was unattainable.

One dark winter evening we caught the bus to Hastensund, where there was a girl who went to Ten Sing, she had blonde hair, was a bit on the chubby side, but was stunningly beautiful, we were interested in her even if she was a year older, we knocked at the door, and then we sat there in her room, chatting shyly about this and that, burning with lust, and on the bus home we were so full of emotion we could barely utter a word.

One weekend mum visited dad in Kristiansand and Lars stayed over with me, we ate crisps, drank Coke, ate ice cream and watched TV, it was in the spring, the night before the first of May, the TV was showing a rock concert that night to keep Oslo kids indoors who might otherwise be wandering the streets and throwing stones. We didn't have any porn magazines, I didn't dare keep any in the house despite the fact that we were on our own, so we had to make do with *Insect Summer* by Knut Faldbakken, the passage I had read so many times the book automatically opened at the right page. We decided we couldn't be alone, we had to invite some girls, and Lars suggested Bente.

'Bente?' I said. 'Which Bente?'

'The one who lives up here,' Lars said. 'She's lovely.'

'*Bente?*' I almost shrieked. 'But she's *younger* than us!'

I had seen her all my life, she had always been smaller, never a girl I had considered. But now she had developed, Lars declared, he had seen, she had breasts and everything. And she was a looker! A real looker!

I hadn't noticed, but now that he said it . . .

We threw on our jackets and ran up the hill and rang her doorbell. She was surprised to see us, but down to our house, no, she couldn't do that, not tonight.

OK, we said, another time then!

Yes, another time.

So back we went and sat down in front of the TV to watch one band after the other while discussing what we saw and all the girls we would have liked to watch it with. Siv from the class, whom I hadn't considered either, suddenly became the focus of our interest, we rang her doorbell too. What would happen afterwards we had no idea.

And so we went on, drifting around, restless, full of ungovernable desire. We read porn magazines, it physically hurt to look at the pictures, they were so close and yet so far, so endlessly far away, not that that prevented them from arousing all these tremendously powerful feelings in us. I felt like shouting as loudly as I could every time I saw a girl, knocking her over and tearing off all her clothes. The thought made my throat constrict and my heart pulsate. It was incredible, the thought that they were naked under the clothes they were wearing beside us, all of them, and they could, theoretically, remove them themselves. It was an impossible thought.

How could everyone walk around knowing that without ultimately running completely amok?

Did they repress it? Were they acting cool?

I couldn't do that. I thought of nothing else, it was all I had in my head from the moment I woke up in the morning to the moment I went to bed at night.

Yes, we read porn magazines. We also played cards, it was out with the pack everywhere and in all situations, we went to friends' homes, we went to the youth club, listened to music, played football, went swimming for as long as it was possible, went apple scrumping, drifted around, hung out here, hung out there and chatted non-stop.

Kjersti?

Marianne?

Tove?

Bente-Lill?

Kristin?

Lise?

Anne Lisbet?

Kajsa?

Marian?

Lene?

Lene's sister?

Lene's *mother*?

Never, later in life, have I had my finger on the pulse the way I had then with the girls living around us in those years. Later I may have doubted whether Svein Jarvoll's *Journey to Australia* was a good or a bad novel, or whether Hermann Broch was a better writer than Robert Musil, but I was never ever in any doubt that Lene was a good-looking girl and that she was in quite a different league from, for example, Siv.

Lars had a lot going on around him as well, he sailed quite a bit with his mother and father, and alone in a Europe dinghy. He was good at skiing, light years better than me, sometimes he went with his father to Åmli or Hovden and he had his old pals out there too, Erik and Sveinung. When he was busy I stayed in my room, played music, read books, talked to Yngve or mum. I never went into the forest, up into the hills, down to the pontoons or into Gamle Tybakken any more.

One Sunday at the end of the winter I cycled out to see Lars. He was going to Åmli with his father and Sveinung to ski down the slalom slope there. I couldn't join them as it had already been planned for a long time. I was so disappointed and it came so unexpectedly that my eyes filled with tears. Lars saw, and I turned away and cycled off. Tears, that was no good, that was the worst.

He rang when I got home. There was room for me too. They could drop by and pick me up. I should have said no to show that I wasn't bothered and should have explained to him that the tears – I had seen from his expression that he didn't like them – were not tears, I had something in my eye, the wind had upset my cornea. But I couldn't, Åmli was a big slalom slope with a lift and everything, I had never been there, so I swallowed my pride and joined them.

His father skied with a 50s elegance I had never seen before.

But the tears had disappointed Lars, and they had disappointed me. Why couldn't they stay away now that I was thirteen years old? Now that they could not be excused?

One woodwork lesson John started to tease me, I cried and was so angry I hit him over the head with a wooden bowl as hard as I could, it must have hurt and I was thrown out of the classroom into the corridor, but he just laughed and came over to me afterwards and apologised, I didn't realise it would make you cry, he said. I didn't mean it. Everyone had seen how feeble and pathetic I was, and suddenly all the efforts I had made to appear tough, to be one of the tough boys, were down the drain. John, who had shown his bum to the teacher on the first day at the new school and who had come in one morning with his eyebrows shaved off and who had started skiving. Everyone was expecting him to be one of those looking for a job while still in the eighth class. He had to be rescued. I tried to rescue myself. Lars had weights in his father's garage and he pumped iron too, and one afternoon I asked if I could have a try.

'Be my guest,' he said.

'How much do you lift?' I said.

He said.

'Can you put the weights on for me?' I said.

'Can't you do that yourself?'

'I don't know how to.'

'OK. Come with me.'

I went downstairs with him. He added the weights and put the bar in position. Looked at me.

'I have to do this on my own,' I said.

'Are you kidding?' he said.

'No. You just run along. I'll be up soon.'

'OK.'

When he had gone I lay down on the bench. I couldn't budge the bar. I couldn't lift it a centimetre. I removed half of the weights. But I still couldn't lift it. A fraction though, perhaps two or three centimetres.

I knew you had to lower the bar onto your chest and raise it with your arms fully stretched.

I removed two more.

But I still couldn't do it.

In the end I removed all of the weights and lay there lifting the bar, and nothing but the bar, up and down a few times.

'How was it?' Lars said as I emerged. 'How much did you manage?'

'Not as much as you,' I said. 'I had to take off two of the weights.'

'Hey, that's not bad!' Lars said.

'Isn't it?' I said.

Through all these years, right from the time when I was with Anne Lisbet in the first class, I thought I had learned something each time. That it would get better and better with every new girl I was with. After Kajsa there would be no more setbacks. After her, yes, it would all be fine, now I knew what it was about and could avoid any more mistakes.

But that was not how it turned out.

I fell in love with Lene. She was in the parallel class. She was the best-looking girl in the school. No contest, she won hands down. She was more beautiful than anyone else, but also shy, and I had never experienced that before. There was a fragility about her it was hard not to be attracted by and dream about.

She had a sister who was in the ninth class called Tove and she was the complete antithesis, although also beautiful, but in a boisterous, provocative, mischievous way. Both were very popular with the boys.

Lene only indirectly though, she was the kind you looked at and pined for in secret. At least I did. Her eyes were narrow, her cheekbones high, cheeks soft and pale, often with a slight flush, she was tall and slim, she held her head at an angle, and often interlaced her fingers as she walked. But she also had something of her sister in her, you could occasionally see it when she laughed, the glint that appeared in her turquoise eyes, and in the obstinacy and unshakeable certainty that sometimes shone through, so difficult to reconcile with the otherwise predominant impression of dreamy fragility. She was a rose, Lene was. I looked at her and started to tilt my head how she did. In this way I made contact with her, in this way we had something in common. I couldn't hope for more really, because I had set her on too high a pedestal to dare make any kind of approach. The thought of asking her to dance, for example, was absurd. Talking to her was unthinkable. I contented myself with looking and dreaming.

Instead I went out with Hilde. She asked me, I said yes, she was in the same class as Lene, she had a broad powerful body, almost masculine, was half a head taller than me, with delicate features and a lovely friendly personality, and she finished with me two days later because, as she put it, you're not in the slightest bit in love with me. With you, there is only Lene. No, I said, you're wrong, but of course she was right. Everyone knew, I thought of nothing else, and when we were in the playground during the break I always knew where she was and who she was with, and that attentiveness couldn't go unnoticed.

One day Lars said he had heard someone say they had heard her say she wasn't at all ill disposed towards me. Despite the fact that I was a jessie. Despite the fact that I had blubbed in the woodwork lesson. Despite the fact that I was slow on the football pitch and could barely manage a bench lift.

I looked at her in the playground, she met my eyes and smiled and turned away with pink cheeks.

I decided that I should strike while the iron was hot. I decided that it was now or never. I decided that I had nothing to lose. If she said no, well, nothing had changed.

If she said yes on the other hand . . .

One Friday, therefore, I sent Lars over to her with a question. They had been in the same class for six years, he knew her well. And he returned with a smile playing around his lips.

'She said yes,' he said.

'Really?'

'Yes, really. Now you're going out with Lene.'

Then it started again.

Could I go over to her now?

I looked in her direction. She smiled at me.

What should I say when I was there?

'Off you go now,' Lars said. 'Give her a kiss from me.'

He didn't push me across the playground, but it wasn't far from it.

'Hi,' I said.

'Hi,' she said.

She looked down; one foot squirmed round on the tarmac.

God, how beautiful she was.

Ay yay yay yay.

'Thank you for saying yes,' my mouth said.

She laughed.

'My pleasure,' she said. 'What lesson have you got now?'

'Lesson?'

'Yes.'

'Err . . . is it Norwegian?'

'Don't ask me,' she said.

The bell rang.

'Will we see each other afterwards?' I said. 'After school, I mean?'

'All right,' she said. 'I've got training in the sports hall. We can see each other afterwards.'

The question was not how this would go, the question was how many days it would last before it stuttered and she brought it to an end. I knew that, but I tried anyway, I had to put up a fight, you could never be sure, and she was present inside me for every single waking minute, partly as a kind of unconstrained, excited feeling, a constant sensation, partly as a more nebulous perception of her essence and character. Yes, I would have to fight, even though I didn't really have anything to fight with. I didn't even know what the fight was about. To keep her, yes, but how? By being myself? Don't make me laugh. No, I would have to draw on others, I realised that, and during these days I sought out the company of others with her so that all the conversation didn't rest on my shoulders. Up to the sports hall with Lene, over to Kjenna with Lene, over to the Skilsø ferry with Lene. We had all been given a Bible at school, the preparations for our confirmation would start next autumn, and it struck me that I could ask her what she had done with her Bible and then I could say I had ditched mine, and I would have a theme going, so that I could ask people I met what they had done with their Bible. Lene listened, Lene followed me, Lene started to get bored. She was a rose, we kissed at a crossroads and we walked hand in hand in the playground, but I was only a little boy and even though I had perfectly even white teeth after the brace had been taken off, that wasn't enough, Lene was bored with me, and one evening when she came to football training with me I saw her leave the spectators' stand and disappear, she was gone for the whole of the last hour, I went in and changed with the others, suspecting that something was wrong, stopped in the entrance hall where the reception desk and the Coke machine were and looked outside: there was Lene Rasmussen, there was Vidar Eiker, they were chatting and laughing, and I could see from the way she was laughing it was over. Vidar Eiker had left school the year before, he was one of the group who hung around at the Fina station, and he had a moped, which he was leaning on at this minute.

I went up into the stand and sat down.

After half an hour or so Hilde came over. She sat down beside me.

'I've got bad news, Karl Ove,' she said. 'Lene's finished it.'

'Yes,' I said, averting my head so that she couldn't see the tears streaming down my cheeks. But she saw them because she stood up as if she had been burned.

'Are you crying?' she said.

'No,' I said.

'You really do love her, don't you?' she said with surprise in her voice.

I didn't answer.

'But Karl Ove,' she said.

I wiped my tears away with one hand, sniffled and drew a slow quivering breath.

'Is she out there now?'

She nodded.

'Shall I walk out with you?'

'No, no. You just go, Hilde.'

As soon as she had gone through the door at the end of the stand I got up, swung my bag onto my back and left. Wiped my tears again, hurried along the corridor, emerged in the entrance hall and opened the door to where they had been standing before.

I bowed my head and walked past.

'Karl Ove!' she said.

I didn't answer, and as soon as they were out of sight I burst into a run.

Lene went out with Vidar, I was crushed for several months, but then spring came and with its immense power it washed everything aside. The year eights and the year nines were at school camp for a week, there were only the year sevens left at school, and a kind of mania spread through the ranks of the boys in those days, we began to attack the girls, one stole up on them from behind and lifted their sweaters while another came at them from the front and groped their naked breasts as they screamed and struggled to get away, but never so loudly that any of the teachers heard. We did this in the corridors between the classrooms, we did it in the playground and we did it on the unpopulated parts of the road to school. There were rumours that Mini, Øystein and others in the Fina crowd had frigged

Kjersti, held her down, pulled down her trousers and stuck a finger inside her, so one evening Lars and I went up to her house, thinking perhaps that we could experience some of the same, but when we rang the bell it was her father who answered, and when Kjersti came down and we asked if we could come in, her lips formed a clear no, we would certainly not be allowed *in*, what were we thinking about?

But the glint in her eyes was even more brazen than that in our own; she understood exactly what we were after. A few weeks later we met at the Boat Fair in Hove, where Lars and I had been at the Trauma stall selling lottery tickets, among them a winning ticket which we put aside and took with us when our stint finished, and we walked around looking at boats and people so as not to arouse suspicion because we had a little scam in mind, then casually stopped by the stall, bought a ticket each and opened them, and while I leaned forward with mine to ask if I had won a prize, Lars swapped his for the winning ticket. Christian and John were manning the stall now and they refused to believe Lars when he passed them the winning ticket. They said it was an old one. We denied this with such vehemence that in the end they agreed to give us half the winnings. We said fine and walked off with the enormous box of chocolates under one arm, bubbling with laughter and tremulous with fear at what we had done. Nearby, we bumped into Kjersti.

'Fancy a walk?' Lars said.

'OK,' Kjersti said, and my body felt so strange when she said that.

We walked through the forest and down to the pebble beach, where we lay down and started on the chocolates.

She was wearing red trousers and a blue padded jacket and she said nothing as I gently stroked the outside of her thigh with my hand. Nor when I stroked the inside. Lars was doing the same on the other side.

'I know what you want,' she said. 'But you're not going to get it.'

'We don't want anything,' I said, swallowing, my throat thick with desire.

'Nothing,' Lars said.

I stroked her crotch, placed my whole hand against it and could have screamed with happiness and frustration. Lars sneaked a hand up to her jacket zip and pulled it down, then put his hand up her jumper. I did the same. Her skin was hot and white, and I felt her breasts in my hand. The nipples were stiff, her breasts firm. I stroked her thigh again, put my hand on her crotch again, but then, gulping repeatedly, I made the mistake of pulling down the zip of her trousers.

'No,' she said. 'What are you thinking of?'

'Nothing,' I said.

She straightened up and pulled down her sweater.

'Any more chocolate?' she said.

'Yes, help yourself,' Lars said, and we sat there eating chocolate and staring across the sea as if nothing had happened. The breakers resembled white snowdrifts the second they crashed against the smooth low rocks. Some seagulls swept past with their wings flapping. When the box was empty we got up and walked back through the forest to the fair. Kjersti said bye, see you later perhaps, and we decided to go home. But to do that we had to drop by the lottery stall to collect our bikes. Øyvind, our coach, was there, and he didn't look happy when he caught sight of us. We denied everything. He said he couldn't prove anything, but he knew what we had done. Why else would we have been content with half the prize? We denied it point blank. He said he was disappointed, he didn't want to have to look at us any more that day, and we cycled home.

On Monday, before school began, Lars lifted up Siv's sweater and I pressed both my hands against her breasts. She screamed and said we were childish and calmly walked off.

In the first lesson, which was Norwegian, we had to borrow a book from the library, read it during the week and then write about it in an essay. I said I had read all the books in the library. Kolloen didn't believe me. But it was true. I could tell him about every book he pulled out. In the end he allowed me to write about another book. Which meant I had nothing to do that lesson. I took out a history book and sat at the desk under the window. Outside, it was misty but warm. The playground was deserted. I flicked through the book and looked at the pictures.

Suddenly I saw one of a naked woman. She was so thin her hips protruded like bowls. All her ribs were visible. Between her legs there was a small black tuft. Behind her there were rows of bunk beds in which I glimpsed other female figures.

My insides shook.

Not because she was so thin but because there was nothing attractive about her, although she was naked, and because on the next page there was a picture of an enormous pile of corpses in front of a deep grave where many bodies lay strewn. What I saw was this: the legs were only legs, the hands were only hands, the noses were only noses, the mouths were only mouths. Something that had been shaped and formed elsewhere was now here, scattered across the ground. When I stood up I felt nauseous and confused. As I had nothing to do I went out and sat against the wall. The sun warmed, despite being covered by mist. The grass growing in the cracks and hollows of the boulder in the middle of the playground, surrounded by walls and tarmac, was long and swayed to and fro in the gentle breeze. The nausea didn't pass, it became associated with what I saw, it became a part of it. The green grass, the yellow dandelions, Siv's bare breasts, Kjersti's fat thighs, the skeletal woman in the book.

I got up and went back in, called Geir and he came over with a quizzical look.

'I've found a picture of a naked woman,' I said. 'Do you want to see it?'

'Of course,' he said, and I opened the book in front of him and pointed to the skeletal woman.

'That's her,' I said.

'Oh my God,' Geir said. 'Ugh.'

'What's the matter?' I said. 'She's naked, isn't she?'

'Oh yuk,' Geir said. 'She looks as if she's dead.'

That was exactly how she looked. Like the living dead. Or death in living form.

The next weekend mum and I went to visit dad. It was odd to see him in his flat. It was on a high floor in a tower block, it was all white, the sun shone in through the windows, filling it completely, and there was so little furniture it almost seemed as if no one was living there.

What did he do here?

He drove us to grandma and grandad's, where we ate, and then he drove us home. No one quite seemed to know when we were going to move, it was dependent on so many factors, the house had to be sold, a new one had to be bought, mum had to find a job, we had to change schools, so I didn't think too much about it. But I had no objection to leaving the estate or the school. It felt as if all my cards had been played. I made mistake after mistake. One day after gym, for example, when I was standing in the corridor outside the classroom, Kjersti came over to me.

'Do you know what, Karl Ove?' she said.

'No,' I said, fearing the worst, for her expression was sardonic.

'We've just been talking about you,' she said. 'And we discovered that not one of the girls in the class likes you.'

I said nothing, I glared at her, filled with a sudden enormous fury.

'Did you hear me?' she continued. 'Not one of the girls in the class likes you!'

I smacked her cheek as hard as I could. The flash of my arm and the following slap, which turned her cheek crimson, caused people to turn their heads.

'You bastard,' she shouted and punched me in the mouth. I grabbed her hair and pulled. She hit me in the stomach, kicked me in the calf and grabbed my hair too, we were a whirl of blows and kicks and hair-pulling, and I, poor, pathetic, miserable little shit, I burst into tears, it all became too much for me, a pathetic sob escaped my mouth; all those who had gathered around us within the space of seconds shouted, he's crying. I heard them, but I couldn't stop myself, and then I felt a heavy hand on my collar, it was Kolloen, he was holding Kjersti in the same way and asked what on earth was going on, are you *fighting*? I said it was nothing, Kjersti said it was nothing and then we were frog-marched into the classroom, each with a teacher's hand in the middle of our backs, me a laughing stock, for I had not only broken the rule about never crying but also the one about never fighting with a girl, Kjersti with the status of a hero, for she had been slapped and hit back, and she didn't cry.

How low can you sink?

Kolloen said we had to shake hands. We did, Kjersti apologised and smiled at me. The smile was not sardonic, it was heartfelt, in a way, as though we were complicit in something.

What did it mean?

*

In the last week of May the heat came, the whole class set off for Bukkevika to go swimming, the sand was white, the sea blue and the sun burned in the sky above us.

Anne Lisbet emerged from the sea.

She was wearing a bikini bottom and a white T-shirt. It was wet, and her round breasts were visible. Her wet black hair shone in the sun. She beamed her broadest smile. I watched her, I couldn't keep my eyes off her, but then I noticed something beside me, and turned my head, and there was Kolloen, he was watching her too.

There was no difference in our gazes, I realised that at once, he saw what I saw and he was thinking what I was thinking.

About *Anne Lisbet.*

She was thirteen years old.

The moment didn't even last for a second, he looked down as soon as I noticed him, but it was enough, and I'd had an insight into something which a moment before I didn't even know existed.

Three days later dad fetched me from school early, we were going off to look at a house, it was twenty kilometres from Kristiansand, by a river, we were considering buying it, now I had to say what I thought and I had to be honest. From the way dad was talking – it had a barn, the house was old, from the 1800s, it was on a big piece of land, you could have a normal garden and a vegetable garden too, there were big old fruit trees growing there, and perhaps we could keep hens, as well as growing our own potatoes, carrots and herbs – I had already decided I would tell him I liked it whether I did or not.

When we arrived, with the sky blue, the grass green and the river glinting down below, I ran from window to window and peered in so that he could see how enthusiastic I was, which was not entirely insincere, just somewhat exaggerated, and the matter was decided. If it was available we would buy it. Mum applied for a job at the nursing college, dad would continue at the *gymnas* and I would start at a new school here. What Yngve would do was less clear. He refused to move. For the first time in his life he stood up to dad. They argued, and that had never happened before. We had never argued with dad. It had been him who told us off, and we were on the receiving end.

But there was Yngve saying no.

Dad was furious.

But Yngve continued to say no.

'I don't want to spend my last year in Kristiansand,' he said. 'Why should I? All my friends are here. I've only got one year of school left. It would be ridiculous to start afresh somewhere new.'

They stood face to face in the living room. Yngve was as tall as dad.

I hadn't noticed before.

'You might think you're grown up, but you're not,' dad said. 'You have to stay with your family.'

'No, I do not,' Yngve said.

'Right,' dad said. 'Can you tell me how you're going to manage? You won't be getting one *øre* from me, you know.'

'I'll take out a loan,' Yngve said.

'Who do you think will give you a loan?' dad said.

'I can apply for a study loan,' Yngve said. 'I've checked.'

'Are you going to take a study loan before you begin to study?' dad said. 'That's very clever.'

'If I must, I must,' Yngve said.

'Where are you going to live?' dad said. 'The house will be sold, you know.'

'I'll rent a bedsit,' Yngve said.

'You do that then,' dad said. 'But you won't get any help from us. Not so much as a krone. Do you understand? If you want to live here, you can, but don't you come running to us for any help. You'll have to manage on your own.'

'OK,' Yngve said. 'I'll be fine.'

And that was what happened.

When the last day of the seventh class came, it had been announced that I was moving and my classmates for seven years had bought farewell presents. First of all I was given a cabbage head, as my name, Karl, as some called me, sounded in the broad dialect we spoke like *kål*, cabbage, which became a nickname. Then I was given a cloth monkey because I looked like a monkey.

That was it.

Then we went through the doors, and I never saw my classmates again.

But it wasn't quite over. That evening there was to be a class party at Unni's. Some of the girls met early that afternoon to get everything ready, and at around six the rest of us cycled over. The party was held in the garden and in the cellar, and as the summer night fell over the hills and all the red roofs of the houses on the estate glinted in the light of the setting sun the party slowly began to degenerate, even though no one was drinking. A year's secret thoughts and desires began to stir. It was simply in the air. Hands wandered under sweaters, not as part of an assault or any brutality, but close by, among the lilac bushes in the garden, amid hot panting, mouths met, mouths kissed, and then some of the girls took off their tops, they walked around with their breasts bobbing, it was a kind of early-puberty orgy which had been slowly building up steam, and the very same girls who only one month earlier had said they didn't like me offered themselves to me, one after the other, they sat on my lap, they kissed me, they rubbed their breasts against my face. The hierarchy the girls had been placed in, with some slowly climbing during autumn and others falling, had no significance here, it didn't make any difference who it was, I pressed my face against their soft white breasts, kissed their dark erect nipples, ran my hands over their thighs and between their legs, and they didn't say no, there wasn't a no in their mouths on this night, instead they leaned forward and kissed me, their eyes were warm and dark but also surprised, as mine must have been, is it really us doing this?

I haven't seen any of them since that summer, and if I search for them on the Net to see what they look like or how life has treated them, there are no hits. They don't belong to that class there, they belong to the class of blue- or white-collar parents who grew up outside the centre and who have presumably remained outside the centre of everything but their own lives. Who I am to them I have no idea, probably a vague memory of someone they once knew in their childhood years, for they have done so much to one another in their lives since then, so much has happened and with such impact that the small incidents that took place in their childhoods have no more gravity than the dust stirred up by a passing car, or the seeds of a withering dandelion dispersed by the breath from a small mouth. And oh, wasn't the latter a fine image, of how event after event is dispersed in the air above the little meadow of one's own history, only to fall between the blades of grass and vanish?

After the removal van had left and we got into the car, mum, dad and I, and we drove down the hill and over the bridge, it struck me with a huge sense of relief that I would never be returning, that everything I saw I was seeing for the final time.

That the houses and the places that disappeared behind me were also disappearing out of my life, for good. Little did I know then that every detail of this landscape, and every single person living in it, would for ever be lodged in my memory with a ring as true as perfect pitch.